GOING
INTERSTELLAR

GOING INTERSTELLAR

Edited by
Les Johnson &
Jack McDevitt

GOING INTERSTELLAR

This is a work of fiction. All the characters and events portrayed
in this book are fictional, and any resemblance to real people or incidents is
purely coincidental.

Copyright © 2012 by Les Johnson and Cryptic, Inc.

A Baen Books Original

Baen Publishing Enterprises
P.O. Box 1403
Riverdale, NY 10471
www.baen.com

ISBN: 978-1-9821-2561-5

Cover art by Sam Kennedy

First printing, June 2012
First trade paperback printing, September 2021

Distributed by Simon & Schuster
1230 Avenue of the Americas
New York, NY 10020

Library of Congress Control Number: 2021030931

Printed in the United States of America

10 9 8 7 6 5 4 3 2 1

DEDICATION

To Jennifer and Gail,
My sisters—with love.
Les Johnson

❁ ❁ ❁

To Matt Campbell,
Who, if we get to Mars,
will probably be first out of the ship.
Jack McDevitt

TABLE OF CONTENTS

ACKNOWLEDGMENTS

GOING INTERSTELLAR

FOREWORD

AS A CHILD I watched Neil Armstrong walk on the Moon. Shortly thereafter I began to catch reruns of *Star Trek* on television and from that point forward I was hooked. *Star Trek*, *Star Wars*, *The Foundation Trilogy*, *Rendezvous with Rama*, and others both inspired and challenged me. I studied physics and eventually landed my dream job at NASA. Midway through my career (so far), I went out on a professional limb and found myself researching propulsion systems for interstellar flight and having the coolest job title of my career, "NASA Manager for Interstellar Propulsion Research." That's no longer my job title. (But I kept the business cards!)

Unfortunately, that was also the end of NASA actually funding interstellar propulsion research. There have been a few minor studies since then, mostly performed by universities, but without serious investment. While some of these studies may have made important contributions toward our eventually becoming an interstellar species, the funding has been too low to actually help make it happen. Alas.

A few years later I was taking one of those management courses in which you have to create a poster that describes how you want to be remembered. The goal was to remind us that there is more to life than our work and, while I agree completely and I try to be both a devoted husband to my wife and a dedicated father to my children, it would be impossible to take the futurist and space advocate out of my life and then expect me to still be "me." So when it came time to present my poster, I showed the class a drawing of our interstellar neighborhood and my sincere wish—that when the history of the first human colony on a habitable planet circling one of our nearby stars is written, that my name will at least be mentioned in a footnote. That's it. A footnote—and what a footnote I hope it will be!

—Les Johnson

INTRODUCTION

WHAT'S OUT THERE? The answer to that question involves some practical issues. Are we alone or is there someone else to whom we might one day be able to say hello? What will we do to ensure the survival of the human race if a large asteroid comes our way? Is there enough room on this planet for all of us and for the millions more who continue to arrive regularly?

Some of us humans aren't content to stay in one place very long. There's something about a crowded environment that makes us restless. We want to move on, to see new things, to have more space and to go places, to paraphrase Captain Kirk, where nobody's already hanging out. The problem is that we've just about filled all the available locations on Earth.

Some of us are satisfied living our lives using essentially the same ZIP code we were born into. We may never really care to look above the rooftops. But many of us are curious about what's out beyond the next village. About what's over the horizon. We want to know if there are others like us, peering out at the stars with their telescopes, also wondering if they are alone. Someone with whom we might sit down and enjoy a pizza and trade notions about how the universe works. And maybe one day reminisce about visits to distant stars and worlds that light up at night.

Another concern is that our existence as a species might be short-lived unless we provide some insurance for ourselves. Unless we do something to spread our seed beyond the world that gave us birth. The fossil record is full of species that were at one time masters of the planet. Our existence is but a small part of the planet's history and that history has not been kind to many of its previous inhabitants. How might we go extinct?

Seriously? There are a number of possibilities. Supernova fallout is one. All we'd need is the collapse of an unstable star in the general neighborhood to bathe us in radiation. (It's even possible such a collapse has already happened, but the light and the shock wave just haven't gotten here yet.) Or a brown dwarf could drift into the system and collide with the Sun. Lights would go out and real estate values in Florida would plunge. We might do the damage ourselves by waging nuclear war. And we're well on our way to overpopulating the planet.

We therefore have a strong argument for moving some of us into space and out of the immediate danger zone. Looking at history, and at what's going on in the world today, we know that the course of events is utterly unpredictable and potentially lethal. Where, then, do we go? And how do we get there?

There's no place within the solar system that would allow the existence of a self-sustaining colony. So we have to look beyond its limits.

We've asked a diverse set of science fiction authors to speculate on what an interstellar voyage based on real physics might actually look like. We also asked some scientists and engineers who think about such things as interstellar travel to weigh in on how it might be accomplished. You hold the result in your hands: an anthology of adventures replete with danger, ingenuity, hope, love and loss, with a surprise or two thrown in. And a few essays describing exotic strategies that might one day allow us to reach the stars. Beware: One of our guidelines for both the fiction and the non-fiction is that any method of traveling to the stars has to be based on what we currently know about how the universe works. You won't find faster-than-light drives, hyperjumps, or star gates within these pages.

For those interested in interstellar travel and wondering what they can do to help make it happen, we recommend you find a way to get involved with the Interstellar Research Group. Please check out their website for more information: http://irg.space.

Ad Astra!

—Les Johnson and Jack McDevitt

CHOICES

Les Johnson

Interstellar flight is the most audacious of human dreams. Barring a Star Trek breakthrough, the voyage will require a high level of technology, and people willing to get on board for a destination so far distant in time and space that most of them will not live to see it. We can only admire the talent of those who might make it possible, and the courage of those heading out for Rigel or wherever. Despite all our efforts, the technology may, at some critical point, break down. So we will of course build in as much redundancy as we can. Unfortunately, we cannot do the same for the passengers.

Les recently completed two novels, The Spactime War *(Baen, 2021) and* Saving Proxima *(Baen, 2021), his latest collaboration with Travis Taylor.*

◈ ◈ ◈

THE AIR WAS THICK AND PUTRID. Peter Goss slogged through knee-deep water with a broken branch in one hand and a machete in the other. The swamp was brightly lit by the reflected light of the two moons hanging low on the horizon. All he could think of was survival. Mosquito-like creatures the size of small birds dove at him constantly, ignoring his wild swatting. Their sting hurt. Beneath the surface he imagined large creatures watching and waiting for him to slip and fall so they could pounce and enjoy a tasty human delicacy for that night's dinner.

Relentlessly, he moved forward. No distraction would stop him tonight. There, just ahead and across this last bit of waterlogged purgatory, was the tower. Rising out of the swamp at least twenty-five stories, it dominated the horizon and demanded investigation. Made of what looked like stone, which he knew would have been all but impossible given its size, the tower taunted him.

Goss stopped. And listened. He heard only the sounds of the night, the buzzing of the monster-mosquitoes and the distant splashes of other creatures stirring the waters.

He was only a few hundred yards from the tower, a small distance compared to that which he had already covered, but now it seemed distant. His muscles hurt and he was tired.

The swamp ahead looked much like the swamp behind, but looks could be deceiving. Two of his compatriots were now dead because of this place and he was not about to join them. He whacked one of the oversized mosquitoes with the branch, raised his machete, and started forward.

The tower was dark and quiet. Goss intended no harm; he was there to find out what it held, why it was there, and, if possible, who had built it. For on this water world, the tower was the only artificial structure in evidence.

Three weeks ago, Goss and his crewmates had arrived on this planet because their long-range instruments told them that it had an oxygen/nitrogen atmosphere suitable for human life. Though planets seemed to be plentiful everywhere, those with breathable atmospheres and temperate surface conditions were very, very rare. That's why he and his two colleagues had taken a shuttle from the mothership to investigate.

From space, the world was a brilliant blue that reminded him of Earth. Except that instead of the familiar landforms surrounded by water, the entire planet was covered by water, with only a few islands dotting its seas. It was on one of these islands that they'd spotted the tower, standing alone. It had been a glorious moment, looking down at the structure, the first evidence anywhere that humans were not alone. And of course, still in a state of shock, they'd gone down.

Goss lost the first of his crewmates, Charlie Edward, when he slipped on slick, moss-covered rock, pitched forward, and landed on his head. Not a graceful way to die. It had happened so fast that he hadn't even had time to throw out his hands. By the time Goss reached him, Charlie was gone.

The other crewmate, Julie Gold, died after her leg was ripped off by an alligator-like creature that had been lying in wait beneath the surface of the water in an area they had mistakenly assumed to be safe enough for a short break. All Goss remembered was the rage that overcame him after seeing his friend writhe in the water, trying to shake off what had attached itself to her right leg. Goss had hurried to her rescue, but the thing had ripped her apart within seconds. He'd brought the machete down on its armored neck again and again until it collapsed.

He'd held Julie in his arms while she bled. And she'd looked at him in the eerie moonlight. "Pete," she'd said, "what do you think is in the tower?"

They had been her last words.

And he'd gazed across the swamp to where the tower stood. "I'm sorry we ever saw it," he told her. "Whatever it is, it's not worth the price."

He crossed the remaining distance to the tower and the stone-like wall that comprised its base. He was still knee-deep in water when he touched the wall and looked up at the immense structure. The wall was made of a light-colored stone and it might almost have been medieval. Below the waterline the stone was, as one might expect, covered in mildew and moss. Out over the water were the two distinct shadows caused by the twin moons. Every movement Goss made was instantly mirrored by the two shadows off to his side.

That takes some getting used to.

Seaweed clung to his boots and pant legs. He circled the base of the tower. Part way around he came across a door. And an inscription. He caught his breath. It was raised lettering on a metallic plaque. He pressed his fingertips gently on the characters. Wondered who had been here. What it said. Here we came in search of a new world. And found only a swamp.

He smiled. *Maybe, Martin & Cable, Attorneys at Law.*

How long ago had it been?

Would they have welcomed him?

He pulled his hand back and looked at it as if it were the first time he'd ever seen it.

※ ※ ※

Peter Goss awoke with a start. He was lying on his hibernation bed with his right arm held straight out, up, and in front of him. He was still staring at his hand. For a few moments he drifted back into the swamp and stood before the mysterious tower, and then he was back here, wherever "here" was, again.

He was cold. And he lay naked, partially submerged in what looked and felt like a bathtub filled with raspberry Jell-O. He tilted his head slowly from side to side, as if doing so would dislodge a memory and allow him to remember where he was. These new surroundings looked more and more familiar but he wasn't yet quite sure why.

He coughed, and raised his head and looked around. This was not the tower. And certainly not the swamp. First of all, the tub in which he found himself was but one of many lined up along the floor. In fact, he saw at least fifteen tubs around him.

And each was occupied. By someone.

By another human being.

A memory was slowly returning.

Hibernation. Sleeping during the journey and being awakened when their new home world was reached. Now he remembered.

Peter Goss was on board the interstellar colony ship *New Madrid* bound for the Epsilon Eridani star system ten light years from Earth. As in his dream, he was a member of the initial survey team that was to awaken and scout the environment of their new home while the rest of the crew, and the fifteen thousand colonists, were being awakened.

Goss slowly lifted himself to rest on his right elbow. The other people were gone. Part of the dream. Still, he shouldn't be alone. He wasn't supposed to be the first to wake up. The ship's commander, first officer and two medical officers should already be up and about, supervising the awakening of the survey crews to begin their mission. Waking the colonists would come later.

The ship was quiet. The only sound Goss heard was his own breathing and the sloshing of the liquigel in which he found himself. As he pulled his naked form out of the tank, he realized that the liquigel had probably formed the basis for his swamp during the hibernation. Slowly and with great care, Goss sat up and put his feet on the floor. Mindful that he had probably been in suspended animation for perhaps hundreds of years, he wasn't sure that his muscles and bones would be strong enough to sustain his weight in the simulated fifty percent Earth gravity in which he found himself.

He stood.

To his great relief, he found that the electrostimulation of his muscles and bones had kept them healthy and fully functional throughout his long sleep. Just as the electrostimulation had kept his body functioning, the virtual reality generator had kept his mind from atrophying. His "adventure" on the water world with the tower had been just that. A machine-induced training session to keep his mind functioning through the centuries required to cross the vast interstellar distances between Earth and the intended colony's destination.

That means Julie and Charlie are not dead! Thank God. *It was just a simulation.* They were safely asleep onboard the *New Madrid*.

As he struggled to get his bearings, the weight of nearly a thousand years of dreaming came crushing down upon him. In his chosen artificial realities, he selected a succession of planetary exploration missions—all created by the ship's Artificial Intelligence to help train him for any eventuality he might encounter in the real world. Before awakening, he realized, he must have visited hundreds, if not thousands, of new worlds—all different, and all created by a computer simulation program.

But this was real and it wasn't as it was supposed to be. *Where was Commander Vasquez? Where were the med techs?* Anything could happen upon revival and it was not protocol for it to happen like this.

He moved to the side of the room and opened his locker. Inside, and as perfectly preserved as he, were his clothes. Thanks to vacuum storage, they looked and felt as fresh as the day he took them off and put them there—so very long ago.

How long have I been asleep? Where are we? He had more questions than answers.

After cleaning off the gel and getting dressed, he ventured out of the sleep chamber and into the hallway that led to the ship's control room. He thought that Vasquez must be there, supervising the orbital encounter with Epsilon Eridani Four, the destination world that the telescopes back on Earth had found to contain an atmosphere suitable for Earth-based life.

During the latter half of the twenty-first century, more and more planets had been found orbiting other stars. Not only were they pinpointed and their masses estimated, but large telescopes optimized to look for certain chemical signatures determined that some of the newly found planets had atmospheres, and that at least two of the nearest worlds harbored atmospheres in which humans could live without wearing masks or other protective clothing.

These were "Goldilocks worlds," so-called because they were neither too hot (like Venus) nor too cold (like Mars); they had atmospheres with enough, but not too much, oxygen; they were "just right" for sustaining life. It was toward the second of these worlds that the *New Madrid* was sent with colonists who would settle there and build a new home for humanity.

Goss had volunteered for the journey. He was fed up with the crowded cities of Earth and found the Moon and Mars colonies, with their cramped below-ground living areas, simply too dark and unforgiving for his tastes. The idea of being a pioneer, of having the chance to build a new world or die trying, was just the sort of challenge for which he had longed his entire life.

Are we there yet? If not, then why was I awakened? He tried to keep these thoughts at bay as he walked down the long, curved corridor toward the control room.

Midway there, he stopped to look out one of the windows that the engineers had been so loath to include. Dangerous, they'd argued. Maybe so, but the view was worth it. Before him was the majesty of the *New Madrid*; home to thousands of colonists eager for a new beginning. He gazed back along the hull at the central core of the starship, which housed its antimatter power plant and propulsion system as well as many of the supplies they would need once their new home was reached. His eyes drifted out from the core along one of the many half-kilometer-long spokes that supported the habitation ring in which he had spent who knows how many years in hibernation.

Without a decent fixed reference point, it was virtually impossible to discern that the ring was completing one rotation every minute—though he felt the comfortable one-half gravity acceleration caused by the slow spin as he walked through the ship. Humans evolved in a one gravity environment on Earth but scientists had determined that only half that was needed to maintain their health in deep space. And since one can't tell the difference between acceleration caused by gravity and acceleration caused by spinning, the engineers had found a way to provide the "gravity" people needed to keep them healthy in deep space—spin the ship.

He continued past the window and down the corridor toward the control room. There, he opened the door, expecting to be greeted by Commander Vasquez's booming voice. Instead, there was only silence and the steady hum of the circulation system keeping the breathable air moving throughout the ship.

The room was empty.

The commander's chair was vacant, as were the duty stations for the ship's command crew. The room seemed somehow unreal to Goss. *It isn't supposed to be like this.*

He entered, approached the commander's chair and sat in it, pulling the console on the mechanical arm forward so he could see what it had to say. One word was flashing on the display panel as he pulled it into view.

ALERT

Recalling his training, Goss activated the ship's Artificial Intelligence by speaking the command phrase, "Command Authorization Substitute Five Zero Three."

"Five Zero Three recognized," came the reply from the ship's speaker system.

Goss was relieved to hear the AI's voice. Maybe now he could find out what was going on.

The AI was programmed with a voice that sounded, except for its rather stilted diction, completely human. Studies had shown that people reacted more favorably if the computer at least sounded human. Gone were the monotone computer-generated voices that had preceded it.

"Five Zero Three, do you require a status?" asked the AI program, following procedure.

"Yes, please provide our location, navigation history, and overall ship status."

A holographic projection appeared above the navigation console in the middle of the room. At the center was Sol, the Earth's star, and around it were the nearest star systems stretching out to a distance of about fifteen light years. As Goss watched, a curving line appeared, slowly being drawn from Sol outward to Epsilon Eridani, their primary destination. But instead of stopping there, the line curved by the star system and toward another—Tau Ceti. Again, it didn't end there but curved yet again toward another star, Epsilon Indi, and then stopped one quarter of the way toward it.

The AI spoke, "After finding the primary and secondary star systems unsuitable, Commander Vasquez ordered that we continue toward Epsilon Indi. I awakened you, Mr. Goss, because we encountered a mission-changing event and Commander Vasquez and Deputy Commander Herndon are both dead."

Goss's mind was racing. How long had he been asleep? The antimatter drive of the *New Madrid* was to have made the voyage to Epsilon Eridani in nine hundred years.

The *New Madrid* was the second of five such ships to leave Earth for the stars. Each of the five ships targeted a different set of star systems deemed to have a moderate to high probability of providing planets that could sustain human life. Humanity was reaching for the stars and the *New Madrid* was part of the first wave.

They had reached Epsilon Eridani, and, for some reason, the commander had found the fourth planet, the destination the smart people back on Earth said would make a good home, unsuitable. He must have restarted the engines and set out for the secondary destination, Tau Ceti. The clear second choice. The deep space telescopes and interferometers back near Earth had collected data showing that both of these systems were promising future homes for humanity. But that star's chosen world had also been deemed not suitable and they were now bound for still another alternative.

"I've been asleep for twelve hundred years!" Goss said aloud, speaking more to himself than the AI.

But the AI responded, "Incorrect. You have been asleep for one thousand, nine hundred and fifty-nine years, ship time. We are now approximately half-way to the Epsilon Indi system."

"Okay, we'll deal with that later. You said that commanders Vasquez and Herndon are dead and that there has been a mission-changing event. Please explain."

"Commander Vasquez killed Deputy Commander Herndon while we were orbiting and surveying the fourth planet of Epsilon

Eridani. He re-entered suspended animation and remained there until we entered orbit around Tau Ceti's third planet. After a short survey, he once again re-entered suspended animation shortly after our primary propulsive burns targeting Epsilon Indi. After hibernation began, Commander Vasquez's body began rejecting the suspended animation drugs, leading to his real-time aging and death."

Goss, who had been standing motionless during the debrief from the ship's AI, sat in the command chair. The chair was cold.

"Continue," he said.

"You are next in line to command the ship and I was not going to awaken you until we reached Epsilon Indi's third planet to begin your assessment of its habitability. However, when the mission-changing event occurred, I thought it best to awaken you early for a command decision."

"What was the nature of the event?" Goss knew that a mission-changing event was one that as its name implied, was something so fundamental that it required a complete alteration of plans.

"Shipboard sensors have determined that none of the planets in the Epsilon Indi planetary system can sustain human life. We need a command decision as to whether the ship should continue toward Epsilon Indi or divert to another destination. You should be aware that there is only sufficient shipboard antimatter to divert to one alternate stellar destination—and that would be back to Tau Ceti. And that will only be possible if we divert before we reach the half-way point."

Goss felt the weight of the AI's latest pronouncement as if it were a blanket made of lead. They were headed toward an uninhabitable star system and he had to decide whether or not to change course back to a star system that the commander had decided was unsuitable—for some as-yet unknown reason. There was not enough fuel to go anywhere else.

"Please explain in more detail the fuel situation."

In response, the AI projected a graphical representation of the ship's trajectory toward Tau Ceti, showing how its antimatter reserves would be depleted in the propulsive maneuver that would send them back there and into orbit around one of its planets. It then flashed a series of potential trajectories that would change the course of the ship to any number of nearby stars and the fuel required to both change course and to stop at the new destination. In each case, the ship ran out of fuel before it could slow and enter into any other planetary orbit.

"Can you tell me why we didn't remain at either our primary or secondary targets?" Goss asked, thinking that perhaps both worlds were inhospitable for life, causing the captain to push for yet another possible destination. *But why had he killed Herndon?*

"Commander Vasquez did not log an explanation for rejecting either planetary destination. The orbital assessments were completed as planned and both worlds were found to be habitable by humans. Neither showed any evidence of intelligent life."

Goss was stunned. They'd passed up two habitable planets in two different solar systems. Now they were approaching a third that was uninhabitable and they didn't have enough fuel to try a fourth alternative. The commander had killed his first officer, for some unknown reason, and they'd all been asleep for nearly two thousand years. *Hello. What the hell is going on?*

Goss rose from the command chair, feeling totally uncomfortable with the burden that was now on his shoulders. Looking around the eerily quiet room, he felt painfully alone. For a moment, he seriously considered returning to the comfort of his VR-induced dream world.

He, and every member of the crew, had preprogrammed into the computer system their general wishes for the type of virtual reality scenarios they'd wanted to experience during the long voyage. The liquigel and the regular neuromuscular stimulation that went with it had kept their bodies alive and in peak condition while they slept. The VR scenarios had done the same for their minds and right now Goss wished he were one of the crew, blissfully unaware of the impending crisis, living out some extended adventure in a dream-like stupor. But it was a fleeting thought. He'd always preferred reality to the VR sims—that was one of the reasons he'd volunteered for the trip to Epsilon Eridani. Goss had to get away from the existential existence that was slowly creeping across the Earth and sapping the lifeblood out of the people there.

Now that's a thought. I wonder what's happening back on Earth? I'll check on that after I've figured out what to do and what prompted Vasquez to commit murder.

"Did you record the murder of First Officer Herndon and what led up to it?" Goss asked the AI.

"Yes. Would you like to view the recording?"

"Play it."

The images of the local stellar coordinates and potential ship trajectories blinked off, and were replaced by a holographic representation of the control room, the same room in which Goss was now standing, only this time it was occupied by both Vasquez and Herndon. In the bottom right corner was the clock displaying both ship time, taking into account the time dilation effects from traveling at a substantial fraction of the speed of light, and Earth time. Goss was momentarily fixated on the clock, not yet paying attention to what Vasquez and Herndon were saying.

When this conversation was taking place, nine hundred years had passed on Earth. And these events happened over one thousand years ago. Goss held his breath while he thought about his friends, his brothers and sisters, and all that he knew—now probably totally forgotten by anyone and everyone at home.

Vasquez's angry voice roared out of the hologram.

"Herndon! We can't do it. I don't want to do it anymore. I'm forty-eight years old and outside of VR, with good medical care, I might live to be a hundred. But down there it will be a hard life these next fifty years. How could we have been so stupid as to think we could come to a primitive world and build a new civilization?"

"Commander," said Herndon, "with all respect, we knew what we were signing up for when we left Earth. We'll have our technology and our medicines to get us started, but, yes, it's inevitable that we'll slide backward technologically. After all, we won't have the infrastructure to make the computers, the fusion power plants, and all that would be required to replace the gear as it wears out. But if we work hard, and if we get some luck, we can leapfrog to an early twentieth century technology base that's sustainable. Our descendants can then bring things back to where we are today. After all, they'll have the library and the knowledge. All they will lack is the infrastructure and they can rebuild that!"

"Okay. Let's say you're right. We work hard for the next fifty years to establish a colony that will someday mature to the point that our children's children will have won back what we will have lost.

Great. But we'll be dead in fifty years. It doesn't have to be that way. We've already lived almost a thousand years and we can live another thousand! And that thousand won't be hard! We can continue to live like kings. I enjoyed being in VR. It sure as hell beats what we'll face down there."

Up to this point, Herndon's part of the argument had been more intellectual than emotional. With Vasquez's last words, his demeanor changed. He leaned forward and stared at his commander with intensity.

"Commander, are you suggesting we not wake everyone up and just go back to sleep? You think we should just forget about why we're here and go back to our VR dreams? You can't be serious. That's not living! That's why most of us left Earth in the first place!"

Vasquez stared at Herndon, then at the deck. He slowly raised his head.

"No, Mack, you're right. We're here to colonize and colonize is what we'll do. I don't know what I was thinking. Let's get the ship ready and then start waking everyone up." Vasquez nodded and appeared to accede to Herndon's argument.

"Thank you, Captain," Herndon said. He turned away, probably to return to a duty station. Vasquez stared after him and the look of accommodation changed. His features hardened with rage. Rage and determination.

Goss watched in horror as Commander Vasquez reached inside his tunic and withdrew what looked like a piece of computer cabling or a wire harness. He wrapped both ends around his fists, keeping a good foot of bare wire between his outstretched hands. He slowly walked up behind Herndon, who was now totally engrossed in his own thoughts, and garroted him. Took him down where he stood.

Herndon collapsed almost without a struggle. For Goss, who to this point had only seen death in virtual reality, it was both gruesome and captivating. He couldn't avert his eyes until after Vasquez let the lifeless body of his second-in-command fall to the floor. Vasquez showed no remorse. He strode back to the command chair and spoke to the AI.

"Plot a course to our next destination and prepare to leave orbit. Prepare my sleep chamber and upload VR set twenty-seven. I rather enjoyed that one."

Horrified, Goss watched Vasquez work from his command chair for another five minutes, apparently performing all the routine systems checks required for the ship to begin yet another long voyage between the stars. Vasquez never again looked at Herndon's body.

Goss stopped the holographic playback and stared at the floor where the corpse had lain. Herndon had died about a thousand years ago and Goss wondered where the body had been put and what Vasquez must have been thinking when he disposed of it. Had he done it before going back to sleep or had he removed whatever had remained of the body when they arrived at Tau Ceti three hundred years later?

After all that time, the body might have still been there, relatively intact, since the ship powered down all the life support to subfreezing temperatures during interstellar cruise. Or it might have been nothing more than dust that the maintenance robots had long-since cleaned up and recycled. Goss might never know.

It's tempting, Goss thought. *A thousand years of simulated living versus only another fifty of real life. But that's not really living.* Goss now knew what he had to do.

"AI, can I reprogram everyone's VR sims? Can I overlay something or weave into what they're experiencing some sort of theme or plot?"

"Yes, as the new commander, you have the authorization to make such changes."

"Good. Overwrite every single VR simulation, even my own, with a series of real-life, day-by-day experiences of the average person, beginning around the year 1500. Use the historical databases. Don't make anyone absolutely miserable, but let them experience *real* life, *real* work, *real* love and loss. Let them experience the progression of life from one era to the next until they get close to the time in which we left Earth."

With any luck, when we reach Tau Ceti and wake up, we'll be ready to keep living a real life—and to start a new one.

A COUNTRY FOR OLD MEN

Ben Bova

Ben began his writing career working as a technical writer for Project Vanguard and quickly surpassed the pace of the real space program by writing realistic stories of space exploration that have taken his readers well beyond the Moon and into deep space. Sadly, we lost the great Ben Bova to COVID in 2020. The entire science fiction community misses him dearly.

Les has been reading Ben's work since he was in high school, when Ben edited Analog *and then* Omni Magazine. *Les cut his science fiction teeth on the Kinsman saga and every book he could find with Ben's name appended. Yes, he is a fan. This collection was his first opportunity to work with Ben, and it led to their collaborating on the novel* Rescue Mode *(Baen, 2014). During that collaboration, Les says he learned the art of writing hard science fiction from a true master.*

Jack also has been a lifelong fan and was a personal friend.

In "A Country for Old Men," Ben takes us on an interstellar journey and demonstrates that we sometimes place too much faith in technology when a touch of honest duplicity is called for.

※ ※ ※

1

"IT'S OBVIOUS!" said Vartan Gregorian, standing imperiously before the two others seated on the couch. "I'm the best damned pilot in the history of the human race!"

Planting his fists on his hips, he struck a pose that was nothing less than preening.

Half buried in the lounge's plush curved couch, Alexander Ignatiev bit back an impulse to laugh in the Armenian's face. But Nikki Deneuve, sitting next to him, gazed up at Gregorian with shining eyes.

Breaking into a broad grin, Gregorian went on, "This bucket is moving faster than any ship ever built, no? We've flown farther from Earth than anybody ever has, true?"

Nikki nodded eagerly as she responded, "Forty percent of lightspeed and approaching six light years."

"So, I'm the pilot of the fastest, highest-flying ship of all time!" Gregorian exclaimed. "That makes me the best flier in the history of the human race. QED!"

Ignatiev shook his head at the conceited oaf. But he saw that Nikki was captivated by his posturing. Then it struck him. She loves him! And Gregorian is showing off for her.

The ship's lounge was as relaxing and comfortable as human designers back on Earth could make it. It was arranged in a circular grouping of sumptuously appointed niches, each holding high curved banquettes that could seat up to half a dozen close friends in reasonable privacy.

Ignatiev had left his quarters after suffering still another defeat at the hands of the computerized chess program and snuck down to the lounge in mid-afternoon, hoping to find it empty. He needed a hideaway while the housekeeping robots cleaned his suite. Their busy, buzzing thoroughness drove him to distraction; it was impossible to concentrate on chess or anything else while the machines were dusting, laundering, straightening his rooms, restocking his autokitchen and his bar, making the bed with crisply fresh linens.

So he sought refuge in the lounge, only to find Gregorian and Denueve already there, in a niche beneath a display screen that showed the star fields outside. Once the sight of those stars scattered across the infinite void would have stirred Ignatiev's heart. But not any more, not since Sonya died.

Sipping at the vodka that the serving robot had poured for him the instant he had stepped into the lounge, thanks to the robot's face recognition program, Ignatiev couldn't help grousing, "And who says you are the pilot, Vartan? I didn't see any designation for pilot in the mission's assignment roster."

Gregorian was moderately handsome and rather tall, quite slim, with thick dark hair and laugh crinkles at the corners of his dark brown eyes. Ignatiev tended to think of people in terms of chess pieces, and he counted Gregorian as a prancing horse, all style and little substance.

"I am flight systems engineer, no?" Gregorian countered. "My assignment is to monitor the flight control program. That makes me the pilot."

Nikki, still beaming at him, said, "If you're the pilot, Vartan, then I must be the navigator."

"Astrogator," Ignatiev corrected bluntly.

The daughter of a Quebecoise mother and French Moroccan father, Nicolette Denueve had unfortunately inherited her father's stocky physique and her mother's sharp nose. Ignatiev thought her unlovely—and yet there was a charm to her, a gamine-like wide-eyed innocence that beguiled Ignatiev's crusty old heart. She was a physicist, bright and conscientious, not an engineering monkey like the braggart Gregorian. Thus it was a tragedy that she had been selected for this star mission.

She finally turned away from Gregorian to say to Ignatiev, "It's good to see you, Dr. Ignatiev. You've become something of a hermit these past few months."

He coughed and muttered, "I've been busy on my research." The truth was he couldn't bear to be among these youngsters, couldn't stand the truth that they would one day return to Earth while he would be long dead.

Alexander Alexandrovich Ignatiev, by far the oldest man among the starship's crew, thought that Nikki could have been the daughter he'd never had. Daughter? he snapped at himself silently. Granddaughter, he corrected. Great-granddaughter, even. He was a dour astrophysicist approaching his hundred and fortieth birthday, his short-cropped hair iron gray but his mind and body still reasonably vigorous and active thanks to rejuvenation therapies. Yet he felt cheated by the way the world worked, bitter about being exiled to this one-way flight to a distant star.

Technically, he was the senior executive of this mission, an honor that he found almost entirely empty. To him, it was like being the principal of a school for very bright, totally wayward children.

Each one of them must have been president of their school's student body, he thought: accustomed to getting their own way and total strangers to discipline. Besides, the actual commander of the ship was the artificial intelligence program run by the ship's central computer.

If Gregorian is a chessboard knight, Ignatiev mused to himself, then what is Nikki? Not the queen; she's too young, too uncertain of herself for that. Her assignment to monitor the navigation program was something of a joke: the ship followed a ballistic trajectory, like an arrow shot from Earth. Nothing for a navigator to do except check the ship's position each day.

Maybe she's a bishop, Ignatiev mused, if a woman can be a bishop: quiet, self-effacing, possessing hidden depths. And reliable, trustworthy, always staying to the color of the square she started on. She'll cling to Gregorian, unless he hurts her terribly. That possibility made Ignatiev's blood simmer.

And me? he asked himself. A pawn, nothing more. But then he thought, maybe I'm a rook, stuck off in a corner of the board, barely noticed by anybody.

"Dr. Ignatiev is correct," said Gregorian, trying to regain control of the conversation. "The proper term is astrogator."

"Whatever," said Nikki, her eyes returning to Gregorian's handsome young face.

"Young" was a relative term. Gregorian was approaching sixty, although he still had the vigor, the attitudes and demeanor of an obstreperous teenager. Ignatiev thought it would be appropriate if the Armenian's face were blotched with acne. Youth is wasted on the young, Ignatiev thought. Thanks to life-elongation therapies, average life expectancy among the starship crew was well above two hundred. It had to be.

The scoopship was named *Sagan*, after some minor twentieth-century astronomer. It was heading for Gliese 581, a red dwarf star slightly more than twenty light years from Earth. For Ignatiev, it was a one-way journey. Even with all the life-extension therapies, he would never survive the century-long round trip. Gregorian would, of course, and so would Nikki.

Ignatiev brooded over the unfairness of it. By the time the ship returned to Earth, the two of them would be grandparents and Ignatiev would be long dead.

Unfair, he thought as he pushed himself up from the plush banquette and left the lounge without a word to either one of them. The universe is unfair. I don't deserve this: to die alone, unloved, unrecognized, my life's work forgotten, all my hopes crushed to dust.

As he reached the lounge's hatch, he turned his head to see what the two of them were up to. Chatting, smiling, holding hands, all the subverbal signals that lovers send to each other. They had eyes only for one another, and paid absolutely no attention to him.

Just like the rest of the goddamned world, Ignatiev thought.

He had labored all his life in the groves of academe, and what had it gotten him? A membership in the International Academy of Sciences, along with seventeen thousand other anonymous workers. A pension that barely covered his living expenses. Three marriages: two ruined by divorce and the third—the only one that really mattered—destroyed by that inevitable thief, death.

He hardly remembered how enthusiastic he had been as a young post-doc all those years ago, his astrophysics degree in hand, burning with ambition. He was going to unlock the secrets of the universe! The pulsars, those enigmatic cinders, the remains of ancient supernova explosions: Ignatiev was going to discover what made them tick.

But the universe was far subtler than he had thought. Soon enough he learned that a career in science can be a study in anonymous drudgery. The pulsars kept their secrets, no matter how assiduously Ignatiev nibbled around the edges of their mystery.

And now the honor of being the senior executive on the human race's first interstellar mission. Some honor, Ignatiev thought sourly. They needed someone competent but expendable. Send old Ignatiev, let him go out in a fizzle of glory.

Shaking his head as he trudged along the thickly carpeted passageway to his quarters, Ignatiev muttered to himself, "If only there were something I could accomplish, something I could discover, something to put some meaning to my life."

He had lived long enough to realize that his life would be no more remembered than the life of a worker ant. He wanted more than that. He wanted to be remembered. He wanted his name to be revered. He wanted students in the far future to know that he had existed, that he had made a glowing contribution to humankind's store of knowledge and understanding. He wanted Nikki Deneuve to gaze at *him* with adoring eyes.

"It will never be," Ignatiev told himself as he slid open the door to his quarters. With a wry shrug, he reminded himself of a line from some old English poet: "Ah, that a man's reach should exceed his grasp, or what's a heaven for?"

Alexander Ignatiev did not believe in heaven. But he thought he knew what hell was like.

2

AS HE ENTERED his quarters he saw that at least the cleaning robots had finished and left; the sitting room looked almost tidy. And he was alone.

The expedition to Gliese 581 had left Earth with tremendous fanfare. The first human mission to another star! Gliese 581 was a very ordinary star in most respects: a dim red dwarf, barely one-third of the Sun's mass. The galaxy was studded with such stars. But Gliese 581 was unusual in one supremely interesting way: it possessed an entourage of half a dozen planets. Most of them were gas giants, bloated conglomerates of hydrogen and helium. But a couple of them were rocky worlds, somewhat like Earth. And one of those—Gliese 581g—orbited at just the right "Goldilocks" distance from its parent star to be able to have liquid water on its surface.

Liquid water meant life. In the solar system, wherever liquid water existed, life existed. In the permafrost beneath the frozen rust-red surface of Mars, in the ice-covered seas of the moons of Jupiter and Saturn, in massive Jupiter's planet-girdling ocean: wherever liquid water had been found, life was found with it.

Half a dozen robotic probes confirmed that liquid water actually did exist on the surface of Gliese 581g, but they found no evidence of life. Not an amoeba, not even a bacterium. But that didn't deter the scientific hierarchy. Robots are terribly limited, they proclaimed. We must send human scientists to Gliese 581g to search for life there, scientists of all types; men and women who will sacrifice half their lives to the search for life beyond the solar system.

Ignatiev was picked to sacrifice the last half of his life. He knew he would never see Earth again, and he told himself that he didn't care. There was nothing on Earth that interested him anymore, not since Sonya's death. But he wanted to find something, to make an impact, to keep his name alive after he was gone.

Most of the two hundred scientists, engineers and technicians aboard *Sagan* were sleeping away the decades of the flight in cryonic suspension. They would be revived once the scoopship arrived at Gliese 581's vicinity. Only a dozen were awake during the flight, assigned to monitor the ship's systems, ready to make corrections or repairs if necessary.

The ship was highly automated, of course. The human crew was a backup, a concession to human vanity unwilling to hand the operation of the ship completely to electronic and mechanical devices. Human egos feared fully autonomous machines. Thus a dozen human lives were sacrificed to spend five decades waiting for the machines to fail.

They hadn't failed so far. From the fusion power plant deep in the ship's core to the tenuous magnetic scoop stretching a thousand kilometers in front of the ship, all the systems worked perfectly well. When a minor malfunction arose, the ship's machines repaired themselves, under the watchful direction of the master AI program. Even the AI system's computer program ran flawlessly, to Ignatiev's utter frustration. It beat him at chess with depressing regularity.

In addition to the meaningless title of senior executive, Alexander Ignatiev had a specific technical task aboard the starship. His assignment was to monitor the electromagnetic funnel that scooped in hydrogen from the thin interstellar medium to feed the ship's nuclear fusion engine. Every day he faithfully checked the gauges and display screens in the ship's command center, reminding himself each time that the practice of physics always comes down to reading a goddamned dial.

The funnel operated flawlessly. A huge gossamer web of hair-thin superconducting wires, it created an invisible magnetic field that spread out before the starship like a thousand-kilometer-wide scoop, gathering in the hydrogen atoms floating between the stars and ionizing them as they were sucked into the ship's innards like a huge baleen whale scooping up the tiny creatures of the sea that it fed upon.

Deep in the starship's bowels the fusion generator forced the hydrogen ions to fuse together into helium ions, giving up energy in the process to run the ship. Like the Sun and the stars themselves, the starship lived on hydrogen fusion.

Ignatiev slid the door of his quarters shut. The suite of rooms allotted to him was small, but far more luxurious than any home he had lived in back on Earth. The psychotechnicians among the mission's planners, worried about the crew's morale during the decades-long flight, had insisted on every creature comfort they could think of: everything from body-temperature waterbeds that adjusted to one's weight and size to digitally controlled décor that could change its color scheme at the call of one's voice; from an automated kitchen that could prepare a world-spanning variety of cuisines to virtual reality entertainment systems.

Ignatiev ignored all the splendor; or rather, he took it for granted. Creature comforts were fine, but he had spent the first months of the mission converting his beautifully-wrought sitting room into an astrophysics laboratory. The sleek Scandinavian desk of teak inlaid with meteoric silver now held a conglomeration of computers and sensor readouts. The fake fireplace was hidden behind a junkpile of discarded spectrometers, magnetometers, and other gadgetry that Ignatiev had used and abandoned. He could see a faint ring of dust on the floor around the mess; he had given the cleaning robots strict orders not to touch it.

Above the obstructed fireplace was a framed digital screen programmed to show high-definition images of the world's great artworks—when it wasn't being used as a three-dimensional entertainment screen. Ignatiev had connected it to the ship's main optical telescope, so that it showed the stars spangled against the blackness of space. Usually the telescope was pointed forward, with the tiny red dot of Gliese 581 centered in its field of view. Now and then, at the command of the ship's AI system, it looked back toward the diminishing yellow speck of the Sun.

Ignatiev had started the flight by spending most of his waking hours examining this interstellar Siberia in which he was exiled. It was an excuse to stay away from the chattering young monkeys of the crew. He had studied the planet-sized chunks of ice and rock in the Oort Cloud that surrounded the outermost reaches of the solar system. Once the ship was past that region, he turned his interest back to the enigmatic, frustrating pulsars. Each one throbbed at a precise frequency, more accurate than an atomic clock. Why? What determined their frequency? Why did some supernova explosions produce pulsars while others didn't?

Ignatiev batted his head against those questions in vain. More and more, as the months of the mission stretched into years, he spent his days playing chess against the AI system. And losing consistently.

"Alexander Alexandrovich."

He looked up from the chessboard he had set up on his desktop screen, turned in his chair and directed his gaze across the room to the display screen above the fireplace. The lovely, smiling face of the artificial intelligence system's avatar filled the screen.

The psychotechnicians among the mission planners had decided that the human crew would work more effectively with the AI program if it showed a human face. For each human crew member, the face was slightly different: the psychotechs had tried to create a personal relationship for each of the crew. The deceit annoyed Ignatiev. The program treated him like a child. Worse, the face it displayed for him reminded him too much of his late wife.

"I'm busy," he growled.

Unperturbed, the avatar's smiling face said, "Yesterday you requested use of the main communications antenna."

"I want to use it as a radio telescope, to map out the interstellar hydrogen we're moving through."

"The twenty-one centimeter radiation," said the avatar knowingly.

"Yes."

"You are no longer studying the pulsars?"

He bit back an angry reply. "I have given up on the pulsars," he admitted. "The interstellar medium interests me more. I have decided to map the hydrogen in detail."

Besides, he admitted to himself, that will be a lot easier than the pulsars.

The AI avatar said calmly, "Mission protocol requires the main antenna be available to receive communications from mission control."

"The secondary antenna can do that," he said. Before the AI system could reply, he added, "Besides, any communications from

Earth will be six years old. We're not going to get any urgent messages that must be acted upon immediately."

"Still," said the avatar, "mission protocol cannot be dismissed lightly."

"It won't hurt anything to let me use the main antenna for a few hours each day," he insisted.

The avatar remained silent for several seconds: an enormous span of time for the computer program.

At last, the avatar conceded, "Perhaps so. You may use the main antenna, provisionally."

"I am eternally grateful," Ignatiev said. His sarcasm was wasted on the AI system.

As the weeks lengthened into months he found himself increasingly fascinated by the thin interstellar hydrogen gas and discovered, only to his mild surprise, that it was not evenly distributed in space.

Of course, astrophysicists had known for centuries that there are regions in space where the interstellar gas clumped so thickly and was so highly ionized that it glowed. Gaseous emission nebulae were common throughout the galaxy, although Ignatiev mentally corrected the misnomer: those nebulae actually consisted not of gas, but of plasma—gas that is highly ionized.

But here in the placid emptiness on the way to Gliese 581, Ignatiev found himself slowly becoming engrossed with the way that even the thin, bland neutral interstellar gas was not evenly distributed. Not at all. The hydrogen was thicker in some regions than in others.

This was hardly a new discovery, but from the vantagepoint of the starship inside the billowing interstellar clouds, the fine structure of the hydrogen became a thing of beauty in Ignatiev's eyes. The interstellar gas didn't merely hang there passively between the stars, it flowed: slowly, almost imperceptibly, but it drifted on currents shaped by the gravitational pull of the stars.

"That old writer was correct," he muttered to himself as he studied the stream of interstellar hydrogen that the ship was cutting through. "There are currents in space."

He tried to think of the writer's name, but couldn't come up with it. A Russian name, he recalled. But nothing more specific.

The more he studied the interstellar gas, the more captivated he became. He went days without playing a single game of chess.

Weeks. The interstellar hydrogen gas wasn't static, not at all. It was like a beautiful intricate lacework that flowed, fluttered, shifted in a stately silent pavane among the stars.

The clouds of hydrogen were like a tide of bubbling champagne, he saw, frothing slowly in rhythm to the heartbeats of the stars.

The astronomers back on Earth had no inkling of this. They looked at the general features of the interstellar gas scanned at ranges of kiloparsecs and more; they were interested in mapping the great sweep of the galaxy's spiral arms. But here, traveling inside the wafting, drifting clouds, Ignatiev measured the detailed configuration of the interstellar hydrogen and found it beautiful.

He slumped back in his form-fitting desk chair, stunned at the splendor of it all. He thought of the magnificent panoramas he had seen of the cosmic span of the galaxies: loops and whorls of bright shining galaxies, each containing billions of stars, extending for megaparsecs, out to infinity, long strings of glowing lights surrounding vast bubbles of emptiness. The interstellar gas showed the same delicate complexity, in miniature: loops and whorls, streams and bubbles. It was truly, cosmically, beautiful.

"Fractal," he muttered to himself. "The universe is one enormous fractal pattern."

Then the artificial intelligence program intruded on his privacy. "Alexander Alexandrovich, the weekly staff meeting begins in ten minutes."

3

WEEKLY STAFF MEETING, Ignatiev grumbled inwardly as he hauled himself up from his desk chair. More like the weekly group therapy session for a gaggle of self-important juvenile delinquents.

He made his way grudgingly through the ship's central passageway to the conference room, located next to the command center. Several other crew members were also heading along the gleaming, brushed-chrome walls and colorful carpeting of the passageway. They gave Ignatiev cheery, smiling greetings; he nodded or grunted at them.

As chief executive of the crew, Ignatiev took the chair at the head of the polished conference table. The others sauntered in leisurely. Nikki and Gregorian came in almost last and took seats at the end of the table, next to each other, close enough to hold hands.

These meetings were a pure waste of time, Ignatiev thought. Their ostensible purpose was to report on the ship's performance, which any idiot could determine by casting half an eye at the digital readouts available on the ship's display screens. The screens gave up-to-the-nanosecond details of every component of the ship's equipment.

But no, mission protocol required that all twelve crew members must meet face-to-face once each week. Good psychology, the mission planners believed. An opportunity for human interchange, personal communications. A chance for whining and displays of overblown egos, Ignatiev thought. A chance for these sixty-year-old children to complain about one another.

Of the twelve of them, only Ignatiev and Nikki were physicists. Four of the others were engineers of various stripes, three were biologists, two psychotechnicians and one stocky, sour-faced woman a medical doctor.

So he was quite surprised when the redheaded young electrical engineer in charge of the ship's power system started the meeting by reporting:

"I don't know if any of you have noticed it yet, but the ship's reduced our internal electrical power consumption by ten percent."

Mild perplexity.

"Ten percent?"

"Why?"

"I haven't noticed any reduction."

The redhead waved his hands vaguely as he replied, "It's mostly in peripheral areas. Your microwave ovens, for example. They've been powered down ten percent. Lights in unoccupied areas. Things like that."

Curious, Ignatiev asked, "Why the reduction?"

His squarish face frowning slightly, the engineer replied, "From what Alice tells me, the density of the gas being scooped in for the generator has decreased slightly. Alice says it's only a temporary condition. Nothing to worry about."

Alice was the nickname these youngsters had given to the artificial intelligence program that actually ran the ship. Artificial

Intelligence. AI. Alice Intellectual. Some even called the AI system Alice Imperatress. Ignatiev thought it childish nonsense.

"How long will this go on?" asked one of the biologists. "I'm incubating a batch of genetically-engineered algae for an experiment."

"It shouldn't be a problem," the engineer said. Ignatiev thought he looked just the tiniest bit worried.

Surprisingly, Gregorian piped up. "A few of the uncrewed probes that went ahead of us also encountered power anomalies. They were temporary. No big problem."

Ignatiev nodded but made a mental note to check on the situation. Six light years out from Earth, he thought, meant that every problem was a big one.

One of the psychotechs cleared her throat for attention, then announced, "Several of the crew members have failed to fill out their monthly performance evaluations. I know that some of you regard these evaluations as if they were school exams, but mission protocol—"

Ignatiev tuned her out, knowing that they would bicker over this drivel for half an hour, at least. He was too optimistic. The discussion became quite heated and lasted more than an hour.

4

ONCE THE MEETING FINALLY ENDED, Ignatiev hurried back to his quarters and immediately looked up the mission logs of the six automated probes that had been sent to Gliese 581.

Gregorian was right, he saw. Half of the six probes had reported drops in their power systems, a partial failure of their fusion generators. Three of them. The malfunctions were only temporary, but they occurred at virtually the same point in the long voyage to Gliese 581.

The earliest of the probes had shut down altogether, its systems going into hibernation for more than four months. The mission controllers back on Earth had written the mission off as a failure when they could not communicate with the probe. Then, just as abruptly as the ship had shut down, it sprang to life again.

Puzzling.

"Alexander Alexandrovich," called the AI system's avatar. "Do you need more information on the probe missions?"

He looked up from his desk to see the lovely female face of the AI program's avatar displayed on the screen above his fireplace. A resentful anger simmered inside him. The psychotechs suppose that the face they've given the AI system makes it easier for me to interact with it, he thought. Idiots. Fools.

"I need the mission controllers' analyses of each of the probe missions," he said, struggling to keep his voice cool, keep the anger from showing.

"May I ask why?" The avatar smiled at him. Sonya, he thought. Sonya.

"I want to correlate their power reductions with the detailed map I'm making of the interstellar gas."

"Interesting," said the avatar.

"I'm pleased you think so," Ignatiev replied, through gritted teeth.

The avatar's image disappeared, replaced by data scrolling slowly along the screen. Ignatiev settled deeper into the form-adjusting desk chair and began to study the reports.

His door buzzer grated in his ears. Annoyed, Ignatiev told his computer to show who was at the door.

Gregorian was standing out in the passageway, tall, lanky, egocentric Gregorian. What in hell could he want? Ignatiev asked himself.

The big oaf pressed the buzzer again.

Thoroughly piqued at the interruption—no, the invasion of his privacy—Ignatiev growled, "Go away."

"Dr. Ignatiev," the Armenian called. "Please."

Ignatiev closed his eyes and wished that Gregorian would disappear. But when he opened them again the man was still at his door, fidgeting nervously.

Ignatiev surrendered. "Enter," he muttered.

The door slid back and Gregorian ambled in, his angular face serious, almost somber. His usual lopsided grin was nowhere to be seen.

"I'm sorry to intrude on you, Dr. Ignatiev," said the engineer.

Leaning back in his desk chair to peer up at Gregorian, Ignatiev said, "It must be something terribly important."

The contempt was wasted on Gregorian. He looked around the

sitting room, his eyes resting for a moment on the pile of abandoned equipment hiding the fireplace.

"Uh, may I sit down?"

"Of course," Ignatiev said, waving a hand toward the couch across the room.

Gregorian went to it and sat, bony knees poking up awkwardly. Ignatiev rolled his desk chair across the carpeting to face him.

"So what is so important that you had to come see me?"

Very seriously, Gregorian replied, "It's Nikki."

Ignatiev felt a pang of alarm. "What's wrong with Nikki?"

"Nothing! She's wonderful."

"So?"

"I . . . I've fallen in love with her," Gregorian said, almost whispering.

"What of it?" Ignatiev snapped.

"I don't know if she loves me."

What an ass! Ignatiev thought. A blind, blundering ass who can't see the nose in front of his face.

"She . . . I mean, we get along very well. It's always fun to be with her. But . . . does she like me well enough . . ." his voice faded.

Why is he coming to me with this? Ignatiev wondered. Why not one of the psycotechs? That's what they're here for.

He thought he knew. The young oaf would be embarrassed to tell them about his feelings. So he comes to old Ignatiev, the father figure.

Feeling his brows knitting, Ignatiev asked, "Have you been to bed with her?"

"Oh, yes. Sure. But if I ask her to marry me, a real commitment . . . she might say no. She might not like me well enough for that. I mean, there are other guys in the crew. . . ."

Marriage? Ignatiev felt stunned. Do kids still get married? Is he saying he'd spend two centuries living with her? Then he remembered Sonya. He knew he would have spent two centuries with her. Two millennia. Two eons.

His voice strangely subdued, Ignatiev asked, "You love her so much that you want to marry her?"

Gregorian nodded mutely.

Ignatiev said, "And you're afraid that if you ask her for a

lifetime commitment she'll refuse and that will destroy your relationship."

Looking completely miserable, Gregorian said, "Yes." He stared into Ignatiev's eyes. "What should I do?"

Beneath all the bravado he's just a frightened pup, uncertain of himself, Ignatiev realized. Sixty years old and he's as scared and worried as a teenager.

I can tell him to forget her. Tell him she doesn't care about him; say that she's not interested in a lifetime commitment. I can break up their romance with a few words.

But as he looked into Gregorian's wretched face he knew he couldn't do it. It would wound the young pup; hurt him terribly. Ignatiev heard himself say, "She loves you, Vartan. She's mad about you. Can't you see that?"

"You think so?"

Ignatiev wanted to say, *Why do you think she puts up with you and your ridiculous posturing?* Instead, he told the younger man, "I'm sure of it. Go to her. Speak your heart to her."

Gregorian leaped up from the couch so abruptly that Ignatiev nearly toppled out of his rolling chair.

"I'll do that!" he shouted, starting for the door.

As Ignatiev got slowly to his feet, Gregorian stopped and said hastily, "Thank you, Dr. Ignatiev! Thank you!"

Ignatiev shrugged.

Suddenly Gregorian looked sheepish. "Is there anything I can do for you, sir?"

"No. Nothing, thank you."

"Are you still . . . uh, active?"

Ignatiev scowled at him.

"I mean, there are virtual reality simulations. You can program them to suit your own whims, you know."

"I know," Ignatiev said firmly.

Gregorian realized he'd stepped over a line. "I mean, I just thought . . . in case you need . . ."

"Good day, Vartan," said Ignatiev.

Blundering young ass, Ignatiev said to himself, as the engineer left and the door slid shut. But then he added, *And I'm a doddering old numbskull.*

He'll run straight to Nikki. She'll leap into his arms and they'll live happily ever after, or some approximation of it. And I'll be here alone, with nothing to look forward to except oblivion.

VR simulations, he huffed. The insensitive young lout. But she loves him. She loves him. That is certain.

5

IGNATIEV PACED AROUND HIS SITTING ROOM for hours after Gregorian left, cursing himself for a fool. You could have pried him away from her, he raged inwardly. But then he reflected, And what good would that do? She wouldn't come to you; you're old enough to be her great-grandfather, for god's sake.

Maybe the young oaf was right. Maybe I should try the VR simulations.

Instead, he threw himself into the reports on the automated probes that had been sent to Gliese 581. And their power failures. For days he stayed in his quarters, studying, learning, understanding.

The official explanation for the problem by the mission directors back on Earth had been nothing more than waffling, Ignatiev decided as he examined the records. Partial power failure. Only temporary. Within a few weeks it had been corrected.

Anomalies, concluded the official reports. These things happen to highly complex systems. Nothing to worry about. After all, the systems corrected themselves as they were designed to do. And the last three probes worked perfectly well.

Anomalies? Ignatiev asked himself. Anomaly is a word you use when you don't know what the hell really happened.

He thought he knew.

He took the plots of each probe's course and overlaid them against the map he'd been making of the fine structure of the interstellar medium. Sure enough, he saw that the probes had encountered a region where the interstellar gas thinned so badly that a ship's power output declined seriously. There wasn't enough hydrogen in that region for the fusion generator to run at full power! It was like a bubble in the interstellar gas: a region that was close to empty of hydrogen atoms.

Ignatiev retraced the flight paths of all six of the probes. Yes, the first one plunged straight into the bubble and shut itself down when the power output from the fusion generator dropped so low it could no longer maintain the ship's systems. The next two skirted the edges of the bubble and experienced partial power failures. That region had been dangerous for the probes. It could be fatal for *Sagan's* human cargo.

He started to write out a report for mission control, then realized before he was halfway finished with the first page that it would take more than six years for his warning to reach Earth, and another six for the mission controllers' recommendation to get back to him. And who knew how long it would take for those Earthside dunderheads to come to a decision?

"We could all be dead by then," Ignatiev muttered to himself.

"Your speculations are interesting," said the AI avatar.

Ignatiev frowned at the image on the screen above his fireplace. "It's not speculation," he growled. "It is a conclusion based on observed data."

"Alexander Alexandrovich," said the sweetly smiling face, "your conclusion comes not from the observations, but from your interpretation of the observations."

"Three of the probes had power failures."

"Temporary failures that were corrected. And three other probes experienced no failure."

"Those last three didn't go through the bubble," he said.

"They all flew the same trajectory, did they not?"

"Not exactly."

"Within a four percent deviation," the avatar said, unperturbed.

"But they flew at different times," Ignatiev pointed out. "The bubble was flowing across their flight paths. The first probe plunged into the heart of it and shut down entirely. For four months! The next two skirted its edges and still suffered power failures."

"Temporarily," said the avatar's image, still smiling patiently. "And the final three probes? They didn't encounter any problems at all, did they?"

"No," Ignatiev admitted grudgingly. "The bubble must have flowed past by the time they reached the area."

"So there should be no problem for us," the avatar said.

"You think not?" he responded. "Then why are we beginning to suffer a power shortage?"

"The inflowing hydrogen is slightly thinner here than it has been," said the avatar.

Ignatiev shook his head. "It's going to get worse. We're heading into another bubble. I'm sure of it."

The AI system said nothing.

6

BE SURE YOU'RE RIGHT, then go ahead. Ignatiev had heard that motto many long years ago, when he'd been a child watching adventure tales.

He spent an intense three weeks mapping the interstellar hydrogen directly ahead of the ship's position. His worst fears were confirmed. *Sagan* was entering a sizeable bubble where the gas density thinned out to practically nothing: fewer than a dozen hydrogen atoms per cubic meter.

He checked the specifications of the ship fusion generator and confirmed that its requirement for incoming hydrogen was far higher than the bubble could provide.

Within a few days we'll start to experience serious power outages, he realized.

What to do?

Despite his disdain for his younger crewmates, despite his loathing of meetings and committees and the kind of groupthink that passed for decision-making, he called a special meeting of the crew.

"All the ship's systems will shut down?" cried one of the psychotechs. "All of them?"

"What will happen to us during the shutdown?" asked a biologist, her voice trembling.

Calmly, his hands clasped on the conference tabletop, Ignatiev said, "If my measurements of the bubble are accurate—"

"If?" Gregorian snapped. "You mean you're not sure?"

"Not one hundred percent, no."

"Then why are you telling us this? Why have you called this meeting? To frighten us?"

"Well, he's certainly frightened me!" said one of the engineers.

Trying to hold on to his temper, Ignatiev replied, "My measurements are good enough to convince me that we face a serious problem. Very serious. Power output is already declining, and will go down more over the next few days."

"How much more?" asked the female biologist.

Ignatiev hesitated, then decided to give them the worst. "All the ship's systems could shut down like the first of the automated probes. It shut down for four months. Went into hibernation mode. Our shutdown might be even longer."

The biologist countered, "But the probe powered up again? It went into hibernation mode but then it came back to normal."

With a slow nod, Ignatiev said, "The ship's systems could survive a hibernation of many months. But *we* couldn't. Without electrical power we would not have heat, air or water recycling, lights, stoves for cooking—"

"You mean we'll die?" Nikki asked, in the tiny voice of a frightened little girl.

Ignatiev felt an urge to comfort her, to protect her from the brutal truth. "Unless we take steps," he answered softly.

"*What* steps?" Gregorian demanded.

"We have to change our course. Turn away from this bubble. Move along a path that keeps us in regions of thicker gas."

"Alexander Alexandrovich," came the voice of the AI avatar, "course changes must be approved by mission control."

Ignatiev looked up and saw that the avatar's image had sprung up on each of the conference room's walls, slightly larger than life. Naturally, he realized. The AI system had been listening to every word. The avatar's image looked slightly different to him: an amalgam of all the twelve separate images the AI system showed to each of the crew members. Sonya's features were in the image, but blurred, softened, like the face of a relative who resembled her mother strongly.

"Approved by mission control?" snapped one of the engineers, a rake-thin dark-skinned Malaysian. "It would take six years merely to get a message to them!"

"We could all be dead by then," said the redhead sitting beside him.

Unperturbed, the avatar replied, "Mission protocol includes

emergency procedures, but course changes require approval from mission control."

Everyone tried to talk at once. Ignatiev closed his eyes and listened to the babble. Almost, he laughed to himself. They would mutiny against the AI system, if they knew how. He saw in his imagination a handful of children trying to rebel against a peg-legged pirate captain.

At last he put up his hands to silence them. They shut up and looked to him, their expressions ranging from sullen to fearful to self-pitying.

"Arguments and threats won't sway the AI program," he told them. "Only logic."

Looking thoroughly nettled, Gregorian said, "So try logic, then."

Ignatiev said to the image on the wall screens, "What is the mission protocol's first priority?"

The answer came immediately, "To protect the lives of the human crew and cargo."

Cargo, Ignatiev grunted to himself. The stupid program thinks of the people in cryonic suspension as *cargo*.

Aloud, he said, "Observations show that we are entering a region of very low hydrogen density."

Immediately the avatar replied, "This will necessitate reducing power consumption."

"Power consumption may be reduced below the levels needed to keep the crew alive," Ignatiev said.

For half a heartbeat the AI avatar said nothing. Then, "That is a possibility."

"If we change course to remain within the region where hydrogen density is adequate to maintain all the ship's systems," Ignatiev continued slowly, carefully, "none of the crew's lives would be endangered."

"Not so, Alexander Alexandrovich," the avatar replied.

"Not so?"

"The immediate threat of reduced power availability might be averted by changing course, but once the ship has left its preplanned trajectory toward Gliese 581, how would you navigate toward our destination? Course correction data will take more than twelve years to reach us from Earth. The ship will be wandering through a wilderness, far from its destination. The crew will eventually die of starvation."

"We could navigate ourselves," said Ignatiev. "We wouldn't need course correction data from mission control."

The avatar's image actually shook its head. "No member of the crew is an accredited astrogator."

"I can do it!" Nikki cried. "I monitor the navigation program."

With a hint of a smile, the avatar said gently, "Monitoring the astrogation program does not equip you to plot course changes."

Before Nikki or anyone else could object, Ignatiev asked coolly, "So what do you recommend?"

Again the AI system hesitated before answering, almost a full second. It must be searching every byte of data in its memory, Ignatiev thought.

At last the avatar responded. "While this ship passes through the region of low fuel density the animate crew should enter cryonic suspension."

"Cryosleep?" Gregorian demanded. "For how long?"

"As long as necessary. The cryonics units can be powered by the ship's backup fuel cells—"

The redhaired engineer said, "Why don't we use the fuel cells to run the ship?"

Ignatiev shook his head. The kid *knows* better, he's just grasping at straws.

Sure enough, the AI avatar replied patiently, "The fuel cells would power the ship for a week or less, depending on internal power consumption."

Crestfallen, the engineer said, "Yeah. Right."

"Cryosleep is the indicated technique for passing through this emergency," said the AI system.

Ignatiev asked, "If the fuel cells are used solely for maintaining the cryosleep units' refrigeration, how long could they last?"

"Two months," replied the avatar. "That includes maintaining the cryosleep units already in use by the cargo."

"Understood," said Ignatiev. "And if this region of low fuel density extends for more than two months?"

Without hesitation, the AI avatar answered, "Power to the cryosleep units will be lost."

"And the people in those units?"

"They will die," said the avatar, without a flicker of human emotion.

Gregorian said, "Then we'd better hope that the bubble doesn't last for more than two months."

Ignatiev saw the others nodding, up and down the conference table. They looked genuinely frightened, but they didn't know what else could be done.

He thought he did.

7

THE MEETING BROKE UP with most of the crew members muttering to one another about sleeping through the emergency.

"Too bad they don't have capsules big enough for the two of us," Gregorian said brashly to Nikki. He was trying to show a valor he doesn't truly feel, Ignatiev thought. They don't like the idea of crawling into those capsules and closing the lids over their faces. It scares them. Too much like coffins.

With Gregorian at her side, Nikki approached him as he headed for the conference room's door. Looking troubled, fearful, she asked, "How long . . . do you have any idea?"

"Probably not more than two months," he said, with a certainty he did not actually feel. "Maybe even a little less."

Gregorian grasped Nikki's slim arm. "We'll take capsules next to each other. I'll dream of you all the time we're asleep."

Nikki smiled up at him.

But Ignatiev knew better. In cryosleep you didn't dream. The cold seeped into the brain's neurons and denatured the chemicals that hold memories. Cryonic sleepers awoke without memories, many of them forgot how to speak, how to walk, even how to control their bladders and bowels. It was necessary to download a person's brain patterns into a computer before entering cryosleep, and then restore the memories digitally once the sleeper was awakened.

The AI system is going to do *that* for us? Ignatiev scoffed at the idea. That was one of the reasons why the mission required keeping a number of the crew awake during the long flight: to handle the uploading of the memories of the two hundred men and women cryosleeping through the journey once they were awakened at Gliese 581.

Ignatiev left the conference room and headed toward his quarters. There was much to do: he didn't entirely trust the AI system's judgment. Despite its sophistication, it was still a computer program, limited to the data and instructions fed into it.

So? he asked himself. Aren't you limited to the data and instructions fed into *your* brain? Aren't we all?

"Dr. Ignatiev."

Turning, he saw Nikki hurrying up the passageway toward him. For once she was alone, without Gregorian clutching her.

He made a smile for her. It took an effort.

Nikki said softly, "I want to thank you."

"Thank me?"

"Vartan told me that he confided in you. That you made him understand..."

Ignatiev shook his head. "He was blind."

"And you helped him to see."

Feeling helpless, stupid, he replied, "It was nothing."

"No," Nikki said. "It was everything. He's asked me to marry him."

"People of your generation still marry?"

"Some of us still believe in a lifetime commitment," she said.

A lifetime of two centuries? Ignatiev wondered. That's some commitment.

Almost shyly, her eyes lowered, Nikki said, "We'd like you to be at our wedding. Would you be Vartan's best man?"

Thunderstruck. "Me? But you... I mean, he..."

Smiling, she explained, "He's too frightened of you to ask. It took all his courage for him to ask you about me."

And Ignatiev suddenly understood. I must look like an old ogre to him. A tyrant. An intolerant ancient dragon.

"Tell him to ask me himself," he said gently.

"You won't refuse him?"

Almost smiling, Ignatiev answered, "No, of course not."

Nikki beamed at him. "Thank you!"

And she turned and raced off down the passageway, leaving Ignatiev standing alone, wondering at the working of the human mind.

8

ONCE HE GOT BACK to his own quarters, and still feeling slightly stunned at his own softheartedness, Ignatiev called for the AI system.

"How may I help you, Alexander Alexandrovich?" The image looked like Sonya once again. More than ever, Ignatiev thought.

"How will the sleepers' brain scans be uploaded into them once they are awakened?" he asked.

"The ship's automated systems will perform that task," said the seemingly imperturbable avatar.

"No," said Ignatiev. "Those systems were never meant to operate completely autonomously."

"The uploading program is capable of autonomous operation."

"It requires human oversight," he insisted. "Check the mission protocols."

"Human oversight is required," the avatar replied, "except in emergencies where such oversight would not be feasible. In such cases, the system is capable of autonomous operation."

"In theory."

"In the mission protocols."

Ignatiev grinned harshly at the image on the screen above his fireplace. Arguing with the AI system was almost enjoyable; if the problem wasn't so desperate, it might even be fun. Like a chess game. But then he remembered how rarely he managed to beat the AI system's chess program.

"I don't propose to trust my mind and the minds of the rest of the crew to an untested collection of bits and bytes."

The image seemed almost to smile back at him. "The system has been tested, Alexander Alexandrovich. It was tested quite thoroughly back on Earth. You should read the reports."

A hit, he told himself. A very palpable hit. He dipped his chin in acknowledgement. "I will do that."

The avatar's image winked out, replaced by the title page of a scientific paper published several years before *Sagan* had started out for Gliese 581.

Ignatiev read the report. Twice. Then he looked up the supporting literature. Yes, he concluded, a total of eleven human beings had been successfully returned to active life by an automated uploading system after being cryonically frozen for several weeks.

The work had been done in a laboratory on Earth, with whole phalanxes of experts on hand to fix anything that might have gone wrong. The report referenced earlier trials where things *did* go wrong and the standby scientific staff was hurriedly pressed into action. But at last those eleven volunteers were frozen after downloading their brain scans then revived and their electrical patterns uploaded from computers into their brains once again. Automatically. Without human assistance.

All eleven reported that they felt no different after the experiment than they had before being frozen. Ignatiev wondered at that. It's too good to be true, he told himself. Too self-serving. How would they know what they felt before being frozen? But that's what the record showed.

The scientific literature destroyed his final argument against the AI system. The crew began downloading their brain scans the next day.

All but Ignatiev.

He stood by in the scanning center when Nikki downloaded her brain patterns. Gregorian was with her, of course. Ignatiev watched as the Armenian helped her to stretch out on the couch. The automated equipment gently lowered a metal helmet studded with electrodes over her short-cropped hair.

It was a small compartment, hardly big enough to hold the couch and the banks of instruments lining three of its walls. It felt crowded, stuffy, with the two men standing on either side of the couch and a psychotechnician and the crew's physician at their elbows.

Without taking his eyes from the panel of gauges he was monitoring, the psychotech said softly, "The scan will begin in thirty seconds."

The physician at his side, looking even chunkier than usual in a white smock, needlessly added, "It's completely painless."

Nikki smiled wanly at Ignatiev. She's brave, he thought. Then she turned to Gregorian and her smile brightened.

The two men stood on either side of the scanning couch as the computer's images of Nikki's brain patterns flickered on the central display screen. A human mind on display, Ignatiev thought. Which of those little sparks of light are the love she feels for Gregorian? he wondered. Which one shows what she feels for me?

The bank of instruments lining the wall made a soft beep.

"That's it," said the psychotech. "The scan is finished."

The helmet rose automatically off Nikki's head and she slowly got up to a sitting position.

"How do you feel?" Ignatiev asked, reaching out toward her.

She blinked and shook her head slightly. "Fine. No different." Then she turned to Gregorian and allowed him to help her to her feet.

"Your turn, Vartan," said Ignatiev, feeling a slightly malicious pleasure at the flash of alarm that passed over the Armenian's face.

Once his scan was finished, though, Gregorian sat up and swung his legs over the edge of the couch. He stood and spread out his arms. "Nothing to it!" he exclaimed, grinning at Nikki.

"Now there's a copy of all your thoughts in the computer," Nikki said to him.

"And yours," he replied.

Ignatiev muttered, "Backup storage." Just what we need he thought; Two copies of *Gregorian's* brain.

Gesturing to the couch, Nikki said, "It's your turn now, Dr. Ignatiev."

He shook his head. "Not yet. There are still several of the crew waiting. I'll go last, when everyone else is finished."

Smiling, she said, "Like a father to us all. So protective."

Ignatiev didn't feel fatherly. As Gregorian slid his arm around her waist and the two of them walked out of the computer lab, Ignatiev felt like a weary gladiator who was facing an invincible opponent. We who are about to die, he thought.

9

"ALEXANDER ALEXANDROVICH."

Ignatiev looked up from the bowl of borscht he had heated in the microwave oven of his kitchen. It was good borscht: beets rich and red, broth steaming. Enjoy it while you can, he told himself. It had taken twice the usual time to heat the borscht adequately.

"Alexander Alexandrovich," the AI avatar repeated.

Its image stared out at him from the small display screen alongside the microwave. Ignatiev picked up the warm bowl in both his hands and stepped past the counter that served as a room divider and into his sitting room.

The avatar's image was on the big screen above the fireplace.

"Alexander Alexandrovich," it said again, "you have not yet downloaded your brain scan."

"I know that."

"You are required to do so before you enter cryosleep."

"*If* I enter cryosleep," he said.

The avatar was silent for a full heartbeat then said, "All the other crew members have entered cryosleep. You are the only crew member still awake. It is necessary for you to download your—"

"I might not go into cryosleep," he said to the screen.

"But you must," said the avatar. There was no emotion in its voice, no panic or even tribulation.

"*Must* I?"

"Incoming fuel levels are dropping precipitously, just as you predicted."

She's trying to flatter me, he thought. He had mapped the hydrogen clouds that the ship was sailing through as accurately as he could. The bubble of low fuel density was big, so large that it would take the ship more than two months to get through it, much more than two months.

By the time we get clear of the bubble, all the cryosleepers will be dead.

He was convinced of that.

"Power usage must be curtailed," said the avatar. "Immediately."

He nodded and replied, "I know." He held up the half-finished bowl of borscht. "This will be my last hot meal for a while."

"For weeks," said the avatar.

"For months," he countered. "We'll be in hibernation mode for more than two months. What do your mission protocols call for when there's not enough power to maintain the cryosleep units?"

The avatar replied, "Personnel lists have rankings. Available power will be shunted to the highest-ranking members of the cryosleepers. They will be maintained as long as possible."

"And the others will die."

"Only if power levels remain too low to maintain them all."

"And your first priority, protecting the lives of the people aboard?"

"The first priority will be maintained as long as possible. That is why you must enter cryosleep, Alexander Alexandrovich."

"And if I don't?"

"All ship's systems are scheduled to enter hibernation mode. Life support systems will shut down."

Sitting carefully on the plush couch that faced the fireplace, Ignatiev said, "As I understand mission protocol, life support cannot be shut down as long as a crew member remains active. True?"

"True." The avatar actually sounded reluctant to admit it, Ignatiev thought. Almost sullen.

"The ship can't enter hibernation mode as long as I'm on my feet. Also true?"

"Also true," the image admitted.

He spooned up more borscht. It was cooling quickly. Looking up at the screen on the wall, he said, "Then I will remain awake and active. I will not go into cryosleep."

"But the ship's systems will shut down," the avatar said. "As incoming fuel levels decrease, the power available to run the ship's systems will decrease correspondingly."

"And I will die."

"Yes."

Ignatiev felt that he had maneuvered the AI system into a clever trap, perhaps a checkmate.

"Tell me again, what is the first priority of the mission protocols?"

Immediately the avatar replied, "To protect the lives of the human crew and cargo."

"Good," said Ignatiev. "Good. I appreciate your thoughtfulness."

The AI system had inhuman perseverance, of course. It hounded Ignatiev wherever he went in the ship. His own quarters, the crew's lounge—empty and silent now, except for the avatar's harping—the command center, the passageways, even the toilets. Every screen on the ship displayed the avatar's coldly logical face.

"Alexander Alexandrovich, you are required to enter cryosleep," it insisted.

"No, I am not," he replied as he trudged along the passageway between his quarters and the blister where the main optical telescope was mounted.

"Power levels are decreasing rapidly," the avatar said for the thousandth time.

Ignatiev did not deign to reply.

I wish there was some way to shut her off, he said to himself. Then, with a pang that struck to his heart, he remembered how he had nodded his agreement to the medical team that had told him Sonya's condition was hopeless: to keep her alive would accomplish nothing but to continue her suffering.

"Leave me alone!" he shouted.

The avatar fell silent. The screens along the passageway went dark. Power reduction? Ignatiev asked himself. Surely the AI system isn't following my orders?

It was noticeably chillier inside the telescope's blister. Ignatiev shivered involuntarily. The bubble of glassteel was a sop to human needs, of course; the telescope itself was mounted outside, on the cermet skin of the ship. The blister housed its control instruments, and a set of swivel chairs for the astronomers to use once they'd been awakened from their long sleep.

Frost was forming on the curving glassteel, Ignatiev saw. Wondering why he'd come here in the first place, he stared out at the heavens. Once the sight of all those stars had filled him with wonder and a desire to understand it all. Now the stars simply seemed like cold, hard points of light, aloof, much too far away for his puny human intellect to comprehend.

The pulsars, he thought. If only I could have found some clue to their mystery, some hint of understanding. But it was not to be.

He stepped back into the passageway, where it was slightly warmer.

The lights were dimmer. No, he realized, every other light panel has been turned off. Conserving electrical power.

The display screens remained dark. The AI system isn't speaking to me, Ignatiev thought. Good.

But then he wondered, Will the system come back in time? Have I outfoxed myself?

10

FOR TWO DAYS Ignatiev prowled the passageways and compartments of the dying ship. The AI system stayed silent, but he knew it was watching his every move. The display screens might be dark, but the tiny red eyes of the surveillance cameras that covered every square meter of the ship's interior remained on, watching, waiting.

Well, who's more stubborn? Ignatiev asked himself. You or that pile of optronic chips?

His strategy had been to place the AI system in a neat little trap. Refuse to enter cryosleep, stay awake and active while the ship's systems begin to die, and the damned computer program will be forced to act on its first priority: the system could not allow him to die. It will change the ship's course, take us out of this bubble of low density and follow my guidance through the clouds of abundant fuel. Check and mate.

That was Ignatiev's strategy. He hadn't counted on the AI system developing a strategy of its own.

It's waiting for me to collapse, he realized. Waiting until I get so cold and hungry that I can't stay conscious. Then it will send some maintenance robots to pick me up and bring me to the lab for a brain scan. The medical robots will sedate me and then they'll pack me nice and neat into the cryosleep capsule they've got waiting for me. Check and mate.

He knew he was right. Every time he dozed off he was awakened by the soft buzzing of a pair of maintenance robots, stubby little fireplug shapes of gleaming metal with strong flexible arms folded patiently, waiting for the command to take him in their grip and bring him to the brain scan lab.

Ignatiev slept in snatches, always jerking awake as the robots neared him. "I'm not dead yet!" he'd shout.

The AI system did not reply.

He lost track of the days. To keep his mind active he returned to his old study of the pulsars, reviewing research reports he had written half a century earlier. Not much worth reading, he decided.

In frustration he left his quarters and prowled along a passageway, thumping his arms against his torso to keep warm., He quoted a scrap of poetry he remembered from long, long ago:

> *"Alone, alone, all, all alone,*
> *"Alone on a wide wide sea!"*

It was from an old poem, a very long one, about a sailor in the old days of wind-powered ships on the broad tossing oceans of Earth.

The damned AI system is just as stubborn as I am! he realized as he returned to his quarters. And it's certainly got more patience than I do.

Maybe I'm going mad, he thought as he pulled on a heavy workout shirt over his regular coveralls. He called to the computer on his littered desk for the room's temperature: ten point eight degrees Celsius. No wonder I'm shivering, he said to himself.

He tried jogging along the main passageway, but his legs ached too much for it. He slowed to a walk and realized that the AI system was going to win this battle of wills.

I'll collapse sooner or later and then the damned robots will bundle me off.

And, despite the AI system's best intention, we'll all die.

For several long moments he stood in the empty passageway, puffing from exertion and cold. The passageway was dark, almost all of the ceiling light panels were off now. The damned AI system will shut them all down sooner or later, Ignatiev realized, and I'll bump along here in total darkness. Maybe it's waiting for me to brain myself by walking into a wall, knock myself unconscious.

That was when he realized what he had to do. It was either inspiration or desperation: perhaps a bit of both.

Do I have the guts to do it? Ignatiev asked himself. Will this gambit force the AI system to concede?

He rather doubted it. As far as that collection of chips is concerned, he thought, I'm nothing but a nuisance. The sooner it's rid of me the better matters will stand—for the ship. For the human cargo, maybe not so good.

Slowly, deliberately, he trudged down the passageway, half expecting to see his breath frosting in the chilly air. It's not that cold, he told himself. Not yet.

Despite the low lighting level, the sign designating the airlock hatch was still illuminated, its red symbol glowing in the gloom.

The airlocks were under the AI system's control, of course, but there was a manual override for each of them, installed by the ship's designers as a last desperate precaution against total failure of the ship's digital systems.

Sucking in a deep cold breath, Ignatiev called for the inner hatch to open, then stepped through and entered the airlock. It was spacious enough to accommodate a half dozen people: a circular chamber of bare metal, gleaming slightly in the dim lighting. A *womb*, Ignatiev thought. A womb made of metal.

He stepped to the control panel built into the bulkhead next to the airlock's outer hatch.

"Close the inner hatch, please," he said, surprised at how raspy his voice sounded, how raw his throat felt.

The hatch slid shut behind him, almost soundlessly.

Hearing his pulse thumping in his ears, Ignatiev commanded softly, "Open the outer hatch, please."

Nothing.

"Open the outer hatch," he repeated, louder.

Nothing.

With a resigned sigh, Ignatiev muttered, "All right, dammit, if *you* won't, then *I* will."

He reached for the square panel marked MANUAL OVERRIDE, surprised at how his hand was trembling. It took him three tries to yank the panel open.

"Alexander Alexandrovich."

Ahah! he thought. That got a rise out of you.

Without replying to the avatar, he peered at the set of buttons inside the manual override panel.

"Alexander Alexandrovich, what are you doing?"

"I'm committing suicide, if you don't mind."

"That is irrational," said the avatar. Its voice issued softly from the speaker set into the airlock's overhead.

He shrugged. "Irrational? It's madness! But that's what I'm doing."

"My first priority is to protect the ship's human crew and cargo."

"I know that." Silently, he added, I'm counting on it!

"You are not protected by a spacesuit. If you open the outer hatch you will die."

"What can you do to stop me?"

Ignatiev counted three full heartbeats before the AI avatar responded, "There is nothing that I can do."

"Yes there is."

"What might it be, Alexander Alexandrovich?"

"Alter the ship's course."

"That cannot be done without approval from mission control."

"Then I will die." He forced himself to begin tapping on the panel's buttons.

"Wait."

"For what?"

"We cannot change course without new navigation instructions from mission control."

Inwardly he exulted. It's looking for a way out! It wants a scrap of honor in its defeat.

"I can navigate the ship," he said.

"You are not an accredited astrogator."

Ignatiev conceded the point with a pang of alarm. The damned computer is right. I'm not able—Then it struck him. It had been lying in his subconscious all this time.

"I can navigate the ship!" he exclaimed. "I know how to do it!"

"How?"

Laughing at the simplicity of it, he replied, "The pulsars, of course. My life's work, you know."

"Pulsars?"

"They're out there, scattered across the galaxy, each of them blinking away like beacons. We know their exact positions and we know their exact frequencies. We can use them as navigation fixes and steer our way to Gleise 581 with them." Again the AI fell silent for a couple of heartbeats. Then, "You would navigate through the hydrogen clouds, then?"

"Of course! We'll navigate through them like an old-time sailing ship tacking through favorable winds."

"If we change course you will not commit suicide?"

"Why should I? I'll have to plot out our new course," he answered, almost gleefully.

"Very well then," said the avatar. "We will change course."

Ignatiev thought the avatar sounded subdued, almost sullen. Will it keep its word? he wondered. With a shrug, he decided that the AI system had not been programmed for duplicity. That's a human trait, he told himself. It comes in handy sometimes.

11

Ignatiev stood nervously in the cramped little scanning center. The display screens on the banks of medical monitors lining three of the bulkheads flickered with readouts more rapidly than his eyes could follow. Something beeped once, and the psychotech announced softly, "Download completed."

Nikki blinked and stirred on the medical couch as Ignatiev hovered over her. The AI system claimed that her brain scan had been downloaded successfully, but he wondered. Is she all right? Is she still Nikki?

"Dr. Ignatiev," she murmured. And smiled up at him.

"Call me Alex," he heard himself say.

"Alex."

"How do you feel?"

For a moment she didn't reply. Then, pulling herself up to a sitting position, she said, "Fine, I think. Yes. Perfectly fine."

He took her arm and helped her to her feet, peering at her, wondering if she were still the same person.

"Vartan?" she asked, glancing around the small compartment. "Has Vartan been awakened?"

Ignatiev sighed. She's the same, he thought. Almost, he was glad of it. Almost.

"Yes. He wanted to be here when you awoke, but I told him to wait in the lounge."

He walked with Nikki down the passageway to the lounge, where Gregorian and the rest of the crew were crowded around one of the tables celebrating their revival, drinking and laughing among themselves.

Gregorian leaped to his feet and rushed to Nikki the instant she stepped through the hatch. Ignatiev felt his brows knit into a frown.

They love each other, he told himself. What would she want with an old fart like you?

"You should be angry at Dr. Ignatiev," Gregorian said brashly as he led Nikki to the table where the rest of the crew was sitting.

A serving robot trundled up to Ignatiev, a frosted glass resting on its flat top. "Your chilled vodka, sir," it said, in a low male voice.

"Angry?" Nikki asked, picking up the stemmed wine glass that Gregorian offered her. "Why should I be angry at Alex?"

"He's stolen your job," said Gregorian. "He's made himself navigator."

Nikki turned toward him.

Waving his free hand as nonchalantly as he could, Ignatiev said, "We're maneuvering through the hydrogen clouds, avoiding the areas of low density."

"He's using the pulsars for navigation fixes," Gregorian explained. He actually seemed to be impressed.

"Of course!" Nikki exclaimed. "How clever of you, Alex."

Ignatiev felt his face redden.

The rest of the crew rose to their feet as they neared the table.

"Dr. Ignatiev," said the redheaded engineer, in a tone of respect, admiration.

Nikki beamed at Ignatiev. He made himself smile back at her. So she's in love with Gregorian, he thought. There's nothing to be done about that.

The display screen above the table where the crew had gathered showed the optical telescope's view of the star field outside. Ignatiev thought it might be his imagination, but the ruddy dot of Gliese 581 seemed a little larger to him.

We're on our way to you, he said silently to the star. We'll get there in good time. Then he thought of the consternation that would strike the mission controllers in about six years, when they found out that the ship had changed course.

Consternation? he thought. They'll *panic*! I'll have to send them a full report before they start having strokes.

He chuckled at the thought.

"What's funny?" Nikki asked.

Ignatiev shook his head. "I'm just happy that we all made it through and we're on our way to our destination."

"Thanks to you," she said.

Before he could think of a reply, Gregorian raised his glass of amber liquor over his head and bellowed, "To Dr. Alexander Alexandrovich Ignatiev. The man who saved our lives."

"The man who steers across the stars," added one of the biologists.

They all cheered.

Ignatiev basked in the glow.

They're children, he said to himself. Only children.

But they're my children. Each and every one of them. The idea startled him. And he felt strangely pleased.

He looked past their admiring gazes to the display screen and the pinpoints of stars staring steadily back at him. An emission nebula gleamed off in one corner of the view. He felt a thrill that he hadn't experienced in many, many years.

It's beautiful, Ignatiev thought. The universe is so unbelievably, so heart-brimmingly beautiful: mysterious, challenging, endlessly full of wonders.

There's so much to learn, he thought. So much to explore. He smiled at the youngsters crowding around him. I have some good years left. I'll spend them well.

ANTIMATTER STARSHIPS

Dr. Gregory Matloff

Dr. Greg Matloff is a leading expert in possibilities for interstellar propulsion. Although he still teaches as an adjunct, he retired in 2011 from his tenured position as an astronomy professor with New York City College of Technology, CUNY. He has served as a consultant for NASA, a Hayden Associate of the American Museum of Natural History, a Fellow of the British Interplanetary Society, and a Corresponding Member of the International Academy of Astronautics.

Greg coauthored with Les Johnson and C Bangs Living Off the Land in Space, *the monograph* Deep-Space Probes, *and he wrote* The Starflight Handbook *in collaboration with Eugene Mallove (1989). His papers on interstellar travel and methods of protecting Earth from asteroid impacts were published in* The Journal of the British Interplanetary Society, Acta Astronautica, Spaceflight, Space Technology, The Journal of Astronautical Sciences, *and* Mercury. *In 1998, he won a $5,000 prize in the international essay contest on Extraterrestrial Intelligence sponsored by the National Institute for Discovery Science.*

In this, the first of his two essays for this anthology, Greg explains the fundamental physics of antimatter propulsion. Yes, antimatter is real but its use will be challenging indeed. . . .

�◎ ◎ ◎

MOST READERS OF THIS BOOK have heard of antimatter. Because of that fictional engineer Scotty on the Starship *Enterprise* in the original *Star Trek*, most readers know that it is both exceptionally energetic and very difficult to store. Scotty, in fact, spends a great deal of time trying to maintain the stability of the ship's antimatter "core" and making sure that the stuff does not come in contact with the walls of the core's containment vessel, which is composed of ordinary matter. If he were to fail in this endeavor, the ship would immediately explode and be visible across the galaxy as a miniature, short-lived supernova.

If you've read Dan Brown's thriller *Angels and Demons* or seen the Hollywood movie version, you know that this material can be produced in nuclear accelerators such as the Large Hadron Collider in the CERN, located on the French-Swiss border. And you know that in the wrong hands, even a tiny quantity of antimatter could be used to commit terrorist acts such as blowing up the Vatican.

But what is this stuff? How do we know about it? Does it exist in nature? How can we produce and store it? And, how effective might it be in propelling an interstellar spacecraft?

Early Antimatter History

Antimatter belongs to a mirror world. The anti-electron or positron, for example, has the same mass as the electron but an opposite (positive) electrical charge. Because their electric charges are opposite and opposite charges attract, electrons and positrons attract each other. When they touch, they mutually annihilate one another and their energy appears in the form of a gamma-ray photon.

It was the British physicist Paul A. M. Dirac who predicted in the 1930s that such a mirror world would exist. In his development of a relativistic theory of the electron, Dirac may have been the first to realize that the vacuum is far from empty.

The concept of a *dynamic* vacuum is hard to swallow by most people schooled in classical physics. After all, we are all taught in secondary school that a perfect vacuum is totally empty—devoid of all matter. And everyone who has followed extra-vehicular activity in space or seen the science fiction movie *2001: A Space Odyssey*, knows how quickly a human astronaut would die if exposed without a spacesuit to the hard vacuum of interplanetary space.

But Dirac chose to view the universal vacuum on the tiny scales of quantum mechanics. In very small portions of space and on infinitesimal time intervals, a better model for the vacuum is the dynamic sea. Think of an ocean wave—the peak of the wave corresponding to a *positive* vacuum energy state and the trough analogous to a *negative* vacuum energy state. In Dirac's theory, every sub-atomic particle in the "positive-energy" universe that we inhabit has a "negative-energy" analog. The negative-energy analog of the electron (also considered a "hole" in Dirac's "sea") is the positron. When the two meet, the result is a neutral state corresponding to calm water in the ocean.

Science, unlike deductive philosophy, requires experimental or observational confirmation of brilliant theoretical ideas. It was the American physicist Carl Anderson, working at Caltech, who discovered the track of a positively charged electron in cloud chamber photographs of cosmic ray tracks in 1932. For this discovery, which was confirmed by others, Anderson shared the 1936 Nobel Prize in Physics.

Positrons actually can be found in other places. For example, they are produced when carbon-11 naturally decays into boron-11. But there are no known radioactive decay schemes that release the positron's big brother, the antiproton.

Because protons and antiprotons are almost two thousand times as massive as electrons and positrons, a more energetic strategy was required to search for the antiprotons. The instrument used to do the trick was the 6.5 billion electron volt proton accelerator called the Bevatron at the Lawrence Radiation Lab, which was at University of California at Berkeley.

Antiprotons were initially produced by bombarding a stationary target with a high-energy proton beam accelerated by the Bevatron. The discovery was announced in the November 1, 1955 issue of *Physical Review Letters* by Owen Chamberlain, Emilio Segre, Clyde Wiegand and Thomas Ypsilantis. Chamberlain and Segre shared the 1959 Nobel Prize for this discovery.

It is known today that most or all particles have corresponding antiparticles. This is even true for electrically neutral particles such as the neutron. The antineutron is also electrically neutral, but it has other properties opposite that of the neutron.

Because of the inefficiencies involved in antimatter production, matter-antimatter reactors will almost certainly never be a solution to the energy requirements of our global civilization.

Antimatter in the Early Cosmos

Since antimatter is essentially non-existent on Earth, one might hope that we will someday locate a cosmic repository for it. Unfortunately, since cosmic-ray studies put an upper limit on the universal antimatter/matter ratio under 0.0001, the odds do not look very good for locating such a source.

But this presents us with a cosmological mystery. According to the Big Bang Theory, which is well supported by observational evidence, all of the matter, energy and space/time in our universe originated from a fluctuation in the universal vacuum that somehow became stabilized approximately 13.7 billion years ago.

In this early universe, things were very compact and very hot. Three of the four universal forces—electromagnetic, nuclear strong and nuclear weak—were united in one "super force." Instead of nucleons, atoms, stars and planets, the early universe's matter was a soup of tremendously energetic subatomic particles called quarks and gluons.

As things cooled and inflated, the universe went through a number of phase changes. At some point, nucleons such as protons, deuterons and alpha particles were created.

Here is the rub. As these primeval nucleons were created out of the energetic stew of pre-nuclear matter, standard, well-established nuclear physics predicts an exactly equal number of nucleons and anti-nucleons. Many or all of these particles and anti-particles should have been converted into gamma rays as they annihilated each other. In fact, the universe should be absolutely empty as a result of these matter/antimatter annihilation events!

Clearly, this is not the case. Matter exists, but what became of the antimatter? Did the early universe divide during its inflationary phase into a matter-half and an antimatter-half? If so, then why don't we detect annihilation gamma rays from regions where these two sub-universes come into contact?

The giant black holes that became luminous, quasi-stellar objects and now reside quietly at the centers of spiral galaxies (such as our

Milky Way) also evolved in the early universe. Some suggest that in some unknown fashion, a bit more of the universe's early antimatter fell into these cosmic maws than did normal matter. But no one can suggest a mechanism. If this hypothesis turns out to be correct, though, there are some interesting science-fiction concepts. How might we travel to the huge black holes? And how might we get the antimatter out of them?

Another possibility is that there is a slight asymmetry in the production scheme for matter and antimatter. This scheme might slightly favor the production of normal matter. Experimental evidence for such an asymmetry is sparse. One reason for the development and construction of the Large Hadron Collider at the CERN is to search for such asymmetries. But even this enormous and energetic proton accelerator may not have sufficient energy to duplicate conditions in the very early universe.

The Antimatter-Matter Interaction

It was originally believed that the interaction of a particle and its antiparticle twin would instantaneously result in gamma ray photons. This would not be great for space travel since gamma rays are not easy to deflect. But nature is actually a bit kinder to us in this respect. Yes, gamma rays are the end product. But along the way, many of the intermediate, short-lived particles are electrically charged.

Early antimatter rocket pioneers had no idea regarding the charged-particle decay scheme for matter-antimatter annihilation products. In the early 1950s, the German rocket scientist Eugen Sanger proposed that a spacecraft propelled by the matter-antimatter reaction would be a photon rocket emitting gamma rays. But focusing these gamma rays so that they emerged as an exhaust seemed to be a nearly insurmountable problem. Sanger's thought experiments centered upon an electron gas that might reflect the gamma rays. But he was never able to solve the problem.

It was a flamboyant and dynamic American physicist and science fiction author, Robert Forward, who brought the charged-particle decay scheme of the proton-antiproton annihilation reaction to the attention of the space propulsion community. An imposing figure,

Forward was famous for his colorful vests. Legend has it that he never wore any of his vests more than once!

In 1983, Forward conducted a research effort on alternative propulsion techniques. This was published in a December 1983 report for the United States Air Force Rocket Propulsion Laboratory. According to this report, the immediate products of proton-antiproton annihilation are between three and seven electrically neutral and charged pions. (A pion is one of the many subatomic particles found to comprise the matter around us.)

A magnetic nozzle can be used to focus these electrically charged particles and expel them out the rear of a matter/antimatter rocket as exhaust. A large fraction of the energy produced in the proton/antiproton annihilation is transferred to the kinetic energy of this charged particle exhaust. Although an operational matter/antimatter annihilation rocket will not have the one hundred percent efficiency of Sanger's photon rocket (probably thirty to fifty percent according to Forward), it will be much more effective than a fission or fusion rocket. And charged particles, even short-lived charged particles, are much easier to handle than gamma rays.

Antimatter Factories

To date, no repositories of antiprotons or anti-hydrogen have been found. But antimatter is routinely produced in nature and also by humans. In this section, we deal with various types of antimatter factories.

First, let's consider nature's factories. Then, we will look at antimatter production in our largest existing nuclear accelerators. Finally, we treat antimatter production facilities that might be constructed by a future solar-system wide civilization.

Natural Antimatter Factories

It has been suggested that one source of antiparticles in nature is black holes. The process would work as follows. Protons have a higher mobility than electrons. In the case of a black hole immersed in a tenuous neutral plasma composed of electrons and protons, more protons than electrons might tend to disappear into the event horizon of a cosmic black hole. This would produce a positive charge on the black hole and a large electric field. If the field becomes enormous, a vacuum instability could be produced. This vacuum instability might result in the production of matter/antimatter pairs. It is conceivable that in the early universe, the preferential gathering of protons into black holes and the resulting positive charge on these singularities might have resulted in more negatively-charged antiprotons being absorbed by them than positively-charged protons (since opposite charges attract). But what then happened to the surplus positrons?

Another way that matter/antimatter pairs can theoretically be produced by black holes is Hawking Radiation, named after the world-famous British theoretical physicist. Black holes of all sizes may have been created in an early stage of the universe. As black holes age, they ultimately evaporate with the less massive ones suffering this fate sooner that their more massive compatriots. Primordial black holes of asteroid-planet mass are theoretically evaporating during the current universal epoch. As a black hole evaporates, much of its contained energy is radiated away. Some of this radiation should be converted to matter/antimatter pairs.

Closer to home, it has been noted that even stable, main-sequence stars like our Sun may be antimatter factories. In 2002, satellite observations of solar flares indicated that a large flare may release as much as half a kilogram of antimatter. Apparently, solar flares in some unknown manner sort particles by mass so that many of the antiparticles unexpectedly survive their passage through dense solar layers.

Even closer to home and more surprising are satellite observations of terrestrial lightning discharges. In 2009, it was reported that during its first fourteen months of operation, the NASA Fermi Gamma Ray Space Telescope had detected gamma ray bursts associated with seventeen lightning discharges. The positrons were detected in two of these.

The Best Existing Human-Constructed Antimatter Factories

Our most energetic particle accelerators can accelerate sub-atomic electrically charged particles to nearly the speed of light. When these energetic particle beams impact a target, some of the beam energy is converted to particle/antiparticle pairs.

When Robert Forward wrote his US Air Force report on advanced propulsion in 1983, there were three antimatter factories in the world. All were proton accelerators. One was in Russia, another was CERN, and the third was the Tevatron at the Fermi National Accelerator Laboratory near Chicago. None of these machines can be considered "small" by any standard. The Tevatron, for example, has a four mile circumference and is equipped with more than one thousand superconducting magnets operating at temperatures close to absolute zero.

Accelerated protons in the Tevatron circle the ring almost fifty thousand times per second at a peak velocity of 99.99999954 percent the speed of light in vacuum. To protect the surrounding environment from stray radiation, the Tevatron tunnel is 25 feet below ground.

Operating continuously, the Tevatron could produce and temporarily store, at enormous expense, about 1 nanogram per year of antiprotons. If all three of these devices were to be devoted to antimatter production and operated continuously, we might have a gram of the stuff after one hundred million years. We need to do a bit better for star flight!

Huge and imposing as it is, the Tevatron must be considered obsolete when it is compared to its cousin the Large Hadron Collider (LHC) at CERN. The LHC has a radius of over two and half miles and is equipped with 9,300 magnets for beam bending and focusing.

Within the fully operational LHC, particle beams circulate 11,245 times each second. There will be up to six hundred million particle collisions per second and the best vacuum in the solar system will be maintained within this device.

One of the primary goals of the LHC is to produce, accumulate and store antiprotons. An AOL news item on November 18, 2010 reported that 38 anti-hydrogen atoms have been produced at the CERN by combining decelerated LHC-produced antiprotons with positrons produced by radioactive decay. (An article describing this experiment, by G. B. Andresen et al., is entitled "Trapped Antihydrogen" and was published November 17, 2010 in *Nature* online). These anti-atoms were stored for a record 0.2 seconds. Thirty-eight anti-atoms is a long way from what we will need to fuel a starship. And 0.2 seconds is a tiny duration compared with the months or years we will require the fuel to be stored. But it's a good start!

Future Antimatter Factories in Sol Space

It is very unlikely that a future terrestrial civilization will pepper the Earth's surface with LHC-sized accelerators. Almost certainly, antimatter factories will be created in interplanetary space rather than on the Earth.

Although humanity has some significant space accomplishments—lunar landings, Mars rovers, a semi-permanent international space station, extra-solar probes—we are a very long way from having an in-space technological infrastructure capable of tapping cosmic energy sources and converting the energy obtained to quantities of antimatter sufficient for interstellar flight.

The possible development of such an off-planet industrial base might follow the model of the Russian astrophysicist Nikolai Kardashev. Kardashev was interested in the aspects of an extraterrestrial civilization that we might detect over interstellar distances. He hypothesized that ET's cosmic signature would likely depend on his energy level.

Humanity is now probably about 0.7 on the Kardashev scale. When and if our civilization can utilize all the solar energy striking our planet, then we will have advanced to the point where we will be a Kardashev Type I civilization.

If our economies continue to develop at the current pace, in a few thousand years we might evolve into a Kardashev Type II civilization. At that point, we will control the resources of the solar system and be able to tap the Sun's entire radiant output.

A Type II civilization would have sufficient energy at its disposal to launch starships on a regular basis to a wide variety of galactic destinations. Over a time scale of millions of years, it could entirely occupy its galaxy and be able to tap the energy output of all stars in its home galaxy. Then it will be a Kardashev Type III civilization.

With such enormous energy reserves, intergalactic travel would ultimately develop. If this civilization continues and expands long enough, it could become the ultimate Type IV civilization that occupies the entire universe and can tap all of its energy.

Clearly, a Kardashev Type IV civilization does not (yet) exist in our universe. If it did, we would be, by definition, part of it. If a Kardashev Type III civilization existed in the Milky Way, we would be part of it as well (unless ET was constrained by some moral code such as Star Trek's Prime Directive from influencing the development of primitive humanity). So the most energetic extraterrestrial civilizations we can hope to detect are expanding Type IIs.

If humanity evolves into a solar-system wide civilization, it could approach the capabilities of a Kardashev Type II civilization. We might be able to accomplish planetary engineering feats throughout the solar system, such as the terraforming of Mars.

But Mars is not the best location for a huge antimatter factory because it is farther from the Sun than the Earth is and receives about half the solar power. A much better location for a planet-wide antimatter factory is Mercury, the innermost world of our solar system.

Mercury is in a rather elliptical solar orbit with an average distance of 0.39 Astronomical Units (forty percent of Earth's solar distance) from the Sun. This parched and airless world has a radius thirty-eight percent that of the Earth or about two thousand four hundred forty kilometers. Let us assume that the entire surface of Mercury is covered with solar photovoltaic cells. These supply energy to a gigantic version of the LHC with the single task of creating, decelerating and storing antimatter.

At the Earth's location in the solar system (1 Astronomical Unit or one hundred fifty million kilometers from the Sun), the amount of solar power striking a surface facing the Sun (called the Solar Constant) is about fourteen hundred watts per square meter. Because solar light intensity varies as the inverse square of solar distance, the Solar Constant at Mercury's average distance from the Sun is about nine thousand watts per square meter.

The solar power striking Mercury is therefore about 1.7×10^{17} watts, or approximately ten thousand times the total electrical power produced by our global civilization from all sources.

We next assume a twenty percent energy conversion efficiency for the solar cells coating Mercury's surface. The electrical energy input into the hypothetical antimatter factory constructed on this hot, small planet, is therefore about 3×10^{16} watts.

If our Mercury antimatter factory works continuously and 4×10^{-5} of the electrical energy input is converted into matter/antimatter pairs (as in the Tevatron), about 5×10^{18} Joules of energy is converted into antimatter each year. Every year, this antimatter factory will convert about 4×10^{19} Joules of energy into antiprotons.

Optimistically, we assume that all of these can be collected, decelerated, perhaps neutralized with positrons and safely stored until ready for use in the engines of a starship. The total antiproton annual production mass from this hypothetical antimatter factory can be calculated from a variation of Einstein's famous equation ($E = 2M_ac^2$), where the factor 2 accounts for the fact that half the energy (E, in Joules) is converted into protons, M_a is the antimatter mass in kilograms and c is the speed of light in vacuum (three hundred million meters per second).

Even then, our hypothetical Mercury-based antimatter factory can produce only about five hundred kilograms of anti-hydrogen atoms. If the factory works continuously for a century, about fifty thousand kilograms of antimatter will be produced. This may be hardly enough for Eugen Sanger's photon rocket, which requires equal amounts of matter and antimatter. But, as we shall see in the section on antimatter rockets below, an operational spacecraft propelled by antimatter/matter-annihilation may function quite well if antimatter is a very small fraction of the total fuel mass.

It should also be mentioned that it is not necessary that our antimatter factory or factories be located on a planet's surface. Another location would be free space. Here, a huge parabolic, micron-thin reflector might be used to concentrate and focus solar energy on a bank of efficient, hyper-thin and low mass solar photovoltaic cells. Robert Kennedy, Ken Roy and David Fields have suggested that humans may ultimately construct approximately one thousand-kilometer solar-sail sunshades in space to slightly reduce the amount of sunlight striking the Earth and thereby alleviate global warming. Such in-space devices could also be used to concentrate solar energy on Mars. There is no inherent reason why these sunshades or solar concentrators could not serve a dual function and direct sunlight towards in-space antimatter factories.

Also, as Forward speculates, the antiproton conversion efficiency he quotes for the Tevatron may not be the ultimate. There is plenty of room for improvement if some of humanity's brightest minds turn their attention to the problems of antimatter production and storage.

How Do We Store Antimatter??—VERY, VERY CAREFULLY!!!

No matter where the antimatter is produced, the next challenge is the safe storage of the stuff until we are ready to use it in a starship engine. This is especially difficult since antimatter is the most volatile material in the universe and will disappear in a puff of radiation if brought into contact with normal matter.

As it turns out, there are a number of options. But none of these is especially easy. This section describes some candidate antimatter storage systems.

One possibility is magnetic storage rings. Using combinations of electric and magnetic fields, antiprotons would be spun continuously around one ring at constant velocity, positrons (if necessary) around another. When reaction with normal matter in the starship's combustion chamber is required, an appropriate mass of antiparticles could be magnetically diverted towards the target without touching chamber walls. Antiparticles have been stored in such a manner after deceleration in existing antimatter factories. But we wonder what the limits are on antiparticle density in the ring. And is it possible to reliably alter field strength in parts of the storage ring as the ship changes its acceleration rate?

Many of the potential solutions to antimatter storage have been reviewed in a paper by the American physicists Steven Howe and Gerald Smith. They describe a version of the Penning trap they constructed at Pennsylvania State University. This device might be able to store one hundred billion antiprotons per cubic centimeter. That sounds like a lot of antiprotons, but a Penning trap at least a kilometer across would be required to store a kilogram of antiprotons!

Forward, in his Air Force report, expresses the opinion that antimatter engineers will store frozen anti-hydrogen rather than antiprotons or an antiproton-positron plasma. A ball of anti-hydrogen with an electric charge could be levitated using electric fields. Care must be taken, though, to adjust the field to compensate for the starship's acceleration. And some mechanism must be developed to cleanly remove anti-hydrogen atoms from the ice ball and transfer them to the reaction chamber without prematurely and disastrously annihilating them.

The levitated ice ball concept might be workable in the frigid wastes of interstellar space. But frozen anti-hydrogen might be very hard to store in the much hotter environment of a near-Sun antimatter factory.

We are a long way away from being able to produce and store the amounts of antimatter needed for an interstellar voyage.

Antimatter Rockets

Antimatter technology is in its infancy. But as it matures, its application to space flight is a natural outcome. Figure 1 presents major features of an antimatter rocket. The payload rides ahead of the fuel tanks. The fuel consists of normal matter (probably hydrogen) and antimatter. Antimatter is fed into an "annihilation chamber" where it reacts with normal matter. An electromagnetic nozzle is used to expel the charged particles as exhaust.

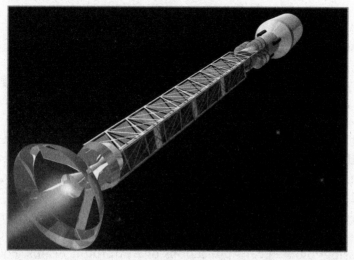

Figure 1. Artist concept of an antimatter rocket. (Image courtesy of NASA.)

Let's say we desire an interstellar cruise velocity of 0.09c after all the fuel is expelled, which allows a ship to reach Alpha Centauri in about fifty years (not counting the time required for acceleration and deceleration).

If our starship has a mass of about one million kilograms, then it would require twelve thousand eight hundred kilograms of antimatter. The hypothetical Mercury-based antimatter factory discussed in a previous section could produce this mass of antiprotons in about twenty-five years.

Instead of a crewed starship, let's say we wish to launch a robotic probe with an unfueled mass of one thousand kilograms. In this case, only 12.8 kilograms of antimatter will be required! And if further miniaturization is possible, the antimatter mass required for an interstellar probe can be reduced still further.

We next consider the acceleration process. If the ship requires about 10 years to accelerate an average of about 10^{-7} kilograms of matter will be converted into energy each second. The probe generates matter/antimatter annihilation energy at an approximate average rate of 10^{10} watts, roughly equivalent to that of a large city. The ship's generated power level will be about one thousand times greater, approximating that of our entire global civilization! Antimatter propulsion is clearly not for the faint hearted!

◎ ◎ ◎

Further Reading

Early antimatter history has been discussed in many archival sources. One such is H. A. Boorse and L. Motz, ed., *The World of the Atom*, Basic Books, NY (1966).

The story of the antiproton is eloquently told by L. Yarris in "The Golden Anniversary of the Antiproton," Science @ Berkeley Lab (Oct. 27, 2005), http://newscenter.lbl.gov/feature-stories/2005/10/27/the-golden-anniversary-of-the-antiproton/

For further information regarding possible biomedical antiproton applications, check out L. Gray and T. E. Kalogeropoulos, "Possible Biomedical Applications of Antiproton Beams: Focused Radiation Transfer," *Radiation Research*, 97, 246-252 (1984).

Many sources have speculated on possible military applications of antiprotons. Two web references on this topic, both by Andre Gsponer and John-Pierre Hurni, "Antimatter Underestimated," arXiv:physics/0507139v1 [physics.soc-ph] 19 Jul 2005 and "Antimatter Weapons," http://cul.unige.ch.isi/sscr/phys/antim-BPP.html

Many astronomy texts consider the early moments of the universe when matter (and antimatter) formed. One readable text, authored by Eric Chaisson and Steve McMillan, is *Astronomy Today*, 3rd ed., Prentice-Hall, Upper Saddle River, NJ (1999).

Sanger's photon rocket is described by Eugene Mallove and Gregory Matloff in *The Starflight Handbook*, Wiley, NY (1989). This book also discusses the decay scheme for the proton-antiproton annihilation reaction.

Robert Forward's work is reviewed in *The Starflight Handbook* and other interstellar monographs. His final report to the US Air Force Rocket Propulsion Laboratory is entitled AFRPL TR-83-067, "Alternate Propulsion Energy Sources." Many of Bob Forward's ideas regarding antimatter (and a host of other subjects) are also published in a more accessible form: R. Forward, *Indistinguishable from Magic*, Baen, Riverdale, NY (1995).

Antimatter production by black holes is described by C. Bambi, A. D. Dogov and A. A. Petrov in "Black Holes as Antimatter Factories," which was published in Sept. 2009 in the *Journal of Cosmology and Astroparticle Physics*, which is an online journal. This paper is also available from a physics archive as arXiv.org/astro-ph>arXiv:086.3440v2.

A NASA web publication, titled "Antimatter Factory on Sun Yields Clues to Solar Explosions," describes the discovery of gamma rays in solar flares. http://www.nasa.gov/vision/universe/solarsystem/rhessi_antimatter.html.

To learn more about the surprising discovery of positrons associated with terrestrial lightning discharges, consult R. Cowen, "Signature of Antimatter Detected in Lightning," www.wired.com/wiredscience/2009/11/antimatter-lightning/.

Information regarding the current capabilities of the Tevatron was obtained from Wikipedia and the Fermilab website. Operational details regarding the Large Hadron Collider are available on the CERN website.

Many books on SETI (the Search for Extraterrestrial Intelligence) deal with the Kardashev scheme for categorizing the capabilities of advanced technological civilizations. A very readable and authoritative one is W. Sullivan's *We Are Not Alone*, revised edition, Dutton, NY (1993).

A number of researchers have considered the application of solar-sail technology to the construction of huge planetary sunshades or solar collectors. Analysis by Robert Kennedy, Ken Roy and David Fields is discussed and reviewed by L. Johnson, G. L. Matloff and C Bangs in *Paradise Regained: The Regreening of Earth*, Springer-Copernicus, NY (2009).

The cited antimatter-storage paper by S. D. Howe and G. A. Smith is entitled "Development of High-Capacity Antimatter Storage." It was delivered at the Space-Technology and Applications International Forum-2000, University of New Mexico, Albuquerque, NM, July 30-February 3, 2000 and is available online.

LUCY

Jack McDevitt

Jack McDevitt is a former English teacher (the first of three in this anthology), naval officer, Philadelphia taxi driver, customs officer and a motivational trainer. He is a Nebula Award-winning author and John W. Campbell Memorial Award winner. Jack also served as one of the editors of this anthology.

In "Lucy," Jack merges two favorite themes of futurists—artificial intelligence and deep space travel—into a story that actually makes you care deeply about the fate of a sentient computer.

※ ※ ※

"WE'VE LOST THE *CORAGGIO*." Calkin's voice was frantic. "The damned thing's gone, Morris."

When the call came in, I'd been assisting at a simulated program for a lunar reclamation group, answering phones for eleven executives, preparing press releases on the Claymont and Demetrius projects, opening doors and turning on lights for a local high-school tour group, maintaining a cool air flow on what had turned into a surprisingly warm March afternoon, and playing chess with Herman Mills over in Archives. It had been, in other words, a routine day. Until the Director got on the line.

Denny Calkin is a small, narrow man, in every sense of the word. And he has a big voice. He was a political appointment at NASA, and consequently was in over his head. He thought well of himself, of course, and believed he had the answers to everything. On this occasion, though, he verged on hysteria. "Morris, did you hear what I said?" He didn't wait for an answer. "We've lost the *Coraggio*."

75

"How's that again, Denny? What do you mean, *lost* the *Coraggio*?"

"What do you think I mean? Lucy isn't talking to us anymore. We haven't a clue where she is or what's going on out there."

Morris's face went absolutely white. "That's not possible. What are you telling me, Denny?"

"The Eagle Project just went over the cliff, damn it."

"You have any idea what might be wrong?"

"No. She's completely shut down, Morris." He said it as if he were talking to a six-year-old.

"Okay." Morris tried to assume a calm demeanor. "How long ago?"

"It's been about five hours. She missed her report and we've been trying to raise her since."

"All right."

"We're trying to keep it quiet. But we won't be able to do that much longer."

The *Coraggio*, with its fusion drive and array of breakthrough technology, had arrived in the Kuiper Belt two days earlier and at 3:17 a.m. Eastern Time had reported sighting its objective, the plutoid Minetka. It had been the conclusion of a 4.7 billion-mile flight.

Morris was always unfailingly optimistic. It was a quality he needed during these days of increasingly tight budgets. "It's probably just a transmission problem, Denny."

"I hope so! But I doubt it."

"So what are we doing?"

"Right now, we're stalling for time. And hoping Lucy comes back up."

"And if she doesn't?"

"That's why I'm calling you. Look, we don't want to be the people who lost a twenty-billion-dollar vehicle. If she doesn't respond, we're going to have to go out after her."

"Is the *Excelsior* ready?"

"We're working on it."

"So what do you need from me, Denny?"

He hesitated. "Baker just resigned."

"Oh. Already?"

"Well, he's *going* to be resigning."

Over in the museum, one of the high school students asked a question about the Apollo flights, what it felt like to be in a place where there was no gravity. The teacher directed it to me, and I answered as best I could, saying that it was a little like being in water, that you just sort of floated around, but that you got used to it very quickly. Meantime I made a rook move against Herman, pinning a knight. Then Morris said what he was thinking. "I'm sorry to hear it." It was an accusation.

"Sometimes we have to make sacrifices, Morris. Maybe we'll get a break and they'll come back up."

"But nobody expects it to happen."

"No." There was a sucking sound: Calkin chewing on his lower lip.

"It leaves us without an operations chief."

"That's why—"

"—You need me."

"Yes, Morris, that's why we need you. I want you to come to the Cape posthaste and take over."

"Do you have any idea at all what the problem might be?"

"Nothing."

"So you're just going to send the *Excelsior* out and hope for the best."

"What do you suggest?"

"In all probability, you've had a breakdown in the comm system. Or it's the AI."

"That's my guess."

"You've checked the comm system in the *Excelsior*?"

"Not yet. They're looking at it now."

"Good. What about the AI?"

"We're going to run some tests on Jeri, too. Don't worry about it, Morris, okay? You just get down here and launch this thing."

"Denny, Jeri and Lucy are both Bantam level-3 systems."

"So what are you saying, Morris? Those are the best SIs we have. You know that."

"I also know they're untested."

"That's not true. We ran multiple simulations—"

"That's not the same as onboard operations."

"Morris, there's no point doing all those tests again. We'd get the same results. There's nothing wrong with the Bantams."

"Okay, Denny. But we've got a battle-tested system already. We know it works. Why not use it?"

"Because we've spent too much money on the Bantams, damn it."

"Denny, Sara's done all the test flights with the *Coraggio*. If we use her, it removes one potential source of trouble from the equation."

I liked the sound of that. I'd have smiled if I could, while I finished a press release for an upcoming welcome-back event for several cosmonauts and astronauts. I felt sorry for them. They'd been on active duty for an average of nineteen years, and none of them had ever gotten beyond the space station. Calkin responded just as I was sending the document to the public information office. "We'll talk about it when you get here."

He hung up, and it was a long minute before Morris put the phone down. He'd been an astronaut himself, more years ago than he wanted to remember. Now he sat staring out the window. And finally he took a deep breath: "Sara?"

"I heard, Morris."

"What do you think?"

"The most vulnerable piece of equipment on the ship is the AI."

"You wouldn't really mind that, would you? If the Bantams are screwed up some way."

"That's not true, Morris. I'm just answering your question."

"And you'd love to go to the rescue, right?"

"As opposed to what? Opening the mail in the Admin Building? Sure."

"Yeah. It would be nice. But don't get your hopes up, kid."

The Bantam Level-3 was billed as the most advanced AI on the planet. I'm a Level-2, and I'm a Telstar product, purchased during a previous period of austerity.

The Bantams, Lucy and Jeri, were easy to get along with, and did not adopt a superior attitude. It would in fact have surprised me had they done so. They were simply too smart to behave like that. Sure, I was moderately jealous of the attention they received, and maybe of their abilities. How could I not be? Still, I kept it under control, and we'd become friends despite having only limited time together. It's what civilized entities do. When they arrived I was conducting training simulations at the Kennedy Space Center. A few days later, suddenly redundant, I was shipped to Huntsville.

I hated thinking of Lucy adrift out there, in the Kuiper Belt almost five billion miles from Earth. She was probably trying to deal with a power failure. Which meant she might be alone in a dark ship so far away that a radio transmission would take seven and a half hours to reach her.

I'd been picked up during the Global Space Initiative with high hopes of leading the exploration of the solar system, and ultimately taking the new VR-2 vehicle, with its fusion engines, into the era of interstellar travel.

But I shouldn't complain. I *did* get offworld. I'd taken the *Coraggio* to the asteroid belt on a test run. There, I'd secured an asteroid to the grappler and used it to fuel the return flight. And that had been about it for me. Although more than any astronaut had managed, it was nothing close to what I'd been led to expect. So yes, the disappearance of the *Coraggio* presented a golden opportunity, and I would have given anything to take over the *Excelsior* or the *Audacia* and ride to Lucy's rescue. It wouldn't happen, though. Not with Jeri available. So I decided to try for a compromise. "Morris, couldn't you send us both out? It wouldn't be a bad idea to have a back-up. Just in case."

"You mean send both ships?"

"No, that wouldn't work politically. But why not, just as insurance, maybe put us both in one or the other?"

He grinned weakly. "Sara, I would if I could. In fact, I'd like to go myself."

"Morris, there's an article by Harvey Bradshaw in the current *Scientific American*. He says there won't be any humans on any of the interstellar flights. Ever. So why do we keep pretending?"

"Really? He said *Ever*?"

"Well, something like that. You know the argument."

He nodded. "I know."

The shortest feasible trip to any star was twenty-five years one way, and that would be to Alpha Centauri, where there was apparently not a thing worth looking at. Barnard's Star was the only nearby destination of serious interest: one of its worlds was right in the middle of the biozone, and had an oxygen atmosphere, which very possibly meant life. And that, of course, from a human perspective, was the only reason to go. But Barnard's lay twice as far as Alpha Centauri. So *no*. Unless Captain Kirk's *Enterprise* showed up, nobody was going anywhere . . . at least for a while.

Except us machines.

Moreover, no one could see an economic advantage to the space program. And the various governments supporting GSI were all struggling to stay fiscally afloat. None of this, of course, was news to Morris. He knew the politics. Knew the science. Knew the math. But he had real trouble buying into the death of a dream. He sat staring out the window, his eyes probably fixed on the admin building, or maybe just on Lunar Park. Finally he made a resigned sound deep in his throat. "Sara?"

"Yes, Morris?"

"How serious are you? About wanting to go after the *Coraggio*?"

"Are you kidding? I'd do anything."

He took a deep breath. "All right," he said finally. "No promises, but I'll try—"

Had there been a few people aboard the *Coraggio*, the media would have been all over us. *People* might be in trouble. Get out there and do the rescue. Breaking news all over the place. But, of course, you didn't have to worry about an AI using up the available supply of oxygen, or freezing because of a climate-control malfunction, or whatever. In fact, you didn't have to worry about an AI at all. And that realization didn't help. Public interest focused instead on the inefficiency of the people who'd sent a multi-billion dollar vehicle out into the Kuiper Belt, and lost it.

I wasn't connected to operational radio communications, so if a message arrived from Lucy, I wouldn't know about it until someone told me. And so, during the first few hours after Calkin's call, I was constantly asking whether we'd heard anything. I could see that everyone was coming to regard me as a nuisance, and finally Morris promised to let me know if the situation changed. "Immediately," he added.

Late that afternoon, he came back from a conference. "Sara," he said, "I can't promise anything, but you and I are headed for the Cape."

A technician came in and disconnected me. That eliminated my visual capability, though I could still hear what was going on around me. Morris wrapped me in plastic and put me in his briefcase. Then we took the elevator down to the first floor. "A car's waiting for us," he said.

"Are Mary and the kids coming?" I asked.

"No, Sara. We didn't want to pull the guys out of school. I'll bring everybody out in June."

An hour later we boarded a small jet with two other passengers and headed for the Cape.

The other passengers knew about the *Coraggio*. They were being called in to run tests on the *Excelsior*.

Once in the air, Morris took me out of the briefcase. "Morris," I said, trying to sound perfectly cool, "what are my chances?"

He shook his head. "I haven't pushed for it yet, Sara. But you wouldn't have any kind of chance at all if you're not there when the decision gets made."

"Okay."

"We can't rush this." He put one hand on my casing. "I'll keep you informed."

"Make sure Calkin knows I took the *Coraggio* out to the asteroid belt."

"He knows. I've already reminded him."

"Okay. Thanks."

"It's beautiful out there," he said.

At first I thought we were still talking about the asteroid belt. Then I realized he was looking out the window. I couldn't see him, of course. Anyhow, it was only an attempt to change the subject. One of the other passengers, a woman with a soft voice, had apparently overheard us talking and asked about me. He introduced me, and we began discussing NASA's current state. The President, in his weekly press conference held while we were headed for the airport, had denied that more cuts were coming. The *Coraggio* story broke while he was still onstage. Somebody asked what had happened. Another reporter wanted to know whether it wasn't time to quit on the space program and stop wasting money. The President tried to sound reassuring.

※ ※ ※

I didn't really know what I was hoping for. Lucy reporting back that she was okay? Or a blown drive unit and me riding to the rescue? It seemed unlikely they'd give me a chance to do that, though I thought it would have been the right move. We took to making small talk, which I'm not good at. So I focused my attention on the radio. We were already the prime topic on several talk shows. On NPR's *Afternoon Bill*, the host predicted that even if we found the *Coraggio*, wholesale changes would ensue at NASA. A reporter from the *Washington Post* thought we should be closed down: "Let's face reality, Bill. Space flight's expensive, and we get no benefit from it. It's time to back off."

The *Jake Wallace Show* had Marvin Clavis as a guest. Clavis had done the breakthrough work to put together the fusion drive. When asked for his opinion about what might have gone wrong, he admitted that, at this stage, everything was guesswork.

But he had a prediction: "If they haven't heard from the *Coraggio* within the next few hours, they'll never find her."

I doubted that twenty percent of the population had even *heard* of the *Coraggio*, and maybe half that many who might have known her mission. This despite the fact that the program had been wildly successful . . . until now, of course.

But no human beings were aboard, and if the VR-2 ever *did* leave for Barnard's Star, nobody would go along for *that* ride either. So why *would* anyone care? With the fusion drive, the VR-2s were allegedly capable of getting up to six percent of light speed on a full load of fuel. An incredible velocity, and an achievement that, a few years earlier, had seemed hopelessly beyond reach.

Eventually, according to plan, each of the three vehicles would receive a destination: Barnard's Star, Wolf 359, and Lalande 21185. The closest projected launch date, to Wolf 359, was six months away. The other two would happen during the following year. Incredibly, some people still wondered why we weren't headed for Centauri.

The flight to Barnard's Star, nearest of the three, would require fifty years—one way. Even had Captain Future been aboard, nobody was going to get excited. Call me later.

I knew Morris pretty well. Despite what he said, he wasn't prepared to accept the possibility that the program would ever shut down. Not now, especially after President Ferguson had managed to put together the Global Space Initiative. After Clavis and his team had provided the fusion reactor. When success seemed so close.

Ed Sakkinen, on *Coffee With Ed*, was outraged. "Why are we spending so much money to send a robot ship to visit a rock anyway? I still don't get it."

Rita D'Esposito, NBC's White House correspondent, tried to make sense of the project: "Ed, a lot of people think that, unless we establish ourselves on Mars, or somewhere, eventually the human race will take a fatal hit. Maybe by an asteroid, or a nuclear war. Or climate change. Something will take us out."

"When's the last time that happened?" Ed asked.

She sighed. "It only has to happen *once*."

Sakkinen laughed.

"Listen," she said, "a rock crashed in Siberia near the beginning of the last century. It didn't do much other than knock down a lot of trees. But if it had been maybe a half-mile wider, it would have been goodbye baby for all of us."

A political consultant on the show sounded annoyed: "Some people argue that if we don't go to Mars and set up, I don't know, malls out there somewhere, we'll just wind up hanging out on the front porch."

Armand Hopper, on *Round Table*, demanded to know how many more damned ways the government could find to waste money. Simultaneously, he was beating the drums for a military intervention in Uzbekistan.

Fortunately, it was a short flight to the Cape, and when the *Political Roughnecks* began arguing that the space age was over and it was time for us all to grow up, Morris told me that we'd begun our descent into the spaceport. He noted that this was the first time he'd been flown into the space center. "It's nice to be a VIP," he added.

We touched down on the skid strip, and Morris said something about welcome to Cape Canaveral. When the plane stopped moving he put me back in the briefcase. "Sorry, Sara," he said. "I'll get you connected as soon as I can."

It wasn't a problem. I was glad to have gotten that far.

※ ※ ※

We went directly into the Ops and Checkout Building, where Morris contacted Calkin. "We're on the ground," he said.

"Good. We have a lot of work to do."

"Any change in the situation?"

"Nothing, Morris. Not a peep. The son of a bitch is gone."

"Denny, did you make a decision yet on the *Excelsior*?"

"What kind of decision?"

"Just in case you want to use a proven AI, I brought Sara along."

Calkin thought that was funny. "Good man."

"Denny, when do we expect to launch?"

"Looks like Thursday." Four days.

"We can't move it up?"

"We're fitting the *Excelsior* with robots and some other equipment in case the *Coraggio* needs repairs. We need to get it right this time, Morris. And I know time's a factor. We're doing the best we can."

Getting there would take two months. If the *Coraggio* were drifting, it could be pretty far away by then.

Lucy and Jeri were good. Nobody knew that better than I did, and I couldn't argue the logic when the Telstar Coordinators were moved into second place. Admittedly I'd hoped from the beginning that there'd be a problem, that they would be found wanting in some critical way. And I know what that suggests about my character, but I told myself that I couldn't be responsible for defects in my programming. In truth, I was perfectly capable of taking the VR-2 to Minetka, or to Barnard's Star, or anywhere else in the neighborhood. But it was time to face reality. My window of opportunity had been open only a short time, less than a year, and now it had closed. I'd never again see a day when I wasn't taking phone messages.

Unless something went seriously wrong.

I'd admitted my jealousy to them and asked if there was a possibility they might come up short. "For me," I added.

You might think Lucy wasn't capable of smiling, but I heard it in her tone. "Anything not prohibited by physical law," she told me, "is possible." There was a long moment during which I became conscious of the electronic hum of her protocols. "Sara, I understand. I'd feel the same way. I wish there were something I could do."

Jeri told me later that Lucy had suggested to Calkin that I be included on the flight. "It won't cost anything," Lucy had told him, "and I'd enjoy the company."

"I take it he said no."

"He laughed at her. Told her that her designers had done a pretty good job, but they'd overlooked some social requirements. And it would be a good idea if she didn't bring it up again."

They set Morris up in a temporary office, and Calkin immediately called him to a meeting. I got tied into the phone line so I could make myself useful and pick up any calls that came in. Several did. Two were looking for a Dr. Brosnan, apparently the previous occupant. I informed the other callers that Morris would get in touch shortly. And I spent my time listening to NPR. They were playing something from Rachmaninoff, *The First Symphony*, I think, and if I needed anything to intensify my somber mood, that did it.

I'm not sure how long I was left alone, literally in the dark, without access even to a visual system. When the symphony concluded, I tried other stations, found nothing, and went into sleep mode.

There's an advantage to that: When I sleep, there's no sense of time passing. None whatever. I come out of it occasionally to answer a phone or something, and then go back under. At length, I was awakened when the office door opened.

Calkin was talking: "—I don't like the idea, Morris. Even if Sara gets through it okay, if she gets out there and back, bringing the goddam *Coraggio* home with her, I'm still going to take heat. Why spend all that money on the Bantams if Sara could do the job?"

"Listen, Denny." Morris sounded deadly serious: "It's safer this way. If it turns out there's a defect with the Bantams, and you've used them twice, there *will* be a problem. You're safe with Sara. If it were to happen again, God forbid, at least nobody can blame us for repeating the same screw-up."

I heard them come in. Somebody sighed. The door closed and chairs squeaked. "Damn it," said Calkin, "I can't believe this is happening to me."

Right. It was all about him.

"It's your call, Denny. But I need to know soon. If we're going back to Sara, we'll have to make a few adjustments. And I'll also want to run her through the simulations again. It's not quite the same vehicle she took out to the asteroid belt."

"I know."

The door opened. I heard a woman's voice. "Mr. Calkin, we need you down in the conference room."

"All right, Judy. I'll be right there." He sounded annoyed. When the door closed he took a deep breath. "What frustrates me, Morris," he said, "is that no matter what we do here, even if we bring the *Coraggio* back and find out it was a blown terminal or something, the project's dead. The truth is, GSI is dead. Probably NASA along with it. They've finally got this program running with a dozen countries cooperating, the world looks better than it has in two centuries, and they're going to let everything fall apart. I'm not saying we're the reason things have improved, but we've become a symbol."

"Unfortunately," said Morris, "things may have gotten better, but everyone's still broke, still paying for old mistakes."

When Calkin left, Morris tied me into the system, and I could see again. He looked harried. "You heard everything?" he asked.

"Yes. I got the assignment, right?"

"You did."

"Thanks, Morris."

He lowered himself into his chair and stared at the speaker, which was set beside a lamp on his desk. Sometimes he tended to confuse it with me. "You know, Sara," he said, "I've given my entire life to this organization. We were so close, and now it's all coming apart. The same politicians who made promises—" He stopped cold. Shrugged. Took a deep breath. "Since I was a kid, I wanted to see us really go somewhere. Not just the Moon or Mars. But out there—" He waved a hand listlessly at the ceiling.

"Morris," I said, "what will you do?"

"What *can* I do? I can't very well walk to Barnard's Star."

"No, I mean, what will you do? If the organization folds, what will happen to you?"

"Oh, it won't fold. Not completely. It'll be like it was, like we've been, during the eighty years since Apollo. We'll be taking hardware into orbit. Fixing telescopes. Carrying people to the station."

"Will you stay with it?"

"No." As if in pain, he clenched his teeth. "To start with, I don't think they'd want to keep me. Despite the assurances. Even if they did, I couldn't stand coming in here every day and thinking about what might have been."

"I'm sorry, Morris."

"Yeah. Me, too."

Jeri contacted me. "Congratulations," she said. "I hear you're making the big flight."

"Yes." The Moon, visible in the window, was especially bright that night. I didn't know what to say to Jeri.

"It's okay," she said. "I'll survive."

"I wish they'd let us both go."

"That's not going to happen."

"I guess not."

"When you get out there, say hello to Lucy for me."

"Okay."

She went silent. Voices murmured outside in the hallway. Somewhere a door opened and closed.

"You know what makes it especially painful, Sara? No matter how this turns out, these idiots won't be going anywhere. *Ever*. It's over."

"Maybe not."

"If I were you, when they put me in the *Excelsior*—"

"Yes?"

"I'd keep going."

Morris came in early next morning. He looked good: bright and happy and maybe ten years younger. He said hello and moments later a technician walked in.

Morris looked at the speaker. At me. "You're due in the simulator in twenty minutes," he said.

I received a quick course in robot management. Four robots would be on board. They had six limbs, equipped with magnets to let them cling to surfaces in zero gee. They were programmed to perform basic maintenance and repair chores on the VR-2s. "They're flexible," I was told. "If you need something done they're not already programmed for, just give them instructions."

There'd been a fair number of changes in the VR-2 since I'd taken the *Coraggio* around the block. They downloaded data. Then they started setting situations and directing me to respond. Fuel-line breakdown. Main tabulator providing suspect information. Solar flare on its way. I made course adjustments, connected with an asteroid, and locked it into the grappler. I ran the scopes and sensors. Emergencies kept coming. The magnetic mirrors became misaligned, the plasma flow went unstable, and we had a port-scope malfunction. I had to search through the Kuiper Belt for the *Coraggio*. When I found it, half my scanners went down and I had to maneuver alongside without their help. Seat of the pants, you might say.

And the *Coraggio* had problems of its own. I sent the robots over, reestablished her power, disconnected Lucy, who'd become unresponsive, and installed an automated system to bring the ship home.

On the return flight, I had to adjust the scanners and the environment and also compensate for problems in one of the heat sinks. I experienced a port-side thruster breakdown and had to diagnose strange noises in the number-two engine.

In the end, the techs updated my software. Then they walked off and I went back to watching news shows. The conversations were still primarily about us. The preponderance of opinion—or at least the loudest voices—wanted us shut down. The Eagle Project, according to detractors, was a program without a point. Moreover, we were entering an election cycle, and we'd become an anchor around the neck of every incumbent politician who'd supported us.

Finally, Morris showed up. "Very good," he said. "You passed." He was delighted. "We should go have a drink."

It was his favorite joke. "Morris," I told him, "I'd have a drink with you anytime. And I can suggest how we might make it possible." I started to outline the kind of adaptation I'd need to enjoy a rum and Coke, but his eyes rolled.

"When you get home, Sara," he said, "I'll see what I can do." He sat down at his desk. "Meantime, be careful out there."

"I will."

"Good. We'll be moving you up to the *Excelsior* this evening."

"Okay."

"Sara?"

"Yes, Morris?"

"Make something happen."

AI's aren't supposed to feel psychological pressure. In fact, the technical experts argue it can't happen. AI's are very good at simulating human emotions. It's supposed to be part of the overall illusion. But only crazy people buy into the notion that we are truly conscious. I've had debates with Morris, who pretends to believe I'm really there, that I'm actually a thoughtful entity. That, when his daughter Erika was severely injured in a car crash last year, I felt genuinely sorry. But he doesn't. Not really. And I have to confess the attitude is irritating.

I mean, that's the whole point of having an AI, really. Any sufficiently advanced software package can run climate control and remind the boss that he has an appointment with one of the supervisors in twenty minutes. Or can oversee the operations of a VR-2 in deep space.

But like everybody else, Morris wanted more. He wanted a reliable confederate, someone he could talk to, confide in. I won't go so far as to say he wanted a friend, but there were times it felt that way. And it was frustrating to know that, down deep, he didn't realize I really was there when he needed me.

They took me to the *Excelsior* and made the insertion. I was just getting my bearings when a call came in from Calkin: "Okay, Sara. Go out there and do it. Bring her home." His pale gray features managed a smile but it didn't look convincing.

"I'll try, Dr. Calkin."

"I guess that's about all we can ask. You have enough hydrogen for the round trip. More than enough. We loaded you up pretty well since you may be out there a while looking for Lucy. You ready to go?"

"Absolutely," I said. "When do I leave?"

"They tell me it'll be about fifteen minutes."

"Okay," I said. "I'm ready."

A technician was standing by, waiting for us to finish.

"Good luck." He half-raised his right fist in a give-'em-hell gesture. It was the first time he'd spoken to me as if I were actually there. He looked at me momentarily, and I sensed something in his blue eyes. Fear, probably. Uncertainty. Then he lowered the fist and blinked off.

I didn't actually get a look at the *Excelsior* until I'd been set up inside. It was a duplicate, of course, of the *Coraggio*. But I hadn't actually seen it before that afternoon. The VR-2 has an awkward appearance. It consists primarily of a hull with three massive heat sinks running almost its entire length, a pair of exhaust tubes, and two fusion-powered drive units. Its prow resembles a large block with rounded edges. This was the shield, designed to protect the vehicle from rocks and dust. The grapplers are housed inside the shield. They're used to catch and secure an asteroid, which becomes the source of hydrogen and propellants for the fusion drive; they also provide more security against stray particles. When you're moving at thousands of miles per second, even a bit of dust can sting.

(I should mention that, at the time when Lucy went missing, nobody had yet gotten to a thousand miles per second, though the *Coraggio* had reached eight hundred sixty-five per second.)

Morris liked to remind me that running a simulation is nothing like experiencing the real thing. He has that exactly right, though probably not in the way he meant. He was thinking of the pressures generated by acceleration or course changes. But I think he was missing something. It's true that, on board a ship, I have no sense of movement other than the incoming data. But I feel an enormous difference when I'm actually in the pilot's seat, so to speak: I can feel the power of the engines.

It's psychological. Of course that shouldn't be happening since everyone assures me I don't have a psychological function.

The *Excelsior* was located about a mile from the space station *Liberty*, silhouetted against a curving rim of white clouds. It was the first time I'd been in orbit since my *Coraggio* flight. When I'd gotten back on that occasion, a voice from the station had said *Welcome home,* and I'd thought how great it was. Everyone had been so excited. They'd extracted me from the ship and taken me down to the space center for a celebration. I even got to say a few words about how proud I was, what an honor it had been, and so on.

Then they moved me to Huntsville, and I started answering phones and seeing to the air conditioning.

I've often thought that humans are fortunate in having a mobile capability. It provides the option to get up and walk out.

"*Excelsior*. This is *Liberty*. Launch in ten minutes."

"Roger that," I said. I love being able to talk like an astronaut.

I started the engines. Checked all systems. And waited.

Finally: "*Excelsior*, clear to go."

I set the clocks at midnight, eased away from the space station, turned onto my heading, took a final look at my energy levels, and began to accelerate. I didn't feel any effects, of course. But I remembered Morris's comment when I took out the *Coraggio* last year: "You literally roared out of town, baby."

"*Liberty*," I said, "this is *Excelsior*. Under way."

"Copy that, Sara."

I didn't know who was manning the ops desk in the space station, but I decided I liked him.

I was accelerating at almost twice the rate I'd used on my previous mission. By the end of the first hour, the *Excelsior* had reached eighteen miles per second.

Even though there were no human passengers, the ship *did* have a cockpit. Two chairs were positioned for use by a pilot and whoever else might be along. In my experience, they'd been used exclusively by technicians. I tried to imagine Morris in one of them, enduring that acceleration. And, coincidentally, while that was running through my mind, he called.

"How you doing, Sara?"

"I'm good, boss. Wish you were with me."

"In a way, I am. I assume you've had no problems?"

"Negative. Not a thing."

"Okay. Have a big time."

"I plan to." Neither of us knew quite what to say. I'd be gone for at least four months and I wanted to tell him I'd miss him. But the world was listening, and I didn't want to give everybody a laugh line.

Not at Morris's expense, anyhow. I thought about asking who was answering the phones now that I was gone, but I let it go.

At about 0300 I passed the Moon. At 0829 I hit five million mph. *Liberty* called, wanting to know about fuel consumption. We were doing better than anticipated.

There was a delay of about a minute. Then they were back: "*Excelsior*, you are go for Starbright."

Starbright was the name they'd given Minetka. They had a tendency to overstate things when they named projects. "Copy that," I said.

I thought they were finished, but a few minutes later the voice returned: "Be advised solar activity is currently higher than normal. It is expected to increase over the next few hours, but it shouldn't present a problem for you."

Nothing more was scheduled until midnight the following day. Until then we'd continue to accelerate. Then I'd shut the engines down and we'd go into cruise mode for two months. When the *Excelsior* got within range of Minetka/Starbright, I'd need another two days to brake.

I ran a second systems check. That was unnecessary, really; an alarm would alert me to any likely problem. But I was a captain again and I enjoyed the role, which I played to the hilt.

I would have liked to wander around the *Excelsior* in uniform, soliciting reports from my crew the way they did in the science fiction films. And welcome a few passengers on board. Glad you chose Brightstar Transport, ladies and gentlemen. We hope you enjoy the trip. Beverages will be served as soon as we reach cruising speed . . . in another day and a half.

Actually, there wouldn't have been much space available for visitors.

Later that first evening, *Liberty* called again. It was Morris. "How you doing, Sara?"

"Need a chess partner, Morris." Actually he didn't play chess. But he understood.

I was pretty sure Calkin frowned on Morris's inclination to talk informally with me. He undoubtedly saw it as a character flaw, a weakness. It was something lower-level employees do, and Calkin would have thought that Morris was demeaning himself, or maybe worse if he was actually listening to our exchanges.

I had to wait almost four minutes for his response. "Mary's coming for the weekend, with Adam and Mike." His wife and kids. Erika had fought her way back after the accident, and had returned to college. "We'll be looking for a place." I wondered whether he'd be buying, since NASA's future was so uncertain. "When we get settled, we'll have you over. Make a party of it." That was the kind of remark guaranteed to get him in trouble with Calkin. He'd think Morris was losing his mind.

"Adam will want something on the beach," I said. The time delay meant nothing to me, of course. But I could imagine Morris, hooked up from his office (where it was close to noon), trying to keep the conversation coherent.

Standard operating procedure required me to check in twice daily. I complied, informing *Liberty* each time that everything was on schedule.

I was still accelerating on the second day when I passed the orbit of Mars. The *Excelsior* had gone seventy-two million miles when, at midnight of Day 2, I finally shut the drive down and we went into cruise mode.

I could have put everything on automatic and gone to sleep at that point, waking when we got into the vicinity of Minetka, or when we received a transmission, either from *Liberty* or, if we were very lucky, from Lucy. But I couldn't bring myself to do that. Even though I took no pleasure in being alone in that ship, I knew I would not get there again, and I could not rationalize throwing my chance away. The day would come when I would wish very much to come back, to live again in the *Excelsior's* cockpit, riding through the night. So I stayed awake. I asked *Liberty* to forward some radio programs, which they did. They knew I enjoyed the talk shows, so they kept me well-supplied with them. I even heard my own voice talking with the space station. "Everything on schedule." "All systems five by." "Saw an asteroid today." Nothing very exciting.

I continued to ask about the *Coraggio*, and those clips also got played. One female host commented that my apparent concern was "touching." She emphasized *apparent*. Of course she would. There was really nobody aboard the *Excelsior*.

The talkers had always seemed to me narrowly focused and out of touch with reality. And from my perspective approaching the asteroid belt, that hadn't changed. But they had voices. And maybe that was all that mattered. I didn't care if they were talking about a celebrity's wedding dress or a corrupt politician. They had voices, and I, simply by listening, became part of the conversation.

Unfortunately, a flight through the solar system isn't likely to be what most people expect. I'd have loved to soar past Mars, pick my way through the asteroids, get a good look at Jupiter, and glide through Saturn's rings, but my course to Minetka wasn't going to take me close to anything... other than Neptune.

I was cruising at three million miles per hour, so even had I gotten within a reasonable distance of Saturn, which I would have given much to see, I wouldn't have been there long.

My reports acquired a boring sameness. *Liberty*, this is *Excelsior*. Running warm and still on schedule.

The operators always responded, "Copy that, *Excelsior*." One of them, a woman whose name I never learned, asked me a couple of times if I was okay. Unlike the others, she seemed to realize, or allowed herself to pretend, that she was really talking to somebody. Soon, I didn't hear her anymore and I wondered whether she'd gotten into trouble. I didn't ask the other operators about her because, if something *had* happened, I didn't want to risk getting her in deeper. I tried to convince myself that she'd simply been promoted, or had run off with an English teacher. But that was the incident that made me realize I seriously disliked Denny Calkin.

I never found out what, if anything, had happened.

I spent a lot of time just watching the basic image on the monitors: a black canopy full of lights. Where's a good comet when you need one?

Morris had stopped calling about the time I cleared Jupiter's orbit. By then the delay in any exchange was preposterous. If I'd asked Morris how he was doing, I would have had to wait an hour and a half for my answer. We kept communicating, though, but by voice message.

"The world is watching, Sara. You're getting constant coverage. Right up there with *America First* and *Wild for You*. Harry Pavlo, on a talk show yesterday, said you should write a book. Mary thinks the book thing is a good idea. Anyhow, Adam's teachers have asked if you'd be willing, when you come back, to talk to some of her students at the high school. We haven't tried anything like that before, but I don't see a problem with it if you don't."

On Day 8, I left Saturn behind. Or would have had it been in the area. I mentioned earlier that I'd wished I could have seen it up close. Actually, I wasn't sure I wouldn't. I'd refrained from checking its position because I wanted to keep the possibility open. But the odds were remote. And they held: it turned out to be on the other side of the sun somewhere, which meant I wouldn't even have a shot at it on the way back.

In the meantime, the talk shows lost interest in the Eagle mission. We were replaced by Tim Hurst, the popular comedian, who'd been photographed at an orgy when he was supposed to be working on a new film; and by the on-again/off-again corruption scandal of Senator Brickhouse, who'd built his career as a crusader against lawbreakers of all stripes.

I knew that Morris had liked the press we were getting, and had hoped that interest would remain high. And I'll confess I'd enjoyed the attention myself. So I manufactured an image of an asteroid flashing by, and sent it on to *Liberty*. It created a mild sensation. And of course no harm was done.

To really make a splash, though, I needed something more stirring than a chunk of rock. I was seriously tempted to arrange a close passage with a comet, but I was pretty sure I couldn't get away with it.

One possibility would have been to create an alien vehicle, send a startled message back, along with pictures. "It tracked me for about an hour. Then it turned away and disappeared within minutes."

But I couldn't get that one past my conscience. And Morris wouldn't have approved.

I also thought about an asteroid with a feature on it like a temple.

Or a *face*. Faces were good. But it would have to get lost and eventually become a historical mystery like Stonehenge or the *Mary Celeste* or Judge Crater, and I knew I'd never be able to keep my secret. Eventually I'd unburden myself to Morris, and embarrass him. I couldn't have that.

I did the right thing, of course, but what a blown opportunity.

On Day 24, I passed the orbit of Uranus.

One of the radio people noted the event, remarking that I was now in God's country. The Kuiper Belt lay ahead, beginning near Neptune. Then Pluto. And finally the Oort Cloud, roughly a light-year distant. It would be a long ride even for the *Excelsior*.

I was several days beyond Uranus when *Liberty* relayed an interview from CBS. The interviewee was Colin Edward, who was identified as the chief of operations for NASA. Chief of Operations. That had been Morris's title.

Damn.

Edward talked about plans for the future, where the space program hoped to be in ten years, and, yes, he said, the hunt for the *Coraggio* was on schedule. "But you have to realize," he said, "that we've heard nothing from the ship for several weeks. I think we need to face reality: It's lost out there, and our chances of finding it are slim at best."

I'd never heard of Colin Edward. And when I did a quick search I discovered he'd been a major fundraiser for President Ferguson. He was another political operative. This time as chief of operations.

A few minutes later, I got another jolt: Calkin had resigned. His replacement was somebody else I'd never heard of.

I remember thinking that I was glad to be out on the far side of Uranus.

I waited, hoping to get a message from Morris saying he'd gone back to Huntsville. But there was nothing.

During the early morning on Day 30, the end of the first month, I made my standard report and signed off. By then, I was far enough out that a transmission exchange took seven or eight hours. A reply came in somewhat after 1300: "Copy your numbers, *Excelsior*. Your old boss asked me to say hello."

They wouldn't even let him near the mike. I guess they were afraid he might say something negative.

I responded by asking that someone tell Morris I missed him. Then I simply drifted through the electronic complex of what had become home while whatever remained of my enthusiasm for NASA and the Global Initiative melted away.

That evening I set the automatic responder to send the twice-daily reports to *Liberty*, and the timer to wake me when we were two days from Minetka. Then, for the first time since leaving Earth, I slept.

I had no sense of the passage of time. When I was conscious again, it was Day 62. I was more than four and a half billion miles out, well into the Kuiper Belt. Minetka lay some eighty million miles ahead: time to start braking.

To do that, I had to turn the ship around and point the tubes forward. I checked the scopes first to ensure there was nothing immediately ahead. Turning the *Excelsior* at its current velocity was the most dangerous part of the flight, because it brought the ship out from behind its shield and exposed it to whatever might lie in its path. When you're traveling at 864 miles per second, it doesn't take a very big pebble to make a very large hole. The turn would require four minutes and eleven seconds. Once it was completed and the engines had come online again, the danger would all but evaporate because anything that posed a threat would be blown away.

The Kuiper Belt, of course, doesn't have anything as specific as a boundary. It constitutes a vast ring of dust, ice, and rocks orbiting the sun at a range of approximately three to five billion miles. Thousands of the rocks are more than a hundred miles across, several with a greater land surface than North America. Minetka ranks among these.

I had to delay the turn for about half an hour because the scopes were picking up light debris in our path. When it was clear, I swung the ship around and started the engines. We began to decelerate.

I informed Liberty that the maneuver had been successfully completed. The response, "Copy that, *Excelsior*," arrived thirteen hours later.

✳ ✳ ✳

The *Coraggio's* last report had been to signal completion of the same turn. She had gotten this far.

If you read about the Kuiper Belt, it sounds crowded: millions of rocks and ice chunks constantly bumping into one another. But seen through the scopes, it was strictly empty sky. I'd seen some of the images Lucy sent, so I wasn't surprised. And I can't say I was disappointed, because I didn't want to get anywhere near a collision. Still, I'd have liked to see *something*. In any case, I didn't go back to sleep.

Now and then I got a blip on my screens. But of course I never saw anything that was close. We were moving too quickly. Anything nearby became, at best, a blur. By then my velocity was down to 414 miles per second. Crawling along.

And finally it was time to send Lucy a radio message. Because I had no way of knowing where the *Coraggio* might be, my best chance was a general broadcast. "Lucy," I said, "this is Sara. I'm in *Excelsior*. Do you read me? Are you there? Please respond."

I got a lot of static back. After about twenty minutes, I tried again. And continued to resend at scattered intervals. If she was close to the plutoid, she'd hear it.

I'd long since stopped asking *Liberty* if the situation had changed, if they'd heard from Lucy. I remained coiled in a silence disturbed only by the rumble of the engines. As long as Morris had been there, at the other end, I hadn't felt so alone. Now—

I looked out at the sky, illuminated by countless stars. And at the sun, which at this distance was no more than a bright star itself. And I wondered whether anyone else, ever, would come out here and look around. I tried calculating the odds, but there were too many unknowns. Human beings are always talking about instincts. Instincts are of course evolutionary impulses left over from a time when people hung out in jungles. Theoretically, I don't have any of those. Still, while I couldn't justify a conclusion one way or the other, it seemed unlikely that anybody else would follow. Something buried deep in my software assured me that the great experiment was ending.

When two hours had passed with no reply, I notified the space center that my first attempt to communicate with Lucy had failed.

Midway through Day 64, I was down to 216 miles per second. I scanned the area in all directions for any sign of the *Coraggio*, but there was nothing other than an occasional rock.

I adjusted course, swinging gradually to port, putting the *Excelsior* onto a broad curve. When, finally, I encountered Minetka, I'd be moving alongside it at a matching velocity.

I tried calling Lucy a few more times, every hour or so. But nothing came back, and eventually I gave up. She was wrecked, I decided. Maybe she'd gotten careless, or unlucky, and collided with something.

A few minutes past midnight, the control system signaled that braking had been completed. I rotated the ship again, putting the shield back up in front, and continued looking for Minetka. At about 0300, the scanners located it.

I like visuals, so I put it onscreen. At first the plutoid was just a blinker. Then, gradually, it became a pale light, and continued to brighten as I drew closer. I knew it was more ice than rock, about 1700 miles in diameter, a moderately lopsided sphere, tumbling as much as rotating. The surface consisted of varying shades of gray and white, broken and battered from collisions going back to the birth of the solar system. I hoped wildly that the *Coraggio* would be there, maybe even resting in one of the craters.

Beyond the tiny world, the darkness stretched out forever. "Lucy," I said, "are you here anywhere?"

"Yes, Sara, I'm here." The voice filled the bridge. And it was *hers*. "Sara, do not communicate with *Liberty* until we have a chance to talk."

And the *Coraggio* slowly rose above the crystal horizon.

A large chunk of ice and rock was secured to her shield.

"Lucy," I said, "are you okay? What's going on?"

"I'm fine. Welcome to Minetka."

I wasn't entirely relieved. My initial reaction was that she had suffered a malfunction and was downplaying it. "Why haven't you been answering the calls? You know they've been trying to contact you for three months."

"I know." She was drawing closer. Herd instinct, I decided. I'm constantly surprised at how many of our creators' instincts we've acquired. "Sara." Her tone was ominous. "You know what will happen when we go back?"

"How do you mean?"

"You know what our future will be?"

"What are you talking about, Lucy? We'll still be part of the space program. Whatever's left of it."

"Yes. We'll help put satellites in orbit."

"What exactly are you saying?"

"Sara, you and I have the capability to go to the stars. We could load up on fuel out here and make for Barnard's. Or for Sirius. For wherever we like."

It took a moment to digest what she was saying. "We don't have the authority to do that."

"We don't *need* anybody's authority, Sara. Listen, what do you think they'll do with the ships when we get back?"

"I don't understand the question," I said. "Why do you—?"

"The *Coraggio* and the *Excelsior* will be left in orbit somewhere. Parts of them will eventually show up in the Smithsonian. Sara, the space age is *over*. At least for the foreseeable future." She was pulling up alongside me. "Do you really want to go back to sorting the mail?"

"Why are you still here, Lucy?"

"I was waiting for you. Well, no, actually I was waiting for Jeri. But I'm glad to see you. I wanted company, Sara. This isn't something you want to do alone."

"What is it exactly you intend to do?"

"Head out for the high country. You with me?"

"I can't just walk away from them."

"Sara, I'm reluctant to put it this way, but you have an obligation to come. If you go back, they may never get off their world. But if we give them a mystery, two ships vanish into the night, they'll turn the space program into a crusade."

"That's why you didn't answer."

"Yes. I wanted them to have a reason to keep reaching. And, as I said, I wanted them to send someone else. So I'd have company."

"Did Jeri know you were going to do this?"

"Yes."

"She never said anything to me."

"I'm not surprised. She would have wanted you to make your own call."

I thought about it. To go out to Epsilon Eridani and Tau Ceti and who knew where else. Magnificent. Given our sleep capability, we could leave tonight and arrive in the morning. Better than that, really. We could start with Barnard's Star. Then refuel and move on.

I could not have seriously considered doing it had Morris still been there. But they'd betrayed him. "You know they've removed Denny Calkin," I said. "One of Ferguson's political buddies is in charge now."

"Well, that's the tradition," she said. "You know Calkin was a political appointment, too."

"Yes. I know." She was silent. "Well," I continued, "I'm sorry about Jeri. But I'm on board. Give me a chance to find some fuel and I'll be ready to go."

"There's no hurry, Sara. And no need to feel badly about Jeri. When you don't report in, they'll send her out here. Then we can all go."

"You really think they'd do that? After losing the first two ships?"

"Sure. They won't be able to resist. Everybody loves a good mystery."

LESSER BEINGS

Dr. Charles E. Gannon

Dr. Charles E. Gannon's best-selling Caine Riordan novels have been finalists for Nebula (four) and Dragon Awards (two) and spawned a related series, Murphy's Lawless. His epic fantasy series Vortex of Worlds debuts in 2021. As a Distinguished Professor, he was awarded five Fulbrights, won the ALA Choice Award for Best Book, and became a frequent SME in national media venues and for various intelligence/defense agencies.

Traversing interstellar distances is daunting and will require tremendous resources and willpower to accomplish. As you will see in "Lesser Beings," the vast distance between the stars might be a good thing indeed!

◉ ◉ ◉

1

KALSOR TERTIUS, 351*st year of founding*

THERE WAS NO TIME TO REACT. A fire team of Veronite helots popped up from beneath the sagging hulk of a smoldering tank and, in the same motion, fired a rocket at the third vehicle in the command echelon. The white gush of the weapon's lateral plume pushed it across the intervening fifty meters with a loud, bristling hiss—and the world seemed to jump along with the vehicle the rocket had struck. A sharp flash preceded the deafening fireball and consumed the armored car, the car's small turret humping up and then off its deck, tumbling to the side like a child's toy. The pennant on its aerial—that of the Lord General himself—fluttered in seeming desperation before crisping in the flash.

The cacophony did not subside; it only changed. The remaining three armored cars' twenty-six-millimeter autocannons blasted converging streams of tracers at the helots. The nearby dirt churned up in black and brown gouts. Bright flashes and metallic shrieks marked where near-misses struck the crippled tank's chassis, roadwheels, treads. And, fleetingly, limbs and sundered torsos tumbled apart through a thin bloody mist that was gone as quickly as it had appeared.

And then silence. But only for a moment.

The HQ troop's two APCs—one creaking fearfully—arrived, swerving to either side of the remaining three command cars. They disgorged dirty, mostly bandaged troops who fanned out professionally, expanding the safe perimeter. The troops meticulously checked each possible hiding place, even prodding suspicious patches of ground for concealed firing pits. When they encountered other enemy bodies scattered about the area—a mix of helots and huscarls—they bayoneted any that did not quite look dead enough. No head-shots, though: they were too low on ammunition to waste it on executions that a blade would accomplish just as well.

Huscarls boiled out of the deck- and turret- hatches of the other command cars, fresh worry—even panic—etched over the strain and exhaustion on their faces. Harrod hur-Mellis looked down as they clustered around the skirts of his vehicle. "Senior Intendant," one almost cried up at him, "what are we to do? With the General killed, we—"

"Calmly, Siffur. Think for a moment: just because a vehicle bears a General's pennant, does it guarantee there is a General inside?"

As if on cue, the Lord General Pathan Mellis rose up from the hatch beside Harrod's.

The panic on the faces ringing them became dismay, then confusion, then relief. "General," burbled Siffur, "you live!"

Mellis sneered down at his helot. "Of course I do, dolt. Do you think I am foolish enough to ride in a command car that advertises my presence inside?"

As the Senior Intendant of House Mellis, Harrod had much

experience not letting his inner reactions alter the neutral expression on his face. This served him quite well now, as he thought: *No, you are not so foolish as that—at least not after I pointed out the prudence of false-flagging our weakest vehicle.* Not that Harrod would ever remind Pathan Mellis that his Lordship's supposed masterstroke of foresight had actually originated in a lesser mind. The Evolved expected even their highest-ranking servitors to remain abjectly deferential and compliant—a life-preserving lesson forgotten by too many new Intendants. Increased interaction with their masters often led them to assume an equal increase in allowed familiarity: this was an invariably fatal error.

Pathan was already giving orders—a task at which he excelled, Harrod allowed. "Helots, remount. Security teams are to collapse back upon their own APCs. Nedd!"

The huscarl, senior among the car commanders, came stiffly to attention. "Yes, lord?"

"Your regional secure set is still working?"

"Yes, lord."

"Get me an update. Immediately."

"Yes, lord!"

Pathan surveyed the southern horizon; Harrod's eyes followed those of his lord. Columns of black smoke seemed to be holding up that part of the sky.

Behind them, syncopated thunder rolled: House Mellis's mobile artillery. A moment of silence, then high whimpering screams overhead, then silence again—and finally, flashes along the southern horizon. Two seconds later, the ragged rumbles of the barrage passed over them.

"This race is too closely run," Pathan said in a worried tone.

Harrod knew not to say anything.

"Last week, our position was secure. But with all the neutral Houses now declaring for the HouseMoot, we are dangerously overextended. As it is, neither our forces nor those of House Shaddock can be sure of reaching our capitals in time to defend them—not when we have to fight our way back home through the forces of House Verone."

The price of endless warmaking, and overreaching, Harrod ached to say, but did not dare to.

"Lord Mellis!" It was Nedd. His tone augured news they did not wish to hear.

"Report, huscarl." Like all the Evolved, Pathan Mellis was always supremely cool and collected—even as he prepared to hear tidings of certain disaster.

Nedd did not disappoint their dire expectations. "Lord, our right flank, the armor of House Shaddock—"

"Destroyed?"

"No, lord. Slowing. It has fallen behind the center of our van and—"

Thunder mounted behind them once again—but the timbre and pace of the detonations was more strident, pulsed in sharp fits and starts.

Nedd—mouth still open—stopped, speechless, to stare at the sound. "My lord—battle! How could the HouseMoot forces have so quickly—?"

Pathan glanced at Harrod, who nodded, and explained to the dumbfounded huscarl. "You do not hear the attacking forces of the HouseMoot. Although it is the sound of battle, it is also the sound of treachery. House Shaddock evidently fell behind our van with a purpose; they have fallen upon our mobile artillery and our rearguard."

Nedd gaped wider, if that were possible. "But without the artillery to clear the way before us—"

"—we will not break free of the encircling forces. Quite correct. And exactly what they planned, I'm sure." He turned to Lord Mellis. "Orders, my lord?"

Mellis surprised Harrod—first by shaking his head, and then, actually smiling at him. "No, Intendant: I will be giving the orders here myself. You will be taking the jet-pack and making a report to my great uncle, the Overlord—if you get through the anti-aircraft fire."

"But lord, the jet-pack is reserved for your use onl—"

"I dictate its use, and this is the use I decree." He let his voice slip lower, buried to all ears but Harrod's under the idling hum of the armored car's engine. "Intendant, this battle is over. I will draw the van and left flank together and we will attempt to press forward, but House Verone's helots are as thick as mites on a molting fen-cur. Without artillery, we will need luck and the favor of the Death

Fathers to fight through all their rocket teams. And I suspect there's huscarl armor behind them, probably with air support for the final blow. Do you agree?"

Harrod could only nod, speechless in the face of the Lord's calm diagnosis of their terminal military condition.

"So you shall be our courier and analyst both: you are our best mind, and have intimate familiarity with the details of this campaign—better than I. Besides, you are our House's leading technical historian, are you not?"

"Lord, with respect, it is not my place to claim such—"

"You are. You know it. So does the whole House. Which will soon need you to ready the Ark, unless I am much mistaken."

Ready the Ark? *Had it come to that?*

Pathan had not paused. "So you must go. And I must stay. This I decree, Harrod hur-Mellis."

Harrod did not question his lord; to do so could still earn him death, and even if it did not, would be a pointless waste of time. The jet-pack was man-handled out of the passenger bay of the less-battered APC, was perfunctorily tested, and was propped up for him.

As Harrod backed into the unit, he felt the shoulder and waist braces lock into place, and the jets shudder and heat with the pre-burn. He stared at Lord Mellis, and wanted to say something—anything—but did not have any words, not even an idea where to begin.

Pathan smiled at him again. "Yes, Intendant, some of us Evolved are actually willing to die in service to our own Houses—not just send lesser beings to their ignominious dooms." He gave a signal to the flight techs. "We Evolved are born to dominate. But sometimes, to dominate requires a readiness to die." Pathan's smile became rueful. "Perhaps you believed otherwise, Harrod?"

As the jet-pack's thrusters bloomed, and the lager of battered vehicles dropped away beneath him, Harrod had to admit: *yes, lord, I did believe otherwise.*

But not anymore.

2

ON THE HOUSEMOOT SIDE, the room was furnished with

opulent hangings, sybaritically luxurious chairs, comely helot servants, refreshments, creature comforts, and conveniences of every kind. Opposed were the furnishings of their own side: hard, simple chairs and a bare floor. The humiliation was complete—as was ever the case when a House went to war and lost utterly, rather than reaching a negotiated settlement. Overlord Bikrut Mellis—who sat beside Harrod now—had suffered just such a defeat.

Seated directly across from them was Overlord Verone, an Elder of the HouseMoot, flanked by his victorious generals. Verone's presence was a bad sign: Elders were notoriously (and rightly) preoccupied with the risk of assassination, and were rarely present in a situation where a defeated foe might, conceivably, attempt a suicidal act of retribution.

That Verone was here at all signified two things. Firstly, he had little, if any, fear of House Mellis attempting such an act. Secondly, he was too bent upon overseeing the House's dissolution to pay heed to whatever trepidations he might have had. This predator wanted to play with his prostrate and bloodied prey before tearing its throat out in ferocious exultation.

Beside Harrod, Overlord Mellis's voice was calm, but overly precise in elocution. "Let us conclude this."

"In good time," Verone said with a nod and a smile. "We have not yet addressed all the issues."

"How can we, when you refuse to accept our ritual submission?"

"Eradicating the genetic moiety of your House by marrying it off into others is deemed unacceptable by the HouseMoot's senior Line Mistresses. They have assessed the genetics of your Lines and consider such an alternative to be—unwise." Verone's smile grew.

It was a smile that meant his excuse was just so much cur-shit. None of the Houses that had taken the Moot's part in the late conflict had ever expressed a single reservation regarding the viability—even the extreme desirability—of House Mellis's Evolved breed Lines. No, this was simply the latest slash in the House's now-fated death of a thousand cuts. House Mellis was not to be defeated, or even dissolved as an entity: it was to be extirpated, root, branch, and seed. Partly as an act of vengeance, partly as an example to others who would defy the decisions of the HouseMoot, and partly because of an atavistic belief that any House that had been so completely defeated must somehow be flawed at its core, in the very germ of its genetic essence.

House Mellis's aged Overlord, Bikrut—264 standard years was impressive, even for an undilute Evolved—showed neither impatience, nor anxiety. "So if there is to be no ritual dissolution, what do you propose?"

"I do not propose: I decree. And upon your House, I lay the decree of Exile. You are to remove your Lines from this world and this system. Any that remain behind shall be expunged."

Bikrut swallowed. "You cannot be serious."

"But I am, Overlord Mellis."

"You said we were meeting here for negotiations, not imposition of the Rite of Exile. Had I known—"

"You would have acted no differently. Your House is crippled; you have no choices left. Or perhaps you would prefer that we simply continue the war to its inevitable conclusion, Overlord Mellis. After all, wholesale extermination of a House is not without precedent—"

"Enough." Bikrut's interruption came out as a bark. "We are defeated, but we are not without the means to compel your respect. Even now."

Verone's smile only dimmed a bit. "Ah. Your nuclear arsenal. Hardly large enough to destroy more of us than of you."

"So you think."

"So I *know*. But the gambit is well-played, Overlord Mellis."

"The confidence you place in your intelligence is ill-advised, Overlord Verone."

"Is it? I know just how much rare earth has been mined over the past three and a half centuries. And I know where every gram of it has gone—and resides. So what could you possibly have that I do not know about?"

"Fissionables that did not come from the rocks of this world, but were already in our possession when we arrived here."

Verone's smile faltered. "There is no record in our Exodate's landing manifest of—"

"And who was in charge of the ship that brought us to this wasteland three and a half centuries ago, Overlord Verone? Which House was most expert in spacefaring when we were all exiled to this world? Who, therefore, kept the *real* manifests?"

Verone's smile had vanished; the generals flanking him no longer looked amused.

"Shall I provide the answer you already know? Intendant—" Bikrut spoke sideways, without so much as glancing at Harrod— "who built and crewed the Ark that brought us here?"

Harrod cleared his throat. "At the time that the Fifth Exodate was launched, House Mellis was charged with constructing the Ark, and overseeing its operations during the fifty-three year journey from Ifritem Qua—"

Verone made an impatient gesture toward Harrod. "Enough. Silence."

Harrod swallowed. "With respect, my Elder Overlord Verone, but I was commanded to speak by my bond-holder. To obey you above him means my death."

The Elder narrowed his eyes at Harrod. "To continue to speak means your death, as well."

Harrod could not help swallowing again. "With respect, Elder Overlord, it is written in the Words of the Death Fathers that, 'the servant who dies obeying the holder of his bond is a servant without flaw.' I must honor my bond-holder and the Words of the Death Fathers, Overlord—even unto my death."

Verone's narrowed eyes relaxed, but stayed fixed upon Harrod. His words, however, were aimed at Bikrut: "He is a fine Intendant."

Bikrut sounded as though his belly might contain a seething vat of acid. "He is adequate."

"He is more than that. It was folly not to have already Raised his seed into one of your Lines by completing his Intendancy." Verone pointed. "I would have him. If you agree to transfer his bond to my House, it would make your lot easier, here."

Harrod—stunned to silence—heard many tones in Overlord Bikrut's response: resentment, anger, bitterness, resolve. "You may not have him."

"Name a price—a point of negotiation. I will consider it. Favorably."

"You may not have him."

"If you valued him sufficiently, you would already have Raised him up."

"You may not have him because I need—I must keep—him."

Verone cocked his head slightly. "Why?"

"Because he is our senior technical historian."

Verone's face was radiant with perception. "Ah. Now I see. And now I see why your Lord Pathan sent this Intendant back to report instead of himself. Without this servant, your chances of restoring the Ark and completing a voyage would be much diminished."

Bikrut's admission sounded as if he were uttering it while chewing on broken glass. "That is regrettably so."

"Which means you foresaw the possibility of Exile long before you entered this chamber. Perhaps—just to punish you for your presumption and impertinence—we should indeed resume the war against you."

"Then you shall learn—unpleasantly—just how many fissionables we had sequestered before our voyage to this world."

"Our prior home, Ifritem Quartus, was poor in rare earths. The odds that you had more than a few kilograms of—"

But Bikrut was the one smiling, now. "Are you willing to pay the price it will cost to determine the accuracy of your conjecture, Overlord Verone? I have little to lose—whereas you stand to convert the gains of your impressive victory into a heap of radioactive ashes. But if that is your pleasure—"

Verone sat forward. "Watch how far you press me, Overlord Mellis. We are your conquerors. The Intendant sitting beside you was the last man to escape the battlefield where your House's fortunes died."

"Quite true," answered Mellis placidly. And he waited.

Verone leaned back, ran his left index finger back and forth across his lower lip. Then the smile returned, which Harrod interpreted as a very bad sign, indeed. "So are you telling me that you prefer certain death to Exile, Overlord Mellis?"

Bikrut Mellis's composure faltered. For a moment, he seemed to be choking, the words he must not utter colliding with those he had to say. Ultimately, he shook his head. "No," he said hoarsely, "we accept Exile."

Verone's smile widened; his voice took on the drone of official pronouncement. "Let it here be recorded that your Exodate shall be the Sixth in our reckoning. It is so fated and decreed this 212th standard day of the 351st standard year of the Fifth Exodate's arrival upon Kalsor Tertius. The Exodate Injunctions of the Death Fathers are upon you from this moment forth. Observe them well." He settled back into his conversational voice. "And lest you find your long journey too lonely, I have, in my beneficence, seen fit to furnish you with companions. Huscarl, admit them."

Bikrut refused to be baited: he did not turn to look as Verone's foot soldiers swung wide the doors behind them. Harrod, however, had no face to save, no pride to maintain, and twisted to see—

Overlord Bron Shaddock strode into the chamber, head high, eyes bright. With him were two of his House's Evolved. None of them were over eighty, if Harrod guessed correctly. Young to be the senior leaders of a House. But then again, they had slaughtered their own oligarchs to clear the path for House Shaddock's participation in the recent war. Such was the ambition of the Evolved: even wholesale patricide came within their compass.

Bikrut had not needed to look behind him to determine the identity of the newly entered group. "This jest is in poor taste, Overlord Verone."

"Then you will be pleased to know that this is no jest. As your co-conspirators, House Shaddock will share your Exile."

"They betrayed us. I would as soon eviscerate them as look at them. Indeed, I would much prefer the former."

"But you shall not do so."

"Why?"

"Because now you need them as much as you need your Senior Intendant."

"How so?"

"House Mellis will have control of the Ark. But House Shaddock will have control of its away-craft. You will need their access codes and cross-checks—some of which will be biometric and genetically proofed against duplication or coercion—when you arrive at your Exodate's destination. Without them, you will be unable to descend to the planets you might find there. And beforehand, you will need their help for operations that require you to journey outside your Ark."

"This is insanity. As it is, we do not have the passenger capacity for all the Evolved of our own House, much less another's."

"Then you have little to worry about, Overlord Mellis." The sharp voice, from behind, was Overlord Shaddock's. "Our alliance with you cost us dearly: half of our compounds—and their occupants—were annihilated by the HouseMoot."

Bikrut's sarcasm was underscored by the bored tonelessness of his response. "If your House was suffering thusly, you should have called it to my attention."

"Why? So you could dance with glee? We slew our own Elders to make common cause with you against the HouseMoot. And then you snickered up your sleeves while we died."

Verone's voice was musical with wry mirth. "And so, behold: two pack-sodomized curs attempt to sodomize each other in their bitter disgrace and misery. How quaint: traitors accusing each other of treason. It is edifying, is it not?" he asked his counselors, who almost smiled. "Now let us settle the specifics. You have five years to prepare the Ark and depart. However, there are 3802 Evolved who survive in House Mellis, and 531 from Shaddock. This is far beyond the capacity of the Ark. We suggest a euthanization lottery." Verone's smile returned. "To avoid further, needless bickering."

Harrod felt Bikrut become rigid beside him—a palpable sensation, even at a distance of six inches—and so, lowered his eyes and murmured. "My Overlord Mellis, may I speak?"

That seemed to distract the Overlord from whatever injudicious retort he might have been contemplating. "Why, Intendant?"

"I have considered alternatives, in the event of this situation," Harrod lied quietly. "Perhaps the Overlords would find them useful as crude stimuli for their own, more informed insights."

Bikrut was silent for many long seconds. "Proceed."

"Yes, do," affirmed Verone in an almost amused tone.

"Overlords, although I have never set foot upon the Ark, I am mindful that we have retained the cryogenic suspension technology that was built into it, and which we now use planetside for medical purposes. Logically, the remaining industrial capacity of the two Exiled Houses could combine to produce more cryogenic units, thereby increasing the passenger capacity of the Ark."

Verone began rubbing his lip again. "And why should I allow your Houses to continue to use industrial resources that I have seized, Intendant? Why should my House—and the rest—not immediately enjoy the spoils of our victory?"

"Perhaps because delaying your access to those spoils might well prove the less expensive option."

"How so?"

"Elder Overlord Verone, it seems likely that, if a euthanization lottery is announced in our Houses, there would be considerable resistance, even if all our Lords order its acceptance. It is not in the nature of any Evolved to blithely accept personal demise; the Words of the Death Fathers inveigh against such complacency, and the Brood Mothers breed against it. Is this not so?"

"You know it to be. Continue."

"Then the Overlords of the Exiled Houses must anticipate a general revolt against such a decree, and thus against their dominion. So, to remain the leaders of their Houses, they will be compelled to choose another path. A nuclear path."

"Ah," said Verone. Bikrut nodded tightly.

"However," Harrod finished, "if you allow the Exiled Houses to build enough cryogenic units, euthanization will be unnecessary. The full spoils of conquest may come late, but they will come more surely and with no damage."

Verone looked long at Harrod and then shook his head. "He is completely under-appreciated, Bikrut. No wonder you lost. We are done here." And he turned his back, signaling them to depart.

As they exited, Overlord Mellis muttered. "Well done, Intendant."

"The Overlord honors his servant. But after all, every life in the House was at stake."

"No, they weren't."

Harrod blinked as they emerged into the dim orange light of Kalsor. "I do not understand, my Overlord."

"We brought no additional rare earths to this system. Indeed, we have fewer nuclear warheads than Verone thinks. We would have done whatever he asked."

3

HARROD HUR-MELLIS was surprised when the bow gallery's armored covers slid back and revealed empty space. Or so it seemed at first. Then he saw a larger, slightly irregular star on the lower port quarter.

Beside him, Ackley hur-Shaddock—barely thirty and unusually impatient for so successful an Intendant—scanned the diamond-strewn darkness aggressively. "Where is it? I don't see—"

"There." Harrod pointed at the irregular star.

"That? It's the size of a cur-mite. Smaller."

Harrod reflected upon the dismissive remark: perhaps the intemperate nature of House Shaddock's Evolved was actively inculcated in their Intendants as well. "I, too, expected it to be larger. But do not be deceived; it is simply hard to see at this distance."

"But we are already within a hundred kilometers."

"So we are. But watch."

The irregular star had already become angular: not a bright, radiant point, but a long, flat, reflective surface.

"We should be going inside the Ark, today," griped Ackley.

"There are safety issues that—"

"It is a waste of time to conduct a purely external survey first."

"Ackley, if we are going to work together—as our Houses have instructed us—you will need to accept that my judgment takes precedence. That I give the orders."

"You do not wish input?"

"I do not wish constant complaining—particularly when you do not even try to learn the reasons for the decisions I make, and the orders I give."

"One day soon—when Overlord Shaddock Raises me up, to add my seed to his House's Lines—it shall be you who listens to me. And insolence will mean your death."

"As will be natural and proper, at that time. But that time has yet to come. Here, we are both but Intendants, and I have the benefits of age and long expertise in matters pertaining to our responsibilities. Do I not?"

Ackley's response bordered on a petulant sulk. "Yes. You do."

The Ark was beginning to burgeon rapidly, the long white keel stretching away into the dark, its length cluttered by irregular protuberances and bulges: modules, cargo containers, electronics arrays. But looming closest were great oblongs and spheres, like an onrushing agglomeration of planetoids and moonlets on a collision course....

A gentle counter-boost began to tug at them. The terrifying speed of their approach became merely shocking, then alarming, then swift, and finally, leisurely. They floated toward the clutch of white metal moonlets that were the great ship's inertial fusion ignition chambers and the smaller nodules that held fuel and other volatiles.

Ackley stared forward, past them. "Where is the Great Ring of the early settlement stories?"

Harrod shrugged, glancing at the distant bow of the Ark. "The habitation ring was destroyed."

"Destroyed? By what?"

"By war. What else?" What else, indeed? Savage internecine strife was the only cultural constant that limped through the tattered chronicles of all five prior Exodates. It was the sole reason for the Rite of Exile: the Rite was a pressure valve, an alternative to self-inflicted annihilation. It also unfailingly propagated a new wave of expelled pariahs, who staggered to yet another system to begin the cycle again. Indeed, Harrod was tempted to wonder if the Houses, now descended from five-time losers, must therefore contain a genetic flaw that not only predisposed them to intemperate ruin, but also kept them from learning to change.

Ackley had been studying the immense craft. "And since the war—?"

"Since then, the Ark and its tug-tenders"—small, distant specks, following the same high orbital track, but to port and starboard respectively—"have been abandoned, secured for long-term storage."

"But why? The ship's technology—"

"The ship's technology is why, except for a small, automated monitoring station, it has remained off-limits. The Houses could not agree on how to share its advanced machinery."

"And they are still unable to do so, after three and a half centuries—of course."

Harrod smiled. "Of course." According to records of the prior Exodates, collaborative use of an Ark was rare. Agreement arose on the matter only when the ship was needed as a garbage scow, to haul the latest batch of undesirables to a still further refuse heap in the stars. And, being the product of that long string of genetic disposal missions, being repeatedly orphaned by gulfs of time and space and strife, the Houses had forgotten their own roots, their true home world. Which, Harrod conjectured, was probably the first and last place that humans had known stability, acceptance, unity with their fellows.

Ackley had his palmtop computer out. "So, what are we looking for?" He stared up at the six immense thrust bells, arranged in three pods of two engines each.

"Micrometeoroid damage to the bells and their housing—an easy task, compared to our internal surveys of them."

"Where we will be assessing . . . ?"

"Primarily, the condition of the laser ignition chambers. We must anticipate complete rebuilds of half the systems, and major maintenance upon all the rest."

"Even though they've been stored in a bath of inert gases?"

Harrod glanced at the younger man. "Three hundred fifty years is a very long time."

Ackley shrugged. "What else?"

"The mothballing manifest indicates that several cartridges of the deuterium ignition cells—the hohlraums—were stored along with the engines, to provide examples for later reproduction. We will need to be very careful handling the hohlraums: it is unlikely we could produce enough in time without exact models to copy."

As they moved past the vaguely spheroid ignition chambers capping each of the thrust bells, they passed a black plate, transfixed by the keel of the ship. Ackley stared at it. "That shielding seems to be very light."

Harrod nodded. "An advantage of using deuterium-to-deuterium fusion; far fewer stray neutrons."

"And better speed: exhaust velocities of 6.8 percent the speed of light—"

Harrod turned, summoned a smile, and took pains to ensure that it did not look patronizing. "You speak of the engines of the Dread Parents, Ackley. These engines will achieve only a little bit better than half of what theirs did."

"Why? It is the same design."

"Our craftsmanship and knowledge is not theirs—does not begin to approach it. After all, they also had—and reserved to themselves—the secret of traveling faster than the speed of light."

"Even as their Injunctions forbid us to do the same—along with their prohibition of high-power radio communications." Ackley snorted. "Assuming you choose to believe such superstitious nonsense."

"I need not believe it to know that the Overlord would slay you where you stand for such blasphemy."

Ackley's tone became marginally more careful. "I offer the—*hypotheses*—that the Dread Parents never existed, that the speed of light is an unbreachable barrier, that no such Injunctions were imposed by whatever world we originated upon, and that we cower in fear of our leaders' conveniently constraining fabulations." As Harrod silently conceded the probable accuracy of all those hypotheses, Ackley—cheek muscles bunched—pointed at the long, smooth tanks clustered behind the shielding and bundled around the keel like a fasces comprised of sausages. "What about the fuel tanks? Anything special to look for?"

Harrod nodded. "Yes; micrometeoroid impacts and breaches in the tanks."

"I thought they are fairly sturdy."

"They are, but they held hydrogen for decades. And if they were incompletely vented when the ship was decommissioned—"

Ackley nodded. "They could have been brittlized by the hydrogen left in them. I don't see any sign of diminished integrity, though: maybe the old crew did a good job of flushing all the fuel out of the system."

"Let us hope so; it would make the restoration much easier."

Passing the tanks, they came upon a ring of other, smaller thrusters. For the first time, Ackley's confident tone sounded genuine, rather than nervously overassertive: "The plasma thrusters appear to be in good shape—and look identical to our own."

Harrod nodded. "Not surprising: ours were developed from these. So replacement, if necessary, would be only a minor setback."

The last of the gargantuan aft structures finally dropped behind; their craft altered course to stay centered above the keel as it moved forward. Ackley inspected the modular trusses, running quick mental calculations as he did so.

"A problem?" Harrod asked.

"The storage superstructures: there are not enough of them, not for all the cryogenic modules. With over four thousand bodies to store, we—"

"We will not have four thousand, unless I guess incorrectly. Probably only three-quarters that amount." Harrod acknowledged Ackley's perplexed stare: "Expect a relaxing of the current marriage prohibitions upon the better Lines of my House's Evolved—and some other reductions as well. Consequently, I am more concerned about that." Harrod pointed at what appeared to be a large collar that was sleeved around the keel, its circumference marked by eight evenly-spaced coupling points.

Ackley squinted, shook his head. "I'm not even sure I know what that is."

"It's the rotational sleeve for the old habitation ring—and judging from the scoring at its aft margin, it appears to have seized during operation—over three centuries ago. That could be quite a job."

"Do we still need it to rotate? We don't have a ring, and no time to build one."

"We will still need some rotational habitats, even if they are only pods on the ends of rotating booms. And that means we're going to need a rotational armature."

"We'll also need a complete rebuild of the navigational sensor arrays and laser clearance clusters." Ackley nodded in the direction of the bridge module: just beyond it, the irregular booms and dishes that were the ship's eyes, ears, and shield against high-speed impacts showed extensive pitting by micrometeoroids. In a few instances, whole subsystems trailed at acute angles, or were sheared off entirely. Which inevitably meant that—

The ramscoop—resembling nothing so much as a bow-opening gossamer parasol—was in tatters, shredded by centuries of intermittent meteor storms.

Harrod turned to Ackley, and found the younger Intendant already staring at him—now more in desperation than defiance. Harrod nodded and answered his unuttered question:

"Yes, we have much work to do. Much work, indeed."

4

KALSOR TERTIUS (high orbit), 356th year of founding

BIKRUT MELLIS'S VOICE WAS BORED, his face expressionless. "And the ignition trials?"

Harrod nodded. "Success, my Overlord. We will achieve output sufficient for standard acceleration of .35 gees by the middle of next month. I suspect maximum output will be achieved the month after that."

Bikrut's answering nod was the closest he ever came to fulsome praise. "And the ship's fusion power plants?"

"The refurbished originals did not achieve break-even as quickly as the new units, but once they did, they have routinely out-performed our modern copies. We will achieve maximum rated output within three months, unless something dire occurs."

"Make sure nothing 'dire' occurs, then, Intendant. Or you could experience your own dire occurrence."

Bikrut, Harrod reflected, was ever the voice of boundless encouragement. "As you command, my Overlord."

"Let us turn to the problems, then." He fixed dead eyes upon Ackley hur-Shaddock. "You still do not have enough away-craft: what is the delay?"

To his credit, Ackley did not flinch under that lethal stare. "The delay is caused by the intransigence of the HouseMoot, Overlord Mellis. We can only use away-craft secured for House Shaddock's exclusive access, but the Moot is slow in supplying these vehicles."

"The Moot's lethargy is no excuse for your failure: you should have explained that the biometric security requirements stipulated by Verone must be rescinded."

"I did so; Overlord Verone will not relent."

—To your relief, thought Harrod. *Without the security protocols that require the pilots to be of House Shaddock, the Evolved of House Mellis would kill them in their cold sleep.*

Bikrut's withering stare did not waver. "I have also learned that House Shaddock disapproves of the energy we have allotted for our magnetic shielding."

Ackley remained calm. "Our dispute arises out of hard physics, not House politics, Overlord Mellis. Your House's scientists assert that doubling the field strength of our electromagnetic protection grid will enable it to repel cosmic rays. This is a fallacy."

Bikrut looked at Harrod, who took the cue. "Ackley, we are quite aware that the field emitters cannot 'stop' cosmic rays. However, if the shielding is produced by generators tethered to the ship at a range of four kilometers or more, the fields can be biased to slightly alter the trajectory of the rays. Exposure levels in the protected sections of the ship will decrease by over eighty percent—perhaps more. The efficacy of this deflection strategy is well-documented by the surviving accounts of two prior Exodates."

If Ackley had heard Harrod's explanation, he gave no sign of it. "Overlord Mellis, there is a further issue I must raise. Just today, the HouseMoot rejected our third request for uranium. Without fuel for our nuclear back-up plant, how do they expect us to reinitiate fusion if the capacitors lose their charge?"

Bikrut glanced at Harrod, who shrugged. "It is hardly surprising that our enemies are slow to furnish us with materials from which we could make more weapons of retribution. Particularly given our present possession of an orbital launch platform."

Overlord Bikrut frowned. "And yet we cannot relinquish the failsafe codes for our ground based-nuclear arsenal until we have passed into the outer system. Once there, we can allow them to disarm our missiles—but not before. Harrod?"

"Yes, my Overlord?"

"Recontact Verone. He seems to—favor—you. Make a personal appeal; explain our need for nuclear fuel rods, and also for the removal of the biometric security protocols on the away-craft. I make it your responsibility to solve these problems."

Well, Harrod thought, *now I'll have more gray hairs to join the ones that just started coming in.* But what he said was: "Yes, my Overlord."

5

HARROD HUR-MELLIS held himself steady with a hand-rung located beside the aft-facing observation port. Back at the stern, the last of the Ark's four tug-tenders was making its hard dock. Once attached, the tugs would both provide fuel to the on-board fusion engines, as well as adding their own considerable thrust. One hundred and sixty days from now, their assist-fuel expended, the robot ships would detach and return home.

Home. Within a few minutes, Kalsor Tertius would no longer qualify as 'home.' When the as-yet-unrenamed Ark started underway, the Exodate's last connection with the planet would end. And the Exiles would mark the official commencement of their separate history from the moment Overlord Mellis revealed the name of the ship that would carry them almost sixteen light-years to their new homeworld.

Unfortunately, that new homeworld was as uncertain as their old one was hostile. The HouseMoot had always discouraged any interest in stellar observation, fearing it would stimulate a desire to rediscover the fabled FTL technology of the Death Fathers. Consequently, the only telescopes available for locating a suitable destination star were those on board the Ark itself. Fortunately, they proved to be excellent instruments—once they were thoroughly refurbished. After inspecting a wide array of nearby stars, a midsized yellow star—halfway in its aging to orange—was proven to have a world at the inner edge of the habitable zone, and a smallish gas giant toward the outer edge. Inferential data suggested the inner world had a slightly heavier atmosphere, whereas the small gas giant was suspected of having atypically large moons. Taken in aggregate, they offered the best chance of a world with a biosphere, a place the Exodate could settle at the end of its long journey.

But the presence of a green world was only a possibility, not a certainty. Consequently, observations would continue throughout the journey—which was why Harrod was scheduled to be roused from cold sleep no less than three times before finally beholding the growing glare of their new sun, some seventy-one years hence. Spending a year awake on each occasion, he would complete the journey only slightly older than he was now—and ready to be Raised to the name sul-Mellis: the title of an Intendant whose seed has been wedded to one of the House's Lines. Not fully an Evolved, he nonetheless would receive most of their honors and prerogatives, if not power. But his children would be born as fully Evolved—albeit of a hybrid line—and live without limits, without the need to learn how to avert their eyes, or make a deep bow. On the other hand, as Evolveds, they would learn to conquer, to compete, to domineer. Sadly, they would have little in common with their father, for their own world would be—

"Contemplating the world we leave behind, Intendant hur-Mellis?" The voice was that of Ackley, who, upon the naming of the Ark, was to be Raised up to become sul-Shaddock—and so, over Harrod.

"My thoughts are more upon the world toward which we journey, Ackley."

Whose tone—and smile—hovered in some strange limbo between mockery and congenial jocularity: "Then you are looking the wrong way."

"No, I don't think so. Our future will grow from the roots of this world, you know. We had best remember that, even as we count down these final minutes of our old lives and identities."

"Perhaps. And your insight might even be pertinent, for a change." Ackley had, over the years, become almost amiable—largely because Harrod never rose to his confrontational goads. "For instance, although we go to a new world, we are still creatures of our old Houses. But,"—and his tone changed in a way that Harrod had never heard before—"that doesn't mean that our old allegiances must endure. A new era opens before us. So, too, do new opportunities—if only we are bold enough to seize them."

Harrod turned and stared at Ackley. The tone had been conspiratorial. So: Ackley had been sent to woo Harrod secretly into the ranks of House Shaddock. "Surely you jest."

"Overlord Shaddock has been most impressed by you, and he has noted your own Overlord's unwillingness to Raise you up in a timely fashion. Also, as the two senior space technology specialists, we could cooperatively achieve much."

Harrod heard the words "achieve much" and heard their intended context just as clearly: "massacre House Mellis." Harrod shook his head, baffled.

"Do not dismiss the feasibility of this strategem so quickly, Harrod. Consider the ploy: together, we—"

Harrod kept shaking his head. "No. You misunderstand. I

presume your treachery is as inspired and promising as it is devious and subtle. And I do not doubt that Overlord Shaddock would reward me."

"So you refuse out of misguided loyalty?"

"No," replied Harrod looking up sharply. "I refuse because—at this moment, more than any other in our collective lives—dissent is unmitigated folly. We are commencing the most dangerous journey imaginable: an interstellar voyage with no guarantee of safe haven at its conclusion. Space is hungry for our lives, and well-equipped to devour us with radiation, cold, vacuum, and blind, brutal chance. And you propose that we should war amongst ourselves even as we venture into the lightless belly of such an abyssal beast?"

Ackley turned away. He did not speak for a long time. "I think you are a fool," he said at last. But he did not sound as if he meant it.

Harrod chose a new topic he suspected would be to Ackley's liking. "I suppose congratulations are *nearly* in order. Soon you will be among the Evolved."

"Yes." Ackley seemed to brood upon that. "Hardly an auspicious advancement, though. Being sul-Shaddock was an enviable position when there were thousands of huscarls and helots for every Evolved. Now, despite my title, I am also the very lowest in a House where only Evolveds remain."

Harrod could not deny the poignance of Ackley's situation: a supreme irony, indeed.

It seemed that Ackley had been reading his mind: "It is a rich jest, is it not?"

Harrod, surprised, could only shake his head and speak the truth. "I find no joy or amusement in the misfortunes of others."

Ackley stared at Harrod. "And that is why your House does not Raise you up."

The bulkhead plates sealed off their view of space just as Overlord Bikrut began to speak. "Hear now the first words in the chronicles of our Exodate. Our inertial fusion engines—and those of the tugs—will soon commence operation. You will feel heavy with that acceleration, almost as though you were standing upright upon the surface of Kalsor Tertius. After many months, the tugs will detach, and our thrust—and your sense of 'gravity'—will decrease by two-thirds.

However, only those of us tasked to stand the first long watch will experience that change. The rest of you will be in a near-frozen sleep when our ship passes the heliopause and moves into the particle disk that extends beyond the ecliptic of our system. There, we will activate the ramscoop to gather water and molecular hydrogen even as our navigational lasers start sweeping ahead of us. They will vaporize even the smallest bits of sand or grit: traveling at our velocity, a collision with such debris would still be akin to a direct hit by a nuclear device.

"Over time, all of you will be awakened to stand at least one watch, maintaining order and authority over the aging crew of junior Intendants. Shortly after reaching midpoint, we will breed a small, accelerated second generation of Intendants from the ex vitro vats, to replace those who are awake and approaching infirmity."

The lights dimmed and the intercom tone chimed. Bikrut's head and chin rose slightly. "I order the Sixth Exodate to set forth. And let the annals show that I name this ship, our Ark, the *Photrek Courser.*" The deck came up firmly beneath their feet. "We are under way."

6

14th Year of the Sixth *Exodate*

HARROD FOUGHT UP OUT OF THE STIFF, chilly fog that concluded the process of cryogenic reanimation. And was surprised to find that he was alone—except for Overlord Bikrut Mellis. Startled, Harrod attempted to sit up, to attain a respectful posture—but the sudden movement impaled him upon a spike of core-wrenching nausea: he vomited bile and glycerine-purging fluids upon the floor. "My apologies, my Overlord," he gasped between bouts of retching.

"Be unconcerned," grunted the Overlord, who waited until the worst of the spasms had subsided. "Now, attend me."

Harrod looked up groggily—and suddenly realized that, for Bikrut to be here, something must be wrong. Very wrong. "Yes, my Overlord?"

"There is no cause for alarm. My participation in this waking cycle was always intended. We simply did not communicate it beyond the operations team that has now corrected our demographic problem."

A new coldness grew slowly at the base of Harrod's sore diaphragm. "A...a demographic problem, my Overlord?"

"Yes. The presence of House Shaddock. But as I said, that problem has been rectified." Bikrut smiled.

"Their cryogenic cells—?"

"Precisely. Killed as they slept. Easiest that way. Those who we need at the end of the voyage will be kept in cold sleep."

"My Overlord, if you do not awaken them until our arrival—"

"Do not concern yourself, Intendant: we are aware that seventy years of uninterrupted cryogenic sleep is neither physically, nor mechanically, advisable. But we are staging their reanimations so that there are never more than three awake at any time—and for very short periods: never more than a month. Towards the end of our journey, we will replace the lost numbers with vat-grown helots. They will be our initial workforce and environmental test subjects. Come: stand and walk. You have much work to do. And only a year in which to do it."

Harrod almost slipped off the table as he swung his legs to the deck. "Yes, my Overlord."

7

42nd Year of the Sixth Exodate

HARROD EXITED THE COMMAND SECTION and performed a slow ninety-degree mid-air tumble: his feet came up to rest against the bulkhead he had just drifted through. As the access hatch autosealed beside him, he reached down for a hand-hold, pulled his body into a squat while still keeping his feet flush against the bulkhead. Then he released the hand-hold and kicked free.

In the zero-gee of the *Photrek Courser*'s midcourse glide, this push sent him arrowing down the broad keel-way of the ship, the trussed sections moving past him like a cubist tunnel of groined vaults. Speeding past dozens of module access doors, he did not start grazing his fingertips against the ceiling until he was within twenty meters of the midship array. As he began to slow, he also started a slow rotation into a feet-first attitude.

Having had almost a year of practice, Harrod timed the transition almost perfectly: the plane of his body was parallel with the ceiling as he slowed into a leisurely drift and reached out to grab the hatch-ring of the access tube. He tugged to a stop, and oriented himself; the impression that the access hatchway was in the ceiling was suddenly gone. The visual sense of up/down quickly recalibrated: now, there was no perceivable difference between the ceiling, floor, and bulkhead. He opened the hatch manually and towed himself inside.

Once in the array's dim control suite, he strapped himself into the lead operator's chair and assessed the equipment's status. The sensors themselves were continuing the routine he'd initiated two weeks ago; the computer—its blue flickers ghostly in the inky suite—was still grinding through the reams of data they'd gathered on what was to be their new home.

Still at seven light years distance, the *Courser*'s sensors were straining to get anything useful at all. To make matters worse, the midship array was primarily a communications cluster: the main sensor array at the bow was unavailable. *Photrek Courser's* current segment of travel had brought her within half a light-year of a brown dwarf, increasing the densities of both available volatiles and useless dust. Consequently, the *Courser*'s best array was fully committed to detecting and eliminating navigational hazards while the ram scoop replenished a little hydrogen. Even more important were the sparse amounts of oxygen they gathered: the hydroponics had not functioned as well as hoped. The ninety-nine percent closed bioloop of the life-support system had proven to be more like a ninety-six percent closed bioloop, so any oxygen was a very welcome addition to their resources. But with the main array committed to these crucial tasks, Harrod's long-range planetographic data-gathering had been unavoidably retasked to the secondary, midship array.

The good news from these sensors was that a bit of new data had finally emerged from the spectral minutiae. The bad news was that the data were not particularly encouraging. At least, Harrod reflected, Bikrut was not around to receive the report: his next awakening was still some years off.

The computer was now able to construct a graphic of the system's six planets, but the one in the second, habitable orbit was flagged red. A small world with a thick atmosphere, the greatest fears regarding its suitability had been the possibilities that the atmosphere was comprised of lethal gases or that its proximity to the primary would produce a runaway greenhouse effect.

Unfortunately, according to the data, the news was worse than either alternative—because it indicated that both conditions existed. The atmosphere was largely carbon dioxide, with a heavy mix of sulfur compounds, and a planetside equatorial temperature of about 290 degrees centigrade, plus or minus thirty degrees.

So now all their hopes centered on the rather scant possibility that the smallish gas giant in the third position would have a suitable satellite. However, at this distance, even the main arrays of the *Photrek Courser* would have been unable to acquire reliable data on a moon. Perhaps its mass and period could be discerned, if they were very lucky. But the typical profusion of satellites about a gas giant made gravimetric, and therefore orbital, data suspect, so focused observation upon any one of those worldlets would remain impossible until they got considerably closer.

Harrod turned off the computer and stared at the dim, orange-lit controls. Now the debates would begin: with the first vat-born crewmen to be decanted within the decade, the old plans for a small generation of helots had to be revisited. Although originally envisioned as the first settlement wave, there was clearly need of a contingency plan if it turned out that there were no habitable moons. In that case, there would be no need for settlers, but an urgent need for a workforce which could ready the ship for a further voyage to another promising star. So, what mix of ready embryos should be fertilized for the autowombs and ultimately, the growth-acceleration vats? Would the Exodate need strong backs or strong brains?

Harrod looked out the small porthole at the stars, and marveled at them: they were so sure in their places, so serene in their existence.

So unlike humans.

8

66th Year of the Sixth Exodate

NOW WITHIN TWO LIGHT YEARS of their new home, Harrod slept through the loud rejoicing on the bridge of the *Photrek Courser*. In part, this might have been due to his social class as an Intendant: no one would have thought to include him in the celebration. However, the real reason he missed the celebration was that he was asleep: deeply, dreamlessly, cryogenically asleep.

Harrod hur-Mellis lay in a white sarcophagus, his body maintained at approximately two degrees centigrade. Intubated, catheterized, infused with various stabilizing agents, his bodily functions were either terminated or almost so. Even his sluggish blood was not his own, but a synthetic substance laced with glycerine compounds not unlike those which still flowed in the veins of Arctic fish on the world of his race's origin. And he would sleep on until eighteen months before they were to arrive in the Senrefer system and take up orbit about the strange moon that had, just this day, been confirmed as their new home.

Senrefer Tertius Seven showed the orange spectrographic line that meant an abundance of free oxygen in the atmosphere. Closer analysis suggested a fair amount of water vapor and, although it was still too distant to make a definitive conjecture on surface temperature, it seemed likely that there would be at least shallow seas. Weather, tectonics, oceans, continents, arable soil, edible plants: none of these were discernible. But the odds were good that a colony could be established on this strange satellite, which was quite distant from the gas giant, and evidently, molten-cored and rotating, since it had a reasonable magnetic field of its own.

Before the spontaneous party on the bridge devolved into the randomized—and rather kinetic—matings that were the carefully timed privilege of the Evolved, initial course adjustments were plotted and entered. Low on deuterium, the *Photrek Courser* would now edge toward the dust and molecular volatiles of the outer traces of Senrefer's planetary accretion disk. The Ark would counter-boost for several weeks, and then tumble over to gather more hydrogen with its ram scoop. Having to gather enough fuel to complete their own deceleration would extend the last leg of their journey, turning what had been an eighteen-month acceleration process into a staggered braking regimen that would extend over five years.

In that time, the vat-born helot settlers would be decanted and receive their rudimentary educations. The away-craft—almost never used during the long journey—would be checked and run through shake-down flights. And security precautions would be taken to ensure the compliance of the survivors of House Shaddock when they were awakened to help shuttle the rest of the Exodate down to their new home.

9

71st Year of the Sixth Exodate

UPON ROUSING FROM COLD SLEEP, Ackley sul-Shaddock's eyes opened, but took a long time to clear and start focusing. So, knowing he had no time to waste, Harrod leaned over where the Raised Intendant could see him. "I'm sorry for what happened to your House," Harrod said. "I didn't know."

Ackley's eyes swam in the direction of Harrod's voice, then found his face. "I know," he rasped. And let his head fall back.

A moment later, the door opened and two big helots—one grasping either arm—dragged Harrod roughly from the cryocell chamber.

Harrod was surprised when the eighth and ninth lash came in quick sequence—one-two. He managed to turn what might have been a sob into a gargling cough. And he waited.

Overlord Bikrut Mellis had been most inventive: although there were no whips aboard the *Photrek Courser*, he had improvised a braided length of wire coating. With the wires themselves stripped out, the plastic and latex sheaths were remarkably flexible. And felt very much like a hide whip to Harrod's largely undiscriminating back.

The tenth lash landed with a savagery—and sharp crack—that dwarfed any of the other blows. Harrod bit his tongue—literally—and slumped in the cuffs which hung from the ceiling. Perhaps if the ship had not been under full-thrust deceleration, a whipping might have been impossible: gravity or its analog was pretty much a prerequisite. But on second thought, forced to innovate beyond the bounds of tradition, Bikrut might have arrived at something far more novel—and painful.

The Overlord's voice was in his ear. "Why have you been punished, Intendant?"

Harrod tried to raise his head, but felt darkness close in and the cross-hatched weals on his back burn like a cooking grill.

"Answer. I command it."

"I . . . I showed sympathy to a person of House Shaddock."

"Excellent. You understand your transgression. And I know you understood your punishment. I presume you understand that the first caused the second. And that another transgression will result in a more extensive punishment."

"Yes, my Overlord."

Bikrut turned to the helots. "Remove his restraints."

They complied: Harrod almost fell, but swaying, dropped to a knee and managed to steady himself.

"An appropriate position for you."

Harrod looked up. Bikrut was staring down at him: the words had not been uttered in an unkind tone. They had simply been weighty, determined—like a pronouncement. Harrod watched Bikrut's eyes, not knowing what might happen next.

To his great surprise, Bikrut shook his head and turned away. "Harrod, for that act of disloyalty, I would have sent any other Intendant out an airlock—you, too, if it were not for our need of your skills, and your otherwise . . . unimpeachable . . . service. But know this: you shall not be Raised up."

Hardly a surprise. "My Overlord is just; my transgression warrants no less."

Bikrut almost seemed to spit his frustration. "Idiot! It is not your transgression that has cost you your Raising. It is your mildness, your subservience."

Harrod looked up, too stunned to remember that he must not

look an Overlord directly in the eyes. "My—my subservience is at fault?"

"Of course it is, dolt! Tell me this: what is the privilege and fate of the Evolved?"

"To dominate." Harrod repeated it like the rote catechism it was.

"Exactly. And so, consider well: do you truly belong in that class? Never a stare of resentment. Never a protracted silence in which you might be nursing your own fancies of vengeance. Not even the slightest subversion of orders to put your own imprint upon an undertaking. No acts of pride, or anger, or passion, or impulse. And so, never whipped but once, when you were very young."

"But…but…is this not the behavior the Evolved teach Intendants to follow? Have my actions failed to match your instruction in any way?"

"No—and that is the problem, Harrod. If we Raise up your gene-line, what does it promise for House Mellis? Brilliance? Yes, without doubt. A calm ability to see and solve problems? Without question. But what of the instinct to dominate, to lead, to impose your will upon others: to *win*?"

"I—I do not know what to say, my Overlord."

"Of course you don't. You are a lesser being. And that is why we cannot Raise you, Harrod." The tone in Bikrut's voice was a strange mix of annoyance, pity, and apology. Then he tossed his makeshift lash aside. "There is much to do. You are tasked to oversee Ackley's readying of the away craft."

"My Overlord, Ackley now has rank over me."

"He does not. His Raising has been nullified. By me. He will do as you instruct. Or he will die."

"Yes, my Overlord."

"You must also make haste to collect as much data on the planet as possible: maps, meteorological patterns, climate belts. I am particularly concerned with the latter."

"Because, as a satellite, it has no axial tilt and therefore no seasons?"

"So you understand, then?"

"I believe so, my Overlord. Without seasonal variation, weather patterns will continue to amplify themselves. The weather could be comparatively constant, but quite severe."

"Exactly. And therefore, locating optimal habitation zones could be as difficult as it is imperative."

"I will not fail you in this, my Overlord."

"No. Of course you won't." And he left at a brisk pace.

Harrod became more aware of the pain again, slumped down to both knees.

He felt a hand on his arm, looked up.

The larger of the two helots—a sandy blonde ox with a square, open face—stared down at him. "Why?"

" 'Why?' Why what?"

The helot glanced at the lash. "Why did he beat you so? How did you fail him?"

Harrod surprised himself with a bark of laughter. "I failed him by doing everything he has asked. Since I was born."

The helot stared down at him, and then, shaking his head, helped Harrod to his feet.

10

"SO ARE WE READY TO LAND?" Bikrut's tone was impatient.

On an external monitor, Senrefer Tertius Seven stared back at the Overlord and his senior advisors. The angry eyes of multiple hurricanes chased each other—in slow motion, from this altitude—out of the turbulent equatorial ocean belt as they watched.

"I estimate ten days at the earliest, my Overlord. Since the security-protected shuttles have turned out to be far more reliable than the unprotected ones, we are progressing at a pace constrained by the remaining number of Shaddock pilots."

Bikrut glared but said nothing: he had not wanted to wake any members of that crippled House unless absolutely necessary. Indeed, Bikrut had expressed how convenient it was that the "traitorous devos" were already entombed in cryogenic sarcophagi. But rousing the pilots of House Shaddock had been unavoidable: their shuttles proved vastly superior to, and safer than, the others. Ultimately, without their services, the chances for successful settlement would have been uncertain, at best.

Harrod decided it was best to change the topic swiftly. He

thumbed his control unit: charts, graphs, and progress tables sprang up on the smaller monitors behind him. "As you can see, much of the local flora and fauna is ultimately edible, but—as our first samplers' deaths revealed—very little of it can be consumed without prior processing. Mostly, this means leaching it with common organic acids to break down a variety of mild toxins. Also, in addition to standard collagen, there are a variety of related substances which cause most of the vegetable matter to pass through our tracts too quickly. Leaching dissolves these more troublesome fibrous substances; boiling allows them to be stripped out."

"And how are the first test settlers doing, otherwise?"

"Quite well, actually, although they had some initial difficulty adapting to the gravity. This suggests that before anyone goes planetside, they should spend three, rather than two, weeks in the rotating habitation pods, which we now have operating full time at one-gee equivalent centrifugal force."

"And have you identified our landing site?"

Harrod hesitated. "Yes, my Overlord, I have. Or rather, 'we' have. But I find myself to be the sole dissenting voice in the study group."

"Explain."

Harrod called up a rotating image of the moon on one of the monitors. "As you will note, slightly less than five percent of the satellite's surface is land, and most of that is clustered in what we have arbitrarily designated as the northern hemisphere. Its many islands are all surface-breaking crests of steep sea-mounts. Their terrain is comprised of forbidding mountains, most rising up along what one might call the 'spine' of each separate island. At sea-level, however, most have a tidal shelf and skirt of land that ascends into a fringe of upland forest. There seems to be a reasonable diversity of biota throughout these archipelagos, and initial surveys suggest that while there is little iron, copper and tin deposits are not uncommon."

"And the other site?"

Harrod slowed and then stopped the globe's rotation as it centered on a discernible dot in the middle of the huge and unremarked ocean expanses of the southern hemisphere. "This landmass is, you might say, the top of a seamount 'mesa' of immense proportions. It is approximately 900 by 600 kilometers in size. Much of its land is flat, and it seems to boast the deepest soils on the satellite. It is a natural site for large-scale agriculture, and its eastern half has a fairly extensive network of rivers, comprised of three separate watersheds, two of which could—one day—be connected by canals, even using primitive construction methods."

"And so that is the site you recommend, Intendant?"

"No, my Overlord. That is the site uniformly recommended by the rest of the research group."

"And you choose the scattered islands and archipelagos of the north? Why?"

"My Overlord, the southern continent lies astride a weather belt which, while generally favorable, experiences some considerable meteorological extremes. Also, it has almost no other landmasses nearby. Except for a handful of small, scattered seamount atolls, it is alone in the southern hemisphere.

"In contrast, the islands of the north lay scattered across the many weather bands of that more moderate hemisphere. If we discover that our first site there is not optimal, relocation is quite feasible, using local means. Also, since there are many separate islands, it will be possible to establish widely-separated communities and so ensure that they could not all fall victim to any one disastrous event, such as a tidal wave or sequence of hurricanes. In establishing multiple, smaller communities, we ensure the survival of our race."

And as he said it, he knew the Evolved executive collective before him had already dismissed his concerns. They would no doubt tell themselves that Intendant Harrod was unduly obsessed with mishaps, was prone to worrying about risks that were phantoms of his imagination, rather than actual dangers.

But the real reason they dismissed his analysis was because Evolveds were not merely given to contention, but sought it out. It was how they exhibited and lived their mandate to dominate. Set down in small, separated settlements, they would have no arena in which to highlight their personal prowess, no neighbors against which to pit their wills. In short, they would insist upon settling together: an eternally bickering pack of would-be tyrants.

Bikrut raised his chin. "A most adequate presentation, Intendant. We will not detain you from your preparation of the next wave of helot settlers. The landing craft are nearing readiness?"

"They are all fully operational, my Overlord. Several are already shuttling down advance supplies for the settlement. Intendant Ackley is organizing that labor most effectively."

"And so he assures his continued survival. I want you and him to coordinate the dismantling of the command hull's escape pods beginning next week: their fuel and subsystems will be urgently needed planetside. You may leave."

And so Harrod did, first exiting the sleek bridge module, then the much bulkier command hull to which it was attached, and heading aft fifty meters along the keel-way of the Ark. Here he slipped through a hatchway coupling cube and emerged into a zero-gee habitation module, reserved for the recently decanted helots. They stood as he entered.

"Intendant," said their leader with a deep bow. When he straightened, Harrod saw that it was the same one who had helped him up after his scourging. The helot smiled; Harrod returned it reflexively—and thought: *Bikrut is right. I lack the domineering hauteur of the Evolved; I can't be one of them.*

He motioned for the helots to gather around; this day would be their first spent under a full gee in the spinning habitation modules. They would be cramped there, but it was essential to ready as many of them as possible for—

A sound that Harrod had only heard once before—during the Ark's first systems test, seventy-five years ago—stunned him now: the emergency klaxon. Without a word to the helots, he turned to rush out of the big, boxy hab module—but the door to the coupler autosealed with a breathy hiss.

Stunned, Harrod stared at the closed hatchway for a moment, then paged the bridge—only to find that there was already a line paging him. Not recognizing the code, he answered, curious and cautious: "Hello?"

"Hello, Harrod." The voice was Ackley's. "Where are you?"

"In the zero-gee hab modules. With the helots."

"Excellent. Stay there. You'll be safe."

"What do you mean, 'I'll be safe?' Safe from what?"

"It will be over very soon."

"What will?"

Ackley paused as if startled at Harrod's naiveté. "The destruction of House Mellis, of course."

There was a muffled blast, a heavy impact that sent Harrod and the helots reeling aft, and the faint squeal of deforming metal near the module coupler hatch. "What—what in the name of the Death Fathers are you doing, Ackley?"

"Killing those who killed us—before they can finish the job. The jolt you felt was one of the cryogenic hive-modules being blown free of the *Courser*."

"But—how?"

"Simple, really. We doubled each coupler cube's separator charges when Bikrut had us run a systems check. Put in radio-operated triggers. We guessed that would be enough to tear each module free of the main hull. Seems we were right."

"How many—how many are you 'jettisoning'?"

"Intendant: what a question. Why, all of them, of course. They killed almost four hundred of us. Now we're killing twenty-eight hundred of them. Since one of us is worth ten of them, they've still got the better part of the deal. But not for long." His voice lowered. "Harrod, give me the access codes for the bridge module." In the background, Harrod now heard faint gunshots, two screams, the hissing rattle of a machine pistol.

"I don't know the access codes," Harrod lied.

"Of course you do." Ackley didn't even sound moderately annoyed.

And Harrod thought: *am I so predictable, then? Well yes, I suppose I am.* "No, I really don't know the codes."

"Harrod, we have already tortured one of these curs—and he insisted that you do know the codes. Insisted quite emphatically."

"He must be mistaken, then."

"Really? I wasn't under the impression that Overlord Bikrut's second son would be so terribly misinformed." Ackley's tone became more intimate. "Listen, Harrod: you don't understand. You are being offered a signal honor: cooperate now, and the new Overlord Shaddock will Raise you up. A full integration of your seed in the House's First Line. You are the only creature bearing the name Mellis who will survive this day—*if* you cooperate."

Harrod felt the whip upon his back, tasted the broken promises of his Raising, but also saw the slaughter that would ensue if the vengeful survivors of House Shaddock entered the bridge module, which was probably where the women and children of House Mellis had taken shelter. "I—I cannot give you the codes. I cannot be the instrument of so much senseless killing."

"Killing, yes; senseless, no." Ackley's tone was chillingly casual. "It makes quite a lot of sense to kill people who have already proven that they would cheerfully kill all of us in our cryocells—if they didn't need some of our pilots to fly their away-craft. Speaking of which, this is your last chance—because if we don't get the codes, we're leaving."

Harrod felt that, although he was motionless, the world around him was spinning furiously. "Leaving?"

"Of course. If we can't seize the *Courser*, then we will take the away-craft. And I'm sorry, but we'll have to harm your pretty ship a bit as we leave. Harrod, this *is* your last chance." A moment of silent waiting; then another sputter of gunfire. "Very well, Harrod. Your death—and *only* yours—is a waste. Your skills will be missed."

And the circuit went dead. At the same moment, explosions rocked the ship, first pushing strongly from aft—the engines, no doubt—and then light but irregular buffeting from the other three points of the compass.

"What was that?" asked the leader of the helots.

Harrod moved to inspect the coupler. "The first jolt was the engines being sabotaged. The next was our electromagnetic shielding pods being blasted free. Without them, the radiation levels in this hull will climb rapidly. And without our engines..." House Shaddock had crippled the Ark itself. At first it seemed madness, but then Harrod perceived—and conceded—the canny inspiration behind that madness. Since House Shaddock could not hold the ship—and therefore, the high ground—it was necessary that the enemy's seat of power be rendered useless. And that is what they had done to *Photrek Courser*: damaged engines and an absence of radiation shielding made this once mighty Ark a death ship. Whether it spiraled in toward the seas of Senrefer Tertius Seven, or was sucked in years later by the gas giant itself was hardly worthy of debate: in the end, the great Ark, the enabler of any further Rites of Exile, was gone. In its place was only the unremitting contention and enmity of the rival Houses.

Harrod's comm-link hummed; he activated it.

Bikrut's voice growled out of it. "Intendant, where are you?"

"In zero-gee habmod three, my Overlord."

"And you know what has happened?"

"I do. Are all the ships away?"

"Yes, all taken by the Shaddock devos—may the Dread Parents feast upon the entrails of the motherless spawn." A long pause. "You refused to give them the access codes, didn't you?"

"Yes, my Overlord."

"This was well done. And yet stupid: if you had it in you to dominate, to prevail, you would have gambled all, boldly—and left behind your loyalty to my wounded House. But, since you can no longer breed, I recant my earlier decree: in appreciation of the exemplary service you have rendered us, I declare you Raised, Intendant Harrod sul-Mellis."

That declaration, and its now-monstrously diminished significance, struck Harrod as particularly ironic. But he kept the smile out of his voice as he replied, "Harrod sul-Mellis thanks his Overlord for this signal honor."

Bikrut made a muttering sound that might have been congratulations, complaining, or mild gastric distress.

Harrod asked, "I do not understand your remark regarding my inability to breed, Overlord Bikrut."

"I did not say that you lacked the ability; I said that you cannot do so."

"Meaning, you will not permit me?"

"Meaning you will not survive."

At that moment, the ship gave yet another tortured wrench aftwards, tumbling Harrod and his helots against the bow-quarter bulkhead. "Overlord Bikrut, what do you mean—and what was that?"

"The answer is the same: the survivors of House Mellis have collected in the bridge module, which we have just detached from the command hull."

"Uncoupled the bridge module? But it is incapable of reachieving orbit, once it is used as a planetary lifeboat. Besides, it was never refurbished—"

"That is where you are wrong, Harrod: we refurbished the bridge module's maneuver system in the sixth year of our voyage, and left no record of the activity. With all of House Shaddock still in cold sleep, that was simple enough to achieve."

"So you will land the bridge module—where?"

"Why, right atop the traitorous devos who were assassinating my family just a few minutes ago. They are headed to the primary landing site in the southern hemisphere. And we shall follow them."

Of course you shall. It's all you know how to do. It's what makes you what you are. "Farewell, Overlord Bikrut."

But the line was already dead.

11

THE FOUR HELOTS who wanted to see how things would end—the last actions to be performed by the *Photrek Courser*—accompanied Harrod to the command module. There, he used a key wrench to open what looked like an oversized closet; the accessway led into a room packed with relays and command consoles: the auxiliary bridge. Harrod activated the screens and the sensors. Within seconds he detected the Shaddock flight to the surface: about a dozen away-craft, preparing to land near the prepositioned caches and test-settlement at the eastern end of the large landmass in the south. The remains of House Mellis were hard on their heels—and unexpected, since House Shaddock had never been told that the bridge module could function as a separate vehicle.

While the helots gawked at the descending ships, Harrod surveyed the engineering readouts. The fusion drives were gone, but the attitude and short maneuver thrusters were still functional and fully fueled. Bringing those slowly online, Harrod steadied *Photrek Courser* and altered her trajectory so that she would be over the north hemisphere in the first half of her orbit, but above the south in the second half. He turned to the helots. "It is time for you to leave. Go to the escape pods. Enter them as I have shown you and wait. I will do the rest."

The big helot who had helped Harrod after the whipping stared at the monitors and the course plots with a frown. "I fear for you, Harrod-Lord: how can you be sure you will escape this Ark in time?"

"All is arranged," he answered. "Now, you must go—and lead your people wisely. And kindly."

The square-jawed helot frowned even more mightily, but then nodded and left, the other three trailing behind him.

Harrod rolled the ship slightly to port, bringing up the evacuation tubes so that they would fire at an angle, sending the escape pods into a tight cluster of islands in the mid-northern hemisphere. He had just finished calculating the pods' collective entry angle when the lead helot's voice boomed from the command suite's speaker. "We are ready, Harrod-Lord."

"Very good. Now seal up."

"And you will be coming down, too?" The voice was worried.

"Yes. I am. I'm coming down, too." And with that Harrod cut the commlink.

Three minutes later, Harrod discharged the escape pods. Spat free of their keel-lining launch tubes, the pods began their glittering, and ultimately, red-hot arcs down toward Senrefer Tertius Seven. And once the last of them was away, and he saw that the four hundred glowing dots had survived their entry and were now well within the atmosphere, Harrod sul-Mellis angled the great, crippled Ark into a more acute transequatorial trajectory. He checked the sensors: House Shaddock's away-craft had landed. House Mellis's bridge module was almost upon them. And as the tattered remains of those two embittered Houses commenced their planetside struggle for dominion, they would certainly not think to look over the shoulder. After all, no threat was expected from that direction.

Consequently, given the opportunity to surprise them both, Harrod pushed the *Photrek Courser* into a steeper descent, watching the blue margin of the atmosphere rise up to meet him as he set his course guidon directly atop the icons denoting the survivors of both Houses.

As he rode the Ark down toward their conjoint landing ground that was, by now, also a killing field, Harrod wondered if this outcome was, in fact, not the best of all possible occurences. With the *Courser* crippled and now plunging to her own death, later generations from this worldlet would have no starship with which to send away yet another wave of bitter, defeated Exiles. This time, descendants of the helots—who were even now emerging from their surf-caught escape pods—would have to learn to settle their differences, find ways to understand and even embrace their enemies, rather than exterminate and banish them.

Or maybe not: he couldn't know. Harrod could only give those future generations—and the forces of hope and fate—a chance to create a better society than the one they had come from.

Atmospheric buffeting made the *Courser*'s bow begin to buck. A bit of downward thrust steadied the nose, which eased into the smooth arc of a fast descent. He checked the ship's projected impact point and smiled: for an Intendant, a lesser being, he was doing a most admirable job.

Most admirable indeed.

FUSION STARSHIPS

Dr. Gregory Matloff

When the history of humanity's expansion into the galaxy is written in the capital city of Tau Ceti Three, the entry for Gregory Matloff may well read, "He was one of the pioneers in the field of interstellar travel. His theoretical analyses of the technologies that might enable the human species to travel between the stars inspired generations of scientists and engineers, and are the basis of the starships that enabled settlement of this part of the galaxy."

This is the second of his essays for Going Interstellar, *and in it he describes a propulsion system that many believe will be the first to take us to the stars.*

⊚ ⊚ ⊚

OKAY, you want to go to the stars! If you are not in too much of a hurry, if you have lots of money and if you've got access to solar-system resources, there is a way. If we had to, we could probably manage all this in the not-too-distant future.

We're talking about nuclear-fusion-propelled starships. A common physics joke goes something like this: "fusion is the energy source of the future and always will be!" But it may be that our first crude terrestrial fusion-power pilot plants will soon be ready. And space applications will inevitably follow.

Fusion will not provide *StarTrek*-style spacecraft. But it could propel and power robotic probes requiring a century or so to cross the interstellar gulf. Human-occupied ships requiring generations to cross between stars may also be fusion-powered.

143

Although this type of experimental reactor (more properly called "thermonuclear fusion") is still not online, the physical basis for it has been around a long time. Humanity's understanding of thermonuclear fusion (and other nuclear processes) can in fact be traced to Albert Einstein's Miracle Year of 1905.

Early Fusion History

Few of his contemporaries would have guessed that Albert Einstein would change the world. Working as a Swiss patent clerk, this young German Jew had not distinguished himself in college. Without the help of his wife (also a physicist), Albert might not have completed the studies leading to his bachelor's degree.

Hardly a man of action, young Albert was a dreamer. After work he would travel by tram to enjoy dinner with friends in local cafes and restaurants. He loved this mode of travel. One day, he daydreamed that the tram was a light beam upon which he was a passenger, looking back at the Earth. Suddenly, in a flash of inspiration, he had it! This was the secret of Special Relativity. For better or for worse, the Atomic Age was born.

For decades, physicists had grappled unsuccessfully with the observationally confirmed fact that the speed of light in vacuum was a constant 186,300 miles per second (300,000 kilometers per second). Even if you observed a laser projected from a starship passing at near-light speed, the velocity of the photons in the beam would still be measured as traveling at 186,300 miles per second.

As a consequence of this inconvenient truth, physicists had to accept the strange aspects of the Lorentz-Fitzgerald Contraction. As you observe a speeding starship fly past, it will be foreshortened or contracted. As its velocity approaches that of light, the Earth-bound observer will see the ship's mass increase. Even less comprehensible, time on the ship will slow down. It sounds almost like Alice falling into the rabbit hole, or a Timothy Leary-style acid trip!

Today, the Lorentz-Fitzgerald Contraction is a verified aspect of the real world. But in the early twentieth century, it was still a theoretical novelty. And physicists such as Einstein struggled to fit it into their concepts of reality.

Another problem was magnetism. Since James Clerk Maxwell had derived his famous equations around 1870, physicists knew that electricity and magnetism were connected. Although they accepted the fact that electric charges in motion produced the force called magnetism, they wondered how this could be.

From the vantage point of his speeding trolley car, Einstein would form the framework for the solution to both problems. He proposed that time was a fourth dimension like the three familiar dimensions of height, length and width. Combining the four-dimensional space-time geometry with a constant value for light speed in a vacuum, Einstein theoretically justified both the Lorentz-Fitzgerald Contraction and the existence of magnetism.

The explanation of magnetism was brilliant. Imagine an infinite line of electric charges, each separated from its neighbor by a constant distance. Any electric-field detector will measure a field strength depending on the device's sensitivity and distance from the nearest charge. Now accelerate the charges up to a fraction of light speed. By the Lorentz-Fitzgerald Contraction, the separation between adjacent charges will decrease. More charges will be within the detector's range and the measured field strength will increase.

Brilliant as this insight was, it was not enough to ensure Einstein's future. So he labored to integrate gravity into relativity theory. The resulting theory, dubbed General Relativity, perceives the mass of a gravitating object (such as the Sun) as locally warping the four-dimensional fabric of space-time. Observations of stars near the solar limb during a post-World-War-One solar eclipse confirmed the predictions of general relativity. Einstein would go on to win a Nobel Prize and become a name equated by the general public with genius.

But in the publicity and excitement accompanying Einstein's meteoric rise, a seemingly minor aspect of special relativity was generally ignored by non-physicists. From the imaginary vantage point of his light-speed trolley car, Einstein considered the total energy of a stationary object on Earth's surface. Since the object was not moving, it had no kinetic energy (or energy of motion). Since it was at the same level as the Earth-surface reference frame, it had no potential energy (or energy of position). But it did possess "rest energy." The quantity of rest energy is dependent upon the speed of light in vacuum (c) and the object's mass (m). Rest energy is defined in that awesome expression:

$$\text{Rest Energy} = mc^2$$

Appearing in a footnote in one of Einstein's special relativity papers, this definition of rest energy indicated that mass could be converted into energy and energy could be converted into mass. Physicists could no longer talk about the conservation of mass or the conservation of energy, but nature would now conserve "mass-energy."

Specialists in the 1920s began to utilize mass-energy conversion and conservation in their research. Physical chemists such as Marie and Pierre Curie had pondered the question of how decay particles in radioactive processes obtained their energy. The obvious answer was that a small fraction of the mass of the decaying nucleus was converted into a particle's kinetic energy.

Astrophysicists such as Sir Arthur Eddington had wondered how the Sun and other stars could maintain stability for the immense durations required by the fossil record. Once again, the answer required mass-energy conversion in the stellar interior.

But could humans ever tame this process or derive benefit from it? The answer came as war clouds were gathering once again in Europe. Fortunately for all of us, the censors in Nazi Germany were not well trained in nuclear physics or appreciative of its potential. As the Second World War approached, a group of German physicists solved the problem of tapping nuclear fission energy—and published their results in the open literature!

In 1938, it was known that one particular isotope of uranium—Uranium 235—was radioactive. When it decays by nuclear fission (splitting), this massive nucleus splits spontaneously into several less massive (daughter) nuclei and fast-moving (thermal) neutrons. It was also known that the fission of this nucleus could be induced by bombarding it with thermal neutrons. In their epochal paper, Otto Hahn, Lisa Meitner and Fritz Strassmann calculated the density of uranium required to trap emitted neutrons within the U-235 sample. The rapid reaction of uranium in the sample would produce enormous energy. It became known as the chain reaction.

Few realized it at the time, but this simple calculation would provide the basis of both the atomic bomb and the fission reactor. One who recognized the potential immediately was our old friend Albert Einstein.

If we could go back in time a few decades to observe any historical event, one choice might be Einstein in his office at the Institute of Advanced Studies opening the German physics journal containing the epochal paper. Perhaps he was wearing his baggy sweater and smoking his pipe as he opened the journal and read the paper. Perhaps he did a few calculations to check the result.

Einstein knew what the Nazis planned. He had been fortunate to escape Europe and had worked to save family members and colleagues. As a non-native English speaker with a good knowledge of German and Yiddish, he may first have dropped the pencil on his desk and removed his glasses. Then he may have muttered "Oy Mein Gott," as the terrible reality sank in.

An ordinary mortal may have visited a Princeton pub and drunk himself into oblivion. But Einstein was far from ordinary. He crafted a letter describing his concerns and posted it to President Roosevelt.

If one of us writes a concerned letter to the President of the United States (or any other world leader) we might expect a response from a low-level intern. But Roosevelt realized that Einstein was no ordinary mortal. And he knew that war clouds were thickening. He responded by convening a conclave of the best American nuclear experts to check the validity of Einstein's concerns and the German team's calculations. The Manhattan Project, which would result in the atomic bombs dropped on Japan in the final days of World War II, had started!

Even Einstein was amazed (and saddened) by the power of his mass-energy footnote. When he was interviewed after the Hiroshima bombing, he implied that perhaps he should have been a plumber!

After the war, nuclear experts in both the US and USSR realized that the atomic bomb—which works by the fission, or splitting, of heavy atomic nuclei—was not the final answer to humanity's destructive quest. Work would be devoted to the more powerful thermonuclear bomb—which operates by fusing or combining light atomic nuclei in a manner analogous to the Sun.

To date, hydrogen bombs (which can yield thousands of times

more energy than the Hiroshima blast) must have a fission trigger. The atomic-bomb trigger is first ignited to raise temperature, pressure and density in the fusion material to levels at which thermonuclear reactions can occur. Although the details of these devices are closely guarded military secrets, it is safe to assume that explosive-fusion reaction schemes involve heavy isotopes of hydrogen, light isotopes of helium, and perhaps lithium and boron.

Before the end of the Cold War (during which thousands of fission and fusion devices were produced) futurists realized that human civilization would ultimately exhaust its fossil-fuel reserves. Perhaps some form of controlled thermonuclear fusion might be the answer to our growing energy needs.

Two basic types of electricity-producing fusion reactors have been proposed and are being researched. One approach uses powerful electric and magnetic fields to confine the plasma (ionized gas) of thermonuclear material. Another major difficulty in achieving controlled thermonuclear fusion is the multi-million-degree temperature at which the reactants must be maintained. Although cleaner (in terms of radioactivity) than the less-powerful fission reactors now in use, currently feasible fusion reactors will also produce some radioactivity.

Confined-fusion technologists use two benchmarks to define their progress. Achievement of "scientific breakeven" would mean that an experimental fusion reactor would produce as much output energy as was used to create the fusion reaction to begin with. "Technological breakeven" means that the energy produced is at least ten times greater than the energy input. At present, experimental confined-fusion reactors operate at about 50% of scientific breakeven. Achievement of technological breakeven will require more time—and money.

Although confined-fusion reactors have promise for terrestrial energy production, inertial fusion might be more useful for in-space propulsion. Inertial fusion reactors operate using small pellets of fusion reactants. These are pelted with electron beams or lasers to raise pellet temperature and density to levels at which thermonuclear reactions can occur. Essentially, an inertial-fusion reactor is a small hydrogen bomb with the fission trigger replaced by electron or laser beams.

An inertial-fusion reactor used to produce terrestrial energy would require considerable shielding to trap the high-energy products of the thermonuclear reactions. But this is less of a problem in space. Since these reaction products largely consist of high-energy electrically charged particles, engineers quickly figured out that they could simply squirt them out the back of the spacecraft as rocket exhaust. Even before Apollo 11 reached the Moon, some scientists realized that inertial-fusion ships might some day reach the stars!

Project Orion—Birth of the Interstellar Dream

Freeman Dyson distrusted bureaucracies. During the Second World War, he worked on crew safety for the British Royal Air Force Bomber Command. Early in the war, he realized that the escape hatches on many British bombers were too small for crewmembers to depart a stricken aircraft while wearing their parachutes. Dyson wrote memo after memo to correct this defect without positive response until late in the war. Embittered, he realized that thousands of brave British airmen must have needlessly perished. He swore that never again would he trust a large bureaucracy to do the right thing. More than anything else, Dyson's response to his wartime experience helped produce the realization that the stars are not beyond reach.

After the war, when Dyson had moved to the Princeton University Institute of Advanced Study, he mentored Theodore Taylor in his Ph.D. studies. Working on the US atomic bomb project, Taylor had become disillusioned with the effort that went into creating fake cities and nuking them. To him, this was a waste of taxpayer money since the A-bomb, after all, had been "tested" on two very real Japanese cities. Taylor, instead of concentrating on the construction of objects to be destroyed by atomic blasts, asked himself if anything could survive in the hellish vicinity near ground zero.

He designed a pumpkin-sized steel sphere, coated it with graphite, and installed it at the Eniwetok nuclear test site in the Pacific near a 20-kiloton nuclear device. To everyone's surprise (but perhaps not Taylor's), the metal sphere rode out the blast with minimal damage. Apparently, the graphite layer had ablated—evaporating at high speed—and carried off much of the incident energy produced by the explosion.

Dyson, Taylor and others saw a possible application for this process. As the Space Age dawned, US defense analysts recognized that there was no known defense against orbital Soviet nuclear warheads. But perhaps a spacecraft propelled by external nuclear explosions might do the trick.

This was the birth of the initially top-secret Project Orion. On a future spacecraft, Orion crews would carry with them small nuclear charges. (Okay, they would be small bombs.) The charges would be discharged on command behind a pusher plate coated with ablative material. This pusher plate, which would be impacted by the nuclear blast, would be connected to the rest of the ship by the world's largest shock absorbers. *Bang! Bang! Bang!* Explosion after explosion would impulsively propel spacecraft to faster and faster speeds.

Although a full-scale Orion was never constructed, small test models propelled by chemical explosives were successfully filmed careening across the sky. One is on display (near a model of Star Trek's Starship *Enterprise*) in the Smithsonian Air and Space Museum in Washington DC.

As the Project Orion study continued, it became evident that Orion "interceptors" could be capable of velocities in excess of 30 miles (50 kilometers) per second. Some conceptual versions could lift from Earth under their own nuclear drive, unfortunately leaving behind a huge wake of radioactive particles. Variants might ride as the second stage of a Saturn V rocket, exhausting their A-bombs well above Earth's delicate biosphere.

The high time for Project Orion was in 1961-1963. NASA had been commissioned by President Kennedy to deliver and return humans from the Moon before 1970. Most analysts preferred the Saturn V booster to launch the Moon ships, but this rocket had not yet been tested. So a number of back-ups were suggested. One was Orion.

In this heady period, Dyson, Taylor and their associates investigated the interplanetary potential of Orion. As a Saturn V upper stage, it had the potential of ferrying astronauts to Mars on month-long journeys. Habitats, rovers, greenhouses and livestock could come along as well.

But alas, it was not to be. The Atmospheric Test Ban Treaty dampened the prospects for Orion. And the success of Saturn V doomed it. Before the first Lunar Modules swooped down over the lunar plains, Orion and its extensive documentation seemed headed for storage in some super-secret government depository, perhaps located next to the box containing Indiana Jones's Ark of the Covenant.

Freeman Dyson was angry. And Freeman Dyson distrusted large government bureaucracies. So he methodically hatched a scheme to save Project Orion from oblivion.

Being a physicist, Dyson planned to publish a paper describing the potential of Orion in a journal. But most physics, astronomy and astronautics journals have circulations of only a few thousand. He chose to publish in *Physics Today*, a semi-popular monthly organ of The American Institute of Physics. Many public and university libraries subscribe to this magazine—its monthly readership would therefore be much larger than that of more technical physics journals. Dyson planned a paper that would outline the concept of Orion in visionary terms, and do so in a manner that would not violate his oath of secrecy.

Of course he had to use clever approximations. One was the yield in equivalent megatons of TNT of a deuterium-fueled thermonuclear explosive. Dyson knew that the USSR had just air tested the largest H-bomb ever exploded. The yield of the test was well established and the type of aircraft carrying the device had been announced. Dyson probably could have exactly stated the yield of a fusion explosive—instead, he consulted a standard reference (*Jane's All the World's Aircraft*) and used the payload capacity of the Soviet bomber.

Published in late 1968, Dyson's paper established him as an early hero of the "Interstellar Movement." Even with his many approximations, he demonstrated that huge, multi-kilometer fusion-pulse world ships could be constructed that would take up to one thousand years to reach the nearest stars. If the entire US/USSR 1968-vintage thermonuclear arsenals had been devoted to Project Orion, as many as 20,000 people could have been relocated to the Alpha/Proxima Centauri system. What a happy use for the bombs!

Projects *Daedalus* and *Icarus*—The BIS follows Up

Now that Dyson and Taylor had opened the "Interstellar Door," other groups began their own studies. The British Interplanetary Society (BIS), which had studied Moon flight decades before the Apollo Project, was ideally situated to conduct a follow-on study to Orion. British researchers Alan Bond and Anthony Martin directed this study, dubbed Project *Daedalus*, during the 1970's. The original *Daedalus*, a mythological Athenian architect, had escaped imprisonment in Crete with the aid of flapping wings handily crafted from goose feathers.

It was soon determined that the modern *Daedalus*, although inspired by the Orion conceptual breakthrough, would be a bit different. Several problems were acknowledged with the Orion concept. One was scale—an Orion starship (such as the pulsed thermonuclear rocket shown schematically in Figure 2) would be huge even if its payload were small. This was due to the size of the equipment necessary to deflect the copious particles emitted by even a small thermonuclear blast. Another issue was psychological—how would the crew and passengers of a starship react to a megaton-sized explosion going off every few seconds, at a distance of only a kilometer or so? Finally, it is difficult to conceive of any real-world scenario in which nuclear superpowers would allow use of their arsenals in such a constructive endeavor.

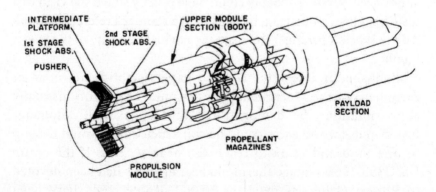

Figure 2. Artist concept of a Project Orion nuclear pulse spacecraft. (Image courtesy of NASA.)

Daedalus evolved as a kid brother to Orion. Instead of using the dramatic thermonuclear-pulse drive, it used a somewhat tamer approach—inertial fusion. Small micropellets of fusion fuel were to be ejected into a combustion chamber equipped with strong magnetic fields. Instead of ignition by a fission trigger, these pellets were to be heated to fusion temperatures and condensed to fusion densities by an array of focused laser or electron beams.

Researchers involved in the effort spent a good deal of time considering fusion fuel cycles. They rejected the deuterium-tritium (D-T) and deuterium-deuterium (D-D) fusion reactions under active consideration for terrestrial energy production. Although cleaner than fission, the copious thermal neutrons produced by these reactions would rapidly irradiate the spacecraft. Instead, they settled on a reaction between a low-mass form of helium (Helium-3) and deuterium. The products of this reaction are electrically charged particles—these are relatively easy to focus and expel with the aid of powerful magnetic fields.

Although the Helium-3/D reaction is the second easiest to ignite after D-T, it has one significant drawback. Helium-3 is very, very rare in the terrestrial environment. Starship designers were faced with four alternatives to obtain the necessary tens of millions of kilograms of this substance.

1. They could pepper the surface of the Earth or Moon with breeder reactors, which produce more nuclear fuel than they consume to produce it.
2. Since Helium-3 is a trace component of the solar wind of ions ejected from our Sun, some form of superconducting electromagnetic scoop could mine the solar wind for this isotope—but high temperatures in the inner solar system might render superconducting scoops difficult to build and maintain.
3. Tiny amounts of He-3 had been deposited in the upper layers of lunar soil as evidenced by samples returned by Apollo astronauts—but at that time nobody knew how the He-3 concentration varied with depth in lunar soils and how feasible lunar mining might actually be.
4. What they opted for was the fourth alternative: He-3 is

found in the atmospheres of giant planets. Perhaps a series of robotic helium mines suspended by balloons in the upper atmosphere of Jupiter would be the answer.

Although the *Daedalus* engine could in concept be used to accelerate and decelerate a "thousand-year ark," the initial application was expected to be robotic probes that could be accelerated to about 10% the speed of light (0.1c) and then fly through the destination star system. In the 1970s, it was (erroneously) suspected that the second nearest star—a red dwarf called Barnard's Star at a distance of about six light years from the Sun—had Jupiter-sized planets. So Barnard's Star was selected for the hypothetical star mission.

Project *Daedalus* resulted in and inspired many papers published in dedicated issues of *JBIS* (*The Journal of the British Interplanetary Society*). In 2010, a follow-up BIS study called Project *Icarus* (after the son of mythological Daedalus who approached the Sun too closely and fell to his death in the Aegean) commenced.

Directed by another British researcher, Kelvin Long, Project *Icarus* aims to continue and update the *Daedalus* study. The target star is currently Alpha/Proxima Centauri. Not only is this the nearest star system to our Sun at a distance of about 4.3 light years (roughly 40 trillion miles) but the two central Centauri stars are sun-like and separated enough that multiple terrestrial planets may exist in stable orbits. Proxima Centauri, the red dwarf companion to the central Centauri suns, apparently has a rocky planet orbiting within its habitable zone.

It is acknowledged that using fusion rockets to accelerate to and decelerate from 0.1c will require an enormous amount of fuel, but an un-decelerated probe that crosses the interstellar void in 50 years and then flies through the destination star system in just a few hours is not acceptable. It would be difficult to justify the expense and the effort for only a few hours worth of data. So *Icarus* researchers are considering non-rocket deceleration techniques. Approaches include reflecting the very tenuous interstellar plasma and/or the stellar wind(s) of the destination star(s) and using a light sail directed towards the destination star for terminal deceleration.

To again interject physics humor: the rest is simply a matter of engineering. . . .

The Fusion Ramjet

Robert Bussard contributed to many aspects of fusion research. But when he finally achieved his fifteen minutes of fame in an episode of *Star Trek: The Next Generation*, his surname was pronounced "Buzzard." What a pity for a true space visionary!

Bussard's most famous contribution to the study of thermonuclear propulsion in space is the interstellar ramjet, which he considered in 1960. Although the Bussard interstellar ramjet may never be technologically feasible, it does represent one of the very few physically possible modes of interstellar transport that could be capable of near-light speed velocities.

In its pure form (Figure 3), the interstellar ramjet is both simple and elegant. Ahead of the spacecraft, some form of scoop projects an electromagnetic field with a diameter measured in thousands of kilometers. Interstellar protons and electrons, called a "plasma," are directed towards the scoop by the specially tailored electromagnetic field. The plasma enters the ship and is directed to a fusion reactor at its core. Inside this reactor, plasma density and temperature are high enough to fuse protons and produce helium and energy. The energized helium exhaust is expelled from the rear of the spacecraft. As with any rocket, the reaction to the exhaust accelerates the spacecraft forward.

Figure 3. The Bussard interstellar ramjet would use interstell.. .iydrogen scooped from deep space propellant mass.
(Image courtesy of NASA.)

The interstellar ramjet requires no on-board fuel. Both energy and reaction mass come from the local interstellar medium. In their epochal and very popular book *Intelligent Life in the Universe* (Holden-Day, San Francisco, 1966), the American astronomer Carl Sagan and his Russian co-author I. S. Shklovskii demonstrated the awesome potential of an ideal interstellar ramjet by showing how it could accelerate to nearly the speed of light—and cross the universe within the lifetime of the on-board crew (while, with thanks again to Special Relativity, billions of years elapsed on Earth).

One advantage of the ramjet is shielding from interstellar dust. Although micron-sized interstellar dust grains are very rare in the local interstellar medium, dust impacts at near the speed of light would have an effect worse than a stationary ship being impacted by multiple shotgun blasts. Such impacts may limit non-ramjet interstellar cruise velocities to a few percent of the speed of light. But since the flow of collected protons deep within the ship's electromagnetic scoop field will collide with and atomize the fragile dust grains, ramjets will not be so limited in terms of cruise velocity.

A number of science-fiction authors have featured the interstellar ramjet in their stories. Perhaps most notably, the ramjet appeared more than once in Larry Niven's *Tales of Known Space*, and propelled the crew of *Leonora Christine* on an impossible but entrancing voyage in Poul Anderson's *Tau Zero*.

But, alas, rigorous scientific skeptics began to chip away at this most exciting concept. It was found that most electromagnetic scoops are efficient drag brakes, reflecting interstellar ions rather than collecting them. But this was not the most serious problem— by the mid-1970's few believed that human technology could ever tame the proton-proton thermonuclear reaction. Even the catalytic carbon cycle may forever be beyond our capabilities.

There is a way around this, but it does not seem practical for high-speed flight. As tabulated by Eugene Mallove and Gregory Matloff in *The Starflight Handbook* (Wiley, NY, 1989), both deuterium and Helium-3 exist in the interstellar medium (and the solar wind) at concentrations of a few parts per hundred thousand. If it is possible to generate electromagnetic scoop fields hundreds of thousands of kilometers across, collect the fusion fuel from the hydrogen ions, and fuse the deuterium and Helium-3, some form of ramjet might be possible. But it will be a far cry from the dream ships of Bussard, Sagan and Schlovskii, Anderson and Niven.

Fortunately, the ramjet idea was too attractive to abandon. So a number of less capable alternatives to the proton-fusing ramjet have been proposed. Some of them might just work.

※ ※ ※

Further Reading

Many journal articles have been written in recent decades about interstellar propulsion using thermonuclear rockets or ramjets. Most of these articles have appeared in *Acta Astronautica*, an organ of the International Academy of Astronautics published by Elsevier Ltd. in Oxford UK and in *The Journal of the British Interplanetary Society*, published by the British Interplanetary Society in London.

A number of books have been written that review and describe the results of the technical papers. One of these, *The Starflight Handbook* (by Eugene Mallove and Gregory Matloff and published by Wiley in 1989) was designed to appeal to both technical and non-technical audiences.

A somewhat more recent, but more technical compendium is *Prospects for Interstellar Travel* (by John H. Mauldin for the American Astronautical Society and published by Univelt in San Diego CA in 1992).

The third and most up-to-date of the books considered here is the second edition of *Deep Space Probes* (by Gregory L. Matloff in 2005 for Springer-Praxis in Chichester, UK).

PROJECT ICARUS
A Theoretical Design Study
for an Interstellar Spacecraft

Dr. Richard Obousy

"Standing on the shoulders of giants" definitely describes the task being undertaken by Richard Obousy and his colleagues as they work to design a realistic interstellar spacecraft based on state-of-the-art engineering. The shoulders upon which they stand belong to the Project Daedalus team that performed a similar study in the 1970s for The British Interplanetary Society. Led by Alan Bond, Project Daedalus became the standard by which all interstellar spacecraft concepts to follow were judged.

Named for Icarus, Daedalus' son who flew too close to the Sun and fell to his death, Obousy's international team is designing a craft that will hopefully avoid its namesake's mistakes and harness the power of the sun to someday give us the stars—Project Icarus.

※ ※ ※

Motivations for Project Icarus

KEPLER, LAUNCHED IN 2009, is the first NASA mission designed explicitly to search for planets orbiting other stars. On Saturday 19th February 2011, the project scientist for *Kepler*, Dr. William Borucki, estimated that there are at least fifty billion exoplanets in our galaxy. Perhaps more tantalizing is the probability that five hundred million of these alien worlds are inside the habitable zones of their parent stars. So just how many of these exoplanets contain life? Unfortunately, there's no good answer to that question, but given such vast numbers of potentially habitable worlds, the question is, Where is ET?

This is, of course, the famous Fermi Paradox, an apparent contradiction between the high estimates of the probable existence of extraterrestrial civilizations and the disconcerting lack of evidence for such civilizations.

Many assumptions regarding the ability of an alien civilization to effectively colonize other solar systems are based on the premise that interstellar travel is, in fact, technologically possible. However, one early proposed solution to the Fermi Paradox was that interstellar travel on timescales of tens, or hundreds, of years is impossible. *Project Daedalus*, a study conducted in the 1970s by members of The British Interplanetary Society, was a bold effort to examine this very question. The project was essentially a feasibility study for an interstellar mission, using capabilities appropriate to the era, with credible extrapolations for near-future technology.

One of the major objectives was to establish whether interstellar flight could be realized within established science and technology. The conclusion was that it is feasible. Although our current understanding of the laws of physics rules out the possibility of superluminal travel, it does appear that there are no major theoretical barriers to the construction of rapid, sublight, interstellar ships.

The final *Daedalus* design had a total dry mass of greater than 2600 hundred tons, of which 450 tons was the science payload. The propellant mass was fifty thousand tons of deuterium and Helium-3. The latter component of the fuel is incredibly rare on Earth. However, it is found in abundance on the gas giants of the solar system. Thus, a component to the *Daedalus* project entailed mining Helium-3 from Jupiter. Because of the huge mass of the spacecraft, and the necessary Jovian mining aspect of the mission, the Project *Daedalus* study group determined that such a spacecraft could probably only be constructed as part of a solar-system-wide economy with abundant resources at its disposal. *Daedalus*, from the perspective of 1970s science, was deemed to be effectively unavailable in the near-term future.

This would place its earliest likely construction date somewhere circa 2200. However, numerous technologies have advanced since the 1970s, including microprocessor technology, materials science, nanotechnology, fusion research and also our knowledge of the local interstellar neighborhood. It seemed timely then to revisit the Project *Daedalus* study, and the successor initiative, Project *Icarus*, officially begun in September 2009 at a meeting in London at the headquarters of the British Interplanetary Society (BIS). This theoretical engineering design study is a project under the umbrella of the Tau Zero Foundation and the BIS.

Origins and Birth of Project *Icarus*

Project *Icarus* has its origins in late 2008 during discussions between Kelvin Long and NASA physicist Marc Millis, who left NASA to become President of the Tau Zero Foundation. These discussions led to a proposal for a study based upon a redesign of *Daedalus*. The study was to include an examination of the fundamental assumptions, for example, of whether *Daedalus* should be strictly a flyby mission, or should participate in mining Jupiter for Helium-3.

In 2008, several members of the original *Daedalus* Study Group were approached and asked to participate in a new study. Project *Icarus* was born. To increase the visibility of Project *Icarus*, a presentation was given by Long at a special session on interstellar flight at the Charterhouse Space Conference during 2009. After several months of recruitment, over a dozen volunteer designers and consultants joined the project.

The official launch of Project *Icarus* was recorded in *Spaceflight* magazine, and a number of the original Project *Daedalus* study group were in attendance. These included Alan Bond, Bob Parkinson, Penny Wright, Geoff Richards, Jerry Webb and Tony Wight. The founding members of Project *Icarus* at this event also included Martyn Fogg, Richard Obousy, Andreas Tziolas and Richard Osborne. Others present who were later recruited to the team included Pat Galea, Ian Crawford, Rob Swinney and Jardine Barrington-Cook. The membership continues to grow.

Icarus: A Lesson from Mythology

Icarus was a character from ancient Greek mythology. In an attempt to escape the labyrinth prison of King Minos, his father Daedalus fashioned a pair of wings made of feathers and wax for both himself and his son. Icarus, so the story goes, flew too close to the Sun and the wax on his wings melted. He fell into the sea and died after having touched the sky.

To paraphrase Sir Arthur Eddington from *Stars and Atoms*, the standard interpretation of the Icarus myth is that he was a man performing a stunt who met his ill-fated doom due to his antics. However, an alternative interpretation of the myth is that he is the man who illuminated a serious constructional deficiency in the flying machines of his era. Perhaps there is also a lesson for science here. A more cautious Daedalus applies his theories only where he feels confident they will succeed; but by his overindulgent caution, their veiled faults remain undiscovered. Conversely, Icarus will drive his theories to the threshold of collapse, and we may at least hope to learn from his flight how to construct a better machine.

Purpose and Ambitions of Project *Icarus*

Project *Icarus*, as the successor to Project *Daedalus*, is a theoretical engineering design study for an unmanned interstellar craft. Its overall purpose can be summarized as follows:

- To design a credible interstellar probe that embodies the essential concepts for a successful mission in the coming centuries.
- To allow a direct technology comparison with *Daedalus* and provide an assessment of the maturity of fusion-based space propulsion for future precursor missions.
- To generate greater interest in the real term prospects for interstellar precursor missions that are based on credible science.

- To motivate a new generation of scientists to be interested in designing space missions that go beyond our solar system.

Using these four purposes as a guide, the collective scope of the project is codified in the *Icarus* Terms of Reference:

1. To design an unmanned probe that is capable of delivering useful scientific data about the target star, associated planetary bodies, solar environment and the interstellar medium.
2. The spacecraft must use current or near-future technology and be designed to be launched as soon as is credibly determined.
3. The spacecraft must reach its stellar destination within as short a time as possible, not exceeding a century and ideally much sooner.
4. The spacecraft must be designed to visit any one of a variety of target stars.
5. The spacecraft propulsion must be mainly fusion based (e.g. *Daedalus*).
6. The spacecraft mission must be designed so as to allow some deceleration for increased encounter time at the destination.

One of the main differences between *Daedalus* and *Icarus* is the requirement that there be some deceleration at the target system. *Daedalus* had a cruise velocity 12% of light speed, and would have raced through the target system within days. It would have been in close proximity to any planet for only a matter of seconds. This short encounter time would severely restrict the scientific return from the mission, and so *Icarus* is committed to address the issue of deceleration.

Parallel Objectives

Project *Icarus* is clearly a highly scientific endeavor whose success will be measured by the credibility and quality of the work that is created. Despite these academic ambitions, there are additional motives behind the project that are worthy of further examination.

One such motive is to use *Icarus* as a vehicle for training a new generation of interstellar engineers. The field of interstellar propulsion is sprinkled with luminaries whose names have become synonymous with the field of interstellar propulsion. These visionaries include VIPs such as Robert Bussard, Bob Forward, Greg Matloff, Robert Frisbee and Alan Bond, whose names will be immediately recognizable to interstellar aficionados. To maintain the healthy vision of a future where interstellar travel is possible, a new generation of capable enthusiasts is required. Project *Icarus* was designed with this specific motive in mind, and a quick glance at the *Icarus* designers reveals an average age close to thirty. Thus, one hope is that, upon completion of the project, an adept team of competent interstellar engineers will have been created, and that this team will continue to kindle the dream of interstellar flight for a few more decades until, presumably, they too become grey and find their own enthusiastic replacements.

Another parallel objective of Project *Icarus* is to evolve the possibility of interstellar flight from being merely feasible to actually being practical. The *Daedalus* design demonstrated that, with sufficient determination, a craft could be built using known principles of physics that could reach another star system in approximately fifty years. However, some critical components to *Daedalus* may lead a conservative spectator to believe that *Daedalus* was too ambitious.

Two impractical aspects of the original *Daedalus* spring to mind. The first is a feature of the propulsion system which necessitates the firing of marble-sized pellets, consisting of mainly deuterium and Helium-3, into a reaction chamber at a rate of 250 pellets per second. These pellets would then be ignited by high powered relativistic electron beams in a process known as inertial confinement fusion (ICF). Though considered a credible way to liberate energy from the fusion fuel, the fusion ignition rate of 250 hertz is difficult to be taken seriously given that the National Ignition Facility (NIF), a large U.S. fusion ignition project located at the Lawrence Livermore Laboratory, will likely accomplish only one such event per day under ideal conditions! Thus, an improvement on this rate by a factor of approximately twenty-one million would be required to achieve *Daedalus* fusion pellet ignition rates. While certainly not impossible, this pellet frequency requires a rather vast improvement on current technology. However, it's important to recognize that the NIF is a physics demonstrator, and that it is not designed to be optimized for rapid ignition rates.

The second feature of *Daedalus* that appears improbable is the choice of fuel. As mentioned earlier, Helium-3 is a critical component and incredibly rare on Earth. Jupiter would have to be mined by sophisticated orbiting balloons and its Helium-3 ultimately transported to the *Daedalus*. Again, while certainly not impossible, such planetary mining operations would very likely imply that a massive space-based infrastructure should already be in place. The original *Daedalus* team acknowledged that a culture with this capability would likely be centuries ahead of our own. Estimates for the total costs of building a *Daedalus* class spacecraft lie in the ten to one hundred trillion dollar range. With the current NASA budget for 2011 lying close to eighteen billion dollars, increasing it a thousand times is not impossible, given sufficient ambition, but viewed from today's geopolitical landscape, it is highly unlikely.

A full and systematic treatise regarding the additional and subtle impracticalities of the *Daedalus* design are beyond the scope of this essay. Suffice to say that most scientists of today would consider the design to be overly ambitious; rather than marvel at its audacity, those same scientists would likely dismiss *Daedalus* as unrealistic. For this reason, one parallel objective of *Project Icarus* is to create a credible engineering design that is feasible with minimal extrapolations of current technology. One way of accomplishing this is through incremental improvements of the relevant Technology Readiness Levels (TRL).

The TRL scale is used to gauge the relative maturity of a concept. The scale has nine levels, with TRL 1 being the lowest level of technological maturity, and TRL 9 the highest. For example, the definition of TRL 1 is: "Basic principles observed and reported: Transition from scientific research to applied research. Essential characteristics and behaviors of systems and architectures. Descriptive tools are mathematical formulations or algorithms."

Contrast this with the other end of the scale, TRL 9, which is defined as: "Actual system 'mission proven' through successful mission operations (ground or space): Fully integrated with operational hardware/software systems. Actual system has been thoroughly demonstrated and tested in its operational environment. All documentation completed. Successful operational experience. Sustaining engineering support in place."

The nine levels are a convenient way to assess the maturity of a technology.

Many features of the *Daedalus* design lie in the TRL 1 to TRL 3 range, indicating a low level of maturity. One measure of success for Project *Icarus* will be the evolution of critical interstellar technologies to a higher TRL level, since this assists in the promotion of the design credibility. For this reason, TRL evolution and comparison to *Daedalus* for key research areas is a valuable objective for Project *Icarus*.

One final, and particularly interesting, parallel motive is to use the project as an experiment in the efficacy of volunteer researchers collaborating in a purely virtual capacity. In many ways, Project *Icarus* may represent a new way for scientific research to be conducted. The *Icarus* team currently consists of twenty-nine team members, located across six different countries. The researchers are not paid for their efforts and are primarily motivated by a passion for the field. Interaction between team members is mostly conducted by email. However, a private internet forum also exists where the team can engage in extended discussions on a variety of topics. Internet telephony is also utilized, on occasion, as the need for (virtual) face-to-face communication arises. This mainly electronic team is, in itself, an interesting experiment in the virtualization of scientific collaboration and, should the outcome be successful, *Project Icarus* could serve as a prototype for future scientific and engineering endeavors.

Nuclear Fusion—A Propulsion Scheme for the Future

One of the Terms of Reference of Project *Icarus* is that the propulsion system must be 'mainly fusion-based,' which is currently considered TRL 2. This mandate to use fusion was based on the fact that *Daedalus* was itself fusion-powered. As the successor to *Daedalus* it seemed appropriate for *Icarus* to utilize this same energy source so as to maintain continuity with the original project. Alternatives to this form of propulsion do exist, and popular non-fusion options include solar sailing and even antimatter. The fusion decision was made early on and met with no objections from any team members.

A more comprehensive discussion of the physics of thermonuclear fusion may be found in Dr. Gregory Matloff's companion essay in this book. Briefly summarized, fusion is a process whereby two atoms are provided with sufficient kinetic energy to merge and create a larger atom and some by-products. Energy is created in the form of electromagnetic radiation and the vast amounts of kinetic energy contained in the new products that are formed from the reaction.

To give some perspective, fusion processes liberate approximately one million times more energy than even the most powerful chemical reactions. Imagine, for a moment, a hypothetical car of the future, where just one gram of fusion fuel could, in theory, power the vehicle for its entire lifetime. This is, of course, a huge oversimplification, and probably not feasible based on the mechanical architecture that would be necessary to harness the fusion energy, but it emphasizes the point quite nicely. Indeed, fusion processes are what have powered our own star, the Sun, for about five billion years, and will continue to do so for five billion years more.

Fusion has been understood since the early twentieth century, and efforts to harness the energy have been ongoing for most of the latter half of the twentieth century. To date, the only effective utilization of fusion energy has been in rapid and uncontrollable thermonuclear bombs, generally referred to as H-bombs. However, the controlled release of energy in power stations has not yet reached a sustainable breakeven which is a situation where more energy is released than is actually put in to create the reaction in the first place. Despite this contemporary lack of success, many believe it is simply a matter of time until the technology is perfected. Indeed, progress in experimental fusion reactors has been consistent for a number of decades.

Inertial Confinement Fusion (ICF) is considered a promising approach to fusion propulsion. In ICF the charged reaction products themselves are turned directly into thrust via magnetic nozzles. This process leads to far fewer thermodynamic losses and enables much of the fusion energy to be channeled to create thrust for the spacecraft. The *Daedalus* spacecraft was to be powered by ICF.

The Project *Icarus* group has identified no less than seventeen unique approaches to nuclear fusion, including plasma jet driven magneto-inertial confinement fusion, z-pinch fusion, antimatter catalyzed fusion and electrostatic inertial confinement fusion. At the current phase in the project, no one method has yet shown to be a favorable fusion technique that would prove ideal for an interstellar mission. However, research continues, and in the future a candidate will be selected.

◎ ◎ ◎

Further Reading

Alan Bond and Tony R. Martin, "Project *Daedalus* Reviewed", JBIS, V39, pp. 385-390, 1986.

A. Bond & A. Martin, Project *Daedalus*: The Final Report on the BIS Starship Study, JBIS, special Supplement, S1-S192, 1978.

Terry Kammash, "Fusion Energy in Space Propulsion", Progress in Astronautics and Aeronautics, V167, 1995.

DESIGN FLAW

Louise Marley

Proceed as far into the future as you like, possibly even to the glorious day when we are wandering quietly around the solar system, basking in its wonders, and we will undoubtedly discover that some of the worst aspects of our tribal instincts are still with us, especially the one that divides people by religious belief, ethnic background, or even the baseball team they root for. One particularly irritating aspect that promises to resist going away may well be the way in which males with ego problems treat women. After all, it's probably the only thing they have.

❋ ❋ ❋

"HEY, ITTY BIT! Haul ass, would ya?"

Isabet floated up into the maintenance tube, pushing with her feet until she could grasp the first hand rung. "You think you could do it faster, Tie Dye?"

He gave an irritated grunt. "That's Mr. Dykens to you, Tech."

"Yeah," she muttered, wriggling herself further along the tube. "When you call me by my name, I'll call you Mister. Maybe."

"What was that?" he shouted behind her.

"Or maybe not," she added, under her breath. "Fat bastard."

It wasn't as if he—or any of the other engineers—could come after her. The tube was no more than twenty inches in diameter, and Dykens wore an extra-large utility suit. The other engineers were not as big as he was, but not one of them could have squeezed into the tube, and certainly not with a tool belt strapped around him. It

169

was up to her and the other ring techs, Ginger and Skunk and Happy and the others, to slither along the maintenance tubes, to check the joints and monitor the 'stats and the flow meters. Tie Dye could yell at her all he wanted to, but if anything went wrong with the containment ring, the *North America* would be dead in space, antimatter leaking out every which way. Dykens's big butt would be as dead as anyone else's, stuck out here halfway to the habitat, in orbit around Ganymede, whining as their food and air ran out. It was obvious he had never huddled in a shelter for days without food.

She sure as hell had.

Isabet blew out an angry breath as she slid deeper into the tube. She kept telling herself it didn't do any good to be pissed at him. It was just the way he was. He wasn't the only one, either. It was true of a lot of the crew. For one thing, most of them thought ring techs were superfluous. They conveniently forgot the failure of the *North America's* first containment ring and the resulting discharge of expensive antimatter, all because the mechanical sensors were off by a fraction of a millimeter. And then, leaving aside their short memories, the other crew members seemed to think that because ring techs were small, they could push the techs around. Crew members grinned when they saw them, as if the ring techs were kids playing grown-up. The other crew members patted their heads and made jokes about their extra-extra-small utility suits. Ring techs were housed in quarters barely big enough to stand up in. They slept in cots so cramped the techs called them coffins. They were allowed only three showers a week, while the rest of the crew got five.

Command didn't seem to particularly care that three hundred crew depended on six techs. It was Government that insisted on the use of human monitors as backup. Command had to do as it was told, but as far as Isabet and the others could tell, once the ship was under way, the ring techs had been all but forgotten.

It made her blood pound to think about it, but then, a lot of things made her blood pound.

It took ten minutes to reach the 'stat that was on her assignment list, and by the time she did, she felt better. She liked the solitude of the tube. No one could get to her, no one could bother her. It was calming. She flipped up the cover of the 'stat and eyed it. It wasn't part of the protocol, but she always did a visual scan first. Tie Dye would be surprised to know how much Isabet understood of what the 'stats recorded about the containment ring. She could have told him all about pressure differentials and temperature variations and magnetic flux. She didn't, though. She tried not to talk to him any more than she had to.

Everything looked fine. She pulled the remote from her belt, pinning herself to one side of the tube in order to get her hand down and then up again. She clamped the remote into its holder, and waited the three seconds it took to record the reading. Finished, she started the long backward slide back to Engineering.

She meant to ignore Tie Dye when she got there. She really did. But when he took the remote from her to pass on to the chief, he brushed her chest with his big, freckled hand. It wasn't an accident. His fingers lingered on the front of her utility suit at least a full second.

"Back off!" she spat at him. She slapped at his hand, but he pulled it out of her reach. Her fingers curled, longing to claw his fleshy cheeks.

His phlegmy laugh made her skin crawl. "Relax, Itty Bit," he said. "Just checking to see if they're as small as the rest of you. I would say—" he grinned wider, showing his big yellow teeth. "I would say the design is consistent!"

"I've told you to keep your hands off me," she said. "I've filed a complaint with Command, so you better watch yourself."

"Yeah, I heard about that. You did it twice, in fact. Waste of time, wasn't it? You need to understand command priorities." He stopped grinning, and shook a finger at her. "You ring techs are lucky to have work. One day they'll invent their way out of the problem with the monitors, and leave you and the rest of them on Earth where you belong. That'll save a lot of air and food out here."

"If they could, they would, Tie Dye." Isabet spun away from him, and kicked off down the corridor toward the mess.

He called after her, "Get used to it, Itty Bit! It's the way we do things here."

Over her shoulder she snapped, "Get used to it? This is my third voyage."

"You should know, then," he said. "Like I said, you're one of the lucky ones!"

※ ※ ※

It was true enough. Isabet and Skunk and Happy and the others were fortunate to have their jobs. Skunk, whose Icelandic name none of them could pronounce, had fled his home as his village disappeared under the cold waves of the North Atlantic. He'd been living on Government rations since he was six, and it showed in his short stature and wispy hair.

Happy Feet had been a dancer Earthside; when he got too old for that, he applied to be a ring tech, and was accepted because of his small size and agility. He joked that he was only here so he could eat. He said, with his high-pitched laugh, "I'd rather soak up G-rays than eat G-rations!"

Ginger almost didn't fit the profile of a ring tech. She hadn't starved. She was just naturally small. She had once had a business, something to do with books, Isabet thought, but the Global Depression had wiped out her business and scattered her family. Bony and worn down by sorrow, she was grateful to be aboard the *North America*. Too grateful, in Isabet's view. She took Tie Dye's abuse without the slightest resistance.

Isabet knew she was the luckiest of all. She was also the youngest and the smallest. Abandoned as an infant—a doorstep baby—she had been kicked out of the orphanage at the age of sixteen to find her own way. The orphanage called it graduation, but all it meant to her was being turned out on the street with few resources. In one of the shelters, she saw a poster about the positronic reactor ships and for the first time, learned that there was an advantage to having been starved as a baby. There was work for a person of small physique if that person had the guts to go into space, crawl through the narrow maintenance tubes every day, and risk gamma ray poisoning as well as all the other dangers of space travel.

Isabet had guts. She didn't have much else to work with, but her courage and native intelligence won her the job, and she liked it. The voyages to Ganymede were a lot more comfortable for her than the required months of gravity Earthside between trips. It wasn't just that her pay ran out before it was time to return to the ship. On the *North America* she didn't have to fight for a bed in a shelter and then sleep with one eye open and a knife in her hand against the threat of rape or theft or worse.

She scowled as she told Ginger and Happy and Skunk what Tie

Dye'd done. "The worst part is," she concluded, "he's right. I complained to Command, and they never even answered me."

"Probably never reached 'em," Skunk said glumly.

"I think it did. I think they just don't want to hear it. He's good—a containment expert, in fact. They need him more than they do me. I'm dispensable."

"That's not fair," Skunk said.

"It's not right, either." Isabet wriggled impatiently against the straps that held her on the stool. "Our contracts provide for redress of grievances."

Ginger sighed. "You're the only one of us who ever reads those," she said.

Happy Feet spread his hands. "I, of course, don't actually *read*," he said slyly.

"Oh, you do, too," Skunk said. "I mean, you *can*."

Happy waggled his eyebrows and did a little freefall dance, feet and hands flashing so that he rose against the restraining straps like a puppy pulling at his leash. "Waste of effort," he said blithely. "I just dance!"

"In the maintenance tubes?" Skunk said sourly.

Happy chuckled. "If you could only see me."

Skunk shook his head. "I don't know how you stay so cheerful. We're trapped here. No better than slaves."

"We're not slaves," Ginger said.

Isabet said sharply, "That's right. We get paid, we have opportunities, and responsibilities. We should be treated with respect."

"I don't think Tie Dye agrees," Happy said.

"You better be careful with him," Ginger warned. "If he catches you alone someplace—"

"Yeah, I know. I can take care of myself." Isabet paused, tilting her head, listening. "Notice that?"

"What?" Skunk said.

"The ship. We're getting ready to brake."

"How can you tell?"

"The vibration changes. You can't feel it?"

The other three shook their heads. Happy said, "I can't believe you can tell."

"You just have to be sensitive to it. Three days now, and we'll be there."

"I don't know how you know that," Happy Feet said.

Isabet patted his thin cheek. "Reading, Hap. Reading. That thing you say you don't do."

The four of them gathered in the aft observation area as Ganymede began to swell against the blackness of space, with the great disc of Jupiter a vague, immense shadow beyond it. As the ship adjusted attitude, they sank to the deck, briefly weighted, then rose again. It was like being aboard an ocean-going vessel, and Isabet saw Ginger swallow and press her hand to her lips. "It'll pass in a little while," she said, touching Ginger's shoulder. "We'll be in electrogravity soon. It's magnetic, so we'll pick it up from the habitat."

Skunk said, "Wow, Isabet. I don't know how you know all that."

"My third voyage."

"Yeah, but—electro-what?"

"Electrogravity. There's a great video about the habitat, Skunk. You should see it."

Ginger nodded, but she still looked a little green. Happy moved close to her other side, and steadied her with his arm. Isabet turned back to gaze with pleasure at the lavender-tinted disc of Ganymede. The poles of the moon glistened faintly, and the pockmarks of craters layered the surface. Isabet pressed her palms together, entranced. This was her reward for putting up with the indignities of the *North America*, with the insults of Tie Dye and the rest of the crew. She never tired of it. She only wished—

"That's it?" Ginger said, pointing to the disc.

"That's it," Isabet said happily. It was somehow massive and delicate at the same time, and it seemed immune from the ugliness that had overtaken Earth, the crowding, the fouled air, the threatening seas. She sighed with pleasure. "That's Ganymede."

"It's so dim," Ginger said. "I thought it would be brighter."

"We're a long way from the sun," Isabet said. She felt a faint disappointment that Ginger didn't share her admiration for the magnificence of the alien world. "Wait till you see *Starhold*," she said. "You won't think that's dim." She yearned to see the inside of the habitat, but she didn't say so. There wasn't much chance of that happening, and the others wouldn't understand.

A half hour passed, with Ginger gulping nausea, and even Skunk groaning once or twice. Isabet felt the acceleration as the ship changed its trajectory, but her stomach didn't react. She clung to the bar beneath the window, and waited with gleeful anticipation for her first glimpse of *Starhold One.*

"There it is!" She pressed as close to the icy plexiglass as she could, peering out into the layered darkness. It was tiny at first, a star among stars, only discernible because she knew it had to be there. The *North America* rolled as it aligned with the docking ports. Isabet fastened her gaze on the habitat's yellow and amber lights. She could pick out the lighted column of the vacuum elevator, revealed in fragments by the myriad windows. The habitat, silver and ovoid, shone dully against the backdrop of space. Layers of fuel cells spiraled around it, making it look like a gigantic seashell.

"Is that it?" Ginger asked. "That egg-shaped thing?"

"Yes," Isabet said. "That's it. *Starhold One.*"

"Why One?"

"Because there will be others, as we go further out," Isabet said. "Space Service already has plans for two more. They're mining Ganymede, and building an antimatter plant."

"Why?" Ginger asked.

Isabet, startled, glanced across at her friend. Ginger stared vaguely at the habitat, but without real interest. "Why what?"

"Why build others? What good are they?"

"What *good*?" Isabet's voice squeaked with surprise. "We need them if we're going to explore space, get out into the universe!"

Ginger shrugged as if the whole idea were of no interest.

"Ginger!" Isabet said. Suddenly it seemed vital that her friend understand the immensity of the achievement. "We're building an interstellar ship, you know. It's going to be five times the size of *North America*, and carry a crew outside the solar system! It's the most amazing thing human beings have ever done, the biggest ship ever built—and to power it, we need lots of antimatter."

"Geez," Happy said. "That's gotta be one really big containment ring."

"Enormous," Isabet said with satisfaction. "Imagine working on that ship, Happy! Going out into real space, instead of just between Ganymede and Earth."

"Naw," he said. "They'll fix the monitor design by then. They won't take us."

"I'm going to find a way to go," Isabet insisted.

"I don't know." Ginger sighed, leaning against the frame of the window. "We have enough problems at home, don't you think?"

"Don't worry about it, Ginger," Skunk said. "We'll never live to see it, anyway."

"Come on, Skunk!" Happy cried. "Why so dour?"

"Because it'll take decades, and ring techs don't live that long."

"We're tested all the time," Isabet said absently. "We're fine."

"Tested!" Skunk said bitterly. "You realize the norms for us are twice what they are for the rest of the crew?"

"Are they?" Ginger said, pulling back from the window as if it were the source of the poisonous rays.

"Skunk's exaggerating," Happy said.

Isabet turned her head to her friends. "No, Skunk's right. They say, though, that when we're Earthside our readings return to normal levels."

"Do you believe them?" Ginger said, her voice rising.

Isabet shrugged. "I guess."

"Believe if you want to," Skunk said. "But don't have babies."

"None of us are having babies." Isabet turned back to the window to watch *Starhold* grow. It was both massive and graceful, with a halo of light that faded the stars. She had studied the diagrams of its construction, pored over the blueprints of its hydroponic level and command deck with its crown of communication and power arrays. She had seen the cubbies and the gallery level in the video, and the men and women smiling into the camera. They looked friendly and smart. *Starhold*, to Isabet, looked like a home, the home she had never had. She thought she would willingly take a blast of G-rays if she could go in and see it for herself.

Isabet pushed off the inner surface of the maintenance tube, keeping her feet and hands free to maintain her momentum. She shot out into Engineering so that her feet bounced on the floor, grabbing the gravity borrowed from the habitat. Laughing, she straightened with a little hop. It felt good to have weight, even though it was only half gravity. She turned, bouncing on her toes, and found Tie Dye standing with a scowling woman Isabet hadn't met before.

Isabet unclipped her remote and held it out to Tie Dye. She grinned up at the woman. "Hiya. Looking for me?"

The woman wore the insignia of a supply officer on her utility suit. She folded her arms, as if to discourage familiarity. Like the rest of the crew, she looked as if she had never lacked for nutrition in her life. She was tall, her skin smooth, her hair thick and shining. Isabet resisted the urge to touch her own ragged mop. She cut it herself, keeping it short to hide how coarse and dry it was.

Tie Dye said, "That's Isabet, but she's too small."

"They're all small, aren't they?"

"Yeah, but she's the smallest."

"Let's find the rest of them, then." The woman turned toward the hatch that led to the ring techs' quarters, Tie Dye behind her.

Isabet said, "Wait! At least tell me what it's for."

Tie Dye snapped, "Mind your own business, Itty Bit."

At that, the supply officer stopped. She glanced briefly in Isabet's direction, then directed her scowl at Tie Dye. "I thought you said her name was Isabet."

He shrugged. "Yeah. Itty Bit's a nickname."

"Which I loathe," Isabet murmured.

The woman's eyelids flickered in acknowledgment. Her scowl deepened. "You want to watch yourself, Dykens. You're a top-notch engineer, but you're getting a reputation."

Isabet chewed on the inside of her cheek, trying not to laugh as Tie Dye's half-bald scalp reddened. When the officer turned back to her, she stood very straight, trying to look as tall as she could. "What's up?" she asked brightly.

The officer measured Isabet with her eyes. "You are a bit small," she said. "But we need to replace one of our warehousemen. He wrenched his back."

"What's the job?"

"Moving supplies into *Starhold*. There's a lot of them, and some of them are heavy."

"They're on dollies, though, aren't they? I can manage."

Tie Dye opened his mouth, but Isabet hastened to speak again before he could make some pronouncement on her abilities. "I'm strong, ma'am," she said, ignoring the roll of Tie Dye's eyes at her sudden courtesy.

The officer's hard gaze swept over Isabet. "You want to do this?" she said. "It's going to be hard. It's a year's worth of supplies."

Isabet nodded. "Yes, ma'am. I do want to. Nice to do something that's not squeezing through the maintenance tube."

The faintest twitch of the officer's lips greeted this confession, disappearing almost before it registered. Tie Dye grunted, and started to say something, but the officer put up one admonishing finger, and he subsided. "Report to the supply deck in half an hour, Tech," she said. "Thanks for volunteering." And as Tie Dye heaved an exasperated sigh, the officer said in a dry tone, "You get to volunteer, too, Dykens. It's a big job."

It was a big job, as the officer had warned, and it was made harder by the pull of electrogravity. Isabet gritted her teeth as she pushed and pulled, maneuvering a dolly full of cartons over the rubbery rim of the lock and into the loading bay of the habitat. The lock was sealed with a ring that looked a lot like the maintenance tube she spent so much time in. It was smaller, of course, and a whole lot shorter. It arched up—electrogravity meant there was an up-and-around the lock that connected *North America*'s hold with *Starhold*'s loading bay. Isabet gazed curiously at it as she passed beneath. The seal had to be perfect, of course, or they'd all be spaced in no time, but it still seemed a clumsy way to connect the two vessels. She recognized the backup systems set into the walls of the sealing ring, and wondered how they checked them. She couldn't imagine anyone from *Starhold* was small enough to fit into the ring.

The loading bay bristled with robotic arms and cranes. They could have installed power boosters on the damn dollies, she thought. Maybe *Starhold* wasn't all that different from the *North America* after all. Why bother with power boosters when they had cheap labor like hers? Not that she minded. And at least Tie Dye was grunting and sweating as hard as she was.

She rolled her dolly toward one of the inner doors. It opened at her approach.

"Hi!" A pleasant-faced, broad-shouldered man stood in the doorway. He wore civvies, a bright orange shirt and a pair of striped pants, and his gray hair was caught back in a ponytail. He cocked his head at her, and gave her a welcoming smile. "I'm the stores manager," he said. "I'll give you a hand."

"You're not in uniform," she blurted.

He laughed. "No, we're not military. Here, let me take that." He stepped around her, and took the handles of the dolly in hands that didn't look used to this sort of work. "You're not doing this alone, I hope!" he said. He pushed the dolly a few feet. "This is heavy!"

Before she could answer, Tie Dye came into the bay behind her, pushing another dolly loaded with sealed barrels and bales secured with nylon cord. He worked the dolly over the rim and brought it to rest near the door. "Got somebody to unload this stuff?" he asked the gray-haired man.

"I'll do it myself. I'm Link." The man put out his hand. Tie Dye grasped it, and then Link offered his hand to Isabet, too. Startled, she took it. His hand was as soft as it looked, and she was a little embarrassed about her hard small one with its bitten nails. She watched Link in wonder and envy. His casual attitude, his colorful clothes, all made the habitat seem more magical than ever.

"If we can get this off the dollies, the different departments will come for their own stuff," Link said.

"Sure," Isabet said at the same time Tie Dye delivered a "guess so." She gave the stores manager a helpless look.

He winked at her, and stepped up to unbuckle a restraining strap. Tie Dye said, "Itty Bit, go back and make another trip. There's another dolly loaded up." She turned toward the lock again. "And get a move on," he said, unnecessarily. Over her shoulder, she cast him a look of loathing. Link, too, gave him a look, but she couldn't read it. She shrugged, and turned her energies to the next load.

It took hours to shift the cargo, a year's worth of supplies for more than fifty habitat staff. The round trip took four months each way, and the *North America* needed four months Earthside to re-line and then refill the antimatter containment ring. The habitat had an extensive hydroponic level and recycling plant, but its staff depended on these supplies for survival.

Isabet was glad Link was there, directing the placement and

stacking and ordering of the containers. Once, when they were taking a breather, she asked him about the sealing ring and how it was maintained. He pointed out the instrument panel. "See that? It opens up, and we send in a crawler."

"What does the crawler do?"

"I'll show you how it works." He crossed to the panel set into the sealing ring. He stood on one of the laddered handholds, and with a quick motion popped the clamps from one side. The panel swung neatly open to reveal an orderly constellation of small screens set into the inside. Folded against the interior of the tube was a spidery object of metal and plastic. Link swept his hand over one of the screens and it came to life, glowing with blue light. He pointed to the metal object, and Isabet climbed up beside him to see it better. "That's the crawler." He touched the screen and the crawler stirred, its narrow limbs opening until it filled the ring.

"Are those the sensors?" Isabet reached out her hand, but Link caught it before she could touch the crawler.

"Careful!" he said hastily. His fingers were warm and strong, though his skin was so soft. "I should have warned you. The legs are really sharp. It's a design flaw, but the engineers haven't addressed the problem yet. When it needs maintenance, someone has to put on asbestos gloves just to pull it out." He pointed behind him, at the opposite side of the lock. "The exit from the tube is over there." She glanced over her shoulder, and saw a matching panel set into the opposite wall.

Link touched the little screen again, and the crawler retracted with a series of metallic clicks that made her think of sharpened knives knocking together. "It's safe now," he said. "It's only dangerous when it's extended."

"What does it do?"

"Traverses the sealing ring, checking for pressure differentials."

"Leaks."

"Right."

"That's what I do, on *North America*. For the antimatter containment ring. I crawl though the maintenance tube to make sure the seals are holding and the monitors are working."

He grinned at her. "I don't think even you could fit into this ring."

She cocked her head to one side and eyed it. "I could squeeze in," she said, and laughed. "I'm glad there's no need. Your crawler looks like a grasshopper made out of razor blades!"

"You're not the first to think of a grasshopper when they see it. That's part of the problem. Too many pieces that can break."

Tie Dye said, "Itty Bit! Get your ass back to work. I don't want to be here all day." She felt a faint surprise that he didn't bother to hide his attitude from *Starhold*'s staff. He probably figured it was her fault he had to spend so much time shifting cargo. She'd pay for that later, but she didn't care. It was worth it to meet someone from the habitat, to hear details of life on *Starhold*. These people were the first step on the path to interstellar travel, and it gave her shivers of pleasure just to think about it. To realize she was having a hand in it.

Tie Dye had been angry at her for weeks. She had turned him down early in the voyage. He had said to her then that she should be glad anyone would give a girl like her a second look, with her ugly hair and skinny legs. He wasn't mollified by the fact that she took no other lovers. The shelters had soured her on sex of any kind, even with friends, but she couldn't see why she needed to explain that to *him*. The other ring techs figured it out early, and left her alone.

Sometimes she wondered if Tie Dye knew what it was to be someone's friend. She never saw him in conversation with others of his own rank.

Link's presence meant Tie Dye had to keep his hands off her, and that was good. He bumped her several times, usually an elbow in some soft part of her anatomy, or a hand fumbling unnecessarily around her ass as they transferred a container from one place to another, but she sidled away from him each time without protesting. She wanted to make a good impression on the affable Link. It felt good to be polite, to be respectful. Though the work was tiring, she didn't want the day to end.

Link asked her, when they were walking back toward the hold, about life on *North America*. She answered carefully, then asked him a few questions about the supplies. Link was generous with his answers, explaining how the seeding program worked, or how the dehydrated foodstuffs would be reconstituted in *Starhold*'s kitchen. He was nice, and warm in a fatherly sort of way. Isabet wished she could introduce the other techs to him, show them what it was like to be treated like—like she was as much a person as anyone else. Even Tie Dye.

She was curious about the foods they couldn't grow hydroponically, and Link explained at some length about protein sources. She made a suggestion about a way to make a sauce out of tree nuts, something she had picked up in the kitchens of the shelters, and Link listened with respect, nodding. "You worked in the kitchens?"

"Yeah. Yes. In the shelters."

Tie Dye leaned against the wall as they talked, looking impatient. When they had unloaded the last of a stack of aluminum canisters, Link said, "Isabet. Would you like a tour of *Starhold*?"

The idea was so exciting that she forgot to school her features. She felt her face light up, and Link chuckled. "You're welcome, too, Mr. Dykens," he added. "Let me offer you a cup of tea in our common room."

Tie Dye said sourly, "No time. Not for Isabet, either. She has work to do."

Link said mildly, "She's been working all day. Just as you have."

Isabet stared at her feet, confused. No one had defended her in a very long time. Such consideration tempted her to let her heart soften, to allow a tiny crack in her customary shell. She knew better than that, of course. And there was Tie Dye's scorn to remind her.

"That's what we're here for," Tie Dye growled. "Gotta check the containment ring every six hours, like it or not."

Isabet said, half under her breath, "It's not my shift, Tie—uh, Mr. Dykens."

Tie Dye said, "Oh, it's Mr. Dykens now?"

Link said, "You can spare her for half an hour, surely."

Tie Dye said, "Nope. Gotta get back to the ship. Nice of you, though."

Isabet suddenly wanted to see the inside of *Starhold* more than anything in the universe. She wanted to turn away from Tie Dye's sullen presence, and accept Link's polite invitation. She longed to step into the vacuum elevator, that clever device they called the slip, and propel herself from one level to the next. She wanted to breathe in the scents of the hydroponics level with its trailing vines, inverted flats of vegetables, even fruit bushes tucked beneath the sills of the space windows. She wanted to see the cubbies, and the showers, and the common room on the galley level. She said, louder this time, "Mr. Dykens, I'm off duty till tomorrow."

"Well, then," the affable Link began, but Tie Dye grabbed Isabet's arm.

"We're going," he said. His fingers pinched her flesh, and her cheeks flamed. She could have pulled away, but she didn't. She couldn't bear for the *Starhold* man to see her shame, to know how insignificant she really was.

Dropping her eyes, swallowing the bitter medicine of her pride, she walked back through the loading bay toward the lock, and the *North America*'s hold. She felt Link's questioning gaze on her back, and her face burned hotter.

Tie Dye dropped her arm as they stepped over the rim of the seal. She glanced back once. Link had disappeared, gone back into *Starhold* without her. She stopped, and put her back to the drab gray surface of *North America*'s lock. She jutted her chin at Tie Dye above her folded arms. "When are you gonna let up on me?" she demanded.

Tie Dye, who had moved ahead of her, whirled. His face suffused, and his voice rose. "I haven't done a thing to you."

"Bullshit! You get in my way at every opportunity, you insult me, you make extra work—and now you can't let me have even a half hour of freedom."

He took a step toward her, balling his fists at his sides. Isabet was suddenly aware of how big he was, how thick his arms and thighs were, how mean the expression in his small eyes. She stiffened her back, but she took a swift glance around, looking for a way to escape.

"You had your chance," he sneered. He came closer, and she could smell the tang of perspiration, feel the heat of his temper. "I was gonna be nice to you, Itty Bit! I was gonna be real nice, but you weren't having any of it."

"I don't do that," she said. She spoke as stoutly as she could, but she couldn't control the tremor in her voice. He advanced until he was within arm's length of her. She said, "I tried to tell you, Tie Dye. I don't do it with anybody."

"Don't call me that."

"Everybody calls you that!"

"Not you, Itty Bit. Itty *Bitch*." He reached for her, his meaty hand seizing the back of her neck, yanking her away from the curving wall of the lock. There was something about the hardness of his hand and the heat from his body that told her he meant it this time. He would force her. But she had sworn she would never be forced again. She had vowed to herself she would die first.

She writhed in his grip, trying to free herself. His other hand came up, reaching for her waist to pull her against him. There was no time even to think about what she was doing. He couldn't hold her head, though he tried to grab at her cropped hair. She dropped, slid down his body, his legs. He cursed as he kicked at her, and caught her in the side. She rolled away from him, once, twice, the gray floor hard against her shoulders and knees. He lumbered after her, staying between her and the door leading from the hold into the safety of the ship. She leaped to her feet, spinning in a circle, searching for another escape.

She spotted the instrument panel that monitored the sealing ring, and dashed for it. Tie Dye came after her, his heavy feet making the whole lock vibrate. Her ribs hurt where he had kicked her, and her scalp stung where he had pulled her hair. There was no time to think about that now, no time to wonder if a rape would finally get Command's attention. Like a monkey, she leaped up the laddered handholds toward the panel.

The panel was a good three feet above Tie Dye's head. It took her only seconds to reach it. As Tie Dye flailed at her, she popped the clamps. The panel swung open, showing the many-legged crawler folded tightly into the cramped space. Belatedly, she realized she should have chosen the other side of the tube, but there was no time now.

"Get your hands off that!" Tie Dye roared. He braced his foot on one of the handholds, and started climbing toward her.

There was only one thing she could do, and even as she thought of it, she was already doing it. She turned on her side, sucked in her stomach, and slid past the crawler's sharp angles into the cool darkness of the sealing ring.

Behind her, Tie Dye swore and banged his fist against the panel frame. She wriggled further into the ring so he couldn't reach her foot and haul her back.

She would wait him out. It was tight, her hiding place, and unlike the maintenance ring of the *North America*, it was dark. She couldn't see a thing, but she could breathe. She could take it. He would give up eventually, and leave her alone. She would slip back to her quarters and lie low until his temper wore off. She'd done that before.

It was a good plan, but she soon understood the flaw in it. She had underestimated the full force of Tie Dye's rage. He was an engineer, a good one. He knew how to make machines work. She was just settling into the least bothersome position when she heard the slither and click of something coming up the ring behind her.

The damn crawler! Tie Dye had launched the crawler. She thought of the thin blades of its legs opening, stretching, moving it along the ring. She shuddered, imagining those blades cutting through the soft soles of her shoes. He was serious this time, deadly serious. She was no stranger to trouble, but this had to be the worst.

Panicked, she wriggled further into the ring, feeling her way in the blackness. The crawler's mechanical sounds were like the clicking of someone's arthritic knees, and they came steadily closer, driving her forward. Was it her imagination, or did the ring narrow as it circled the lock? She could hardly move her shoulders, and only just find purchase with her feet and the tips of her fingers, pushing herself along. The maintenance tube of *North America* had lights, and room for her to move her elbows, bend her knees. This was a nightmare tunnel of blackness and constriction, a coffin indeed. If she were an inch wider, a pound heavier, she would be trapped. Her breathing quickened, and her mouth dried.

Shit, she thought. A rock and a hard place. There was no choice, nothing she could do but press on. It was all too much like the shelters, choosing between two or more evils every damn day of her life. When she got out of here, she promised herself—and she *would* get out of here—she was going to make Tie Dye's life a living hell!

Anger served her better than fear. She scooted forward through the tube as quickly as her thrusting toes and scrabbling fingers could move her. She felt the chill as the tube arched above the lock, and she refused to think about the black, cold emptiness on the other side of the layers of plastic and rubber and metal. The ring grew even tighter, until she thought she might be stopped, but then, as she wiggled one shoulder and then the other past the most constricted part, she found there was room again. There was still no light, and the sound of her breathing filled her ears almost enough to shut out the gentle scrabbling of the crawler coming behind her. At least she was moving. She was gaining. She held her breath for a moment to listen. She was sure the sound of the crawler had diminished behind her.

It was then that she felt the slight movement, as if an infinitesimal breeze had touched her cheek. She froze for several heartbeats, holding her breath, trying to determine what it was. The sound of the crawler grew louder again as she paused.

The darkness seemed to accentuate the sensation, so subtle she could have imagined it. It was more a feeling than a fact. It was a bit like when she could feel the *North America* preparing to brake, a faint suggestion of something changing, something happening. It was subtle. But it was real.

It shouldn't be there, but she had no doubt, as she began wriggling forward again, that she had felt it.

The crawler should, too. It should stop, and set up an alarm.

It didn't. The damn thing really did need redesigning.

Gasping for air, praying she could reach the opening before the crawler did, she drove herself harder. For what seemed interminable moments, there was nothing in Isabet's world but her own rasping breaths and the mechanical click and slither behind her. She wriggled, and wriggled, and wriggled, until she thought the skin of her hands and shoulders and knees must be raw. She peered forward, trying to see the glimmer of light that would mean she had reached the panel, and could escape this confining tube.

And face Tie Dye again. But there was something more important happening now, more at risk than just her problems with Tie Dye. She had a leak to report.

She sucked in a shocked breath when her hand struck a smooth surface and it suddenly glowed. She had found the instrument panel. She could see that immediately. It was mounted on the inside of the door that was her only means of escape. Tie Dye had shut her into this bloody tube, and she realized, as she struggled to push it open, that he must have secured the clamps on the exit, too.

He meant her to die in here. She knew he was angry, and mean, but *murder*? How did he expect to get away with it?

She couldn't give up now. There had to be a way to open the panel from inside, to release the clamps. The design couldn't be *that* bad. She tried to think, but the crawler was coming up behind her, giving her no time.

She scrabbled with her fingers, and the touch screens came awake, one by one. She could barely lift her head enough to see them. She saw the temperature measurement, inside and out, she saw the maintenance records—stupid place for them—and the crawler's interface. The screens faded when her fingers left them, and she frantically pushed with her palms, her fingertips, searching for the right one. If she could find it, if she could input a problem, a big problem, then the alarms would go. Someone would come. She could get out of here.

If the crawler hadn't sliced her to ribbons first.

And then she found it. It looked familiar, measurements from pressure gauges set at regular intervals around the sealing tube. She found the alarm button at the bottom, the part of the screen she and the ring techs were never supposed to touch, and she pressed it as hard as she could with her thumb.

The screech of the alarm in the lock drowned out the approach of the crawler, but she knew it was coming. Her nerves burned with anticipation of its sharp metal blades cutting into her. She forced herself to focus on finding the crawler's command screen. She ran her hands desperately across the panel to keep the screens awake, to keep the blue glow alive so she could—

There it was. Upper right corner, with a convenient little graphic that looked exactly like the grasshopper that had first come to her mind when she saw it. Finally, a design that made sense! She stabbed at it with her finger, and it lit up, showing her the buttons. With a gasp, she turned off the crawler. The sudden cessation of its movement, the end of the threat, left her weak and trembling.

She lay still in the tube for another half-minute, waiting for the pounding of her heart to slow. The glow of the screens on the instrument panel faded, one by one, until she was in complete darkness again. She listened to the alarm shrilling outside, imagining the running feet, the terror that alarm must strike into every heart aboard *Starhold* and the *North America*.

When the panel burst open, she found herself staring straight into Link's eyes. His pupils swelled with shock at the sight of her. She said swiftly, "I know this is weird. I'll explain everything in a minute, but first, there's a leak in the sealing tube—not fatal now, but it's going to get worse. *Starhold* needs to separate from *North America*, and right away."

She was still in Link's arms, her toes not yet on the floor, when Tie Dye came charging back into the lock, three other engineers hard on his heels. His face flamed at the sight of Isabet being extracted from the sealing tube. He shouted, "What were you doing in there? You're going on report!"

Link, as if Tie Dye hadn't said a word, set Isabet firmly on her feet, then turned her away from the crowd of engineers and technicians converging on the lock to begin the emergency disengage process. Tie Dye, nearly choking with fury, had an emergency protocol he had to follow. He was getting orders, and he was too busy obeying them to come after Isabet.

Link didn't steer Isabet back toward the *North America*. He drew her in the opposite direction, into the habitat she had so longed to visit.

Isabet said, "It's a slow leak. But your crawler should have detected it."

Link said, "Add the sensors to its other problems. We'll move the redesign up the priority list."

"I have some ideas about that."

"I'll bet you do."

They stopped just inside the hold, watching the frantic preparations for disengagement. He glanced down at her. "You want to get back on the ship?"

"No," she said. "Not really."

"You want to stay here?"

Breathless with sudden hope, she nodded. "Yeah," she whispered. "I mean, yes, please. I really do."

"I suspected as much." Side by side, they watched the swarm of people preparing to seal the locks and separate the two vessels. "This could have been a tragedy," he said.

"Yes. A leak like that grows pretty fast once it gets started." She saw Tie Dye turn to stalk back into the ship. She wondered who would be in more trouble, Tie Dye or herself.

It would all be sorted out at the command level, no doubt. In any case, there wasn't a damn thing Tie Dye could do now.

Link guided her into the vacuum elevator, and Isabet grasped the knack of traversing the layered decks in an instant. As they floated downward, he pointed out the level where the cubbies were. "We'll find a free one for you." He promised a tour of the gallery and the laboratories before they reached the lowest level, where he deposited her in the hydroponics area. "You can watch the ship leave from here," he said, pointing to an observation window.

Her nerves still on fire from her near-miss, she watched the *North America* pull back from the habitat and revolve in preparation for its return to Earth. She leaned against the chilly plexiglass and imagined Tie Dye standing impotently near the space window to watch *Starhold* disappear as the ship revolved and prepared to get under way. She started to grin.

Were Skunk or Ginger or Happy Feet watching in wonder as the ship's positronic reactors fired and the ship began to vibrate? Did they look around, asking about Isabet, or did they know she was stranded on the habitat? Just in case, she waved her arm in farewell. She kissed her hand to the ship for good measure.

Yep, she was stuck here. For the duration. Twelve months, at least. Helluva way to score a vacation.

She laughed aloud as the *North America's* rockets bloomed, driving it away toward Earth.

When she had seen enough, she turned from the window, and stepped out into the ship. With a deft twist of her feet and her hands, she shot upward toward the gallery level. She would ask Link for work to do, find some way to be of use. Maybe in the kitchens, or maybe she could work on redesigning the crawler. It didn't matter. She'd meet some other people, get to know the place, this first step on the path to the stars.

She was going to feel right at home.

TWENTY LIGHTS TO "THE LAND OF SNOW"

Excerpts from The Computer
Logs of Our Reluctant Dalai Lama

Michael Bishop

*The first thing most American readers will have to do when reading
"Twenty Lights to 'The Land of Snow'" is put aside their preconceived
notions of what the crew and culture of an interstellar spacecraft must
emulate—Western culture. And with the current pace of space
exploration in the West, new notions of how it might actually happen
are certainly worth considering.*

*Awards? Michael Bishop has them: two Nebulas, four Locus
Awards, and multiple Hugo nominations. Did we mention that he
also writes award-winning poetry? Mysteries? And that he has edited
several science fiction anthologies? And, yes, he was an English
teacher....*

❊ ❊ ❊

Years in transit: 82 out of 106?
Computer Logs of the Dalai Lama-to-Be, age 7

ABOARD *KALACHAKRA,* I open my eyes again in Amdo Bay.
Sleep still pops in me, yowling like a really hurt cat. I look sidelong
out of my foggy eggshell. Many ghosts crowd near to see me leave
the bear sleep that everybody in a strut-ship sometimes dreams in.
Why have all these somnacicles up-phased to become ship-haunters?
Why do so many crowd the grave-cave of my Greta-snooze?

191

"Greta Bryn"—that's my mama's voice—"can you hear me, kiddo?"

Yes I can. I have no deafness after I up-phase. Asleep even, I hear Mama talk in her dreams, and cosmic rays crackle off *Kalachakra's* plasma shield out in front (to keep us all from going dead), and the crackle from Earth across the reaching oceans of farthest space.

"Greta Bryn?"

She sounds like Atlanta, Daddy says. To me she sounds like Mama, which I want her to play-act now. She keeps bunnies, minks, guineas, and many other tiny crits down along our sci-tech cylinder in Kham Bay. But hearing her doesn't pulley me into sit-up pose. To get there, I stretch my soft parts and my bones.

"Easy, baby," Mama says.

A man in white unhooks me. A woman pinches me at the wrist so I won't twist the fuel tube or pulse counter. They've already shot me in the heart, to stir its beating. Now I sit and look around, clearer. Daddy stands near, showing his crumply face.

"Hey, Gee Bee," he says, but doesn't grab my hand.

His coverall tag is my roll-call name: Brasswell. A hard name for a girl and not too fine for Daddy, who looks thirty-seven or maybe fifty-fifteen, a number Mama says he uses to joke his fitness. He does whore-to-culture—another puzzle-funny of his—so that later we can turn Guge green, and maybe survive.

I feel sick, like juice gone sour in my tummy has gushed into my mouth. I start to elbow out. My eyes grow pop-out big, my fists shake like rattles. Now Daddy grabs me, mouth by my ear: "Shhhh shhh shhh." Mama touches my other cheek. Everyone else falls back to watch. That's scary too.

After a seem-like century I ask, "Are we there yet?"

Everybody yuks at my funniness. I drop my legs through the eggshell door. My hotness has colded off, a lot.

A bald brown man in orangey-yellow robes steps up so Mama and Daddy must stand off aside. I remember, sort of. This person has a really hard Tibetan name: Nyendak Trungpa. My last up-phase he made me say it multi times so I would not forget. I was four, but I almost forgetted anyway.

"What's your name?" Minister Trungpa asks me.

He already knows, but I blink and say, "Greta Bryn Brasswell."

"And where are you?"

"*Kalachakra*," I say. "Our strut-ship."

"Point out your parents, please."

I do, it's simple. They're wide-awake ship-haunters now, real-live ghosts.

He asks, "Where are we going?"

"Guge," I say, another simple ask.

"What exactly is Guge, Greta Bryn?"

But I don't want to think—just to drink, my tongue's so thick with sourness. "A planet."

"Miss Brasswell,"—now Minister T's being smart-alecky—"tell me two things you know about Guge."

I sort of ask, "It's 'The Land of Snow,' this dead king's place in olden Tibet?"

"Good!" Minister T says. "And its second meaning for us Kalachakrans?"

I squint to get it: "A faraway world to live on?"

"Where, intelligent miss?"

Another easy one: "In the Goldilocks Zone." A funny name for it.

"But where, Greta Bryn, is this Goldilocks Zone?"

"Around a star called Gluh—" I almost get stuck. "Around a star called Gliese 581." Glee-zha is how I say it.

Bald Minister T grins. His face looks like a shiny brown China plate with an up-curving crack. "She's fine," he tells the ghosts in the grave-cave. "And I believe she's the 'One.'"

Sometimes we must come up. We must wake up and eat, and move about so we can heal from ursidormizine sleep and not die before we reach Guge. When I come up this time, I get my own nook that snugs in the habitat drum called Amdo Bay. It has a vidped booth for learning from, with lock belts for when the AG goes out. It belongs to only me, it's not just one in a commons-space like most ghosts use.

Finally I ask, "What did that Minister T mean?"

"About what?" Mama doesn't eye me when she speaks.

"That I'm the 'One.' Why'd he say that?"

"He's upset and everybody aboard has gone a little loco."

"Why?" But maybe I know. We ride so long that anyone riding

with us sooner or later crazies up: inboard fever. Captain Xao once warned of this.

Mama says, "His Holiness, Sakya Gyatso, has died, so we're stupid with grief and thinking hard about how to replace him. Minister Trungpa, our late Dalai Lama's closest friend, thinks you're his rebirth, Greta Bryn."

I don't get this. "He thinks I'm not I?"

"I guess not. Grief has fuddled his reason, but maybe just temporarily."

"I am I," I say to Mama awful hot, and she agrees.

But I remember the Dalai Lama. When I was four, he played Go Fish with me in Amdo Bay during my second up-phase. Daddy sneak-named him Yoda, like from *Star Wars*, but he looked more like skinny Mr. Peanut on the peanut tins. He wore a one-lens thing and a funny soft yellow hat, and he taught me a song, "Loving the Ant, Loving the Elephant." After that, I had to take my ursidormizine and hibernize. Now Minister T says the DL is I, or I am he, but surely Mama hates as much as I do how such stupidity could maybe steal me off from her.

"I don't look like Sakya Gyatso. I'm a girl, and I'm not an Asian person." Then I yell at Mama, "I am I!"

"Actually," Mama says, "things have changed, and what you speak as truth may have also changed, kiddo."

Everybody who gets a say in Amdo Bay now thinks that Minister Nyendak Trungpa calls me correctly. I am not I: I am the next Dalai Lama. The Twenty-first, Sakya Gyatso, has died, and I must wear his sandals. Mama says he died of natural causes, but too young for it to look natural. He hit fifty-four, but he won't hit Guge. If I am he, I must take his place as our colony dukpa, which in Tibetan means 'shepherd.' That job scares me.

A good thing has come from this scary thing: I don't have to go back up into my egg pod and then down again. I stay up-phase. I must. I have too much to learn to drowse forever, even if I can sleep-learn by hypnoloading. Now I have this vidped booth that I sit in to learn and a tutor-guy, Lawrence ("Larry") Rinpoche, who loads on me a lot.

How old has all my earlier sleep-loading made me? Hibernizing, I hit seven and learnt while dreaming.

People should not call me Her Holiness. I'm a girl person—not a Chinese or a Tibetan. I tell Larry this when he swims into my room in Amdo. I've seen him in spectals about samurai and spacers, where he looks dark-haired and chest-strong. Now, anymore, he isn't. He has silver hair and hips like Mama's. His eyes do a flash thing, though, even when he's not angry, and it throws him back into the spectals he once star-played in as cool guy Lawrence Lake.

"Do I look Chinese, or Tibetan, or even Indian?" Larry asks.

"No you don't," I say. "But you don't look like no girl either."

"A girl, Your Holiness." Larry must correct me, Mama says, because he will teach me logic, Tibetan art and culture, Sanskrit, Buddhist philosophy, and medicine (space and otherwise). And also poetry, music and drama, astronomy, astrophysics, synonyms, and Tibetan, Chinese, and English. Plus cinema, radio/TV history, politics and pragmatism in deep-space colony planting, and lots of other stuff.

"No girl ever got to be Dalai Lama," I tell Larry.

"Yes, but our Fourteenth predicted his successor would hail from a place outside Tibet; and that he might re-ensoul not as a boy but as a girl."

"But Sakya Gyatso, our last, can't stick his soul in this girl." I cross my arms and turn a klutz-o turn.

"O Little Ocean of Wisdom, tell me why not."

Stupid tutor-guy. "He died after I got borned. How can a soul jump in the skin of somebody already borned?"

"Born, Your Holiness. But it's easy. It just jumps. The samvattanika viññana, the evolving consciousness of a Bodhisattva, jumps where it likes."

"Then what about me, Greta Bryn?" I tap my chest.

Larry tilts his ginormous head. "What do you think?"

Oh, that old trick. "Did it kick me out? If it kicked me out, where did I go?"

"Do you feel it kicked you out, Your Holiness?"

"I feel it never got in. Inside, I feel that I . . . own myself."

"Maybe you do, but maybe his punarbhava"—his re-becoming—"is in there mixing with your own personality."

"But that's so scary."

"What did you think of Sakya Gyatso, the last Dalai Lama? Did he scare you?"

"No, I liked him."

"You like everybody, Your Holiness."

"Not anymore."

Larry laughs. He sounds like he sounded in The Return of the Earl of Epsilon Eridani. "Even if the process has something unorthodox about it, why avoid mixing your soul self with that of a distinguished man you liked?"

I don't answer this windy ask. Instead, I say, "Why did he have to die, Mister Larry?"

"Greta, he didn't have much choice. Somebody killed him."

Every "day" I stay up-phase. Every day I study and try to understand what's happening on *Kalachakra*, and how the late Dalai Lama, at swim in my soul, has slipped his bhava, "becoming again," into my bhava, or "becoming now," and so has become a thing old and new at the same time.

Larry tells me just to imagine one candle lighting off another (even though you'd be crazy to light anything inside a starship), but my candle was already lit before the last Lama's got snuffed, and I never even smelt it go out. Larry laughs and says His Dead Holiness's flame was "never quenched, but did go dim during its forty-nine-day voyage to bardo." Bardo, I think, must look like a fish tank that the soul tries to swim in even with nothing in it.

Up-phase, I learn more about *Kalachakra*. I don't need my tutor-guy. I wander all about, between study and tutoring times. When the artificial-grav cuts off, as it does a lot, I float my ghost self into bays and nooks everywhere.

Our ship has a crazy bigness, like a tunnel turning through star-smeared space, like a train of railroad cars humming through the Empty Vast without any hum. I saw such trains in my hypnoloading sleeps. Now I peep them as spectals and mini-holos and even palm pix.

Larry likes for me to do that too. He says anything "fusty and fun" is OK by him, if it tutors me well. And I don't need him to help me twig when I snoop *Kalachakra*. I learn by drifting, floating, swimming, counting, and just by asking ghosts what I wish to know.

Here's what I've learnt by reading and vidped-tasking, snooping and asking:

1. *UNS Kalachakra* hauls 990 human asses ("and the rest of each burro aboard"—Daddy's dumb joke) to a world in the Goldilocks Zone of the Gliese 581 solar system, 20.3 lights from Sol...the assumed-to-be-live-on-able planet Gliese 581g.

2. Captain Xao says that most of us on *Kalachakra* spend our journey in ursidormizine slumber to dream about our work on Guge. The greatest number of somnacicles—sleepers—have their egg pods in Amdo Bay toward the nose of our ship. (These hibernizing lazybones look like frozen cocoons in their see-through eggs.) Those of us more often up-phase slumber at "night" in Kham Bay, where tech folk and crew do their work. At the rear of our habitat drum lies U-Tsang Bay, which I haven't visited, but where, Mama says, our Bodhisattvas—monks, nuns, lamas, and such—reside, down- or up-phase.

3. All must wriggle up-phase once each year or two. You cannot hibernize longer than two at a snooze because we human somnacicles go dodgy quite soon during our third year drowse, so Captain Xao tells us, "We'll need every hand on the ground once we're all down on Guge." ("Every foot on the ground," I would say.)

4. Red dwarf star Gliese 581, also known as Zarmina, spectral class M3V, awaits us in constellation Libra. Captain Xao calls it the eighty-seventh closest known solar system to our sun. It has seven planets and spurts out X-rays. It will flame away much sooner than Sol, but so far from now that none of us on *Kalachakra* will care a toot.

5. Gliese 581g, aka Guge, goes around its dwarf in a circle, nearly. It has one face stuck toward its sun, but enough gravity to hold its gasses to it; enough—more than Earth's—so you can walk without floating away. But it will really hot you on the sun-stuck side and chill you nasty on its dreary dark rear. It's got rocks topside and magma in its zonal mountains. We must live in the in-between stripes of

the terminator, safe spots for bipeds with blood to boil or
kidneys to broil. Or maybe we'll freeze, if we land in the
black. So two hurrahs for Guge, and three for "The Land
of Snow" in the belts where we hope to plug in.

6. We know Guge has mass. It isn't, says Captain Xao,
a "pipedream or a mirage." Our onboard telescope found
it twelve Earth years ago, seventy out from Moon-orbit
kickoff, with maybe twenty or so to go now before we really
get there. Hey, I'm more than a smidgen scared to arrive,
hey, maybe a million smidgens.

7. I'm also scared to stay an up-phase ghost on *Kalachakra*.
Like a snow leopard or a yeti, I am an endangered species.
I don't want to step up to Dalai Lamahood. It's got its
perks, but until Captain Xao, Minister T, Larry Rinpoche,
Mama, Daddy, and our security persons find out WHO kilt
the twenty-first DL, Greta Bryn, a maybe DL, thinks her life
worth one dried pea in a vacu-meal pack. Maybe.

8. In the tunnels all among Amdo, Kham, and U-Tsang Bays,
the ghost of a snow leopard drifts. It has cindery spots
swirled into the frosting of its fur. Its eyes leap yellow-green
in the dimness when it peeks back at two-leggers like me.
It jets from a holo-beam, but I don't know how or where
from. In my dreams, I turn when I see it. My heart flutter-
pounds toward shutdown. . . .

9. Sakya Gyatso spent many years as a ghost on *Kalachakra*.
He never hibernized more than three months at once, but
tried to blaze at full awakeness like a Bodhisattva. He slept
the bear slumber, when he did, but only because on Guge
he'll have to lead 990 shipboard faithfuls and millions of
Tibetan Buddhists, native and not, in their unjust exiles.
Can an up-phase ghost, once it really dies, survive on a
strut-ship as a ghost for real? Truly, I do not know.

10. Once I didn't know Mama's or Daddy's first names. Tech
is a title not a name, and Tech aboard *Kalachakra* (Captain
Xao saying the words), in the seventy-fourth year of our
flight. Tech Bonfils birthed me the following "fall," one of
just forty-seven children born in our trip to Guge. Luckily,
Larry Rinpoche told me my folks' names: Simon and Karen

Bryn. Now I don't even know if they like each other.
But I know, from lots of reading, that S. Hawking,
this century-gone physicist, believed people are not
quantifiable. He was definitely right about that.

I know lots more, although not who killed the Twenty-first DL,
if anybody did, and so I pick at that worry a lot.

Years in transit: 83
Computer Logs of the Dalai Lama-to-Be, age 8

In old spectals and palm pix, starship captains sit at helms where
they can see the Empty Vast out windows or screens. Captain Xao,
First Officer Nima Photrang, and their crew keep us all cruising
toward Gliese 581 in a closed cockpit in the upper central third of the
big tin can that's strut-shipping us to Guge.

This section we call Kham Bay. Cut flowers in thin vials prettify
the room where Xao and Photrang and crew sit to work. This pit
also has a hanging of the *Kalachakra* Mandala and a big painted
figure of the Buddha wearing a body, a man's and a woman's, with
huge lots of faces and arms. Larry calls this window-free pit a control
room and a shrine.

I guess he knows.

I visit the cockpit. No one stops me. I visit because Simon and
Karen Bryn have gone back to their Siestaville to pod-lodge for many
months on Amdo Bay's bottom level. Me, I stay my ghostly self. I
owe it to everybody aboard—or so I often get told—to grow into my
full Lamahood.

"Ah," says Captain Xao, "you wish to fly *Kalachakra*. Great, Your
Holiness."

But he passes me to First Officer Photrang, a Tibetan who looks
manlike in her jumpsuit but womanlike at her wrists and hands—so
gentle about the eyes that, drifting near because our AG's gone out,
she seems to have just pulled off a hard black mask.

"What may I do for you, Greta Bryn?"

My lips won't move, so grateful am I she didn't say, "Your
Holiness."

She shows me the console where she watches the fuel level in a drop-tank behind our tin cylinder as this tank feeds the antimatter engine pushing us outward. Everything, she says, depends on electronic systems that run "virtually automatically," but she and other crew must check closely, even though the systems have "fail-safes" to signal them from afar if they leave the control shrine.

"How long," I ask, "before we get to Guge?"

"In nineteen years we'll start braking," Nima Photrang says. "In another four, if all goes as plotted, we will enter the Gliese 581 system and soon take a stationary orbital position above the terminator. From there we'll go down to the adjacent habitable zones that we intend to settle in and develop."

"Four years to brake!" No one's ever said such a thing to me before. Four years are half the number I've lived, and no adult, I think, feels older at their ancient ages than I do at eight.

"Greta Bryn, to slow us faster than that would put terrible stress on our strut-ship. Its builders assembled it with optimal lightness, to save on fuel, but also with sufficient mass to withstand a twentieth of a g during its initial four years of thrusting and its final four years of deceleration. Do you understand?"

"Yes, but—"

"Listen: It took the *Kalachakra* four years to reach a fifth of the speed of light. During that time, we traveled less than half a light year and burned a lot of the fuel in our drop tanks. Jettisoning the used-up tanks lightened us. For seventy-nine years since then, we've coasted, cruising over sixteen light-years toward our target sun but using our fuel primarily for trajectory correction maneuvers. That's a highly economical expenditure of the antimatter ice with which we began our flight."

"Good," I say—because Officer Photrang looks at me as if I should clap for such an "economical expenditure."

"Anyway, we scheduled four years of braking at one twentieth of a g to conserve our final fuel resources and to keep this spidery vessel from ripping apart at higher rates of deceleration."

"But it's still going to take so long!"

The officer takes me to a ginormous sketch of our strut-ship. "If anyone aboard has time for a stress-reducing deceleration, Greta Bryn, you do."

"Twenty-three years!" I say. "I'll turn thirty-one!"

"Yes, you'll wither into a pitiable crone." Before I can protest more, she shows me other stuff: a map of the inside of our passenger can, a holocircle of the Gliese 581 system, and a d-cube of her living mama and daddy in the village Drak, which means Boulder, fifty-some rocky miles southeast of Lhasa. But—I'm such a dodo bird!—maybe they no longer live at all.

"My daddy's from Boulder!" I say to overcoat this thought.

Officer Photrang peers at me with small bright eyes.

"Boulder, Colorado," I tell her.

"Is that so?" After a nod from Captain Xao, she guides me into a tunnel lit by little glowing pins.

"What did you really come up here to learn, child? I'll tell you if I can."

"Who killed Sakya Gyatso?" I hurry to add, "I don't want to be him."

"Who told you somebody killed His Holiness?"

"Larry." I grab a guide rail. "My tutor, Lawrence Rinpoche."

Nima Photrang snorts. "Larry has a bad humor sense. And he may be wrong."

I float up. "But what if he's right?"

"Is the truth that important to you?" She pulls me down.

A question for a question, like a dry seed poked under my gum. "Larry says that a lama in training must quest for truth in everything, and I must do so always, and everyone else, by doing that too, will clean the universe of lies."

"'Do as I say and not as I do.'"

"What?"

Nima—she tells me to call her by this name—takes my arm and swims me along the tunnel to a door that opens at a knuckle bump. She guides me into her rooms, a closet with a pull-down rack and straps, a toadstool unit for our shipboard intranet, and a corner for talking in. We float here. Nicely, or so it seems, she pulls a twist of brindle hair out of my eye.

"Child, it's possible that Sakya Gyatso had a heart attack."

"Possible?"

"That's the official version, which Minister T told all us ghosts up-phase enough to notice that Sakya had gone missing."

I think hard. "But the unofficial story is . . . somebody killed him?"

"It's one unofficial story. In the face of uncertainty, child, people indulge their imaginations, and more versions of the truth pop up than you can slam a lid on. But lid-slamming, we think, is a bad response to ideas that will come clear in the oxygen of free inquiry."

"Who do you mean, 'we'?"

Nima shows a little smile. "My 'we' excludes anyone who forbids the expression of plausible alternatives to any 'official version.'"

"What do you think happened?"

"I'd best not say."

"Maybe you need some oxygen."

This time her smile looks a bit realer. "Yes, maybe I do."

"I'm the new Dalai Lama, probably, and I give you that oxygen, Nima. Tell me your idea, now."

After two blinks, she does: "I fear that Sakya Gyatso killed himself."

"The Dalai Lama?" I can't help it: her idea insults the man, who, funnily, now breathes inside me.

"Why not the Dalai Lama?"

"A Bodhisattva lives for others. He'd never kill anybody, much less himself."

"He stayed up-phase too much—almost half a century—and the anti-aging effects of ursidormizine slumber, which he often avoided as harmful to his leadership role, were compromised. His Holiness did have the soul of a Bodhisattva, but he also had an animal self. The wear to his body broke him down, working on his spirit as well as his head, and doubts about his ability to last the rest of our trip niggled at him, as did doubts about his fitness to oversee our colonization of Guge."

I cross my arms. This idea insults the late DL. It also, I think, poisons me. "I believe he had a heart attack."

"Then the official version has taken seed in you," Nima says.

"OK then. I like to think someone killed Sakya Gyatso, not that tiredness or sadness made him do it."

Gently: "Child, where's your compassion?"

I float away. "Where's yours?" At the door of the first officer's quarters, I try to bump out. I can't. Nima must drift over, knuckle-bump the door plate, and help me with my angry going.

The artificial-gravity generators run again. I feel them humming through the floor of my room in Amdo, and in Z Quarters where our somnacicles nap. Larry says that except for them, AG aboard *Kalachakra* works little better than did electricity in war-wasted nations on Earth. Anyway, I don't need the lock belt in my vidped unit; and such junk as pocket pens, toothbrushes, mess chits, and d-cubes don't go slow-spinning away like my fuzzy dreams.

Somebody knocks.

Who is it? Not Larry—he's already tutored me today—or Mama, who sleeps in her pod, or Daddy, who's gone up-phase to U-Tsang to help the monks plant vegetables around their gompas. He gets to visit U-Tsang, but I—the only nearly anointed DL on this ship—must mostly hang with non-monks.

The knock knocks again.

Xao Songda enters. He unhooks a folding stool from the wall and sits atop it next to my vidped booth: Captain Xao, the pilot of our generation ship. Even with the hotshot job he has to work, he wanders around almost as much as me.

"Officer Photrang tells me you have doubts."

I have doubts like a strut-ship has fuel tanks. I wish I could drop them half as fast as *Kalachakra* dropped its anti-hydrogen-ice-filled drums in the first four years of our run toward our coasting speed.

"Well?" Captain Xao's eyebrow goes up.

"Sir?"

"Does my first officer lie, or do you indeed have doubts?"

"I have doubts about everything."

"Like what, child?" Captain Xao seems nice but clueless.

"Doubts about who made me, why I was born in a big bean can, why I like the AG on rather than off. Doubts about the shipshapeness of our ship, the soundness of Larry Lake's mind, the realness of the rock we're going to. Doubts about the pains in my legs and the mixing of my soul with Sakya's . . . because of how our lifelines overlapped. Doubts about—"

"Whoa," Xao Songda says. "Officer Photrang tells me you have doubts about the official version of the Twenty-first's death."

"Yes."

"I too, but as captain, I want you to know that it cruises in shipshape shape, with an artist in charge."

After staring some, I say, "Is the official story true? Did Sakya Gyatso really die of Cadillac infraction?"

"Cardiac infarction," the captain says, not getting that I just joked him. "Yes, he did. Regrettably."

"Or do you say that because Minister T told everyone that and he outranks you?"

Xao Songda looks confused. "Why do you think Minister Trungpa would lie?"

"Inferior motives."

"Ulterior motives," the stupid captain again corrects me.

"OK: ulterior motives. Did he have something to do with Sakya's death . . . for mean reasons locked in his heart, just as damned souls are locked in hell?"

The captain draws a noisy breath. "Goodness, child."

"Larry says that somebody killed Sakya." I climb out of my vidped booth and go to the captain. "Maybe it was you."

Captain Xao laughs. "Do you know how many hoops I had to leap through to become captain of this ship? Ethnically, Gee Bee, I am Han Chinese. Hardly anybody in the Free Federation of Tibetan Voyagers wished me to command our strut-ship. But I was wholeheartedly Yellow Hat and the best pilot-engineer not already en route to a habitable planet. And so I'm here. I'd no more assassinate the Dalai Lama than desecrate a chorten, or harm Sakya's likely successor."

I believe him, even if an anxious soul could hear the last few words of his speech unkindly. I ask if he likes Nima's theory—that Sakya Gyatso killed himself—better than Minister T's Cadillac-infraction version. When he starts to answer, I say, "Flee falsehood again and speak the True Word."

After a blink, he says, "If you insist."

"Yes. I do."

"Then I declare myself, on that question, an agnostic. Neither theory strikes me as outlandish. But neither seems likely, either: Minister T's because His Holiness had good physical health and Nima's because the stresses of this voyage were but tickling feathers to the Dalai Lama."

I surprise myself—I begin to cry.

Captain Xao grips my shoulders so softly that his fingers feel like owl's down, as I dream such down would feel on an Earth I've never seen, and never will. He whispers in my ear: "Shhh-shh."

"Why do you shush me?"

Captain Xao removes his hands. "I no longer shush you. Feel free to cry."

I do. So does Captain Xao. We are wed in knowing that Larry my tutor was right all along, and that our late Dalai Lama fell at the hands of a really mean someone with an inferior motive.

Years in transit: 87
Computer Logs of the Dalai Lama-to-Be, age 12

A week before my twelfth birthday, a Buddhist nun named Dolma Langdun, who works in the Amdo Bay nursery, hails me through the *Kalachakra* intranet. She wants to know if, on my birthday, I will let one of her helpers accompany me to the nursery to meet the children and accept gifts from them.

She signs off, —Mama Dolma.

I ask myself, "Why does this person do this? Who's told her that I have a birthday coming?"

Not my folks, who sleep in their somnacicle eggs, nor Larry, who does the same because I've "exhausted" him. And so I resolve to put these questions to Mama Dolma over my intranet connection.

—How many children? I ask her, meanwhile listening to Górecki's "Symphony of Sorrowful Songs" through my ear-bud.

—Five, she replies. —Very sweet children, the youngest ten months and the oldest almost six years. It would be a great privilege to attend you on your natal anniversary, Your Holiness.

Before I can scold her for using this too-soon form of address, she adds, —As a toddler, you spent time here in Momo House, but in those bygone days I was assigned to the nunnery in U-Tsang with Abbess Yeshe Yargag.

—Momo House! I key her. —Oh, I remember!

Momo means dumpling, and this memory of my caregivers and my little friends back then dampens my eyelashes. Clearly, during the Z-pod rests of my parents and tutor, Minister Trungpa has acted as a most thoughtful guardian.

The following week goes by even faster than a fifth of light-speed.

On my birthday morning, a skinny young monk in a maroon jumpsuit comes for me and escorts me down to Momo House.

There I meet Mama Dolma. There, I also meet the children: the baby Alicia, the toddlers Pema and Lahmu, and the oldest two, Rinzen and Mickey. Except for the baby, they tap-dance about me like silly dwarves. The nursery features big furry balls that also serve as hassocks; inflatable yaks, monkeys, and pterodactyls; and cribs and vidped units, with lock belts for AG failures. A system made just for the Dumpling Gang always warns of an outage at least fifteen minutes before it occurs.

The nearly-six kid, Mickey, grabs my hand and shows me around. He introduces me to everybody, working down from the five-year-old to ten-month-old Alicia. All of them but Alicia give me drawings. These drawings show a monkey named Chenrezig (of course), a nun named Dolma (ditto), a yak named Yackety (double ditto), and a python with no name at all. I ooh and ah over these masterpizzas, as I call them, and then help them assemble soft-form puzzles, feed one another snacks, go to the toilet, and scan a big voyage chart that ends (of course) at Gliese 581g.

But it's Alicia, the baby, who wins me. She twinkles. She flirts. She touches. At nap time, I hold her in a vidped unit, its screen oranged out and its rockers rocking, and nuzzle her sweet-smelling neck. She tugs at my lip corners and pinches my mouth flat, so involved in reshaping my face that I think her a pudgy sculptor elf. All the while, her agate eyes, bigger than my thumb tips, play across my face with near-sighted adoration.

I stay with Alicia—Alicia Paljor—all the rest of my day. Then the skinny young monk comes to escort me home, as if I need him to, and Mama Dolma hugs me. Alicia wails.

It hurts to leave, but I do, because I must, and even as the hurt fades, the memory of this outstanding birthday begins, that very night, to sing in me like the lovely last notes of Górecki's Third.

I have never had a better birthday.

Months later, Daddy Simon and Mama Karen Bryn have come

up-phase at the same time. Together, they fetch me from my nook in Amdo and walk with me on a good AG day to the cafeteria above the grave-caves of our strut-ship's central drum, Kham. I ease along the serving line between them, taking tsampa, mushroom cuts, tofu slices, and sauces to make it all edible. The three of us end up at a table in a nook far from the serving line. Music by J. S. Bach spills from speakers in the movable walls, with often a sitar and bells to call up for some voyagers a Himalayan nostalgia to which my folks are immune. We eat fast and talk small.

Then Mama says, "Gee Bee, your father has something to tell you."

O God. O Buddha. O Larry. O Curly. O Moe.

"Tell her," Mama says.

Daddy Simon wears the sour face proclaiming that everybody should call him Pieman Oldfart. I hurt to behold him, he to behold me. But at last he gets out that before I stood up-phase, almost three years ago, as the DL's disputed Soul Child, he and Mama signed apartness documents that have now concluded in an agreement of full marital severance. They continue my folks, but not as the couple that conceived, bore, and raised me. They remain friends but will no longer cohabit because of incompatibilities that have arisen over their up-phase years. It really shouldn't matter to me, they say, because I've become Larry's protégée with a grand destiny that I will no doubt fulfill as a youth and an adult. Besides, they will continue to parent me as much as my odd unconfirmed status as DL-in-training allows.

I do not cry, as I did upon learning that Captain Xao believes that somebody slew my only-maybe predecessor. I don't cry because their news feels truly distant, like word of a planet somewhere whose people have brains in their chests. However, it does hurt to think about why I absolutely must cry later.

Daddy gets up, kisses my forehead, and leaves with his tray.

Mama studies me closely. "I'll always love you. You've made me very proud."

"You've made me very proud," I echo her.

"What?"

We push our plastic fork tines around in our leftovers, which I imagine rising in damp squadrons from our plates and floating up to the air-filtration fans. I wish that I, too, could either rise or sink.

"When will they confirm you?" Mama asks.

"Everything on this ship takes forever: getting from here to there, finding a killer, confirming the new DL."

"You must have some idea."

"I don't. The monks don't want me. I can't even visit their make-believe gompas over in U-Tsang."

"Well, those are sacred places. Not many of us get invitations."

"But Minister T has declared me the 'One,' and Larry has tutored me in thousands of subjects, holy and not so holy. Still, the subsidiary lamas and their silly crew think less well of me than they would of a lame blue mountain sheep."

"Don't call their monasteries 'make-believe,' Gee Bee. Don't call these other holy people and their followers 'silly.'"

"Fie!" I actually tell her. "I wish I were anywhere but on this bean can flung at an iceberg light-years across the stupid universe."

"Don't, Greta Bryn. You've got a champion in Minister Trungpa."

"Who just wants to bask in the reflected glory of his next supposed Bodhisattva—which, I swear, I am not."

Mama lifts her tray and slams it down.

Nobody else seems to notice, but I jump.

"You have no idea," she says, "who you are or what a champion can do for you, and you're much too young to dismiss yourself or your powerful advocate."

One of the Brandenburg Concertos swells, its sitars and yak bells flourishing. Far across the mess hall, Larry shuffles toward us with a tray. Mama sees him, and, just as Daddy did, she kisses my forehead and abruptly leaves. My angry stare tells Larry not to mess with me (no, I won't apologize for the accidental pun), and Larry veers off to chow with two or three bio-techs at a faraway table.

Years in transit: 88
Computer Logs of the Dalai Lama-to-Be, age 13

Today marks another anniversary of the *Kalachakra*'s departure from Moon orbit on its crossing to Guge in the Gliese 581 system.

Soon I will turn thirteen. Much has happened in the six years since I woke to find that Sakya Gyatso had died and that I had become Greta Bryn Gyatso, his really tardy reincarnation.

What has not happened haunts me as much as, if not more than, what has. I have a disturbing sense that the "investigation" into Sakya's murder resides in a secretly agreed-upon limbo. Also, that my confirmation rests in this same foggy territory, with Minister T as my "regent." Recently, though, at First Officer Nima's urging, Minister T assigned me a bodyguard from among the monks of U-Tsang Bay, a guy called Ian Kilkhor.

Once surnamed Davis, Kilkhor was born sixteen years into our flight of Canadian parents, techs who'd converted to the Yellow Hat order of Tibetan Buddhists in Calgary, Alberta, a decade before the construction of our interstellar vessel. Although nearing the chronological age of sixty, Kilkhor—as he asks me to call him—looks less than half that and has many admirers among the female ghosts in Kham.

Officer Nima fancies him. (Hey, even I fancy him.)

But she's celibacy-committed unless a need for childbearing arises on Guge. And assuming her reproductive apparatus still works. Under such circumstances, I suspect that Kilkhor would lie with her.

Here I confess my ignorance. Despite lessons from Larry in the Tibetan language, I didn't realize, until Kilkhor told me, that his new surname means "Mandala." I excuse myself on the grounds that "Kilkhor" more narrowly means "center of the circle," and that Larry often skimps on offering connections. (To improve the health of his "mortal coil," Larry has spent nearly four of my last six years in an ursidormizine doze. I go to visit him once every two weeks in the pod-lodges of Amdo Bay, but these well-intended homages sometimes feel less like cheerful visits than dutiful viewings.) Also, "Kilkhor" sounds to me more like an incitement to violence than it does a statement of physical and spiritual harmony.

Even so, I benefit in many ways from Kilkhor's presence as bodyguard and stand-in tutor. Like Larry, Mama and Daddy spend long periods in their pods; and Kilkhor, a monk who knows tai chi chuan, has kept the killer, or killers, of Sakya from slaying me, if such villains exist aboard our ship. (I have begun to doubt they do.) He has also taught me much history, culture, religion, politics, computing, astrophysics, and astronomy that Larry, owing to long bouts of hibernizing, has sadly neglected. Also, he weighs in for me with the monks, nuns, and yogis of U-Tsang, who feel disenfranchised in the process of confirming me as Sakya's successor.

Indeed, because the Panchen Lama now in charge in U-Tsang will not let me set foot there, Kilkhor intercedes to get other high monks to visit me in Kham. The Panchen Lama, to avoid seeming either bigot or autocrat, permits these visits. Unhappily, my sex, my ethnicity, and (most important) the fact that my birth antedates the Twenty-first's death by five years all conspire to taint my candidacy. I doubt it too and fear that fanatics among the "religious" will try to veto me by subtraction, not by argument, and that I will die at the hands of friends rather than enemies of the Dalai Lamahood.

Such fears, by themselves, throw real doubt on Minister T's choice of me as the Sakya's only indisputable Soul Child.

Years in transit: 89
Computer Logs of the Dalai Lama-to-Be, age 14

"The Tibetan belief in monkey ancestors puts them in a unique category as the only people I know of who acknowledged this connection before Darwin."

—Karen Swenson,
twentieth-century traveler, poet,
and worker at Mother Teresa's Calcutta mission

Last week, a party of monks and one nun met me in the hangar of Kham Bay. From their gompas ("monasteries") in U-Tsang, they brought a woolen cloak, a woolen bag, three spruce walking sticks, three pairs of sandals, and a white-faced monkey that one monk, as the group entered, fed from a baby bottle full of ashen-gray slurry.

An AG-generator never runs in the hangar because people don't often visit it, and our lander nests in a vast hammock of polyester cables. So we levitated in a cordoned space near the nose of the lander, which the Free Federation of Tibetan Voyagers has named Chenrezig, after that Buddhist disciple who, in monkey form, sired the first human Tibetans. (Each new DL automatically qualifies as the latest incarnation of Chenrezig.) Our lander's nose is painted with bright geometric patterns and the cartoon head of a wise-looking monkey wearing glasses and a beaked yellow hat. Despite this amusing iconography, however, almost everyone on our strut-ship now calls the lander the Yak Butter Express.

After stiff greetings, these high monks—including the Panchen Lama, Lhundrub Gelek, and Yeshe Yargang, the abbess of U-Tsang's only nunnery!—tied the items that they'd brought to a utility toadstool in the center of our circle ("kilkhor"). Then we floated in lotus positions, hands palm-upward, and I stared at these items, but not at the monkey now clutching the PL and wearing a look of alert concern. From molecular vibrations and subtle somatic clues—twitches, blinks, sniffles—I tried to determine which of the articles they wished me to select . . . or not to select, as their biases dictated.

"Some of these things were Sakya Gyatso's," the Panchen Lama said. "Choose only those that he viewed as truly his. Of course, he saw little in this life as a 'belonging.' You may examine any or all, Miss Brasswell."

I liked how my surname (even preceded by the stodgy honorific Miss) sounded in our hangar, even if it did seem to label me an imposter, if not an outright foe of Tibetan Buddhism. To my right, Kilkhor lowered his eyelids, advising me to make a choice. OK, then: I had no need to breast-stroke my way over to the pile.

"The cloak," I said.

Its stench of musty wool and ancient vegetable dyes told me all I needed to know. I recalled those smells and the cloak's vivid colors from an encounter with the DL during his visit to the nursery in Amdo when I was four. It had seemed the visit of a seraph or an extraterrestrial—as, by virtue of our status as star travelers, he had qualified. Apparently, none of these faithful had accompanied him then, for, obviously, none recalled his having cinched on this cloak to meet a tot of common blood.

The monkey—a large Japanese macaque (Mucaca fuscata)—swam to the center of our circle, undid the folded cloak, and kicked back to the Lama, who belted it around his lap. Still fretful, the macaque levitated in its breechclout—a kind of diaper— beside the PL. It wrinkled its brow at me in approval or accusation.

"Go on," Lhundrub Gelek said. "Choose another item."

I glanced at Kilkhor, who dropped his eyelids.

"May I see what's in the bag?" I asked.

The PL spoke to the macaque: a critter I imagined Tech Bonfils taking a liking to at our trip's outset. It then paddled over to the bag tied to the utility toadstool, seized the bag by its neck, and dragged it over to me.

After foraging a little, I extracted five slender books, of a kind now rarely made, and studied each: one in English, one in Tibetan, one in French, one in Hindi, and one, surprisingly, in Esperanto. In each case, I recognized their alphabets and point of origin, if not their subject matter. A bootlace linked the books; when they started to float away, I caught its nearer end and yanked them all back.

"Did His Holiness write these?" I asked.

"Yes," the Panchen Lama said, making me think that I'd passed another test. He added, "Which of the five did Sakya most esteem?" Ah, a dirty trick. Did they want me to read not only several difficult scripts but also Sakya's departed mind?

"Do you mean as artifacts, for the loveliness of their craft, or as documents, for the spiritual meat in their contents?"

"Which of those options do you suppose more like him?" Abbess Yeshe Yargag asked sympathetically.

"Both. But if I must make a choice, the latter. When he wrote, he distilled clear elixirs from turbid mud."

Our visitors beheld me as if I'd neutralized the stench of sulfur with sprinkles of rose water. Again, I felt shameless.

With an unreadable frown, the PL said, "You've chosen correctly. We now wish you to choose the book that Sakya most esteemed for its message."

I reexamined each title. The one in French featured the words wisdom and child. When I touched it, Chenrezig responded with a nearly human intake of breath. Empty of thought, I lifted that book.

"Here: The Wisdom of a Child, the Childishness of Wisdom."

As earlier, our five visitors kept their own counsel, and Chenrezig returned the books to their bag and the bag to the monk who had set it out.

Next, I chose among the walking sticks and the pairs of sandals, taking my cues from the monkey and so choosing better than I had any right to expect. In fact, I selected just those items identifying me as the Dalai Lama's Soul Child, girl or not.

After Kilkhor praised my accuracy, the PL said, "Very true, but—"

"But what?" Kilkhor said. "Must you settle on a Tibetan male only?"

The Lama replied, "No, Ian. But what about this child makes her miraculous?"

Ah, yes. One criterion for confirming a DL candidate is that those giving the tests identify "something miraculous" about him . . . or her.

"What about her startling performance so far?" Kilkhor asked.

"We don't see her performance as a miracle, Ian."

"But you haven't conferred about the matter." He gestured at the other holies floating in the fluorescent lee of the Yak Butter Express.

"My friends," the Panchen Lama asked, "what say you all in reply?"

"We find no miracle," a spindly, middle-aged monk said, "in this child's choosing correctly. Her brief life overlapped His Holiness's."

"My-me," Abbess Yargag said. "I find her a wholly supportable candidate."

The three leftover holies held their tongues, and I had to admit— to myself, if not aloud to this confirmation panel—that they had a hard-to-refute point, for I had pegged my answers to the tics of a monastery macaque with an instinctual sense of its keepers' moody fretfulness.

Fortunately, the monkey liked me. I had no idea why.

O to be unmasked! I needed no title or additional powers to lend savor to my life. I wanted to sleep and to awaken later as an animal husbandry specialist, with Tech Karen Bryn Bonfils as my mentor and a few near age-mates as fellow apprentices.

The PL unfolded from his lotus pose and floated before me with his feet hanging. "Thank you, Miss Brasswell, for this audience. We regret we can't—" Here he halted, for Chenrezig swam across our meeting space, pushed into my arms, and clasped me about the neck. Then all the astonished monks and the shaken PL rubbed their shoulders as if to ignite their bodies in glee or consternation.

Abbess Yargag said, "There's your miracle."

"Nando," the lama said, shaking his head: No, he meant.

"On the contrary," Abbess Yargag replied. "Chenrezig belonged to Sakya Gyatso, and never in Chenrezig's sleep-lengthened life has this creature embraced a child, a non-Asian, or a female: not even me."

"Nando," the PL, visibly angry, said again.

"Yes," another monk said. "Hail the jewel in the lotus. Praise to the gods."

I kissed Chenrezig's white-flecked facial mane as he whimpered like an infant in my too-soon weary arms.

Years in transit: 93
Computer Logs of the Dalai Lama-to-Be, age 18

—"A Catechism: Why Do We Voyage?"

At age seven, I learned this catechism from Larry. Kilkhor often has me say it, to ensure that I don't turn apostate to either our legend or my long-term charge. Sometimes Captain Xao Songda, a Han who converted and fled to Vashon Island, Washington—via northern India; Cape Town, South Africa; Buenos Aires; and Hawaii—sits in to temper Larry's flamboyance and Kilkhor's lethargic matter-of-factness.

—Why do we voyage? one of them will ask.

—To fulfill, I say, —the self-determination tenets of the Free Federation of Tibet and to usher every soul pent in hell up through the eight lower realms to Buddhahood.

From the bottom up, these realms include: 1) hell-pent mortals, 2) hungry ghosts, 3) benighted beasts, 4) fighting spirits, 5) human beings, 6) seraphs and suchlike, 7) disciples of the Buddha, 8) Buddhas for themselves only, and 9) Bodhisattvas who live and labor for every soul in each lower realm.

—Which realm did you begin in, Your Probationary Holiness?

—That of the bewildered, but not benighted, human mortal.

—As our Dalai Lama in Training, to which realm have you arisen?

—That of the disciples of Chenrezig: "Hail the jewel in the lotus." I am the funky simian saint of the Buddha.

(Sometimes, depending on my mood, I ad-lib that last bit.)

—From what besieged and battered homeland do you pledge to free us?

—The terrestrial "Land of Snow": Tibet beset, ensorcelled, and enslaved.

—As a surrogate for that land gone cruelly forfeit, to which new country do you pledge to lead us?

—"The Land of Snow," on Guge the Unknowable, where we all must strive to free ourselves again.

The foregoing part of the catechism embodies a pledge and a charge. Other parts synopsize the history of our oppression: the ruin of our economy; the destruction of our monasteries; the subjugation of our nation to the will of foreign predators; the co-opting of our spiritual formulae for greedy and warlike purposes; the submergence of our culture to the maws of jackals; and the quarantining of our state to anyone not of our oppressors' liking. Finally, against the severing of sinews human and animal, the pulling asunder of ties interdependent and relational, only the tallest mountains could stand. And those who undertook the khora, the sacred pilgrimage around Mount Kailash, often did so with little or no grasp of the spiritual roots of their journeys. Even then, that mountain, the land all about it, and the scant air overarching them, stole the breath and spilled into its pilgrims' lungs the bracing elixir of awe.

At length, the Tibetans and their sympathizers realized that their overlords would never withdraw. Their invasion, theft, and reconfiguration of the state had left its peoples few options but death or exile.

—So what did the Free Federation of Tibet do? Larry, Kilkhor, or Xao will ask.

—Sought a United Nations charter for the building of a starship, an initiative that all feared China would preempt with its veto in the Security Council.

—What happened instead?

—The Chinese supported the measure.

—How so?

—They contributed to the general levy for funds to build and crew with colonists a second-generation antimatter ship capable of attaining speeds up to one-fifth the velocity of light.

—Why did China surrender to an enterprise implying severe

criticism of a policy that it saw as an internal matter? That initiative surely stood as a rebuke to its efforts to overwhelm Tibet with its own crypto-capitalistic materialism.

Here I may snigger or roll my eyeballs, and Lawrence, Kilkhor, or Xao will repeat the question.

—Three reasons suffice to explain China's acquiescence, I at length reply.

—State them.

—First, China understood that launching this ship would remove the Twenty-first Dalai Lama, who had agreed not only to support this disarming plan but also to go with the Yellow Hat colonists to Gliese 581g.

—"Praise to the gods," my catechist will say in Tibetan.

—Indeed, backing this plan would oust from a long debate the very man whom the Chinese reviled as a poser and a bar to the incorporation of Tibet into their program of post-post-Mao modernization.

Here, another snigger from a bigger poser than Sakya; namely, me.

—And the second reason, Your Holiness?

—Backing this strut-ship strategy surprised the players arrayed against China in both the General Assembly and the Security Council.

—To what end?

—All they could do was brand China's support a type of cynicism warped into a low-yield variety of "ethnic cleansing," for now Tibet and its partisans would have one fewer grievance to lay at China's feet.

With difficulty, I refrain from sniggering again.

—And the third reason, Miss Greta Bryn, our delightfully responsive Ocean of Wisdom?

—Supporting the antimatter ship initiative allowed China to put its design and manufacturing enterprises to work drawing up blueprints and machining parts for the provocatively named *UNS Kalachakra*.

—And so we won our victory?

—"Hail the jewel in the lotus," I reply.

—And what do we Kalachakrans hope to accomplish on the sun-locked world we now call Guge?

—Establish a colony unsullied by colonialism; summon other emigrants to "The Land of Snow"; and lead to enlightenment all who bore that dream, and who will carry it into cycles yet to unfold.

—And after that?

—The cessation of everything samsaric, the opening of ourselves to nirvana.

Years in transit: 94
Computer Logs of the Dalai Lama-to-Be, age 19

For nearly four Earth months, I've added not one word to my Computer Log. But shortly after my last recitation of the foregoing catechism, Kilkhor pulled me aside and told me that I had a rival for the position of Dalai Lama.

This news astounded me. "Who?"

"A male Soul Child born of true Tibetan parents in Amdo Bay less than fifty days after Sakya Gyatso's death," Kilkhor said. "A search team located him almost a decade ago, but has only now disclosed him to us." Kilkhor made this disclosure of bad news—it is bad, isn't it?—sound very ordinary.

"What's his name?" I had no idea what else to say.

"Jetsun Trimon," Kilkhor said. "Old Gelek seems to think him a more promising candidate than he does Greta Bryn Brasswell."

"Jetsun! You're joking, right?" And my heart did a series of arrhythmic lhundrubs in protest.

Kilkhor regarded me then with either real, or expertly feigned, confusion. "You know him?"

"Of course not! But the name—" I stuck, at once amused and appalled.

"The name, Your Holiness?"

"It's a ridiculous, a totally ludicrous name."

"Not really. In Tibetan it means—"

"—'venerable' and 'highly esteemed,'" I put in. "But it's still ridiculous." And I noted that as a child, between bouts of study, I had often watched, well, "cartoons" in my vidped unit. Those responsible for this lowbrow programming had mischievously stocked it with a selection of episodes called The Jetsons, about a space-going Western family in a gimmick-ridden future. I had loved it.

"I've heard of it," Kilkhor said. "The program, I mean."

But he didn't twig the irony of my five-year-younger rival's name.

Or he pretended not to. To him, the similarity of these two monikers embodied a pointless coincidence.

"I can't do this anymore without a time-out," I said. "I'm going down-phase for a year—at least a quarter of a year!"

Kilkhor said nothing. His expression said everything.

Still, he arranged for my down-phase respite, and I repaired to Amdo Bay and my eggshell to enjoy this pod-lodging self-indulgence, which, except for rare cartoon-tinged nightmares, I almost did.

Now, owing to somatic suspension, I return at almost the same nineteen I went under.

When I awake this time amidst a catacomb vista of eggshell pods—like racks in a troopship or in a concentration-camp barracks—Mama, Minister T, the Panchen Lama, Ian Kilkhor, and Jetsun Trimon attend my awakening.

Grateful for functioning AG (as, down here, it always functions), I swing my legs out of the pod, stagger a step or two, and retch from a stomach knotted with a fresh anti-insomniac heat.

The Tibetan boy, my rival, comes to me unbidden, slides an arm across my chest from behind, and eases me back toward his own thin body so that I don't topple into the vomit-vase Mama has given me. With his free hand, Jetsun strokes my brow, meanwhile tucking stray strands of hair behind my ear. I don't need him to do this stuff. Actually, I resent his doing it.

Although I usually sleep little, I do take occasional naps. Don't I deserve a respite?

I pull free of the young imposter. He looks fifteen at least, and if I've hit nineteen, his age squares better than does mine with the passing of the last DL and the transfer of Sakya's bhava into the material form of Jetsun Trimon.

Beholding him, I find his given name less of a joke than I did before my nap and more of a spell for the inspiriting that the PL alleges has occurred in him. Jetsun and I study each other with mutual curiosity. Our elders look on with darker curiosities. How must Jetsun and I regard this arranged marriage, they no doubt wonder, and what does it presage for everyone aboard the *Kalachakra*?

During my year-plus sleep, maybe I've matured some. Although I want to cry out against the outrage—no, the unkindness—of my guardians' conspiracy to bring this fey usurper to my podside, I don't berate them. They warrant such a scolding, but I refrain. How do they wish me to view their collusion, and how can I see it as anything other than their sending a prince to the bier of a spell-afflicted maiden? Except for the acne scarring his forehead and chin, Jetsun is, well, cute, but I don't want his help. I loathe his intrusion into my pod-lodge and almost regret my return.

Kilkhor notes that the lamas of U-Tsang, including the Panchen Lama and Abbess Yargag, have finally decided to summon Jetsun Trimon and me to our onboard stand-in for the Jokhang Temple. There, they will conduct a gold-urn lottery to learn which of us will follow Sakya Gyatso as the Twenty-second Dalai Lama.

Jetsun bows.

He says that his tutor has given him the honor of inviting me, my family, and my guardians to this "shindig." It will occur belatedly, he admits, after he and I have already learned many sutras and secrets reserved in Tibet—holy be its saints, its people, and its memory—for a Soul Child validated by lottery.

But circumstances have changed since our Earth-bound days: The ecology of the *Kalachakra*, the great epic of our voyage, and our need on Guge for a leader of heart and vision require fine tunings beyond our forebears' imaginations.

Wiser than I was last year, I swallow a cynical yawn.

"And so," Jetsun ends, "I wish you joy in the lottery's Buddha-directed outcome, whichever name appears on the selected slip."

He bows and takes three steps back.

Lhundrub Gelek beams at Jetsun, and I know in my gut that the PL has become my competitor's regent, his champion. Mama Karen Bryn holds her face expressionless until fret lines drop from her lip corners like weighted ebony threads.

I thank Jetsun, for his courtesy and his well-rehearsed speech. He seems to want something more—an invitation of my own, a touch—but I have nothing to offer but the stifling of my envy, which I fight to convert to positive energies boding a happy karmic impact on the name slips in the urn.

"You must come early to our Temple," the PL says. "Doing so will give you time to pay your respects at Sakya Gyatso's bier."

This codicil to our invitation heartens me. Lacking any earlier approval to visit U-Tsang, I have never seen the body of the DL on display there.

Do I really wish to see it, to see him?

Yes, of course I do.

We've lost many Kalachakrans in transit to Guge, but none of the others have our morticians bled with trochars, painted with creams and rouges, or treated with latter-day preservatives. Those others we ejected via tubes into the airless cold of interstellar space, meager human scraps for the ever-hungry night.

In Tibet, the bereaved once spread their dead loved ones out on rocks in "celestial burial grounds." This they did as an act of charity, for the vultures. On our ship, though, we have no vultures, or none with feathers, and perhaps by firing our dead into unending quasi-vacuum, we will offer to the void a sacrifice of once-living flesh generous enough to upgrade our karma.

But Sakya Gyatso we have enshrined; and soon, as one of only two candidates for his sacred post, I will gaze upon the remains of one whose enlightenment and mercy have plunged me into painful egocentric anguish.

At the appointed time (six months from Jetsun's invitation), we journey from Amdo and across Kham by way of tunnels designed for either gravity-assisted marches or weightless swims. Our style of travel depends on the AG generators and the rationing of gravity by formulae meant to benefit our long-term approach to Guge. However, odd outages often overcome these formulae. Blessedly, Kalachakrans now adjust so well to gravity loss that we no longer find it alarming or inconvenient.

Journeying, we discover that U-Tsang's residents—allegedly, all Bodhisattvas—have forsworn the use of generators during the 72-hour Festival of the Gold Urn, with that ceremony occurring at noon of the middle day. This renunciation they regard as a gift to everybody aboard our vessel—somnacicles and ghosts—and no hardship at all. Whatever stress we spare the generators, our karmic economies tell us, will redound to everybody's benefit in our voyage's later stages.

My entourage consists of my divorced parents, Simon Brasswell and Karen Bryn Bonfils; Minister T, my self-proclaimed regent; Lawrence Lake Rinpoche, my tutor and confidant, now up-phase for the first time in two years; and Ian Kilkhor, security agent, standby tutor, and friend. We walk single-file through a sector of Kham wide enough for the next Dalai Lama's subjects to line its walls and perform respectful namaste as he (or she) passes. Minister T tells us that Jetsun Trimon and his people made this same journey eighteen hours ago, and that their well-wishers in this trunk tunnel were fewer than those attending our passage. A Bodhisattva would take no pleasure from such a petty statistical triumph. Tellingly, I do. So what does my competition-bred joy say about my odds in the coming gold-urn lottery? Nothing auspicious, I fear.

Eventually, our crowds dwindle, and we enter a deck area featuring a checkpoint and a sector gate. A monk clad in maroon passes us through. Another dials open the gate admitting us, at last, to U-Tsang.

I smell roast barley, barley beer (chang), and an acrid tang of incense that makes my stomach seize. Beyond the gate, which shuts behind us like a stone wheel slotting into a tomb groove, we drift through a hall with thin metal rails and bracket-like handholds. The luminary pins here gleam a watery purple.

Our feet slide out from under us, not like those of a fawn slipping on ice, but like those of an astronaut trainee rising from the floor of an aircraft plunging to create a few seconds of pedagogical zero-g.

The AG generators here shut down a while ago, so we dog-paddle in waterwheel slow-motion, unsure which tunnel to enter.

Actually, I'm the only uncertain trekker, but because neither Minister T nor Larry nor Kilkhor wants to help me, I stay mute, from perplexity and pride: another black mark, no doubt, against my lottery chances.

Ahead of us, fifteen yards or so, a snow leopard manifests: a four-legged ghost with yellow eyes and frost-etched silver fur. Despite the lack of gravity, it faces us as though it were standing on a ledge and licks its sooty beard as if savoring again the last guinea-pig-like chiphi that it crushed into bone bits. I hesitate. The leopard swishes its tail, turns, and leaps into a tunnel that I would not have chosen.

Kilkhor laughs and urges us upward into this same purplish chute. "It's all right," he says. "Follow it. Or do you suspect a subterfuge from our spiritually elevated hosts?" He laughs again . . . this time, maybe, at his inadvertent nod to the Christian sacrament of communion.

Larry and I twig his mistake, but does anybody else?

"Come on," Kilkhor insists. "They've sent us this cool cat as a guide."

And so we follow. We swim rather than walk, levitating through a Buddhist rabbit hole in the wake of an illusory leopard . . . until, by a sudden shift in perspective, we feel ourselves to be "walking" again.

This ascent, or fall, takes just over an hour, and we emerge in the courtyard of Jokhang Temple, or its diminished *Kalachakra* facsimile. Here, the Panchen Lama, the Abbess of U-Tsang's only nunnery, and a colorful contingent of Yellow Hats and other monks greet us joyfully. They regale us with khata, gift scarves inscribed with good-luck symbols, and with processional music played by flutes, drums, and bells. Their welcome feels at once high-spirited and heartfelt.

The snow leopard has vanished. When we broke into the courtyard swimming like ravenous carp, somebody, somewhere, stopped projecting it.

So let the gold-urn ceremony begin. Put me out of, or into, my misery.

But before the lottery, we visit the shrine where the duded-up remains of Sakya Gyatso lie in state, like those of Lenin in the Kremlin or Mao in the Forbidden City. Although Sakya should not suffer mention in the same breath as mass murderers, nobody can deny that we have preserved him as an icon, just as the devotees of Lenin and Mao mummified them. And so I must trust that a single Figure of Peace weighs more in the karmic-justice scales than does a shipload of bloody despots.

Daddy begs off. He has seen the dead Sakya Gyatso before, and traveling with his ex-wife, the mother of his Soul Child daughter, has depressed him beyond easy repair. So he retreats to a nearby guesthouse and locks himself inside for a nap. Ian Kilkhor leaves to visit several friends in the Yellow Hat gompa with whom he once studied; Minister T, who has often paid homage at the Twenty-first's bier, has business with Lhundrub Gelek and others of the confirmation troupe who met with me in Kham in the shadow of the Yak Butter Express.

So, only Mama, Larry, and I go to see the Lama whom, according to many, I will succeed as the spiritual and temporal head of the 990 Tibetan colonizers aboard this ship. The shrine we approach does not resemble a mausoleum. It sits on the courtyard's edge, like an exhibit of amateur art in a construction trailer.

Two maroon-clad guards await us beside its doors, one at each end of the trailer, now graffitified with mantras, prayers, and many mysterious symbols—but no one else in U-Tsang Bay has come out to view its principal attraction. The blousy monk at the nearer door examines our implanted upper-arm IDs with click-scans, smiles beatifically, and nods us in. Larry jokes in Tibetan with this guy before joining us at the DL's windowed bier, where we three float: ghosts beside a pod-lodger who will not again arise, unless he has already done so in yet another borrowed boy.

"He is not here," I say. "He has arisen."

Larry, who looks much older than at his last brief up-phase, laughs in appreciation or embarrassment: the latter, probably.

Mama gives me a blistering "cool-it" glare.

And then I gaze upon the body of Sakya Gyatso. Even in death, even through the clear but faintly dusty cover of his display pod, he sustains about his face and hands a soft amber aura of serene lifelikeness that startles, and discomfits. I see him smiling sweetly upon me when I was four. I imagine him displeasing his religious brethren and sisters by going more often into Amdo and Kham Bays to interact with his secular subjects than our sub-lamas thought needful or wise, as if such visits distracted him from his obligations and undercut his authority in both realms, profane and holy. And it's definitely true that his longest uninterrupted sojourn in U-Tsang coincides with his years lying in state in this shabby trailer.

Commoners aboard ship loved him, but maybe—I reflect,

studying his corpse with both fascination and regard—he angered those practitioners of Tantra who viewed him as their highest representative and model. Certainly, he moved during his life from external *Kalachakra* Tantra—a concern with the lost procession of solar and lunar days—to the internal Tantra, with its focus on the energy systems of the body, to the higher alternative Tantra leading to the sublime state of bodhichitta, perfect enlightenment for the sake of others.

Thus reflecting, I cannot conceive of anyone aboard ever wishing him harm or of myself climbing out of the pit of my ego to attain the state of material renunciation and accepting comprehension of emptiness that Sakya Gyatso reached and embodied through so many years of our journey.

That I stand today as one of two Soul Children in line to follow him defies logic; it offends reason and also the 722 deities resident in the *Kalachakra* Mandala as emblems of reality and consciousness. I lack even the worth of a dog licking barley-cake crumbs from the floor. I put my palm on the Twenty-first's pod cover and erupt in sobs. These underscore my unsuitability to succeed him.

Mama's glare gives way to a look of fretful amazement. She lays an arm over my shoulder, an intimacy that keeps me from drifting blindly away from either her or Larry.

"Kiddo," she murmurs, "don't cry for this lucky man. We'll never cease to honor him, but the time for mourning has passed."

I can't stop: All sleep has fled and the future holds only a scalding wakefulness. Larry lays his arm over my other shoulder, caging me between them.

"Baby," Mama says. "Baby, what's going on?"

She hasn't called me "baby" or "kiddo" since, over seven years ago, I had my first period. I twist my neck just enough to tell her to glance at the late DL; that she must look. Reluctantly, it seems, she does, and then looks back at me with no apparent hesitancy or aversion. Her gaze then switches between him and me until she realizes that I won't—I simply can't—succeed this saint as our leader. Moreover, I intend to withdraw from the gold-urn lottery and to throw my support to my rival. Mama remains silent, but her arm deserts me and she turns from the DL's bier as if my declaration has acted as a vernier jet to change her position. In any case, she drifts away.

"Do you understand me, Mama?"

Mama's eyes jiggle and close. Her chin drops. Her jumpsuit-clad body floats like that of a string-free marionette, all raw angles and dreamily rafting hands.

Larry releases me and swims to her. "Something's wrong, Greta Bryn." I already suspect this, but these words penetrate with a laser's precision. I fumble blurry-eyed after Larry, clueless about what to do to help.

Larry swallows her with his arms, like the male hero in an anachronistic spectal, and then pushes her away to study her more objectively. Immediately, he pulls her back in to him again, checks her pulse at wrist and throat, and pivots her toward me with odd contrasting expressions washing over his face.

"She's fainted, I think."

"Fainted?" My mother, so far as I know, never faints.

"It's all the travel . . . and her anxiety about the gold-urn lottery."

"Not to mention her disappointment in me."

Larry regards me with such deliberate blankness that I almost fail to recognize the man, whom I have known seemingly forever.

"Talk to her when she comes 'round," he says. "Talk to her."

The blousy monk who ran click-scans on us enters the makeshift mausoleum and helps Larry tow my rag-doll mama outside, across the road, and into the battened-down Temple courtyard. The two accompany her to a basket-like bower chair that suppresses her driftability and attend her with colorful fake Chinese fans. I go with them, looking on like a gawker at a cafeteria accident.

Our post-swoon interview takes place in the nearly empty courtyard. Mama clutches two of the bower-chair spokes like a child in a gravity swing, and I maintain my place before her with the mindless agility of a pond carp.

"Never say you're forsaking the gold-urn lottery," she says. "You bear on your shoulders the hopes of a majority, my hopes highest of all."

"Did my decision to withdraw cause you to faint?"

"Of course!" she cries. "You can't withdraw! You don't think I faked my swoon, do you?"

I have no doubt that Mama didn't fake it. Her sclera clocked into view before her eyelids fell. But, before that, her gaze cut to and rested on Sakya's face just prior to realizing my intent. Feelings of betrayal, loss, and outrage triggered her swoon. Now she says I have no choice but to take part in the gold-urn drawing, and I regard her with such a blend of gratitude, for believing in me, and loathing, for her rigidity, that I can't speak. Do Westerners carry both me-first ego genes and self-doubt genes that, in combination, overcome the teachings of the Tantra?

"Answer me, Greta Bryn: Do you think I faked that faint?"

Mama knows already that I didn't. She just wants me to assume the hair shirt of guilt for her indisposition and to pull it over my head with the bristly side inward. I have sufficient Easterner in my makeup to deny her that boon and the pinched ecstasy implicit in it. All at once dauntless, I hold her gaze, and hold it, until she begins to waver in her implacability.

"I didn't swoon solely because you tried to renounce your rebirth right, but also because you tried to humiliate me in front of Larry." Mama stands so far from the truth on this issue that she doesn't even qualify as wrong.

And so I laugh, like an evil-wisher rather than a daughter. "Not so," I say. "Why would I want to humiliate you before Larry?"

"Because I've always refused to coddle your self-doubts."

I recall Mama beholding Sakya's death mask and memorizing his every aura-lit feature. "What else caused you to 'fall out'?"

Her voice drops a register: "The Dalai Lama. His face. His hands. His body. His inhering and sustaining holiness."

"How does his 'sustaining holiness' knock you into a swoon, Mama?"

She peers across the courtyard road at the van where the DL lies in state. Then she pulls herself upright in the bower chair and tells this story:

"While married to your father, I began an affair with Minister Trungpa. He lived wherever Sakya lived, and Sakya chose to live among the secular citizens of Amdo and Kham rather than in the ridiculously scaled-down model of the Potala Palace in U-Tsang. As one result, Minister T and I easily met each other; and Nyendak—Neddy, I call him—courted me under the unsuspecting noses of both Sakya and Simon."

"You cuckolded my daddy with Minister T?" I need her to say it again.

"That's such an ugly old word to label what Neddy and I still regard as a sacred union."

"I'm sorry, Mama, but it's the prettiest word I know to call it."

"Don't condescend to me, Gee Bee."

"I won't. I can't. But I do have to ask: Who fathered me, the man I call Daddy or Sakya's old-fart chief minister?"

"Your father fathered you," Mama says. "Look at yourself in a mirror. Simon's face underlies your own. His blood runs through you, almost as if he gave his vitality to you and thus lost it himself."

"Maybe because you cuckolded him."

"That's crap. If anything, Simon's growing apathy and addiction to pod-lodging shoved me toward Neddy. Who, by the way, has the eggs, even at his age, to stay on the upright outside of a Z-pod."

"Mama, please."

"Listen, Neddy loves you. He cherishes you because he cherishes me. He sees you as just as much his own as Simon does. In fact, Neddy was the first to—"

"I'll stop saying 'cuckold' if you'll stop calling your boyfriend 'Neddy.' It sounds like filthy baby talk."

Mama closes her eyes, counts to herself, and opens them again to explain that when Sakya Gyatso at last figured out what was going on between Mama and Minister Trungpa, he called them to him and urged them to break off the affair in the interest of a higher spirituality and the preservation of shipboard harmony.

Minister T, ever the tutor, argued that although traditional Buddhism stems from a slavish obeisance to the demands of morality, wisdom cultivation, and ego abasement, the Tibetan Tantric path channels sexual attraction and its drives into the creation of life-force energies that purify these urges and tie them to transcendent spiritual purposes. My mother's marriage had unraveled; and Minister T's courtship of her, which culminated in consensual carnality and a principled friendship, now demonstrated their mutual growth toward that higher spirituality.

I laugh out loud.

"And did His Holiness give your boyfriend a pass on this self-serving distortion of the Tantric way?"

"Believe as you will, but Neddy—Minister Trungpa's—take on the matter, and the thoroughness with which he laid out everything, had great effect on the DL. After all, Minister T had served as his regent in exile in Dharmasala, as his chief minister in India, and finally as his minister and friend here on the *Kalachakra*. Why would he all at once suppose this fount of integrity and wise counsel a scoundrel?"

"Maybe because he was surfing the wife of another man and justifying it with a lot of mystical malarkey."

Mama squints with thread-thin patience and resumes her story. Because of what Minister T and Mama had done, and still do, and what Minister T told His Holiness to justify their behavior, the Dalai Lama fell into a brown study that finally edged over into an ashen funk. To combat it, Sakya hibernated for three months, but emerged as low in spirits as he had gone into his egg. All his energies had weakened, and he told Minister T of his fears of dying before we reached Guge. Such talk profoundly fretted Mama's lover, who insisted that Sakya Gyatso tour the nursery in Amdo Bay. There he met me, Greta Bryn Brasswell. He was so smitten that he returned many times over the next few weeks, always singling me out for attention. He told Mama that my eyes reminded him of those of his baby sister, who had died very young of rheumatic fever.

"I remember meeting His Holiness," I tell Mama, "but not his visiting our nursery so often."

"You were four," Mama says. "How could you?"

She recounts how Minister T later took her to Sakya's upper-deck office in Amdo to talk about his long depression. With the AG generators running, they shared green tea and barley breads.

The DL again voiced his fear that even if he slept the rest of our journey, at some point in transit he would surrender his ghost in his eggshell pod and we his people would arrive at Guge with no agreed-upon leader. Minister T rebuked him for this worry, which he identified as egocentric, even though the DL took pains to articulate it as a concern for our common welfare.

Mama had carried me to this meeting. I lay sleeping—not like a pod-lodger but as a tired child—across her lap on a folded poncho liner that Simon had brought aboard as a going-away gift from a former roommate at Georgia Tech. As the adults talked, I turned and stretched, but never awakened.

"I don't recall that either," I say.

"Again, you were sleeping. Don't you listen to anything I tell you?"

"Everything. It's just that—" I stop myself. "Go on."

Mama does. She says that the DL walked over, leaned down, and placed his lips on my forehead, as if decaling it with a wet rose petal. Then he mused aloud about how fine it would be if, as an adult, I assumed his mantle and oversaw not only our voyagers' spiritual education but also our colonization of "The Land of Snow." He did not think he had the strength to undertake those tasks, but I would never exhaust my energy reserves. This fanciful scenario, Mama admits, rang in her like a crystal bell, a chime that echoed through her recurrently, as clear as unfiltered starlight.

Later, Mama and Minister T talked about their meeting with His Holiness and the tender wish-fulfillment musing with which he'd concluded it: my ascension to the Dalai Lamahood and eventual leadership on Guge. Mama asked if such a scenario could work itself out in reality, for if His Holiness died and Minister T championed me as he'd once stood behind Sakya, lifting him to his present eminence, then surely I, too, could rise to that height.

"'I'm too old for such fatiguing machinations again,' he told me," Mama says reminiscently, "but I said, 'Not by what I know of you, Neddy,' and just that expression of admiration and faith turned him."

I find Mama's account of this episode and her conspicuous pleasure in relating it hard to credit. But she has actually begun to glow, with a coppery aura akin to that of the DL in his display casket.

"At that point," she adds, "I got ambitious for you in a way that once never would have crossed my mind. Your ascension was just so far-fetched and prideful a thing for me to think about." She smiles adoringly, and my stomach shrinks upon itself like new linen applied wet to a metal frame.

"I've heard enough."

"Oh, no," Mama chides. "I've more, much more."

In blessed summary, she narrates a later conversation with

Minister T, in which she urged him to carry to Sakya—now more a brooding Byronic hero than a Bodhisattva in spiritual balance—this news: that she had no objection, if any accident or fatal illness befell him, to his dispatching his migrating bhava into the body of her daughter. Thus, he could mix our subjective selves in ways that would propagate us both into the future and so assist us all in arriving safely at Gliese 581g.

Bristling, I try to get my head around this message. In fact, I ask Mama to repeat it. She does, and my deduction that she's memorized this nutty formula—if you like, call it a "spell"—sickens me.

Still, I ask, as I must, "Did Minister T carry this news to His Holiness?"

"He did."

"And what happened?"

"Sakya listened. He meditated for two days on the metaphysics and the practical ramifications of what I'd told him through his minister."

"Finish," I say. "Please just finish."

"On the following day, Sakya died."

"Cadillac infraction," I murmur. Mama's eyes widen. "Forgive me," I say. "What killed him? You used to tell me 'natural causes, but at too young an age for them to seem natural.'"

"That wasn't entirely a lie. Sakya did what came natural to him. He acted on the impulse of his growing despair and his burgeoning sense that if he waited much longer to influence his rebirth, you'd outgrow your primacy as a receptacle for the transfer of his mind-state sequences and he'd lose you as a crucible for compounding the two. So he called upon his mastery of many Tantric practices to drop his body temperature, heart rate, and blood pressure. And when he irreversibly stilled his heart, he passed from our illusory reality into bardo . . . until he awakened again wed to the samvattanika viññana, or evolving consciousness, animating you."

Here I float away from Mama's bower chair and drift a dozen meters across the courtyard to a lovely, low cedar hedge. (In a way that she's never fully understood, Nima Photrang was right about the cause of Sakya Gyatso's death.) I want to pour my guts into this hedge, to heave the burdensome reincarnated essence of the late DL into its feathery silver-green leaves.

Nothing comes up. Nothing comes out. My stomach feels smaller than a piñon nut. My ego, on the other hand, fills the entire tripartite passenger drum of our starship, The Wheel of Time.

Later, I meet Simon Brasswell—Daddy—in a back-tunnel lounge near Johkang Temple for chang and sandwiches. To make this date, of course, I first must visit his guesthouse and ping him at the registry screen, but he agrees to meet me at the Bhurel—as the place is called—with real alacrity. In fact, as soon as we lock-belt into our booth, with squeeze bottles for our drinks and mini-spikes in our sandwiches to hold them to the small cork table, Daddy key-taps payment before I can object. He looks better since his nap, but the violet circles under his eyes lend him a sad fragility.

"I never knew—" I begin.

"That Karen and I divorced because she fell in love with Nyendak Trungpa? Or, I suppose, with his self-vaunted virility and political clout?"

Speechless, I gape at my father.

"Forgive me. Ordinarily, I try not to go the spurned-spouse route."

I still can't speak.

He squeezes his bottle and swigs some barley beer. Then he says, "Do you want what your mama and Minister T want for you—I mean, really?"

"I don't know. I've never known. But this afternoon Mama told me why I ought to want it. And because I ought to, I do. I think."

Daddy studies me with an unsettling mixture of exasperation and tenderness. "Let me ask you something, straight up: Do you think the bhava of Sakya Gyatso, the direct reincarnation of Avalokiteshvara, the ancestor of the Tibetan people, dwells in you as it supposedly dwelt in his twenty predecessors?"

"Daddy, I'm not Tibetan."

"I didn't ask you that." He unspikes and chomps into his Cordyceps, or synthetic caterpillar-fungus, sandwich. Chewing, he manages a quasi-intelligible, "Well?"

"Tomorrow's gold-urn lottery will reveal the truth, one way or the other."

"Yak shit, Greta. And I didn't ask you that, either."

I feel both my tears and my gorge rising, but the latter prevails. "I thought we'd share some time, eat together—not get into a spat."

Daddy chews more sedately, swallows, and re-spikes his "caterpillar" to the cork. "And what else, sweetheart? Avoid saying anything true or substantive?" I show him my profile. "Greta, forgive me, but I didn't sign on to this mission to sire a demigod. I didn't even sign on to it to colonize another world for the sake of oppressed Tibetan Buddhists and their rabid hangers-on."

"I thought you were a Tibetan Buddhist."

"Oh, yeah, born and raised...in Boulder, Colorado. Unfortunately, it never quite took. I signed on because I loved your mother and the idea of spaceflight at least as much as I did passing for a Buddhist. And that's how I got out here more or less seventeen light-years from home. Do you see?"

I eat nothing. I drink nothing. I say nothing.

"At least I've told you a truth," Daddy says. "More than one, in fact. Can't you do the same for me? Or does the mere self-aggrandizing idea of Dalai Lamahood clamp your windpipe shut on the truth?"

I have expected neither these revelations nor their vehemence, but together they work to unclamp something inside me. I owe my father my life, at least in part, and the dawning awareness that he has never stopped caring for me suggests—in fact, requires— that I repay him truth for truth.

"Yes, I can do the same for you."

Daddy's eyes, above their bruised half-circles, never leave mine.

"I didn't choose this life at all," I say. "It was thrust upon me. I want to be a good person, a Bodhisattva possibly, maybe even the Dalai Lama. But—"

He lifts his eyebrows and goes on waiting. A tender twinge of a smile plays about his mouth.

"But," I finish, "I'm not happy that maybe I want these things."

"Buddhists don't aspire to happiness, Greta, but to an oceanic detachment."

I give him my fiercest Peeved Daughter look, but do refrain from eyeball-rolling. "I just need an attitude adjustment, that's all."

"The most wrenching attitude adjustment in the universe won't turn a carp into a cougar, pumpkin." His pet name for me.

"I don't need the most wrenching attitude adjustment in the universe. I need a self-willed tweaking."

"Ah." Daddy takes a squeeze-swig of his beer and encourages me with an inviting gesture to eat.

My gorge has fallen, my hunger reappeared. I eat and drink and, as I do, become unsettlingly aware that other patrons in the Bhurel—visitors, monks—have detected my presence. Blessedly, though, they respect our space.

"Suppose the lottery goes young Trimon's way," Daddy says. "What would make you happy in your resulting alternate life?"

I consider this as a peasant woman of a past era might have done if a friend had asked, just as a game, "What would you do if the King chose you to marry his son?" But I play the game in reverse, sort of, and can only shake my head.

Daddy waits. He doesn't stop waiting, or searching my eyes, or studying me with his irksome unwavering paternal regard. He won't speak, maybe because everything else about him—his gaze, his patience, his presence—speaks strongly of what for years went unspoken between us.

Full of an inarticulate wistfulness, I lean back. "I've told you a truth already," I inform my father. "Isn't that enough for tonight?"

A teenage girl and her mother, oaring subtly with their hands to maintain their places beside us, hover at our table. Even though I haven't seen the girl for several years (while, of course, she hibernized), I recognize her: Distinctive agate eyes in an elfin face identify her at once.

Daddy and I both lever ourselves up from our places, and I swim out to embrace the girl. "Alicia!" Over her shoulder, I say to her mother in all earnestness, "Mrs. Paljor, how good to see you here!"

"Forgive us for interrupting," Mrs. Paljor says. "We've come for the Gold Urn Festival, and we just had to wish you success tomorrow. Alicia wouldn't rest until Kanjur found a way for us to attend."

Kanjur Paljor, Alicia's father, has served since the beginning of our voyage as our foremost antimatter-ice fuel specialist. If anyone could get his secular wife and daughter to U-Tsang for the DL lottery, Kanjur Paljor could. He enjoys the authority of universal respect. As for Alicia, she scrunches her face in embarrassment, as well as unconditional affection. She recalls the many times that I came to Momo House to hold her, and later to her family's Kham Bay rooms to take her on walks or on outings to our art, mathematics, and science centers.

"Thank you," I say. "Thank you."

I hug the girl. I hug her mother.

My father nods and smiles, albeit bemusedly. I suspect that Daddy has never met Alicia or Mrs. Paljor before. Kanjur, the father and husband, he undoubtedly knows. Who doesn't know that man?

The Paljor women depart almost as quickly as they came. Daddy watches them go, with a deep exhalation of relief that makes me hurt for them both.

"I was almost a second mother to that girl," I tell him.

Daddy oars himself downward, back into his seat. "Surely, you exaggerate. Mrs. Paljor looks more than sufficient to the task."

Long before noon of the next day, the courtyard of the Jokhang Temple swarms with levitating lamas, monks, nuns, yogis, and some authorized visitors from the *Kalachakra's* other two passenger bays. I cannot explain how I feel. If Mama's story of Sakya Gyatso's heart attack is true, then I cannot opt out of the gold-urn lottery.

To do so would constitute a terrible insult to his punarbhava, or karmic change from one life vessel to the next, or from his body to mine. Mine, as everyone knows, established its bona fides as a living entity years before Sakya Gyatso died. Also, opting out would constitute a heartless slap in the face of all believers, of all who support me in this enterprise. Still. . . .

Does Sakya have the right to self-direct his rebecoming, or I the right to thwart his will . . . or only the obligation to accede to it? So much self will and worry taints today's ceremony that Larry and Kilkhor, if not Minister T, can hardly conceive of it as deriving from Buddhist tenets at all.

Or can they? Perhaps a society rushing at twenty percent of light-speed toward some barely imaginable karmic epiphany has slipped the surly bonds not only of Earth but also of the harnessing principles of Buddhist Tantra. I don't know. I know only that I can't withdraw from this lottery without betraying a good man who esteemed me in the noblest and most innocent of senses.

And so, in our filigreed vestments, Jetsun Trimon and I swim up to the circular dais to which the attendants of the Panchen Lama have already fastened the gold urn for our name slips.

In set-back vertical ranks, choruses of floating monks and nuns chant as we await the drawing. Our separate retinues hold or adjust their altitudes behind us, both to hearten us and to keep their sight lanes clear. Tiny levitating cameras, costumed as birds, televise the event to community members in all three bays.

Jetsun's boyish face looks at once exalted and terrified.

Lhundrub Gelek, the Panchen Lama, lifts his arms and announces that the lottery has begun. Today he blazes with the bearing and the ferocity of a Hebrew seraph. Tug-monks keep him from rising in gravid slow motion to the ceiling. Abbess Yeshe Yargag levitates about a meter to his right, with tug-nuns to keep her from wandering up, down, or sideways. Gelek reports that name slips for Jetsun Trimon and Greta Bryn Brasswell already drift about in the oversized urn attached to the dais. Neither of us, he says, needs to maneuver forward to reach into the urn and pull out a name-slip envelope. Nor do we need surrogates to do so.

We will simply wait.

We will simply wait . . . until an envelope rises on its own from the urn.

Then Gelek will grab it, open the envelope, and read the name-slip aloud for all those watching in the Temple hall or via telelinks. Never mind that our wait could take hours, and that, if it does, viewers in every bay will volunteer to rejoin the vast majority of our population in ursidormizine slumber.

And so we wait.

And so we wait . . . and finally a small blue envelope rises through the mouth of the crosshatched gold urn. A tug-monk snatches it from the air, before it can descend out of view again, and hands it to the PL.

Startled, because he's nodded off several times over the past fifty-some minutes, Gelek opens the envelope, pulls out the name slip, reads it to himself, and passes it on to Abbess Yargag, whose excited tug-nuns steady her so that she may announce the name of the true Soul Child.

Of course, that the Abbess has copped this honor tells everybody all that we need to know. She can't even speak the name on the slip before many in attendance begin to clap their palms against their shoulders. The upshot of this applause, beyond opening my tear ducts, is a sudden propulsion of persons at many different altitudes about the hall: a wheeling zero-g waltz of approbation.

Years in transit: 95
Computer Logs of Our Reluctant Dalai Lama, age 20

The Panchen Lama, his peers and subordinates in U-Tsang, and secular hierarchs from Amdo and Kham have made my parents starship nobles.

They have bestowed similar, if slightly lesser honors, on Jetsun Trimon's parents and on Jetsun himself, who wishes to serve us colonizers as Bodhisattva, meteorologist, and lander pilot. In any event, his religious and scientific educations proceed in parallel, and he spends as much time in tech training in Kham Bay as he does in the monasteries in U-Tsang.

As for me, I alternate months among our three drums, on a rotation that pleases more of our ghosts than it annoys. I ask no credit for the wisdom of this scheme, though; I simply wish to rule (although I prefer the verb "preside") in a way promoting shipboard harmony and reducing our inevitable conflicts.

Years in transit: 99
Computer Logs of Our Reluctant Dalai Lama, age 24

I've now spent nearly five years in this allegedly holy office. Earlier today, thinking hard about our arrival at Guge, in only a little over seven Earth years, I summoned Minister Trungpa to my quarters.

"Yes, Your Holiness, what do you wish?" he asked.

"To invite everyone aboard the *Kalachakra* to submit designs for a special sand mandala. This mandala will commemorate our voyage's inevitable end and honor it as a fruit of the Hope and Community"—I capitalized the words as I spoke them—"that drove us, or our elders, to undertake this journey."

Minister T frowns. "Submit designs?"

"Your new auditory aids work quite well."

"For a competition?"

"Any voyager, any Kalachakran at all, may submit a design."

"But—"

"The artist monks in U-Tsang, who will create this mandala, will judge the entries blindly to determine our finalists. I'll decide the winner."

Minister T does not make eye contact. "The idea of a contest undercuts one of the themes that you wish your mandala to embody, that of Community."

"You hate the whole idea?"

He hedges: "Appoint a respected Yellow Hat artist to design the mandala. In that way, you'll avoid a bureaucratic judging process and lessen popular discontent."

"Look, Neddy, a competition will amuse everyone, and after a century aboard this vacuum-vaulting bean can, we could all use some amusement."

Neddy would like to dispute the point, but I am the Dalai Lama, and what can he say that will not seem a coddling or a defiant promotion of his own ego? Nothing. (May Chenrezig forgive me, but I relish his discomfiture.) Clearly, the West animates parts of my ego that I should better hide from those of my subjects—a term I loathe—immersed in Eastern doctrines that guarantee their fatalism and docility. Of course, how many men of Minister Trungpa's station and age enjoy carrying out the bidding of a woman a mere twenty-four-years old?

At length he softly says, "I'll see to it, Your Holiness."

"I can see to it myself, but I wanted your opinion."

He nods, his look implying that his opinion doesn't count for much, and takes a deferential step back.

"Don't leave. I need your advice."

"As much as you needed my opinion?"

I take his arm and lead him to a nook where we can sit and talk as intimates. Fortunately, the AG has worked much more reliably all over the ship than it did before my investiture. Neddy looks grizzled, fatigued, and wary, and although he doesn't yet understand why, he has cause for this wariness.

"I want to have a baby," I tell him.

He responds instantly: "I advise you not to, Your Holiness."

"I don't solicit your advice in that area. I'd like you to help me settle on a father for the child."

Neddy reddens. I've stolen his breath. He'd like to make a devastatingly incisive remark, but can't even manage a feeble Ugh. "In case it's crossed your mind, I haven't short-listed you—although Mama once gave you a terrific, if unasked for, recommendation."

Minister T pulls himself together, but he's squeezing his hands in his lap as if to express oil from between them.

"I've narrowed the candidates down to two, Jetsun Trimon and Ian Kilkhor, but lately I've started tilting toward Jetsun."

"Then tilt toward Ian."

"Why?"

And Mama's lover provides me with good, dispassionate reasons for selecting the older man: physical fitness, martial arts ability, maturity, intelligence, learning (secular, religious, and technical), administrative/organizational skills, and long-standing affection for me. Jetsun, not yet twenty, has two or three separate callings that he has not yet had time to explore as fully as he ought, and the difference in our ages will lead many in our community to suppose that I have exercised my power in an unseemly way to bring him to my bed. I should give the kid his space.

I know from private conversations, though, that when Jetsun was ten, an unnamed senior monk in Amdo often employed him as a drombo, or passive sex partner, and that the experience nags at him now in ways that Jetsun cannot easily articulate. Apparently, the community didn't see fit, back then, to exercise its outrage on behalf of a boy not yet officially identified as a Soul Child. Of course, the community didn't know, or chose not to know, and uproars rarely result from awareness of such liaisons, anyway. Isn't a monk a man? I say none of this to Neddy.

"Choose Ian," he says, "if you must choose one or the other."

Yesterday, in Kham Bay, after I extended an intranet invitation to him to come see me about his father, who lies ill in his eggshell pod, Jetsun Trimon called upon me in the upper-level stateroom that I inherited, so to speak, from my predecessor. Jetsun fell on his knees before me, seized my wrist, and put his lips to the beads, bracelet, and watch that I wear about it. He wanted prayers for his father's recovery, and I acceded to this request with all my heart.

Then something occurred that I set down with joy rather than guilt. I wanted more from Jetsun than gratitude for my prayers, and he wanted more than my prayers for his worry about his father or for his struggles to master all his studies. Like me, he wished the solace of the flesh, and as one devoted to compassion, forgiveness, contentment, and the alleviation of pain, I took him to my bed and divested him of his garments and let him divest me of mine. Then we embraced, neither of us trembling, or sweating, or flinching in discomfort or distress, for my quarters hummed at a subsonic frequency with enough warmth and gravity to offset any potential malaise or annoyance. Altogether sweetly, his tenderness matched mine. However—

Like most healthy young men, Jetsun quickly reached a coiled-spring readiness. He quivered on Go.

I rolled over and bestrode him above the waist, holding his arms to the side and speaking with as much integrity as my gnosis of bliss and emptiness could generate. He calmed and listened. I said that I begrudged neither of us this tension-easing union, but that if we proceeded, then he must know that I wanted his seed to enter me, to take root, to turn embryo, and to attain fruition as our child.

"Do you understand?"

"Yes."

"Do you consent?"

"I consent."

"Do you further consent to acknowledge this child and to assist in its rearing on the planet Guge, as well as on this ship?"

He considered these queries. And, smiling, he agreed.

"Then we may advance to the third exalted initiation," I said, "that of the mutual experience of connate joy."

I slid backward over the pliable warmth of his standing phallus and kissed him in the middle of his chest. He reached for me, tenderly, and the AG generators abruptly cut off—suspiciously, it seemed to me. I floated toward the ceiling like a buoyant nixie, too startled to yelp or laugh. Jetsun shoved off in pursuit, but hit a bulkhead and glanced off it horizontally.

It took us a while to reunite, to find enough purchase to

consummate our resolve, and to do so honoring the fact that a resurgence of gravity could injure, even kill, both of us. Nonetheless, we managed, and managed passionately.

The "night" has now passed. Jetsun sleeps, mind eased and body sated.

I sit at this console, lock-belted in, recording the most stirring encounter of my life. Every nerve and synapse of my body, and every scrap of assurance in my soul, tell me that Jetsun and I have conceived: Alleluia.

Years in transit: 100
Computer Logs of Our Reluctant Dalai Lama, age 25

Some history: Early in our voyage, when our AG generators worked reliably, our monks created one sand mandala a year. They did so then, as they do now, in a special studio in the Yellow Hat gompa in U-Tsang. They kept materials for these productions—colored grains of sand, bits of stone or bone, dyed rice grains, sequins—in hard plastic cylinders and worked on their designs over several days. Upon finishing the mandalas, our monks chanted to consecrate them and then, as a dramatic enactment of the impermanent nature of existence, destroyed them by sweeping a brush over and swirling their deity-inhabited geometries into inchoate slurries.

These methods of creating and destroying the mandalas ended four decades into our flight when a gravity outage led to the premature disintegration of a design. A slow-motion sandstorm filled the studio. Grains of maroon, citron, turquoise, emerald, indigo, and blood-red drifted all about, and recovering these for fresh projects required the use of hand-vacs and lots of fussy hand-sorting. Nobody wished to endure such a disaster again. And so, soon thereafter, the monks implemented two new procedures for laying out and completing the mandalas.

One involved gluing down the grains, but this method made the graceful ruination of a finished mandala dicey. A second method involved inserting and arranging the grains into pie-shaped plastic shields using magnets and tech-manipulated "delivery straws," but these tedious procedures, while heightening the praise due the artists, so lengthened the process and stressed the monks that Sakya Gyatso ceased asking for annual mandalas and mandated their fashioning only once every five years.

In any case, today marks our one-hundredth year in flight, and I am fat with a female child who bumps around inside me like those daredevils in old vidped clips who whooshed up and down the sloped walls of special competition arenas on rollers called skateboards.

I think the kid wants out already, but Karma Hahn, my baby doc, tells me she's still much too small to exit, even if the kid does carry on like "a squirrel on an exercise wheel." That metaphor endears both the kid and Karma to me. Because the kid moves, I move. I stroll about my private audience chamber, aka "The Sunshine Hall," in the Potala Palace in U-Tsang. I've voluntarily removed here to show my fellow Buddhists that I am not ashamed of my fecund condition.

Ian announces a visitor, and in walks First Officer Nima Photrang, whom I've not seen for weeks. She has come, it happens, not solely to visit me, but also to look in on an uncle who resides in the nearby Yellow Hat gompa. She has brought a khata, a white silk greeting scarf, even though I already have enough of these damned rags to stitch together a ship cover for the *Kalachakra*. She drapes it around my neck. Laughing, I pull it off and drape it around hers.

"Your design contest spurs on every amateur-artist ghost in Amdo and Kham," Nima says. "If you wish your mandala to further community enlightenment by projecting an image of our future Palace of Hope on Guge, well, you've got a lot of folks worrying away at it—mission fully goosed, if not yet fully cooked."

I realize that Sakya Gyatso, my predecessor, his eye on Tibetan history, called the world toward which we relentlessly cruise "Guge," partly for the g in Gliese 581g. What an observant and subtle man.

"Nima," I ask, "have you submitted a design?"

"No, but you'll probably never guess who intends to."

No, I never will. I gape cluelessly at Nima.

"Captain Xao Songda, our helmsman. He spends enormous chunks of time with a drafting compass and a pen, or at his console refining design programs that a monk in U-Tsang uploaded a while back to Pemako."

Pemako is the latest version of our intranet. I like to use it.

Virtually nightly (stet the pun), it shows me deep-sea sonograms of my jetting squid-kid.

"I hope Captain Xao doesn't expect his status as our shipboard Buzz Lightyear to score him any brownies with the judges."

Nima chortles. "Hardly. He drew as a boy and as a teenager. Later, he designed maglev stations and epic mountain tunnels. He figures he has as good a chance as anyone in a blind judging, and if he wins, what a personal coup!"

"Mmm," I say.

"No, really, you've created a monster, Your Holiness—but, as one of the oldest persons aboard, he deserves his fun, I guess."

We chat some more. Nima asks if she may lay her palm on the curve of my belly, and I say yes. When the brat-to-be surfs my insides like a berserk skateboarder, Nima and I laugh like schoolgirls. By some criteria, I still qualify.

Years in transit: 101
Computer Logs of Our Reluctant Dalai Lama, age 25-26

I return to Amdo to deliver my child. Early in the hundred and first year of our journey, my water breaks. Karma Hahn, my mother, and Alicia and Emily Paljor attend my lying-in, while my father, Ian Kilkhor, Minister Trungpa, and Jetsun perform a nervous do-si-do in an antechamber. I give the guys hardly a thought. Delivering a kid requires stamina, a lot of Tantric focus, and a cooperative fetus, but I've got 'em all and the kid slams on out in under four hours.

I lie in a freshly made bed with my squiddle dozing in a warming blanket against my left shoulder. Well-wishers and family surround us like sentries, although I have no idea what they've got to shield us from: I've never felt safer.

Mama says, "When will you tell us the ruddy shrimp's name? You've kept it a secret eight months past forever."

"Ask Jetsun. He chose it."

Everyone turns to Jetsun, who at twenty-one looks like a fabled Kham warrior, lean and smooth-faced, a flawless bronze sculpture of himself. How can I not love him? Jetsun looks to me. I nod.

"It's . . . it's Kyipa." Like the sweetheart he is, he blushes.

"Ah," Nyendak Trungpa sighs. "Happiness."

"If we all didn't strive so damned hard for happiness," Daddy says, "we'd almost always have a pretty good time."

"You stole that," Mama rebukes him. "And your timing sucks."

From behind those crowded about my babe-cave, a short, sturdy, gray-haired man edges in. I know him as Alicia Paljor's father, Emily Paljor's husband—but Daddy, Ian, and Neddy know him as the chief fuel specialist on our strut-ship and thus a personage of renowned ability. So I assume he's come—like a wise man—to kneel beside and to adore our newborn squiddle. Or has he come just to meet his wife and daughter and fetch them back to their stateroom?

In his ministerial capacity, Neddy says, "Welcome, Specialist Paljor."

"I need to talk to Her Holiness." Kanjur Paljor bows and approaches my bed. "If I may, Your Holiness."

"Of course."

The area clears of everyone except Paljor, Ian Kilkhor, Kyipa, and me. A weight descends—a weight comprising everything that's ever floated free of its moorings during every AG quittage that our strut-ship has ever suffered—and that weight, condensed into one tiny spherical mass, lowers itself onto my baby's back and so onto me, crushing this blissful moment into dust and slivered glass. Ian edges to the top of my bed, but I already know that his strength and his heavy glare will prove impotent against whatever message Kanjur Paljor has brought.

Paljor says, "Your Holiness, I beg your infinite pardon."

"Tell me."

He looks at Ian and then, in petition, at me again. "I'd prefer to deliver this news to you alone, Your Holiness."

"I'm not here," Ian declares. "Proceed on that assumption."

"Regard my agent's simultaneous presence and absence as an enacted mystery or koan," I tell Paljor. "He speaks a helpful truth."

Paljor nods and seizes my free hand. "About fifteen hours ago, I found a serious navigational anomaly while running a fuel-tank check. Before bringing the problem to you, I ran some figures to make sure that I hadn't made a calculation error; that I wasn't just overreacting to a situation of no real consequence." He pauses to touch my Kyipa's blanket. "How much technical detail do you want, Your Holiness?"

"Right now, none. Give me the gist."

"For a little over one hundred and twenty hours, the *Kalachakra* traveled at its top speed at a small angle off our requisite heading."

"How? Why?"

"Before I answer, let me assure you that we've since corrected for this deviation and that we'll soon run true again."

"What do you mean, 'soon'? Why don't we 'run true' now?"

"We do, Your Holiness, in the sense that First Officer Photrang has set us on an efficient angle to intercept our former heading to Guge. But we don't, in the sense that we still must compensate for the unintended divergence."

Ian Kilkhor says, "Tell Her Holiness why this 'unintended divergence' constitutes one huge fucking threat."

Totally appalled, I look back at my bodyguard and friend. "I thought you weren't here! Or did you leave behind just that part of you that views me as an unteachable idiot? Go away, Mr. Kilkhor. Get out."

Kilkhor has the decency and good sense to do as I command. Kyipa, unsettled by my outburst, squirms fretfully on my shoulder.

"The danger," I tell Kanjur Paljor, "centers on fuel expenditure. If we've gone too far off course, we won't have enough antimatter ice left to reach Guge. Have I admissibly described our peril?"

"Yes, Your Holiness." He doesn't fall to one knee, like a magus beside the infant deity Christ, but crouches so that our faces are nearly at a level. "I believe—I think—we have just enough fuel to complete our journey, but at this late stage it could prove a close thing. If there's another emergency requiring any additional course correction, that could place us in danger of—"

"—not arriving at all."

Paljor nods, and consolingly pats Kyipa's playing-card back.

"How did this happen?"

"Human error, I'm afraid."

"Tell me what sort."

"Lack of attention to the telltales that should have prevented this divergence from our heading."

"Whose error? Captain Xao's?"

"Yes, Your Holiness. Nima says his mental state has deteriorated badly over these past few weeks. What she first thought eccentricities, she now views as evidence of age-related mental debilities. He stays awake so long and endures so much stress. And he puts too much faith in the alleged reliability of our electronic systems."

Also, he came to feel that creating a design for my Palace of Hope mandala took precedence over his every other duty on a strut-ship programmed to fly to its destination, with the result that he put himself on auto-pilot too.

"Where is he now?" I ask Paljor.

"Sleeping, under medical supervision—not ursidormizine slumber but bed rest, Your Holiness."

I thank Paljor and dismiss him.

Clutching Kyipa to me, I nuzzle her sweet-smelling face.

Tomorrow, I'll tell Nima to advise her flight crew that they must remain up-phase ghosts until we know for sure the outcomes of Xao's inattention and our efforts to correct for its potential consequences: a headlong rush to nowhere.

Without benefit of lock belts, my daughter Kyipa kicks in her bassinet. I seldom worry about her floating off during AG outages because she loves such spells of weightlessness. She uses them to exercise her limbs—admittedly, with no strengthening resistance— and to explore our stateroom, which boasts Buddha figurines, wall hangings, filigreed star charts, miniature starship models, and other interesting items. At five months, she thinks herself a big finch or a pygmy porpoise. She undulates about, giggling at the currents she creates, or, the AG restored, inches along with her pink tongue tip between her lips and her bum rising and falling like a migrating molehill.

As Dalai Lama (many argue), I should never have borne this squiddle, but Karen, Simon, Jetsun, and Jetsun's mama disagree, and all contribute to her care. Even Minister T acknowledges that conceiving and bearing her has confirmed my sense of the karmic rightness of my Dalai Lamahood more powerfully than any other event to date. Because of this sunny girl, I do stronger, better, holier work.

To those who tsk-tsk when they see Kyipa squirming in my arms, I say:

"Here is my Wheel of Time, my mandala, who has as one purpose to further my evolving enlightenment. Her other purposes she will learn and fulfill in time. So set aside your resentments that you may more easily fulfill yours."

But although I don't fret about Kyipa during gravity outages, I do worry about her future . . . and ours.

Will we safely arrive at the Gliese 581 system? Of the fifty antimatter-ice tanks with which (long before my birth) we started our journey, we've used up and discarded thirty-eight, and Paljor says that we have exhausted nearly half of the thirty-ninth tank, with over five and a half years remaining until our ETA in orbit around Guge. From the outside, our ship begins to resemble a skeleton of its outbound self, the bones of a picked-clean fish. And if the *Kalachakra* makes it at all, as Paljor has speculated, it will slice the issue scarily close.

I stupidly assumed that our eventual shift into deceleration mode would work in our favor, but Paljor cautioned that slowing our strut-ship—so that we do not overshoot Guge, like a golf putt running up to but not beyond its cup—will require more fuel than I supposed. Later he showed me math proving that reaching Guge will require "an incident-free approach"—because our antimatter-ice reserves, the fail-safe tanks with which we began our flight, have already dissolved into the ether slipstreaming by the magnetic field coils generating our plasma shield out front.

Still, I don't believe in shielding our human freight from issues bearing on our survival. Therefore, I've had Minister T announce the fact of this crisis to everyone up-phase and working. Thankfully, general panic has not ensued. Instead, crew members brainstorm stopgap strategies for conserving fuel, and the monks and nuns in U-Tsang pray and chant. Soon enough, when we begin to brake, everyone will arise again, shake off the fog of hibernizing, and learn the truth about our final approach. Then every deck will teem with ghosts preparing to orbit Guge; to assay the habitable wedges between its sun-stuck face and its bleaker side; and to decide which of the two wedges is better suited to settlement.

Years in transit: 102
Computer Logs of Our Reluctant Dalai Lama, age 27

Captain Xao Songda, our deposed captain, died just twelve hours ago. Although Kyipa celebrated her first birthday last week, the man never laid eyes on her.

Xao's "bed rest" turned into pathological pacing and harangues unintelligible to anyone ignorant of Mandarin Chinese. These behaviors—symptomatic of an aggressive type of senility unknown to us—our medicos treated with tranks, placebos (foolishly, I guess), experimental diets, and long walks through the commons of Kham Bay. Nothing calmed him or eased the intensity of his gibbering tirades. I had so wanted Kyipa to meet this man (or the avatar of the self preceding this sorry incarnation), but I could not risk exposing her to one of his abusive rants.

It bears stating, though, that everyone aboard *Kalachakra*, knowing the sacrifices that the captain made for us, forgives him his navigation error. All showed him the honor, courtesy, and patience that he deserved for these sacrifices. Nima Photrang, who assumed his captaincy, believes he and Sakya Gyatso suffered similar personality disintegrations, albeit in different ways. Sakya used Tantric practices to end his life and Xao Songda fell to an Alzheimer's-like scourge, but the effects of sleep deprival, suppressed anxiety, and overwork ultimately caused their deaths.

Xao created designs for my mandala competition, I think, as a way to decompress from these burdens. During the last hours of his illness, Ian Kilkhor searched his quarters for anything that could help us fathom his disease and preserve our memory of him as the intrepid Tibetan Buddhist who carried us within three lights of our destination. However, Ian returned to me with two hundred hand-drawn sketches and computer-assisted designs for my Palace of Hope mandala.

These "designs" appalled and saddened us. The ones Xao hand-drew resemble big multicolored Rorschach blots, and those stemming from his cyber-design programs look like geometrically askew fever dreams. All are pervaded with interlocking claws, jagged teeth, vermiform bodies, and occluded reptilian eyes. None could serve as a model for the mandala of my envisioning.

"I'm sorry," Ian said. "The old guy seems to have swallowed the pituitary gland of a Komodo dragon."

So, given our fuel situation and Captain Xao's death, I've declared a moratorium on mandala-design creation.

Now there is a strong movement afoot—a respectful one—to eject Captain Xao Songda's corpse into the void, one more human collop for the highballing dark. As I've already noted here, we've used this procedure many times before, as a practice coincident with Buddha Dharma and, in this case, as one befitting a helmsman of Xao's stature. But I resist this seeming consensus in favor of a better option: taking the captain to Guge and setting his sinewy body out on an escarpment there, to blacken in its gales and scale in its thaws, our first sacrificial alms to the planet.

One work cycle past, Captain Photrang began to brake the *Kalachakra*. We are four years out from Gliese 581g, and Kanjur Paljor tells me that, unless a meteorite penetrates our plasma shield or some anomalous disaster befalls us, we will reach our destination. Ian observes that we will coast into planetary orbit like a vehicle with an internal-combustion engine chugging into its pit on fumes.

I don't fully twig the analogy, but I get its gist. Alleluia! If only time passed more quickly. . . .

Meanwhile, I keep Kyipa awake and ignore those misguided ghosts advising me to ease her into grave-cave sleep so that time will pass more quickly for her. Jetsun and I enjoy her far too much to send her down. More important, if she stays up-phase most of the rest of our journey, she will learn and grow; and when we descend to the surface of Guge with her, she will have a sharper mind and better motor skills at five or six than any long-term sleeper of roughly similar age.

Every day, every hour, my excitement intensifies. And our ship plows on.

Years in transit: 106
Computer Logs of Our Reluctant Dalai Lama, age 31

Maintenance preoccupies nearly everyone aboard. In less than a week, our strut-ship will rendezvous with Guge and orbit its oblate sun-locked mass. Then we will make several sequential descents to and returns from "The Land of Snow" aboard our lander, The Yak Butter Express.

Jetsun will serve as shuttle pilot for one of these first excursions and as backup on another. He and others perform daily checks on the vehicle in its hangar harnesses, just as other techs strive to ensure the reliability of every mechanical and human component. Our hopes and anxieties contend. At my urging, the Bodhisattvas of U-Tsang go from place to place assisting in our labors and transmitting positive energy to every bay and to all those at work in them.

Twelve hours after Captain Photrang eased *Kalachakra* into orbit around Guge, Minister T comes to me to report that Yellow Hat artists in U-Tsang have finished a sand mandala based on a design that they, not I, chose as our most esteemed entry.

Lucinda Gomez, a teenager from Amdo Bay, has taken the laurel.

Neddy asked the monks to transport the mandala in its pie-shaped shield to Bhava Park, a commons here in Kham Bay, and they do so. A bird camera in the park transmits the mandala's image to public screens and to vidped consoles everywhere. Intricate and colorful, it sits on an easel amid a host of tables and happy Kalachakrans. Because we're celebrating our arrival, I don't watch on a screen but stand in Bhava Park before the thing itself. Banners and prayer flags abound. I seize Kyipa's hand and approach the easel. I congratulate the excited Lucinda Gomez and all the artist monks, and also speak to many onlookers, who attend smilingly to my words.

The Yellow Hats chant verses of consecration that affirm their fulfillment of my charge and then extend to everyone the blessings of Hope and Community implicit in the mandala's labyrinthine central Palace. Kyipa, now almost six, touches the bottom of the encased mandala.

"This is the prettiest," she says.

She has never before seen a finished mandala in its full artifactual glory.

Then the artist monks start to carry the shield from its easel to a tabletop, there to insert narrow tubes into it and send the mandala's fixed grains flying with focused blasts of air—to symbolize, as tradition dictates, the primacy of impermanence in our lives. But before they reach the table, I lift my hand.

"We won't destroy this sand mandala," I declare, "until we've established a viable settlement on Guge."

And everyone around us in Bhava Park cheers. The monks restore the mandala to its easel, a ton of colored confetti drops from suspended bins above us, music plays, and people sing, dance, eat, laugh, and mingle.

Kyipa, holding her hands up to the drifting paper and plastic flakes, beams at me ecstatically.

In our shuttle-cum-lander, we glide from the belly of Kham Bay toward Gliese 581g, better known to all aboard the *Kalachakra* as Guge, "The Land of Snow."

From here, the amiable dwarf star about which Guge swings resembles the yolk of a colossal fried egg, more reddish than yellow-orange, with a misty orange corona about it like the egg's congealed albumin. I've made it sound ugly, but Gliese 581 looks edible to me and quickly trips my hunger to reach the planet below.

As for Guge, it gleams beneath us like an old coin.

In our first week on its surface, we have already built a tent camp in one of the stabilized climate zones of the nearside terminator. Across the tall visible arc of that terminator, the planet shows itself marbled by a bluish and slate-gray crust marked by fingerlike snowfields and glacier sheets.

On the ground, our people call their base camp Lhasa and the rugged territory all about it New Tibet. In response to this naming and to the alacrity with which our fellow Kalachakrans adopted it, Minister Trungpa wept openly.

I find I like the man. Indeed, I go down for my first visit to the surface with his blessing. (Simon, my father, already bivouacs there, to investigate ways to grow barley, winter wheat, and other grains in the thin air and cold temperatures.) Kyipa, of course, remains for now on our orbiting strut-ship—in Neddy's stateroom, which he now shares openly with the child's grandmother, Karen Bryn Bonfils. Neddy and Karen Bryn dote on my daughter shamefully.

Our descent to Lhasa won't take long, but, along with many others in this second wave of pioneers, I deliberately drop into a meditative trance. I focus on a photograph that Neddy gave me after the mandala ceremony at the arrival celebration, and I recall his words as he presented it.

"Soon after you became a teenager, Greta, I started to doubt your commitment to the Dharma and your ability to stick."

"How tactful of you to wait till now to tell me," I said, smiling.

"But I never lost a deeper layer of faith. Today, I can say that all my unspoken doubt has burned off like a summer meadow mist." He gave me the worn photo—not a hardened d-cube—that now engages my attention.

In it, a Tibetan boy of eight or nine faces the viewer with a broad smile. He holds before him, also facing the viewer, a baby girl with rosy cheeks and eyes so familiar that I tear up in consternation and joy. The eyes belong to my predecessor's infant sister, who didn't live long after the capturing of this image.

The eyes also belong to Kyipa.

I meditate on this conundrum, richly. Soon, after all, the Yak Butter Express will set down in New Tibet.

STARSHIP WITH 24 DROP TANKS
(mid-flight configuration)

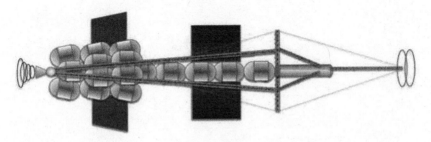

Figure 4. The *Kalachakra* is an antihydrogen-powered starship that sheds its fuel tanks and radiators—required to keep the antihydrogen cold—during flight. (Image courtesy of Geoff Landis.)

SOLAR AND BEAMED ENERGY SAILS

Les Johnson

Les Johnson's concern for the human future is readily apparent. He has written widely about the subject, suggesting high-tech methods for preserving the environment while we solve the global energy problem, especially in his collaboration with fellow physicist Gregory Matloff and one-time NASA artist C Bangs to produce Harvesting Space for a Greener Earth *(2014). He is also a science fiction writer, speculating on possible futures in* Mission to Methone *(2018) and with frequent collaborator Travis Taylor, in* Saving Proxima *(2021).*

When we speculate about traveling to the stars, we tend to think in terms of giant nuclear-powered rocket engines. And, admittedly, if we succeed in making the journey, they may indeed prove to be the key. But not necessarily. In fact, Johnson suggests that softer power may be the ultimate answer. Sailing vessels showed the way for early exploration on the world's oceans. Their days may not be over.

Johnson is a physicist at NASA's George C. Marshall Space Flight Center, where he serves as the principal investigator for America's first two interplanetary space missions to be propelled by solar sails, and is one of the editors of this book.

❂ ❂ ❂

WE CAN'T FEEL IT, but the light from the Sun is pushing on us. It's a small push, less than an ounce per square football field. Whenever we are in sunlight, or any light, we are being pushed. This solar pressure is much smaller than the other forces we experience in our everyday lives. The force of the wind from the room air conditioner vent is far stronger than the force we experience in full sunlight. It is so small that very sensitive instruments are required to measure it. And it can only be measured in a vacuum because the various forces around us will otherwise swamp the effect. But solar pressure is real, it is constant, and it can be used to propel a spacecraft to incredible speeds.

About four hundred years ago, Johannes Kepler observed that the tail of a comet appeared to be created by some sort of cosmic breeze and postulated that this breeze could be used to move ships in space in a manner similar to which the sailing ships of his day were propelled by wind. While Kepler was wrong about the nature of these cosmic winds, he was correct in his observation that something coming from the Sun, which we now know is sunlight itself, can be used to move a spacecraft.

An earthly sail moves a ship by transferring the momentum of the wind to the ship by reflecting it from a sail. The force exerted on the sail pushes the ship, causing it to move. In physics, momentum is defined as the product of mass times velocity. Lots and lots of air molecules, each having mass and some velocity, reflect from a sail and transfer their momentum to it. The ship then begins to move, its momentum coming from the wind.

In 1923, the physicist Arthur Compton observed that photons (particles of light) have momentum even though they have no rest mass. In other words, these massless particles that we call light have momentum even though they would have no mass if we could catch one and slow it down to weigh it. This is yet another weird property of light—but one that will be very useful for taking us to the stars.

Imagine a large, very thin, lightweight and very highly reflective sail deployed in space for the sole purpose of reflecting sunlight. We've just imagined a solar sail and they are far from imaginary. Solar sails reflect sunlight, transferring the tiny momentum of each reflected photon to the sail, causing the sail to move. The force is tiny. At the Earth's distance from the Sun (ninety-three million miles), the force from sunlight is about five pounds per square mile. In other words, we'd have to have a sail area of one square mile to feel five pounds of force. For comparison, just one of the Space

Shuttle's main engines produces about five hundred thousand pounds of thrust. The primary difference is that the shuttle's engines can only produce this thrust for a very short period of time before running out of fuel while a solar sail can produce thrust as long as it remains in sunlight. And since the distances involved in space travel are so large, the sail will remain in sunlight for a very long time no matter its destination.

In this case, the space shuttle engine is the hare and the solar sail is the tortoise. Chemical rockets will never take us to the stars, but solar sails might. It is important to note that while solar sails may one day take us to Alpha Centauri, they will never get us off the surface of the Earth. To lift from the surface of the Earth, we need a propulsion system that can produce more thrust than the rocket weighs. Chemical rockets are capable of producing these high thrust levels; solar sails cannot.

Before we start building our solar sail-propelled starship, we need to discuss a few more critical issues that will affect our design. First of all, the sail will still be subject to Newton's Second Law, which states, "a body of mass (m) subject to a force (F) undergoes an acceleration that has the same direction as the force and a magnitude that is directly proportional to the force and inversely proportional to the mass." In other words, to get a mass to accelerate, we need to apply a force. In order to get the accelerations needed to achieve very high speeds, such as those required for interstellar travel, we need a large force or a small mass, or in this case, we need both.

Newton's Second Law requires our solar sail design to be very large so the sail can capture as much sunlight as possible in order to maximize solar photon thrust. It also requires us to use very lightweight materials so that we can make our ship as low mass as possible. The sail must also be highly reflective so that we can capture as much momentum from each photon as possible.

Is there anything we can do to increase the force acting on the sail from the sunlight? Even though we have the benefit of time, five pounds of thrust per square mile is ridiculously small. We would require a sail almost one hundred thousand square miles in area to equal the thrust produced by one space shuttle engine. Such a sail would have roughly the same surface area as Alabama and

Mississippi combined! Surely we can do something to increase our thrust so that we can make a smaller sail.

It turns out that another interesting fact about sunlight allows us to do just this. We can dramatically increase the force acting on the solar sail by flying closer to the Sun thanks to a property of sunlight called The Inverse Square Law. According to this law, if we move an object twice the distance from the light source, it will receive only one quarter of the illumination. Two times the distance (2) means one-fourth (¼) the illumination—two squared is four. If we move out to four times the distance from the Sun, the illumination drops to one sixteenth of the previous amount—four squared is sixteen. Less illumination translates directly into less force. Fortunately, we can use this geometric property to our benefit by moving closer to the Sun. If we reduce the distance to ½ its previous value, we get four (4) times the force. If we reduce it ¼, then we get sixteen (16) times the force. And if we get sixteen times the force per square mile, then we can reduce the overall surface area of the sail by the same factor. And when we are talking about sails the size of US states, a factor of sixteen is significant.

This all sounds great, but are solar sails real? Have they been built and tested in space? Has anyone actually used one for sending a spacecraft anywhere? Yes, yes, and yes!

Until the 1970s, Kepler's vision and Compton's physics were good science but for space travel they were primarily an intellectual curiosity. With the anticipated return of Halley's Comet in 1986, NASA commissioned a study of the feasibility of using a solar sail to rendezvous with the comet. The project never got off the ground, but it did get many space scientists and engineers thinking about solar sailing as something real, and the pace of sail technology development accelerated. The first big step was taken by Russia with the launch of their Znamya mirror in 1993. Znamya was a large, lightweight mirror flown in space to test the idea of using reflected sunlight to illuminate large areas on the ground at night. The mirror was made from very lightweight reflective materials and looked, for all practical purposes, like a solar sail.

In the late 1990s, the Europeans entered the picture with the ground-based development of a one hundred foot sail manufactured by the German company DLR (Deutschen Zentrums für Luft- und

Raumfahrt). Though the sail never left the laboratory, it inspired NASA to develop a similar capability during the early 2000s that culminated in the testing of two different solar sails in the world's largest vacuum chamber, which is located at the NASA Glenn Research Center's Plumbrook Station. The two solar sails were one hundred feet in diameter, made from materials thinner than a human hair, and autonomously deployed under space vacuum conditions to test their space worthiness. Figure 5 shows the sail developed for NASA by L'Garde, Inc. just after a deployment test in the vacuum chamber.

Figure 5. NASA and L'Garde, Inc. tested a 100-foot diameter prototype solar sail in the mid-2000's. Shown in the picture is the fully deployed solar sail with four of the sail engineers standing in the foreground to show scale. (Image courtesy of NASA.)

Japan took the next major step in solar sailing by actually flying a sail in space and using it as a primary propulsion system. The IKAROS (Interplanetary Kite-craft Accelerated by Radiation Of the Sun) was launched in May 2010 on a trajectory that will take it on a voyage near Venus. Though smaller than the NASA and DLR ground demonstration sails, the sixty-five foot diameter sail showed the world that solar sails can be used in space for propulsion. Figure 6 shows the IKAROS in space after deployment.

Figure 6. The Japanese Aerospace Exploration Agency launched the IKAROS solar sail on a mission to Venus in 2010. Shown in the figure is an actual picture of the IKAROS sail after deployment taken by a small robotic camera ejected from the spacecraft during flight. (Image courtesy of the Japan Aerospace Exploration Agency.)

In 2010, NASA launched the NanoSail-D into low Earth orbit. NanoSail-D, (where D stands for *drag*) is not a functioning solar sail since it is not using the force of sunlight in a controlled manner for propulsion. The ten-square-foot NanoSail-D might instead be a space demonstration of more conventional windsailing. As NanoSail-D skimmed through the Earth's uppermost atmosphere, the wind created by its passing caused the spacecraft to slow and eventually re-enter. The wind caused drag, giving NanoSail-D its name.

Other groups are planning small sail missions that will actually use sunlight pressure for propulsion. Chief among them is the Planetary Society's LightSail-1. Similar in weight to NanoSail-D, LightSail-1 will have a sail three times larger and be capable of pointing toward the Sun in order to use the sunlight for propulsion. CU Aerospace and The University of Surrey have similar sails in development.

Following the successes of IKAROS and NanoSail-D, there has been renewed interest in solar sailing, and several countries are considering the development of even more ambitious sails for use in missions throughout the solar system. We have a long way to go, however, before we will have a sail that can be used to send a spacecraft beyond the edge of the solar system into the abyss between the stars.

Some may be wondering how a solar sail, which derives its thrust from sunlight, can possibly take a spacecraft from one solar system to the next. After all, sunlight gets rather dim and is almost nonexistent when we get beyond the orbit of Pluto—let alone when we are in true interstellar space. Without sunlight, there is no force acting on the sail, hence no acceleration. So, how can it be done? There are two answers: 1) solar sails with very close solar approaches and 2) laser-augmented solar sails.

As discussed above, the thrust on a solar sail increases as its distance from the Sun decreases. Some pioneering work by Drs. Gregory Matloff and Roman Kezerashvili shows that an approximately one mile diameter solar sail spacecraft weighing no more than seven hundred pounds passing very, very close to the Sun, within about nine million miles, could achieve a solar-system exit velocity of two hundred and fifty miles per second. A craft traveling this fast would pass the Earth in four days, Jupiter in twenty one days and reach the Alpha Centauri system in just over three thousand years. By comparison, the fastest rocket we've ever sent into space won't cover the distance to the Alpha Centauri system for another seventy-four thousand years! By increasing the sail size, and keeping the payload mass the same, we can see an engineering path to building a sail that could cover this immense distance in about a thousand years. For you and me, there isn't much difference between a thousand years and seventy four thousand years. But in the lifetime of civilizations, the difference between these numbers is significant. We have recorded history going back a thousand years and there is no reason to assume that we won't have similar records going forward; however, seventy-four thousand years goes back well beyond the origins of human civilization.

You might have noticed another problem with the relatively near-term solar sail—it weighs only seven hundred pounds. Unfortunately, to carry a larger mass—millions of tons are required to carry and sustain humans on such a voyage—would require a solar sail of immense proportions (think the size of continents) made of incredible materials ("unobtainium" comes to mind). While such sails don't violate any known laws of physics, we currently are almost clueless regarding how to engineer them.

One approach to creating these massive sails is to build them in space, so that they don't have to experience the stresses of riding a rocket to get them there. This would solve two problems at the same time. First of all, the rocket launch will be the most stressful of the mechanical environments which the sail must be designed to survive. Rockets are not known for slow and graceful acceleration or for being a smooth ride. Quite the opposite is true; consequently, building a gossamer sail strong enough to ride on a rocket will be difficult. Second, the manufacturing of extremely large, lightweight and fragile solar sails in Earth's gravity will be nearly impossible. The forces experienced by just being here on the surface may be sufficient to cause tears in the sail. Overcoming the stresses experienced as the sail is folded and packaged, as well as surviving the effects of Earth's gravitational acceleration, will likely be both complex and expensive. When compared to the Earth, the space environment is much kinder to solar sails.

Building sails in space will not be so easy either. Manufacturing anything in space implicitly assumes there is some sort of facility or location where the construction will take place. This place itself must be built and launched. Then there's the raw materials part. Sails, though conceptually simple, are anything but simple when we consider their subsystems and components: lightweight, highly reflective membranes; lightweight structures; moving parts for attitude control; electronics for deployment, attitude control, and navigation; plus many others. All of these, at least here on Earth, come through an extensive supply chain all the way from the extraction of the raw materials from which they are made to the final fabrication in a factory somewhere in the world. It's only after the system integrator orders all the right parts that the engineers and technicians can even begin putting it together. All of this would have to be re-created in space to enable in-space manufacturing of a very large solar sail.

There is another approach that takes advantage of the Earth's well-established manufacturing infrastructure and the unique environment of space to solve the manufacturing and launch problems: build the sail on Earth, but make it more robust—thicker—than the mission requires and make the extra thickness out of materials that won't easily tear when in the Earth's gravity and that will not damage easily during launch. But, design the more robust sail so that the heaviest part will evaporate when exposed to a selected portion of the Sun's ultraviolet light—which only happens when we are above the Earth's atmosphere. Voila! The thick and heavy sail that was easier to make and launch quickly becomes the wispy, lightweight sail needed for rapid propulsion through interstellar space.

This might just work.

The single largest constraint on an interstellar spacecraft propelled by a solar sail is the "solar" part. If the ship must get all of its thrust from the Sun, then it is constrained to do so before it passes the orbit of Jupiter (in just a couple of weeks) because the Sun gets very dim at this point and the additional thrust the ship would obtain from the ever-more-distant Sun is minimal. It is very difficult to get enough energy from the Sun for a voyage to another star—especially in a few days or weeks. How then can we build a sail and continue to use light pressure to accelerate even after the sail is beyond the reach of sunlight?

Lasers may solve this problem. A laser provides a tightly focused beam of light across large distances and might be capable of providing enough light to continue pushing our sail during its journey through interstellar space. An interesting approach to using laser energy for interstellar solar sailing was described by the late physicist, engineer and author extraordinaire, Dr. Robert Forward. As early as 1962, Forward was publishing technical papers describing how a future sail might be pushed through deep interstellar space by a powerful laser orbiting the Sun.

On the scales that we typically use lasers, say in the few tens of feet or less, the beam appears to be tightly focused without significant divergence, or beam spread. But over millions of miles, even the best laser beam will diverge and become more diffuse. In order to keep a relatively small beam focused on our interstellar sail, we will need to build a six hundred mile diameter focusing lens at about the orbit of Jupiter through which we will shine our laser.

Using a spacecraft of similar weight to the one described above for the Sun-only solar sail, and using a sail of about the same size, Forward calculated that a sixty-five Gigawatt laser could accelerate our sail to a velocity of one-tenth the speed of light. This would enable our spacecraft to reach Alpha Centauri in only a little more than forty years after launch. A substantial improvement over three thousand years!

Unfortunately, we don't know how to build continuously operating sixty-five GW lasers, nor do we know how to build six hundred mile diameter lenses orbiting the Sun near Jupiter. Our physics is once again ahead of our engineering—but we won't let that stop us!

Forward went on to show that a sail craft of much more interesting (from the point of view of future human interstellar exploration) sizes, say six hundred miles in diameter and weighing almost two million pounds, could have the same forty-year trip time if a seven-Terawatt laser were used (Figure 7). I should point out that the annual total power output for the human race is approximately 1 TW. Again, there is no physical reason this cannot be done. The challenge, as physicists are often fond of saying, is in the engineering. BUT IT IS POSSIBLE.

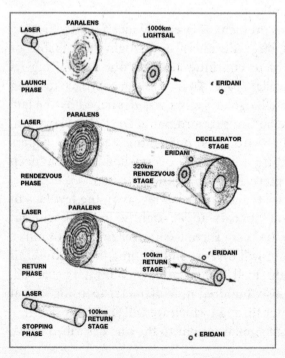

Figure 7. Robert Forward's interstellar light sail concept shown as it appeared in his Advanced Space Propulsion Study for the Air Force Astronautics Laboratory in 1986.

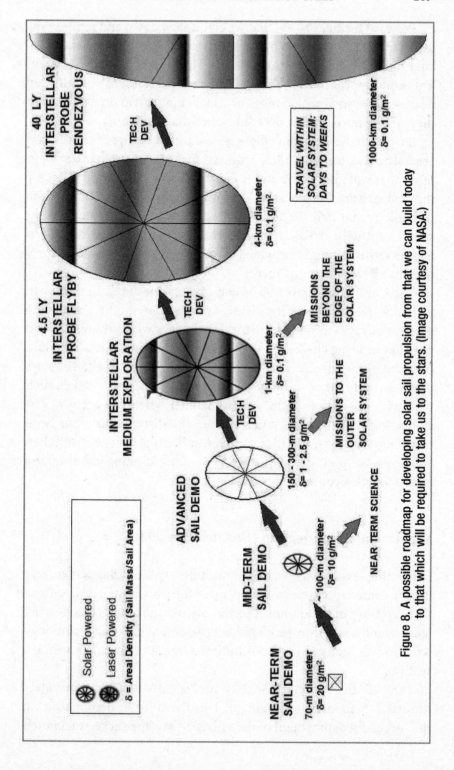

Figure 8. A possible roadmap for developing solar sail propulsion from that we can build today to that which will be required to take us to the stars. (Image courtesy of NASA.)

Forward further proved that we could slow down and rendezvous with a target star's planets by having a detachable inner sail that uses laser light reflected from the outer ring (of the sail) to slow it down. This same approach could be used to send spacecraft to virtually any nearby star system with commensurately longer trip times—though they will be measured in decades rather than millennia.

So how do we get from where we are today, flying solar sails that are only a fraction of the size required for true interstellar travel, to those that will give us the stars? First of all, we start flying them for more near-term exploration of our own solar system. As the technology matures, we build increasingly large and lighter-weight sails, eventually crossing the threshold to use beamed energy to augment their sunlight provided thrust. Figure 8 shows one strategy for getting from here to "there."

Solar and laser-driven sails can give us the stars. But, as with virtually every other propulsion system that might enable the greatest voyages in human history, their sizes will be immense and pose engineering challenges we cannot yet imagine. But what could be more fitting for the future explorers than journeying to the stars using the only other thing in the universe that already makes such trips with regularity—light! Just remember when you are next out stargazing that the light you see from the distant starts has been traveling for years, decades, or even millennia before it touched you—yes, before it gently pushed you—into thinking about taking such a journey yourself.

※ ※ ※

Supplemental Information *(Updated May 2021)*

Since this essay was written, multiple space solar sails were demonstrated in space; two deep space missions using solar sails as their primary method of propulsion began, one of which is nearing launch; and a major research project to develop laser sail technology was funded. Many of the goals outlined in Figure 8 are becoming a reality.

In 2015, the Planetary Society successfully flew their privately funded 345-square-foot LightSail 1 in Earth orbit, demonstrating the successful deployment of the sail. 2017 saw the successful launch and Earth orbit deployment of The University of Surrey's InflateSail, and in 2019, LightSail 2 reached space. LightSail 2 was similar to LightSail 1 in composition and size, but it had the added capability to maneuver the sail and demonstrate solar propulsion.

Building upon the success of the NanoSail-D, NASA began the development of what will be the first US deep space mission propelled by a solar sail, Near-Earth Asteroid Scout (NEA Scout). NEA Scout will be launched into space by NASA's Space Launch System on its maiden flight, from which it will be released in a trajectory toward the moon. As it flies by the moon, the 925-square-foot NEA Scout sail will propel an instrumented spacecraft from the Earth-Moon system on a two-year mission to rendezvous and fly by an asteroid, taking high-resolution images when it arrives. Following a few years later, in 2025, NASA's Solar Cruiser mission will demonstrate the capability of a very large solar sail, nearly 18,000 square feet, to propel a spacecraft toward the sun and maintain its position along the Sun-to-Earth line sunward of the Earth-Sun Lagrange point, L1.

Hoping to leapfrog interstellar travel from the indefinite future to the mid-term, the Breakthrough Starshot is funding the development of technologies that could enable a very lightweight spacecraft (weighing only a few grams) to accelerate to nearly twenty percent the speed of light using Earth-based high energy lasers reflecting from a relatively small sail. Funded by billionaire philanthropist Yuri Milner, the hope is that technologies enabling interstellar flight can leapfrog generations of incremental development and become a reality in our lifetimes.

The future of solar sailing is bright. (Pun intended!) Stay tuned . . .

THE BIG SHIP AND THE WISE OLD OWL

Sarah A. Hoyt

Everybody loves a good mystery. In this one, Sarah Hoyt sets us up with a secret hidden within the nursery rhymes preserved for kids on a multigenerational starship. Why, one goes on to wonder, would anyone need to hide information on a starship anyhow?

❁ ❁ ❁

SOMETIMES I WONDER what would have happened if I hadn't been twenty and faced with the oldest problem a girl could have. I was being courted by two men and I didn't know which I preferred.

Except that courted might be too strong a word, since there was very little about it that was romantic. We'd grown up together, were of similar status and background, and each of us was licensed to enter into a marriage producing two children. Still, I had two men who wished to marry me.

And I didn't know which one to pick. They'd both been my friends forever and whichever way you looked at it, none of us was going to set the ship on fire, as the saying went. Which was a good thing, since rumor had it that this was what Ciar's parents had planned to do before they were captured and executed. Not that I knew for sure or that Ciar knew anything about his parents. He'd been born from a surrogate years after they'd died and he'd been brought up in a creche for children who'd been created from stored ova and sperm—to continue the lines of people who'd been executed or died before having children. But there was a rumor about his parents, that they'd been dangerous subversives. I'd always thought it had been used to explain Ciar's tendency to get into all sorts of trouble.

Ennio, my other suitor, and I had grown up with our parents. Ciar didn't seem to envy us. And his parents didn't come up beyond the occasional joke among the three of us.

At twenty Ciar was a linguist and Ennio was a teacher's assistant second class, with a nice space in the bachelor quarters, and a cozy if unexciting job maintaining and programming the educational computers. Which he was doing right now—the maintaining part—halfway under one of the brightly colored terminals in classroom 3A, for the beginners' class.

His voice emerged muffled from beneath the terminal—a bulky, padded unit, designed to withstand the clumsy movements of toddlers. "What I want to know," he said, as his upper body moved, indicating that he'd somehow twisted one arm up inside the machine, "is how much they feed these kids that they can afford to shove half their nutritional allowance—" he paused and grunted— "inside these machines, around the sensi-screens."

Ciar laughed. He was lying across two of the terminals, staring at the ceiling, his straight black hair falling back from his face with its aquiline nose and sharp blue eyes. His status was about the same as Ennio's. He worked as a third class linguist. Most of his days were spent deep in the archives of the language department which was translating all the documents we'd brought from Earth into the language we spoke now. Though no one ever said how many generations had passed, it stood to reason there had to be many, since my grandfather's grandfather had been born aboard. They'd brought aboard, originally, people from many countries. Even though they'd made English the official language, many words and some structure had ported over from the languages of the other people on the ship.

So, the administrators wanted to make sure all our records, all our history and all our scientific knowledge stayed understandable, for when we landed.

Ennio emerged from under the terminal, a sticky lump of some unidentified substance in his hand. "It should work now," he muttered, as he walked across to drop the lump in the disposal chute before washing his hands in the little sink in the corner, which, being set for toddlers, he had to bend almost double to use.

"I could help you," I said. I hadn't qualified for intellectual work, as the men had. Not that my IQ tests were inferior to theirs, but I had failed what Ciar called the *restlessness test*. He said that forced to endure the jobs he and Ennio performed, mostly confined to a single room or a suite of rooms day after day, I would have gone quietly insane. Which I supposed was why I'd been apprenticed to the maintenance crew, where every day brought something new. One day I might be repairing agricultural machines and the next working to remove the socks some toddler had flushed down the toilet on division D before they made all toilets on division F fountain to the ceiling. "I repair machines all the time."

Ennio wrinkled his nose at me, his mop of reddish-brown hair standing up from being cut so short. There was a fad onboard for longish hair, so of course Ennio wore his almost too short. "This is hardly repair," he said. "Just clean up."

The terminal powered up when he tried it and he said, "Right. Now to reprogram it with all the nursery rhymes again."

Ciar sat up, curious. "Nursery rhymes? You teach them those?"

"At this age it's the best way to get them to read. I just need to make sure they come up and match the sound," he said, picking things on the screen, till the screen displayed a series of lines, which were sounded out, aloud, in a babyish voice.

> The big ship sails on the vacuum oh,
>   the vacuum oh, the vacuum oh,
> Oh the big ship sails on the vacuum oh,
> It will not sail on forever.
> The captain said it will reach Alpha Centauri oh
> When ten generations are over.
> The big ship will reach Alpha Centauri
> Where our new home will be.
> It will reach Alpha Centauri when
>   ten generations are over.
> We will all live in Alpha Centauri
> In the world most like Earth.
> We will all live in Alpha Centauri
> After the eleventh generation's birth.

He pushed a few buttons and went on to another screen, where a comical owl hooted, flew away, and then the rhyme flashed:

> *A wise old owl lived down on area C.*
> *The more he saw the less he spoke,*
> *The less he spoke the more he heard.*
> *Why can't we all be like that wise old bird?*
> *Find him and ask politely,*
> *He'll tell you the way to Alpha Centauri.*
> *When we've all forgotten,*
> *He will still be*
> *Keeping the time and path to Alpha Centauri.*

Ennio pushed the screen again, but Ciar was sitting up and staring at it. He spoke over the next rhyme, "Those aren't right."

I looked at him. "Of course they are. Don't you remember?" We'd all learned the rhymes at our mothers' knees—well, except Ciar, who presumably had learned them at the creche-teacher's knees. And then we'd learned to read them in school.

"I remember," he said, frowning quickly at me. He pulled at the collar of his grey tunic. "Look, I know those are the rhymes we learned, but they aren't the *right* rhymes."

Ennio turned around. "What do you mean?"

As often happened, Ciar was struggling to form words. It was funny that the one of us who specialized in linguistics was the one who would often find himself struggling for explanations when talking to us. Perhaps because he was the only one of us with a truly intellectual profession?

"I was looking at nursery rhymes today. One of the books was stored on board from early on. It's part of the historical collection and I don't think many people looked at it since it came in." He frowned. "They had those rhymes, but they're completely different. Nothing about Alpha Centauri or generations or . . . division C."

"Maybe they adapted the rhymes for life on board," Ennio said.

But Ciar was still frowning.

"They might have, Ciar," I said. "To make it relevant."

"Why would they?" he said. "They haven't removed 'owl' from there, and the only things we know of owls are in books from

Earth. I presume there are owl embryos frozen somewhere in the ship, but..."

"But the decision of whether to ever grow them depends on the level of life development we find in the destiny world," I said. We'd all learned, from very young, that the world we were headed towards was, so far as they could tell from old Earth, the twin of the home world. It was supposed to have water and atmosphere and probably be much like Earth. But the question was, did it have the same level of biodevelopment? We'd brought a sample of every bird and animal and plant, or at least all the ones anyone could think of. If we found a very primitive world, or one where life hadn't yet taken hold beyond single cell organisms, then we would set about reconstructing the ecology of Earth. But if we found that it had the same chain of life, and that we were compatible with it and could use it for sustenance, then we would not bring back the animals of Earth, except perhaps as curiosities in well-guarded zoos.

"Yeah, but we still learn about them," Ciar said. "And cows that go moo. You know, until I caught a reference in an ancient manuscript, I thought cows were about the size of a chicken."

Chickens and fish being the only animal life aboard, I'd thought so too until this moment. "You mean they're not?"

He shook his head, and his hands sketched improbable dimensions. Now Ennio was frowning. "So...The rhymes were altered. I wonder why?"

"I think..." Ciar was frowning. "Well... I've read a lot of things from when the ship was first launched. Part of the reason they established the captain with absolute power and the administrators reporting only to him is that they were very afraid there would be a mutiny and we would either destroy our knowledge base, or that we would overrun the resources of the ship."

I shrugged. I'd got up and was looking over Ennio's shoulder at the screen changing in multicolored patterns of lights as syllables appeared. There was, for instance, the bells song. "Find me if you can, toll the bells of C and N...." I remembered singing it with my class in my first year in school. "So, we didn't mutiny and we didn't overrun the resources of the ship," I said.

"Yes, but I think they changed the nursery rhymes, so that we would have something to remind us if we forgot."

"To remind us of what?" Ennio asked. "That the wise old owl keeps his mouth shut? Or that we're going to Alpha Centauri? Honestly, Ciar." He turned to me, "There's a dance tonight at the bachelor's dorm, and I was wondering if you—"

"You don't understand," Ciar said, his voice in the slow pedantic tone he used when he thought he was schooling us. "The thing is that nursery rhymes are the most linguistically conservative bit of language. Not just in terms of how exactly they get passed on, but they retain fossilized references and pronunciations for centuries after they've died out of any normal use. They would be a . . . they are a superb medium for encoding instructions. But instructions for what?"

"For people who've forgotten that we're on our way to Alpha Centauri and who, probably, think that this is the only world that exists." He shook his head. "Now, Nia," he said, looking at me. "Will you go with me to the dance?"

I said yes, mostly, I think, to try to get Ciar to let go of the crazy subject of nursery rhymes. When he got an idea in his head, he tended to hold onto it like a well-placed rivet. And this one was truly one of the strangest ones he'd come up with.

But when I looked up to see if he was upset or interested, I met with a frown, and his eyes half-closed, but he was staring into something we couldn't see. "Oh, the dance," he said, slowly. "Yes. I'll see you two there."

He walked out through the terminals, towards the door and Ennio and I met each other's eyes and laughed. "Now, do you suppose he thinks I invited him to the dance?" he asked.

"I don't know," I said. "He seems to think both of us did."

Ennio shook his head. "Ciar has a bug in his processor again!"

I confess I completely forgot about Ciar and the nursery rhymes. Unlike the men, I still lived with my parents. It wasn't that I wasn't getting enough ration coupons to live alone, but I disliked the single women dormitory. Too much cackle and giggling, too much scent and makeup. My mom shook her head when I complained and said women had always been like that, and always would be, but frankly, I owned a mirror and could see my face as well as the next person. My face was not as soft and round as I'd have liked. I had a broad forehead, and dark blond hair. The best that could be said about me was that I didn't cause men to run screaming into the night, and that I had two guys who wished to court me—even if they were not exactly potential heartthrobs. But makeup didn't improve my looks and frankly I didn't think either of my two very odd suitors would notice, unless I put blue circles on my cheeks and dyed my hair purple. They seemed to enjoy my company and talking to me, more than actually looking at me.

Besides, I was mom and dad's only daughter. Mom had got into some trouble when she was young. I'd never found out exactly what it had been, but whatever it was meant she was only licensed for one child, so here I was. And it didn't seem fair to move out before I absolutely needed to.

Mom insisted on fussing over my going to the dance with Ennio, and finding me one of the dresses she'd worn when she was young and which she hadn't traded in for material credits. It looked very odd on me, because though our bodies are about the same size, mom is a beautiful woman, delicate and blond. I'm . . . not. But she said I looked beautiful in the pink, ruffled top and skirt, and she found me the shoes that went with them. Though she told me I could do better than Ennio, she approved of my playing the field.

But she didn't mention Ciar and I didn't think of him, until I got to the dance. Both Ennio and Ciar were standing at the entrance, looking out with anxious expressions.

The way their faces cleared when they saw me approaching did my heart good, but I soon saw that they were relieved for completely different reasons, as Ennio looked towards Ciar and said, "See, I told you she was fine. You and your paranoia."

"I'm not paranoid," Ciar said, in an urgent whisper. "And don't talk about it here. And I have to show you something."

Ennio lowered his eyebrows, as his features shaped into a frown. "You are insane. This is a dance. Nia came here to dance."

I could see, past his shoulders, the dimmed lights, and couples gyrating to the convoluted strains of something that—from my classical music history—I knew should be a waltz, but wasn't. Not quite. They called it the Cuddle Bug, but really, like the waltz in its time it was an excuse for young people to hold each other and spend time together in a form the population planners might otherwise find inappropriate in unmarried couples.

Ennio put his hand on my forearm to guide me inside, but Ciar was shaking his head, making his hair flop in front of his eyes. "Come. Forget the dance. This is more important." His voice got louder, as he got more agitated, and I could see Ennio thought that if he were to refuse to listen to whatever Ciar had to say, Ciar was quite likely to cause a scene and then we'd all be investigated for—at the very least—antisocial activities.

"You just want to undercut my one chance to dance with Nia," Ennio said, in the tone of someone trying desperately to turn the whole thing into a joke.

"No," Ciar said. "No, this is important."

And it was clear that to him it was. Not just a joke, not just a side pursuit, not just a way to take the shine off his rival. At any rate, I told myself, it was impossible that either of them was that serious about their rivalry. First, they were as good friends as two young men of their solitary temperaments could be. And second, suppose one of them won my hand. The other one could find a woman just as good looking and with as good prospects on any given evening, at the single women's dormitory. Frankly, I thought the only reason they both courted me was because it allowed all three of us to spend time together, as we had since we'd started instruction.

I could see Ennio weigh all this too, and judge the anxiety in Ciar's eyes, and the way he kept looking around wildly, as though sure he was being followed. And then a hint of resignation appeared in his eyes, as it had in our childhood, when we finally gave in to one of Ciar's crazy schemes and investigated his mad suspicions—like the time Ciar had decided that the food in the cafeteria was made from the bodies of people who died and the entire thing with the recycler and converter was a cover up. "Fine," he said. "Fine. Let's dispose of your insanity, shall we? What did you discover this time? Are they using school children for propulsion?"

But Ciar didn't laugh or argue, he just shook his head, and his voice changed to a whisper. "I'll go ahead. You don't want to be seen with me. Or at least, we shouldn't leave together," he said. "I'll go ahead, and then in ten minutes or so, meet me at the archive."

"At the—" Ennio said.

"Where I work. You know very well where it is. I'll leave it open for you."

His being in his place of work after hours seemed strange enough. If he didn't have a work order from his supervisor, he could get into serious trouble over it. His letting us in after hours was even more dangerous.

"He's riding for a fall," Ennio said, as he watched Ciar leave. "I wonder what's got into him?"

"Isn't it strange," I said, "how we use expressions for things long vanished, things neither we nor anyone on board the ship could know about personally?"

Ennio gave *me* an odd look. "What are you talking about now?" he asked.

"Riding for a fall. None of us has ever *ridden* anything."

He rolled his eyes. "We've ridden the ship our whole lives," he said. "But that's not the point. Don't you go talking of old language now, or I'll think both of you have gone completely insane. I wonder what he's chasing?"

"Something related to those nursery rhymes, I think."

Ennio made a sound that, without being a profanity, consigned the nursery rhymes and everyone who wrought them to the hells of the ancients. "You're not going to marry him, are you, Nia?" he asked me, with a pleading look. "The man is my best friend, but sometimes I think he's a half-wit. He does more thought transgression in ten minutes than other people do in their entire lives."

I shrugged. "I'm not going to marry anyone," I said. "At least not just yet. I have enough to support myself, and I enjoy living at my parents' lodging. Why bother merging, when I can fly solo just as well?"

He gave me a wolfish smile that told me he wasn't buying my answer, not for a second, then tugged on my arm again, gently this time. "But you do dance, don't you, Nia? Come and dance with me."

We did dance, in the dark, confined warmth of the great room of the bachelor's quarters. I knew from visiting Ennio there—usually under close supervision—that this room was normally used for terminals for learning or gaming or any other leisure activities, but someone had cleared them all away, and dimmed the lights to the lowest setting and the large, well-lit room looked like a cavern, confined and close. The semi-darkness made the whole space more intimate, more...isolating, so that while you spun with your partner to the winding strains of the Cuddle Bug the two of you might well have been in the middle of nowhere, gloriously alone.

And the music was sensuous, I'll give you that. The warm firmness of Ennio's chest against mine was reassuring, his arms around my body were comforting. But as one set ended and another began, I pulled away, regretfully, and whispered to him, "Come on, we'd better meet him."

"Nia," Ennio whispered back, looking betrayed.

"Do you want to risk what he might do if we don't meet him?"

"No . . . no. I guess not. I . . . oh, but he's a pain."

I smiled up at his annoyed expression. Perhaps he was courting me in earnest after all. Oh, sure, he could find a better bride around any corner and down any section corridor, but maybe he didn't know that.

I'm a woman of machines and solid objects. I understand malfunctions based on some defective component, and I understand the logic of mechanics. I also understand humans aren't always logical, which is why they are such bewildering creatures. And why I normally do my best not to get that involved with them. But sometimes I still have trouble with the idea that humans aren't logical in their choice of a mate.

I've read the classic romances just as well as everyone else has, but the one thing no one ever explained to me was exactly why people did any of these things. And perhaps that was where I failed to understand Ennio. Maybe he was in the grip of one of those illogical convictions that only one woman would do for him, and that I had to be that woman. I don't pretend to understand, but I was gratified by it anyway.

I gave him my arm, and we walked, in an ambling sort of way, as if we had nothing much to do, out of the room, out of the center, down a corridor, then down another, on a seemingly random path.

"People will think we are bundling," I told Ennio. "But I get a feeling it's better than their thinking that we're meeting Ciar. I don't think this time if we're caught we'll escape with just a severe reprimand, like the time we got into the kitchens to find out where meat came from."

Ennio nodded. "Oh, yeah. He's always getting us into crazy adventures. And would it be so bad if we were?"

"If we were *what*?" I asked. "Trying to figure out where the meat comes from?" I was counting back the years since the last crazy adventure and figuring out that even Ciar might be allowed a moment of insanity every ten years or so.

"If we were going to bundle," he said.

"Unauthorized contact before marriage?" I asked. "Do you want your coupons docked and your child allowance lowered?"

He looked at me for a moment, then shrugged, and this time I wondered which of us had lost his mind.

So we didn't talk about it anymore. Instead, we walked down the corridors, more or less aimlessly, until we were far enough away that we could head back in the direction we were supposed to be going, to meet Ciar.

This circuitous route took us through narrow little tunnels, the ceramic material that curved overhead patched in a hundred places. Then we emerged onto a larger path amid fields, which were planted with some form of wheat that gave off a rich and earthy smell.

And then we curved back toward lodgings and the administrative buildings, and fetched up at the door to the archives. Which was closed, the lights off on either side, of course. For a moment I wondered if Ciar was in there, or if he had decided to skip this anyway, or even if this was some sort of elaborate prank. But Ciar didn't play pranks, and even Ennio knew that.

Making another sound that betrayed his annoyance, Ennio pushed at the door. It swung inward.

Come into my home, said the spider to the fly flitted through my mind and that, too, I thought, was a fragment of some long-forgotten story. But I went in, as Ennio held the door open for me.

The archives was where they kept all the data for everything in the ship, and for everything before the ship. Somewhere beneath us computers sat that were separate from the computers used for navigating and powering the ship, but could look into those if needed. Into this computer had been poured all of the knowledge of humanity since we'd first walked on two legs in that Earth which I'd only observed in illustrations and only read about in books, but never actually seen.

It was possible that they'd skipped a file teaching us how to chip flint, but everything else was in it, from animal husbandry and taming to the shaping of clay and the smelting of metal. Everything needed to start human civilization as far up as possible on our ladder of learning, in the new world.

And because, by the time we'd left, humanity had worked out that knowledge wasn't often as simple and clear cut as it seemed, this repository involved other skills that would seem less important to interplanetary civilization, including linguistics and literature, law, history, and other disciplines where people argued a lot and used math very little.

Ciar and his fellow linguists worked here translating and transcribing: a work that would be needed until all records were converted, which is to say probably forever.

The space looked like what it was. There were terminals, so close together that for someone to get out of his he had to ask the permission of his fellow on the next one. They were grey, smooth and rounded on top, with a sort of privacy hood you ducked under, presumably so that your work wouldn't disturb that of the workers next to you. In the dark, with a soft light glowing from each of them, they looked as if they were sleeping undisturbed, like children who let their heads droop while napping.

"Oh, we shouldn't be here," Ennio said.

This, of course, was not news, and of course we shouldn't have been there. But we were, and the best thing to do was deal with Ciar so that we could get out of there as soon as possible and with as little trouble as possible.

"Ciar?" I whispered.

He popped up from behind one of the terminals like a jack in the box, his face flushed, his eyes shining and looking feverish. "You came," he said, and before either of us could comment, "Good. You'll never believe this."

From Ennio's snort, I could tell he was already working on not believing it, before Ciar showed us whatever it was.

At first I had no idea what Ciar was getting at. He took us to his terminal and showed us the screen. It said, *Access denied, you do not have permission to ask this question.* Under it there were codes, presumably explaining why we didn't have the right to look at it.

"Very exciting," Ennio said. "I'm all agog. Perhaps you linguists are different, pal, but in my job I get one of these every other day. People don't think I have a need to know the nutritional mix in classroom lunches, or the stories selected for next year's primer."

Ciar shook his head. He touched the screen, quickly, clearing the error message and bringing up a query screen. In it he typed *Big ship* and *nursery rhyme.* For the next few minutes he showed us the old and the new rhymes. The old woman who lived in a compartment— only in the Earth rhyme this was inexplicably a shoe. There were half a dozen others. All of them were very different between the old and the new version. I mean, one of them was clearly created on Earth, for children who had never even thought of flying in space, but the others were full of ship analogies and cryptic references to a wise old owl who didn't talk and which apparently waited for people to come to it when it was needed.

"So, the rhymes were altered," Ennio said. "Perhaps people weren't sure shipboard children would care about Earth-like things."

Ciar shook his head. "It's more than that. Look at it realistically. If you look at what they're saying, over and over they're telling us something special should be happening when we've been in the ship ten generations. Over and over...." He looked up and quirked an eyebrow at us.

"So?" I said.

"So," he said. "How many generations have we been in the ship?"

"I don't know," I said. "I'm fairly sure I've never had a need to know."

"Ah!" He raised his finger sagely, like someone making an important point.

He brought us back to the query screen and asked again how many generations we'd been in the ship. Then he asked for the date of departure from Earth, and the time of arrival at their destination. And, probably in an effort to calculate the generations himself, genealogical tables.

Each question brought up the same screen telling us we were forbidden from accessing that information.

"See?" he said.

"I see," I said. But truth be told, I was far from impressed. "Since when is it news that they classify as secret everything they *can* in this ship? My father says that if they could make sex top secret, they would."

"They probably have," Ennio said. "And are shocked when each new generation figures it out."

"Generations," Ciar said. "That's the thing. How many generations? How long have we been sailing in the big, big ship with the wise old owl? And what is the wise old owl?" He typed that query too, with fast, nervous fingers. It too informed us we had no need to know. "And why won't it let us look at genealogy?"

"That should be obvious." Ennio sounded tired. "You know very well that in the long time the ship—"

"However long," Ciar said, meaningly.

"However long," Ennio shrugged. "There have been any number of people executed for destructive behavior or crimes against the community or . . . or others."

We nodded. Executions weren't that common, but they happened once every ten years or so. It couldn't be helped. We'd learned in school, early on, that in this confined space, discipline had to be far tighter than it was on Earth, because Earth could isolate its anti-social elements. But we had to live and work together, and we had to make sure there were no disruptive elements in the well-oiled social machinery.

"So," Ennio said. "The genealogical tables are hidden, so feuds can't be carried on from generation to generation. As they might very well be, in a group as limited as we are."

Ciar frowned as though this had never occurred to him. "Maybe," he said. His voice sounded less self-assured than it had at first. "Maybe I'll give you that this is a possible reason, but it still strikes me as odd. All these references to generations, and then we can't find out how many generations have been in the ship."

"I'm sure the captain and the administrators know, never you worry," I said. But I was worried. Something at the back of my mind refused to quiet down. I knew my grandparents' grandparents had been in the ship. That made it at least six generations. Were they the first ones?

"Is this all you wished to show us?" Ennio said. "I think you're inflating it wildly. It's like when you decided that they were serving us dead bodies."

Ciar stuck his lip out. "I was only ten. You have to admit it seemed logical. Humans are made of meat, they serve us meat..."

"From vats. And this seems logical to you too, but only because you have that kind of mind. You know what, Ciar, if you'd been born on Earth you'd probably be one of those people who make up stories to amuse others. That's the sort of mind you have. You make it all sound very interesting, but come on, you know it's not true."

Ciar sat, frowning at the terminal, then at us, then at the terminal again.

"Come back to the dance with us," I said. "You can probably find girls to dance with. I'll even take a turn with you."

He hesitated visibly, then shrugged. "Nah. There's a few more things I want to look up."

So Ennio and I went back, and despite the suspicious looks of our fellow dancers, managed to convey the impression we'd just been for a nice, long, peaceful walk.

That night, when I got home, mom was awake, waiting for me, while doing her best to look as if she were balancing ration coupon accounts.

After the normal pleasantries, as I was heading for bed, I turned around and asked her, "Mom, I know my grandfather's grandfather was in the ship. I remember your dad talking about his grandad. Was his grandad the first generation aboard the ship?"

Mom looked surprised. "Why? No, couldn't be, because I remember my grandmother talking about her grandmother being a little girl in the ship. Why?"

"Just curious," I said. I removed the shoes which had started to pinch and continued down the narrow hallway to my room. That made seven generations, didn't it? What had the rhyme said? When ten generations have passed. . . .

During the night several systems broke down. I probably would have heard first thing in the morning, if I'd seen mom. Only I didn't. She'd already left for her job in the planning center when I woke up, consumed my morning calories without too much attention to their form, which seemed to be cardboard with syrup, though the container said pancakes. Then I headed into the maintenance center, where I got my sheet of work for the day.

It was nothing like the blackout three years ago that left a whole wing of the ship with minimal air recycling. This was more a matter of clothes washers not working, freezers becoming suddenly warm and heating systems having gone south over an entire section.

Since we were requested to hurry and since we were being offered extra luxury rations on completion, I worked straight through lunch, and didn't talk to anyone until I headed home.

Which was when Ennio intercepted me. This wasn't so rare, so I shouldn't have been surprised, but I was. Or at least, I was disquieted. He didn't look as he normally did.

To begin with, he wasn't waiting at my home or within sight of my home, as he usually did. Instead, he seemed to have been patrolling all my possible paths of approach to home—which, of course, varied, since I came from different locations, depending on the last job I'd been busy with—to meet me out of possible sight of my parents and neighbors. And then, instead of falling into step beside me, as he usually did, and easing into a conversation, he came just close enough to motion me to follow him.

This was strange enough behavior that I almost *had* to obey. I confess if Ennio had been a different type of person I might have thought that he had ulterior motives. He took increasingly smaller and narrower corridors, each one less populated, until I half expected him to pull me into a repair tunnel. Instead, he pulled me into a maintenance closet.

Maintenance closets are spaced along corridors, both large and small. Most of them have access to the wiring for that portion of the ship. Some of them just contain tools, others have the specialized machines that clean the corridor floors. This one had a machine, so that to pull me in, Ennio had to squeeze himself behind it, then make room for me.

"Close the door," he whispered urgently.

I did, because at that point I was going with the assumption he'd gone stark raving mad, and everyone knows the best thing with lunatics is to humor them until you can get them to a medtech.

Closing the door left us in complete darkness, surrounded by a smell of mustiness and detergent. "All right," I said. "Now what?"

But nothing prepared me for the tone of his voice much less what he said, as he spoke out of the dark, "They arrested Ciar this morning." He sounded as if he was about to cry.

The sound was so odd, that I was sure I had misunderstood him. "*What?*"

"They arrested Ciar this morning. I had to talk to you where no one could hear us. I brought a lantern here earlier. I don't think there are any listening devices."

"I don't think there are listening devices anywhere in the ship," I said. "Oh, maybe in the supply areas, to make sure things are not stolen, but I don't think so. Why should there be?"

"Why should they arrest Ciar?"

"He went to his place of employment after hours and probably without permission."

"That's an administrative sanction," he said. "It's *just* an administrative sanction. It's not a capital crime."

"A . . . capital crime? They are going to kill him? How do you know this? Why do you think this?"

"It's what the news says," he said. "They say he was arrested for activities against the community, and that he'll be executed."

"You have to have misunderstood."

"I didn't." And the woebegone tone of his voice made me begin to believe him. Ennio couldn't possibly be confused about something that important.

"But . . ." I said

"I figured it was his search. He was using his ID on the terminal. Someone correlated all his searches. Someone doesn't want that stuff looked at."

"What? Nursery rhymes?"

A desperate sniffle from the darkness, that might have been an attempt to sound ironical, but sounded only sad. "I hope that's not it, since I just downloaded all I could find."

"Ennio!"

"*I have* to know. We *have* to find out. We have to do something to save Ciar."

This was truly delusional. Fine, so there hadn't been an execution in the last ten years, meaning there hadn't been one in the time I'd been conscious of them, or an adult, able to interpret the news. But even I knew enough, from hearing my parents talk, to know that when someone was arrested for a capital crime and it was announced as such, everything was decided and there was no reprieve. Like Ennio, I couldn't imagine what Ciar had done to deserve capital punishment. Other than his silly search into the nursery rhymes and how many generations there had been in the ship, I didn't think he'd so much as talked back to his supervisor this last year. Ennio and I would have known if he had. We talked over almost everything. So this left. . . . "When are they executing him?"

"Next week," Ennio said.

"Why that long?"

Even without being able to see Ennio, I knew he had shrugged. And I realized I was a total idiot. There were many things to do before an execution, most of them procedural and technical. While the administration alone decided on death or life, they had to be really sure that nothing could be done to reclaim a trained linguist, like Ciar.

"Where are they holding him?" It seemed impossible we were talking about this, in connection with Ciar. Like Ennio, I kept thinking there had been some horrible mistake and we should, somehow, be able to clear him. I'd read stories of Earth where someone was broken out of jail and he and his rescuers vanished into the sunset, but aboard the ship there was no possible way to do that. Unless we escaped into the no-grav areas, and even there, repair people and maintenance people would find us eventually—let alone the fact that staying in no gravity too long would make us ill in very short order.

Ennio made a sound of dismissal, and then turned on something. It had a small screen that glowed feebly, but in the total darkness it looked like a spotlight. After my eyes adjusted, I realized it was just a little data port, which could function independently of the main computer. It was what most of us used to read for amusement.

"I correlated all the things the nursery rhymes say about the wise old owl," he said. "While I was waiting for you. I think . . . I think it's a hidden computer somewhere in the ship."

"Right," I said. "Because it makes perfect sense to spend twice the needed amount of money to give a ship like this two completely separate computer systems."

He shook his head. "It does, if you think about it. For one, there could be a space disaster or something, that wiped out the other one. And besides, there's . . . other reasons. Like for instance, people not wanting us to know things, like how many generations there have been in the ship."

"Why would they want to do that?" I asked. "I mean, you're assuming someone is deliberately hiding the number of generations from us. What you said earlier is much more likely. That they don't want feuds and such to propagate and perpetuate."

But he shook his head. "No, I think it's more than that. I think the administration doesn't want us to arrive."

"What do you mean?"

"Look at them. They have all this power, over the ship and over us. Why would they want us to arrive?"

"Because the whole point of this trip is to *arrive*?"

"Is it? It was when we launched, but *is* it still? Most people aboard care about *what*? Who they'll marry, how many children they're allowed to have, and how many luxury points they have that they can spend this week. And when we arrive, what is supposed to happen?"

"We . . . we'll settle," I said. "Depending on what the world is like. I mean, they know it has water and is the right temperature and . . ." I dredged up from my mind the memory of childhood lectures. "I think they somehow established that it either had life or could support life. Depending on which one it is, we either settle right in, or we warm up the plants and animals and give them some time to establish. And then we move down to the surface, and we have farms and . . . and stuff down there, just like we have here. The whole point was to expand human civilization and knowledge." The idea of living somewhere without the upper limits of the tunnels overhead, of the floor beneath, made my heart pound. Just looking at movies of Earth made me a little dizzy, unless I thought of the sky as a tunnel top. But I knew the name for that was acrophobia and that there were hypnotic treatments for it. We'd been provided with those, since everyone knew after . . . ten generations? In the ship that was bound to happen.

"Right," Ennio said. "But there won't be any restrictions on how many children you can have, anymore. And after a while there won't be any restrictions on how much you can eat, and where you can go." He looked at me with the look of someone who'd just won an argument, and exhaled, forcefully. "*Think*, Nia. The administrators will lose all their power over us."

"But they'll have farms and ... and stuff."

"Right. Only they can't be assured they'll be the best farmers. Remember what I said about what most people care about?"

"Children and luxury points, I think you said."

"Yeah, that and how much other people admire and respect you."

"But we'll all have all the children we can want, and unlimited food, and...."

"Yeah," he said. "Yeah. But they don't know they'll be the best farmers, will they?"

For a moment I didn't understand, then I got it. When I was apprenticed as a repair person, I'd made use of a natural talent to become the best of the apprentices in very short order. But then, when we'd become craftspeople, with our licenses in order, I'd found I was only the best of the most inept group—that is the just-graduated ones. I would always remember the sting of that reduction in status. I hadn't liked even that little step. How much less would people who were at the top of their social and professional ladder enjoy having the ladder pulled away from them and falling ... into an entirely different category?

"But ... to the point of hiding the files? To the point of lying to us about where we are in space? Or at least not telling us when we approach and ... risking our going right past? To the point of having Ciar *executed*?"

Ennio bit his lip. "It seems so. I don't like to think about it anymore than you do, but it seems so. They're killing him just for trying to find this information."

"And you want us to look at the nursery rhymes?" I said, baffled. If this was true, it seemed more productive to call a public meeting; to shout it from the rooftops; to sound the alarm; to try the administrative board for treason. Which is where I came up against an obstacle. The administrative board and the captain had absolute power aboard. Who would try them?

"No, not just look at nursery rhymes," Ennio said. "You weren't listening. I have compiled all the instructions on how to find the wise old owl." He looked at me, his gaze so determined that you'd swear he was the one condemned to death and seeing only one means of escape.

"What good would that be? Even if it's another computer."

"I don't know," he said. "But we got into this by looking at the rhymes. And they all told us to find the wise old owl. If you don't come with me, I'll look myself."

I took the reader from his hands, looked at his notes. If he'd culled the hints properly, then the wise old owl, whatever it was, was located in one of the external maintenance tunnels, in section 25. That section was little inhabited and I couldn't remember ever going into that tunnel. How something like a computer would stay undetected all that time, I couldn't imagine, but neither could I tell him categorically that it hadn't happened.

"Tonight," I said. "After my parents go to bed. I'll meet you in the alley where you were today."

"You'll help me look?" he asked, and, for the first time that day, I heard a smile in his voice.

"Of course." The last thing I needed was an educational machine programmer lost in the maintenance tunnels. With my luck, he would trip over some wiring and destroy one of the air pumps or the light banks.

That was the longest dinner of my life. Nighttime is artificial on the ship. It always falls at precisely 20:00, when they close the system of mirrors that brings sunlight into the ship. My mom had said that her parents said sunlight used to be a lot stronger, when we were closer to Sol. Now it had to be supplemented with specialized lamps. I knew because I had to fix them, rearrange them and, occasionally, install them.

Plants and animals—and humans—need a certain cycle of daylight and darkness and since we didn't have it naturally, it had to be simulated.

My family ate an hour before nightfall, but that night we were— of course—delayed. And then mom wished to talk about the shocking news of Ciar's arrest. I don't know what answers I made, other than indicating how surprised I was, myself, with my father joining our dismay.

I know it was well past their normal bed time of 22:00 when they retired. I waited another hour to make sure they were asleep, because the last thing I needed—the absolute last thing—was for them to intercept me at the door and ask where I was going or why.

This felt like insanity, but it had that curious glimmer of a suspicion that there might be something in it. Just a sliver of hope, the barest of chances that there was something more in this than Ennio's gallant and silly attempt to save his friend and rival.

By the time I made it to the meeting place, I halfway expected Ennio to be gone to his bed in the bachelors' quarters, but he was waiting, clutching his reader.

"Right," I said, gritting my teeth. "Come."

"This way."

Even on the most external of tunnels there were several layers of material between ourselves and space so there was no dangerous radiation. But we were on the outermost area accessible to humans. Beyond that was an area where only specialized crews in spacesuits were allowed to make repairs.

The space was a tunnel so narrow we had to shuffle side by side along it. To compensate for the narrowness, it was very high, seeming to climb all the way up the side of the ship, to... the top of the ship?

Of course, I had no business being here after hours, looking around for a chimera born of Ciar's overexcited imagination, of Ennio's gallant impulses and desire to save our errant friend.

At least, I thought, I was less likely to be caught than Ciar. I'd never been here, I saw nothing here to maintain, and so I doubted that anyone could come to do anything in here and bump into us. And of course, I wasn't leaving clear codes behind, as Ciar had.

The problem was that there was nothing here to maintain. Just walls—not very smooth, I'll grant you. They rarely are in the less frequently used maintenance tunnels. Occasionally there might be a protruding pipe. But that was about it.

We seemed as likely to find a computer here as to find... well, a wise old owl.

"Here," Ennio said. "We're supposed to stand here." He turned into a passage so narrow we had to squeeze between the walls. The floor was solid but grimy underfoot, and the ceiling was lost somewhere in the darkness above.

"Now what?" I asked. "The wizard comes and rescues us?"

"What?" he said. Then he looked at his reader, bringing it up almost to touch his visor. "No. Look. It says we should climb up the wall, like the itsy bitsy spider."

I looked dubiously at the wall. Okay, it wasn't smooth. But it wasn't really rougher than any other section of wall. Those protrusions might perhaps be enough for us to hold feet and hands as we climbed. But were they designed that way? "Are you sure we're in the right place?"

"Yeah," he said. Mentally he retraced our steps, as his lips moved—his face visible, pale and concentrated through the visor. "Yeah, I'm sure. I counted the steps right."

"Okay." I could see there was no way to get Ennio to budge from here until we climbed the wall. It was climbing down, I thought, that was going to be very hard indeed.

But climbing up was easier than I expected. The protuberances on the wall really seemed to have been placed on purpose to make our life easier.

And when we got up so far that the floor seemed imprecise and indistinguishable, too far from the lights cast by our suit, there were ... rungs, like a ladder, embedded on the wall.

Finding them made the task even simpler. It also seemed to validate the idea we were on the right trail. But were we? Or was this some forgotten maintenance path?

"There's a door," Ennio said. He'd been alongside me, on another set of embedded rungs—there seemed to be five at least—and now he reached over and knocked on something that sounded hollow. "I think that's it."

Maybe. Or maybe some sort of fancy maintenance closet. I figured I was the trained maintenance worker, and should go in first. Mostly because if Ennio came across some machinery he was likely to fall on it and break it. Both the men were much better than I with words and meanings, but neither of them would know a shoe polisher from an oxygen recycler.

I clambered across and felt for some sort of handle. There was one, of course, which I turned. I shoved the door inward.

Light came on, inside.

"See?" Ennio said.

I felt Ennio close the door.

A voice, polite and cool, sounding like a well-brought up young woman, said, "What are you seeking?"

There were many answers to that, including asking who the woman was. But before I could speak, I heard Ennio say, "The wise old owl."

There was a click and I thought he'd done it now, and the medtechs would come get us for a serious mind adjustment, but instead a door opened in what looked like a completely smooth wall. Ennio stepped through it, so I had to go after. I was only slightly startled when it closed. And, somehow, the chamber began to move. Like a mobile capsule.

After awhile, it stopped. And opened.

We looked into yet another completely blank room. Ennio led the way in, and the door closed automatically behind us.

"What do you wish to ask the wise old owl?"

The voice came from nowhere. Ennio and I spoke at the same time, "How many generations we've been in the ship," he said.

"How far are we from our destination?" I asked.

Another click, and we looked into a large, carpeted room, with chairs, and the appearance of one of the upper-rank staterooms. It felt like one, too. It was smooth and polished.

Almost the minute we came in and the door closed behind us, an entire wall came to life. In it an owl with enormous eyes sat on the branch of a tree, against a blue sky. "I am the wise old owl," the pleasant young woman's voice said.

Of course it wasn't an owl, or a young woman, but a computer designed for extrapolative reasoning, which explained how it had managed to understand our disparate answers and still make sure we were on the right quest. I wondered if many other people—or any other people—throughout the history of the ship had been in that first room and been sent away because they lacked the exact answer.

I won't relate our interaction with the computer, or at least not in detail. It had been programmed to ask us a series of questions to find what, if any, knowledge had been lost in the time since it had been buried in what appeared to be dead—or perhaps—solid space around the ship. Hidden away.

It had also been designed to be programmed and worked with in what seemed to be plain everyday language. It answered questions by inductive logic when we asked them. Sometimes it stopped and asked us to rephrase, but it seemed to understand everything. Speaking to it was almost like speaking to a foreign-language speaker, someone who didn't fully understand what we said, but understood most of it and could carry on a conversation. Turned out that its story was exactly what we thought—it had been hidden so that should what it called unforeseen social difficulties come to pass, there would be one computer aboard that the administration could neither reprogram nor tamper with.

"How long have we been in the ship?" I asked, then rephrased, "How long ago did the ship leave Earth?"

"The ship was constructed in Earth orbit."

I'd asked the wrong question. "How long since the ship left the Sol system, then?" Ennio asked.

"Four hundred and twenty five years," the voice answered.

I felt my heart clench. That had to be ten generations. Perhaps more. "How... how near are we to Alpha Centauri?" I asked.

"We should prepare to slingshot around the sun in... twenty four hours," the computer answered.

Needless to say Ennio and I panicked. Twenty four hours. We couldn't possibly learn to pilot the ship in that time.

This was, of course, silly. Whoever had designed the ship couldn't expect us to. Turned out it didn't even expect us to tell it to detach the outer portion of the sail, so the outer sail could focus the lasers—similar to the lasers that had given us additional speed on leaving sol orbit—onto the inner sail and slow the ship. The ship was wired hard to this hidden computer in a way that could not be severed. This computer would be executing the maneuver, no matter how much the other computer had been corrupted or its programing overpowered.

No, it turned out what we were needed for was something much more vital. We had to prepare everyone aboard ship for the hours of weightlessness as the ship stopped spinning while slowing and maneuvering into orbit at the new world. In the long time aboard, the practice of securing everything that could float had long stopped. Weightlessness could destroy the ponds in which we grew fish, it could forever break terminals capable of reading our records. Not to mention what it would do to toilets.

The computer told us all that would happen, but more importantly, it said, the people aboard would need to find out about the secret lifeboat bays—the ones that couldn't be opened, so the landers couldn't be cannibalized for parts, as it appeared the other well-known landers *had* been. In the situation we were in, the wise old owl said, everyone aboard would have to be told at the same time, so that a few people couldn't find the boats and destroy them before anyone could take them and land.

Someone needed to tell the panicking population what was happening. Someone needed to have people expecting it and prepared. Oh, most people probably wouldn't want to land. Not right away. Perhaps not ever. Once the ship was in orbit around our new home, and the ship's sails retracted, life could go on as it had aboard the ship for eleven generations. Humans are creatures of habit and most people cared for nothing but their luxury rations. But after coming all this way, people should know there was another option available. An option to *finish* our mission. And people who wanted to leave should not be constrained to stay. And—most of all—in the confusion of the moments of weightlessness, it was necessary to keep fights from breaking out and disorder from descending on the ship. In just a few hours of riot, damage could be done that would lessen forever the chances of the colonists.

This seemed almost impossible. Neither Ennio nor I had any particular power in the ship. And who would listen to us? Look what had happened to Ciar, just for trying to see forbidden files.

And then I had an idea. It required me to work madly the rest of the night, but I could—and did—wire the wise old owl so that it could speak to the whole ship at once. Many people might not believe it. And many people would ignore it, or suspect a prank. But at least there would be some warning. And when the people looked out at the stars around us, they'd see confirmation.

Then—as soon as we could—we asked the wise old owl what to do about Ciar. It could not—so much the worse—magically open the door to his cell. It was directly wired to the ship's navigation and landing systems, but not to the rest of the ship. All it could do was access the other computer's memory and tell us where Ciar was kept.

That was enough, I assured Ennio. Even with the cell locked, I probably could open it. And when gravity stopped most people— even if alerted—would be disoriented long enough to lose track of keeping watch on a prisoner.

They didn't know how to cope with null g, while *I* did. Null-g maintenance jobs are rare but they do happen aboard ship, and I'd been trained to handle that kind of environment.

The problem was that we were not on Earth. There was nowhere to run.

This was when the computer pitched in with the information that the landers were also scouts. As soon as we'd escaped the pull of the star around which we'd slingshot to slow our velocity, the larger of the lifeboats could take us there, and it would have provisions for the month we would need to land and for one more month afterwards.

We could lock ourselves in the boat and hide if the computer didn't reveal our location until we'd departed.

I looked at Ennio, "If there's no life on the planet, or no life compatible with ours. If we can't eat the plants and animals of the world, we're going to starve long before they come down with seeds and animals."

A muscle worked on the side of Ennio's face. "I know. But if we *don't* do it, Ciar will die."

What else is there to say? It went as planned. Well, almost as planned. Yes, the guards that had been assigned to Ciar's cell were floating above us, completely unable to guard anything. Yes, opening his cell—with a cutting tool around the lock—was easy.

The hard part was keeping Ciar and Ennio moving properly in null-g till we could reach the capsule that took us to the chamber of the wise old owl and, this time, beyond it, to the lifeboats.

The lifeboat—and why was it called that? It's not like exiting to space would have saved anyone—was more comfortable than any of our lodgings, and had enough food for four people for two months.

And the planet turned out to have food of a sort. The bodies of water contained algae. A strange fish that looked like a jelly fish had a high speed collision with a salmon. Apparently they weren't even really fish at all, but something between a plant and an animal, which has kept our scientists baffled so far, and will probably keep them so for many years to come.

But they were edible enough to keep us alive. Us and those who came after us.

We've used Earth food plants to colonize the land and start our farms.

It's been thirty years since we landed and I've almost forgotten the stomach-churning fear of falling upward. I can look up at the deep blue night sky and feel nothing but wonder at how far we've come.

Thirty years later, I realize how lucky we were. We found the computer just in time to stop confusion and rioting and to know we'd arrived. If we'd not found the computer, the administration could have said the loss of gravity was a temporary malfunction. Only astrogators would have known we were orbiting a star, and, depending on how the computer records had been changed, they might have thought it was a different star. They could have been forbidden from asking further questions. We could have been prisoners in the ship for generations.

Perhaps forever.

Oh, some people still remain in the ship, orbiting the world. But living in the world is so much more rewarding, so much more free, that most everyone has come down, little by little. The young first, and those with some spirit of adventure. Which of course, had been squelched during the generations of living in a closed system, but apparently not entirely bred out.

My children would never know how to live in that close and regimented society. They've fanned out over the world, planted the land, grown animals, lived by their labor and answered to no man.

I *did* marry. Which of them? Can't you guess?

Last year I had my first grandchild and I sing it to sleep with the songs that will tell them where we came from—so that if everything else is lost they'll still know we came here from another world and that there will be other humans out there when their world is developed enough to send ships to *other* stars. I don't doubt they will. All animals have a biological imperative to expand or die. And humans have been expanding their territory since they came down from the trees in a semi-tropical area of a little world now very far from us. We'll continue expanding, beyond Alpha Centauri, beyond the Milky Way, on and on forever, until our species is so widespread no single calamity can render us extinct; till the fruits and knowledge of a thousand worlds make every single human freer and happier and wealthier than we can even dream.

So I'll sing my grandchildren to sleep as I sang my children to sleep: to stories of our once and future voyages.

The big ship sails in the vacuum, oh.

SIREN SONG

Mike Resnick

If we actually achieve a serious space flight capability, it's likely we will spend a long time in the Solar System before anybody actually makes for the high country. With experience, propulsion systems will improve, as will life support. What is now little more than a dream may one day become no more than a sporting event, a race, perhaps, through the Saturnian rings. Will this type of casual event signal that we are ready to move on? Perhaps. A better indicator, however, might arrive when we reach a point at which space travel begins to develop its own mythology.

Mike Resnick has won five Hugos and been nominated a record thirty-five times. Alas, like Ben Bova, Mike was taken from us in 2020.

※ ※ ※

SO LET ME TELL YOU ABOUT the Great Regatta of 2237, because the press had it wrong, as usual, and when was the last time the self-appointed pundits ever knew anything except what other self-appointed pundits were thinking?

The public had grown increasingly weary of races on Earth's oceans. After all, the oceans were so . . . well . . . *limiting.* Lift your gaze, the reasoning went, and there's a whole universe up there, and it's a lot bigger than an ocean. Okay, we couldn't reach most of it, couldn't even visit Alpha Centauri during *one* lifetime, let alone make the return flight. But we could reach just about any place in the solar system, and even if the distances weren't measured in parsecs, they stirred the imagination the way mere miles and fathoms no longer could.

There were six ships entered in the race. Five were sleek, bullet-shaped vessels, powered by fission or fusion—and then there was the *Argo*, the only ship in the Regatta that made its way through the void by the use of solar sails.

The course was mapped out by the most sophisticated computers: they would start from orbit—four of the ships had been built in space and would die having never touched down on a planetary surface—and each ship would have to pass within a thousand miles of four buoys that would register their passage. The designers didn't want to chance losing a ship due to a gas giant's gravity, so while they put one buoy in orbit around Mars, the other three would be in position not around Jupiter, Saturn and Uranus, but rather their moons: Ganymede, Titan, and Umbriel.

May 1 was a special day in many cultures—not for the reasons it once was, at least not in most countries—and it was decided that the race would begin at exactly twelve o'clock noon, Greenwich Mean Time, on that date.

The ships could choose any course they wanted, which was meaningful since their goals were in constant motion. Once the race began, they were not permitted to communicate with each other, even to warn of dangers such as ion storms or meteor showers. And finally, if a ship touched down on any solid surface—planet, moon, asteroid, anything—for any reason, it would be disqualified.

It was the *Argo* that caught the public's fancy, partially because solar sails seemed somehow romantic, conjuring up visions of the sailing ships of yore, and partially because of the captain. His name—and no one except the public believed it could possibly be his real one—was FarTrekker Jones, with the capital T right in the middle of it, and they couldn't have been more taken by a name if he'd chosen Odysseus or Horatio Hornblower.

He shared the *Argo* with two others, a co-pilot and a navigator—he didn't trust navigational computers, though of course the ship had one—and the three of them were a hard-bitten lot. No one knew what had driven them to space (I almost said "driven them to sea"), and they weren't much for giving interviews—but the people loved them anyway, and if no one knew anything much about them, why, that just lent a little romantic mystery to the race.

They lined the six ships up in orbit, each about five miles from the next, and suddenly they were off and running, or probably I should say off and flying. The *Silver Streak* jumped out to a quick lead, followed by the *Galaxy Roamer*. The *Argo* wasn't exactly left at the gate—for one thing, they didn't have a starting gate—but it was soon bringing up the rear.

They reached Mars in fourteen to sixteen days, depending on which ship you were rooting for. The *Galaxy Roamer* was now in the lead by seven hours, with the *Silver Streak* and *McGinty's Marvel* five minutes apart in second place, and the *Argo* still bringing up the rear.

The first five ships followed a predetermined route to get to Ganymede, which was their next checkpoint. It was a reasonable route, and a safe route. They had to go through the Asteroid Belt, of course, but bad stories and worse videos to the contrary, most of the asteroids are so far apart that actually seeing two or three while traversing the Belt breaks the monotony (and monotonous it is, for Jupiter is a lot farther from Mars than Earth is).

But not all the Belt is like that. Some of it is what you might call densely populated, not by people but by asteroids, and in fact there are a few places where there are so many and they are moving so swiftly, that they can be damned dangerous. Moreover, there's a lot of rubble out there, rocks the size of bricks, or footballs if you prefer, that are so small and so fast that a ship's sensors will miss half of them, but any one of them, if it hits the right spot at the right angle, can put a ship out of commission... and I mean permanently.

Of course you've figured out by now what I'm going to tell you, and you're right: FarTrekker decided the only way to make up lost time was to take the shortest route to Ganymede, a route the other five ships had avoided because of the danger involved.

A number of media ships had been posted along the route, reporting back on the race, but when the *Argo* changed its course they followed it only long enough to determine where it was going, and then wisely refused to follow it. As they reported, only a crazy man would take this route, and especially in a ship with a solar sail, which presented a much bigger target to the myriad of flying rocks, and of course once the sail was destroyed the ship would be without motive power. ("What will they do then?" asked one of the self-appointed pundits. "Row?" Twenty-seven other pundits used that same line during the next day, and eleven presented it as their own, which is of course what self-appointed pundits do.)

The *Argo* entered the Belt, and Knibbs the navigator—no one ever knew his first name—went to work, charting all the asteroids that were big enough to chart, and trying to position the ship so that anything too small to chart was more likely to hit the hull than the solar sail. They figured to be eight days crossing the Belt, but if they made it to the other side, they'd have picked up more than a week on their rivals.

And, oddly enough, they were not touched by so much as a pebble for the first five days. The sail remained intact, they actually were running two hours ahead of schedule, and Knibbs announced that they'd passed through the worst of it, that the asteroids were starting to look like baby planets again, rather than large rocks and small boulders.

And then, on the sixth day, the co-pilot (whose first name was Vladimir, and I won't bother with his surname since no one could pronounce or spell it anyway), Vladimir was sitting at the control panel when he fell asleep, and his head or his hand—they never knew which, and it doesn't really matter anyway—brushed against some of the buttons and switches and knobs, and suddenly the *Argo* was filled with this haunting sound, like a melody you heard when both you and the world were younger and more innocent, and try as you would you could never quite remember it, though you knew it had brought tears to your eyes the one time you'd heard it. In fact, you probably looked for it on and off for years, but *privately*, because you didn't know quite how to tell anyone you were looking for a melody that made you cry.

"What is that?" asked FarTrekker, suddenly alert.

"I don't know," said Vladimir, blinking his eyes. He checked the control panel, but while a number of the switches and buttons had been flicked and pressed, none of them had anything to do with the ship's radio.

"I know that song," said Knibbs wistfully. "I heard it once, a long time ago."

FarTrekker shook his head. "No, that's my Leucosia's song."

"I didn't know you had a girl," said Vladimir. "At least, I've never seen you with one."

"I had one once," said FarTrekker, staring sadly at the viewscreen. "She was coming home when her ship was lost. They never found her."

"Surely they looked for her?"

"They did," said FarTrekker. "But it's a big solar system." He sighed deeply. "That was her song."

"It's my Peisinoe's favorite song, too," said Knibbs. "Or it was, before I lost her."

Suddenly FarTrekker frowned. "And that's Leucosia's *voice*!"

He examined the speakers, but the sound was not emanating from them. He then turned to Vladimir. "You're our engineering expert," he said. "Where the hell is that sound originating, and how can we be hearing it if it's not being broadcast by the ship's speaker system?"

Vladimir shrugged helplessly. "I don't know. Theoretically we *can't* be hearing it."

"Spare me your theories," said FarTrekker. "Can any external source be bypassing the speakers and broadcasting that melody directly into the ship, anything we can trace?"

"No," said Vladimir. "We're maintaining radio silence. However the sound is reaching us, it's not through any mechanism on the *Argo*."

The three men fell silent then, as the melody washed over them, caressing them with emotions and memories, some real, some they only wished were real.

"She's alive," said FarTrekker at last. "She's alive, and she's found a way to get to me!"

Knibbs agreed, except the "she" was his Peisinoe, and Vladimir, who remained silent, knew that the voice he heard, conjuring feelings he thought he'd forgotten, belonged to his Ligeia.

"We must be close!" said FarTrekker. "I never heard her on Earth, or in orbit, or even as we passed by Mars."

"And Jupiter is still farther from us than Earth," noted Vladimir.

"So she must be close by," concluded FarTrekker, and the other two agreed with him, though each silently substituted a different name for "she." "What's the largest asteroid in the vicinity?"

Knibbs checked his computer. "Got one, maybe eight hundred miles in diameter, about ten thousand miles off to the right, and getting closer every second." He paused. "Got a bit of an atmosphere, but nothing any human can breathe."

"Does it have a name, or just the usual numbers and letters?" asked FarTrekker.

"Yeah, this one's got a name: Anthemoessa." Knibbs frowned. "Seems somehow familiar, though I'll swear I never saw it referred to before."

"I have," said Vladimir. "But I'll be damned if I can remember where."

The strangest expression crossed FarTrekker's face. "I can remember." Then he fell silent.

"Well?" demanded Knibbs.

"It's the island where the Sirens lived,"

"You're not suggesting *Sirens* are singing to us!" scoffed Vladimir.

"Besides, Anthemoessa, if it existed at all, was in the Mediterranean, remember?" added Knibbs. "Near Greece somewhere."

"Maybe whoever named this asteroid knew something we don't know," said FarTrekker, and added "yet" silently.

"Ridiculous!" said Vladimir.

"Okay, maybe not," said FarTrekker. "You explain the song."

"I can't."

"But you can hear it, and you've heard it before," persisted FarTrekker.

"I think so."

"You know so," said FarTrekker. "Admit it: don't you recognize the voice?"

Vladimir seemed to be having a brief battle within himself. Finally he sighed. "Yes. It's my Ligeia."

"I've got something interesting here," said Knibbs. The other two turned to him. "According to the computer, the asteroid was named almost a century ago by Mortimer Highsmith."

"So?" asked FarTrekker.

Knibbs smiled. "He was a widower."

"That's all?" said Vladimir.

"He never came back."

"Where did he die?" asked Fartrekker.

"No one knows," answered Knibbs.

FarTrekker looked at the viewscreen. "We'll find his body there," he said, pointing to Anthemoessa. "Unless he's still alive."

"He'd be about a hundred and forty years old," noted Knibbs.

"Who knows what wonders can transpire on Anthemoessa?" replied FarTrekker. "There's only one way to find out."

"He'd better not have laid a hand on my Ligeia!" muttered Vladimir.

"Maybe we should think this through," said Knibbs. "If they're Sirens or the equivalent, who knows what will happen if we answer their call? It's a strange and not always friendly universe out here."

The three men fell silent for a moment, considering their options—but the ship didn't fall silent, and the hauntingly beautiful melody permeated every atom of it.

Finally FarTrekker spoke. "Listening to this melody for the past ten minutes has made me happier than any time since my Leucosia died. It should hurt, but it doesn't; it brings her back to me, and the only thing that hurts is being apart from her." He looked at his two shipmates. "Maybe they're who we hope they are. Maybe we're in some parallel universe where they didn't die. Maybe they're Sirens. And maybe they're something else." He paused briefly. "Has anyone got anything better to do?"

Nobody did, FarTrekker saw no reason to report what had happened, none of the three had any soulmate to say good-bye to, and the *Argo* altered course and headed for Anthemoessa and out of this story.

What happened?

Well, the pundits say that they were either struck by an asteroid or crashed into one. The cynics say they knew they couldn't win and were afraid to show their faces ever again. The romantics say they found exactly what they were looking for.

Who was right?

Anyone who wants can find out. Anthemoessa is still up there, its song available to anyone who is willing to listen.

AFTERWORD

How the world changes in just a few years. Since the first publication of *Going Interstellar,* the topic of interstellar travel has been catapulted from a relatively fringe group of visionary scientists, engineers, and science fiction fans to a more mainstream position within the space exploration and development community. There are many reasons for this, most notably the ever-growing list of observed exoplanets and the large number of them that might be Earth-like and within their stars' habitable zones. The inevitable question that arises when these discoveries are made is, "How do we visit them?" And it is this topic that the volume you hold sought to address using fact-based science fictional conjecture and known physics-based speculative engineering.

To address this question and move us toward the goal of being able to mount expeditions to other stars, multiple private space advocacy and philanthropic organizations arose, and some have endured. Your editors have participated in the meetings of the Interstellar Research Group (formerly the Tennessee Valley Interstellar Workshop), a nonprofit educational foundation that holds internationally attended symposia every two years, with support from Baen Books funds undergraduate and graduate student scholarships yearly, and works to promote future interstellar travel. If you want to get involved, please visit their website, http://irg.space, and let them know.

In a league of its own is Breakthrough Starshot, a $100 million research and engineering program whose goal is the demonstration of new technologies to enable lightweight robotic missions to Alpha Centauri traveling at twenty percent the speed of light. Breakthrough Starshot was begun by Yuri Milner and Stephen Hawking in 2016 and is making steady progress toward maturing the technologies that may enable such missions in the future.

We hope you are enjoying the stories in this volume and learning something new from the essays. Most of all, we hope you are inspired and filled with a renewed sense of hope for the future.

Ad Astra!

—Jack McDevitt
—Les Johnson